IN SICKNESS AND IN HEALTH

FIONA SUSSMAN

Legend Press Ltd, 51 Gower Street, London, WC1E 6HJ
info@legendtimesgroup.co.uk | www.legendpress.co.uk

First Published in New Zealand in 2022 by David Bateman Ltd | Unit
2/5 Workspace Drive, Hobsonville, Auckland 0618, New Zealand |
www.batemanbooks.co.nz

Print ISBN 9781915643476
Ebook ISBN 9781915643483
Set in Times.
Cover design by Rose Cooper | www.rosecooper.com

Former GP **Fiona Sussman** was born in South Africa and now lives in New Zealand.

Her short story *A Breath, A Bunk, A Land, A Sky* was shortlisted for the 2020 Commonwealth Writers' Prize. Her debut novel *Shifting Colours* was published by Allison & Busby in the UK and by Berkley in the US under the title, *Another Woman's Daughter.* Her second novel, *The Last Time We Spoke* (Allison & Busby) was translated into Polish and won the Ngaio Marsh Award for Best Crime Novel in New Zealand. *Addressed to Greta* (Bateman Books 2020) won the NZ Booklovers Award for Best Fiction.

Her new novel, *In Sickness and In Health*, is a finalist for the Ngaio Marsh Award for Best Crime Novel.

Follow Fiona
@FionaSussman

and visit
www.fionasussman.co.nz

For Pete

CHAPTER 1

ELIOT BARD

Eliot stopped, his breath whistle-sucking in his ears, his face thumping hot. He looked back down the stairs diving through the vegetation. The water was no longer visible.

'Hurry, Eliot. Hurry!' he wheezed, starting up the hill again.

Stumbling, frantic footsteps. Up. Up. All pain in his calves, his chest, his groin. The staircase seemed so much longer than before.

Then, over the noise of his breath and the pounding in his head, something else.

He stopped again. Leant forward, hands on his thighs, head tilted. Voices. And the thud and judder of feet on the pathway.

Glancing up, he saw a streak of black against the sun-bleached green of bamboo. He cast about in panic, then launched into the undergrowth. The soil was loose and slippery. He let out a grunting cry as he started to slide.

Shush, Eliot!

He grabbed wildly at branches and plants, and grass, which kept pulling away in clumps. Then he was on all fours, trying to disentangle himself from a Morning Glory vine.

The voices were close. Men's voices.

Scrunching his eyes shut, Eliot rolled himself into a ball.

The pounding on the pathway stopped. Just breathing.

Thick, wet breathing that was outside of Eliot's head and outside of his chest. Breathing that belonged to someone else.

He opened an eye.

Two men were standing on the path, their faces shiny with sweat. One was dressed all in black, his mouth a small rectangle of teeth. The other wore grey shorts and a yellow sports shirt.

'You okay there, fella?'

Friend or foe?

Eliot opened both eyes. The man in yellow looked quite a lot like Mr Roy, his former woodwork teacher – Golden Retriever eyes and ears like big, kind commas.

Eliot took a gulp of air. Wiped his mouth with his arm. Pointed down the slope.

'Down there. She's down there.'

CHAPTER 2

STAN ANDINO

Three months earlier

'Tickets for Air Supply go on sale tomorrow,' Carmen said, scraping up smudges of the chocolate-chilli fondant she and Stan had shared. 'You guys interested?'

They were the last two couples in the restaurant. The waitstaff hovered. 'Air Supply,' Stan groaned. 'You're not putting me through that again.'

Austin and Tibbie laughed. Neither had ordered dessert. Tibbie was very careful with her figure.

'Why does music always have to be your choice?' Carmen snapped.

Stan sighed. 'It can't be more than five years since we saw them. Once a decade is enough for me.'

Carmen swung around, her face flushed. 'Not with me you didn't!'

'Yes. At The Civic. Remember how we thought they were lip-synching?'

'I think I'd know if I'd seen my favourite group live in concert. Don't know who you went with. It certainly wasn't me.'

Stan saw Tibbie shoot Austin a wide-eyed glance.

'No more wine for you, Mrs Andino,' Stan said quickly, patting Carmen on the thigh and signalling for the waiter to bring the bill. 'Better let these guys clear our table so they can go home.'

Carmen swiped away his hand. 'Don't shut me up like that.'

'Woah, just teasing, love.'

Carmen turned back to their friends. 'So, do you or don't you want to join us?'

'Uh, sure,' Tibbie said, fiddling with her vintage brass bracelet. 'What's the date?'

Stan thought that the wide Brutalist cuff looked out of place on Tibbie's delicate wrist. He wondered if she'd inherited it from her mother; it didn't seem her usual style.

'Thirtieth of April at the Bruce Mason, so there'll be no battling traffic to get across the bridge.'

Austin took out his phone and scrolled through his diary. 'Sorry. I've got a medico-legal dinner that night. Tibs, you're invited, too. Looks like we'll have to give it a miss,' he said with a wink.

Stan wasn't sure for whom the wink was intended, but regardless, in true diplomatic fashion, Austin had calmed the waters.

'Thanks for thinking of us,' Tibbie said, resting a hand on Carmen's arm.

Carmen shrugged. 'Looks like it's just me who'll be lip-synching to "I'm All Out of Love".'

CHAPTER 3

AUSTIN LAMB

Two days later Austin found himself again seated across the table from Stan, this time in The British Isles. The place was heaving, which was a surprise considering it was a Monday night.

He undid his top button and took a swig of his IPA. What would it be like to go to work in jeans and an oversized T-shirt? he wondered. Just thinking about Stan's attire made Austin feel itchy and unsettled. The nebulous sagginess of it. A business shirt and chinos were Austin's first pins on the corkboard of an ordered day. Even as a med student he'd refused to swot at home in his pyjamas. Success in life was about playing the part, about actively shaping each day. *Live the life you aspire to achieve*.

He wondered what it was that Stan wanted to talk to him about. The guy had not been his usual laidback self at dinner on Saturday. Tibbie had also noticed, commenting on the drive home how subdued their friend had seemed.

Stan had been pretty consistent in the twenty-four years Austin had known him. An agreeable coaster. Not easily riled. Not easily enthused. A man without ambition or agenda. What you saw was what you got.

It had been awkward with him in the beginning, Stan being a rather late addition to an already tight three-way friendship

– Austin, Tibbie and Carmen – *Friends forever* scrawled in their high-school leaving book. Neither Austin nor Tibbie were too pleased when Carmen's new beau had arrived on the scene, disrupting the cosy threesome. They'd had Carmen all to themselves for almost eight years and were reluctant to have to share her. She was their on-call sounding board. A dependable third wheel. There to fill the gap when Austin was working long hours, or Tibbie was away. Carmen's outrageous confidence and irreverence imported a liveliness into their very respectable lives. Austin had sometimes wondered whether the success of his relationship with Tibbie was predicated on Carmen's presence, like seasoning was to a good meal.

So when Stan Andino started dating Carmen, he had his work cut out for him trying to win over her two best friends. Austin, in particular, made no bones about his disdain for the guy. Tibbie was more forgiving. In retrospect, it would have been impossible for anyone, let alone a podgy pottery teacher, to meet the bar Austin had set for their friend.

Despite Austin's initial misgivings, however, Stan proved a good foil for Carmen: his chilled approach the perfect antidote to her frenetic energy and drive. And she, of course, had been good for Stan in so many ways, not the least being keeping him on track when his lackadaisical work ethos threatened to sabotage the requirements of a regular life.

Over the years the four had shared some significant milestones and traumas. Austin had safely delivered the Andino twins, recognised the mole on Carmen's thigh for what it was, and stitched Stan's hand back together when he almost took off his thumb with the hedge trimmer. And Carmen and Stan had been there for Austin after he missed out on selection for the Plastic Surgery training scheme. Not that he'd been too devastated; just a timing thing, really. In retrospect, General Practice proved very fulfilling. Carmen had also been a huge support to Tibbie when she spiralled into depression after her brother Angus died from an overdose.

Despite a substantial difference in the couples' bank balances, the four had holidayed together a few times over the years – supposedly the true measure of a friendship. They also had a standing arrangement for dinner on the first Saturday of every month, a tradition which they'd observed for years.

'Good value, the feed on Saturday,' Stan began, wiping beer froth off his beard. 'Just sorry the evening ended a bit abruptly. Carmen so tetchy and all.'

Austin put up a hand, halting Stan's apology. 'Air Supply has a lot to answer for.'

'The thing is,' Stan said, rubbing his palms down his thighs, 'she's been like this a lot lately. Flying off the handle for no good reason. Critical of everything I do. And moody like you wouldn't believe.' He dug his thumbnail into the wooden table, indenting a crescent-shaped scar. 'I've even found myself wondering if she's... if she's... I don't know, having an affair.'

'Welcome to life under the golden arches,' Austin said with a smile.

'The golden arches?'

'The big M.'

Stan was still confused. 'McDonald's?'

'Menopause, my friend. It's a turbulent time for our women. And the households they rule.'

'Menopause!' Stan flushed. 'You think so? But... but Carmen still gets her monthly.'

'Things can start going awry quite some time before the big shebang,' Austin said, with a wry grin. 'My advice is: buckle yourself in for the ride. It's bound to be a bit rocky. If you hold on tight, you should come out the other end relatively unscathed.'

Stan's frown melted.

Austin felt gratified by his friend's obvious relief. It was good to have solved at least one problem of the day with ease. It had been a particularly difficult afternoon clinic, no diagnosis straightforward.

He pulled out a handkerchief and dabbed the table where condensation from his glass had collected.

'And find yourself a good florist,' he said, rubbing the stubble on his chin with distaste. Since the age of sixteen he'd had to shave twice a day, and he got his neck and back waxed monthly.

Stan gave a half-hearted chuckle.

'I can have a chat with her next time she's in to see me,' Austin offered. 'Some of my patients get by with very little help, while others really struggle as the feel-good hormones drain out of their lives. Replacement therapy can be a godsend in such instances. It restores a sense of humour to many a desperate household.'

As if in synchrony with their conversation, a woman at a table across from them let out an own-the-room laugh, followed by several loud whoops.

Austin turned, then tossed his head back and raised his glass in her direction.

'Abby Manderson,' he said, answering Stan's quizzical expression. 'Can recognise that laugh a mile away.'

Stan shook his head.'You know everyone.'

'Comes from living in the same suburb as my practice,' Austin said. 'It has its pros and cons, though, let me tell you. Sometimes I'd prefer to travel under the radar.'

'Dr Austin Lamb, local celebrity,' Stan ribbed.

Austin gave a self-deprecating laugh. 'Sure. World-famous in Rothesay Bay.'

Nonetheless, the comment gave him a little boost. If his parents could see him now! Though that would be the only plus in reconnecting with them: seeing the look on their faces when they realised he'd made something of himself, despite them.

He glanced at his watch, took another mouthful of beer, then pushed the bottle aside. 'I'm going to have to do a runner, Stan. Still got a housecall on the way home.'

'Sure. Absolutely. Hey, thanks a ton for swinging by. Really appreciate it. I knew you'd have a sensible take on things.'

'We guys have got to stick together,' Austin said.

Stan leant forward and lowered his voice. 'Has Tibbie… I mean, has she got it, too?'

'You make it sound like some disease,' Austin said, almost embarrassed by Stan's schoolboy discomfort. He pushed his chair back. 'Don't worry about it. Carmen will be fine.'

Stan stood up. Fumbled in his back pocket. 'My shout.'

'Cheers,' Austin said, and headed out into the night.

CHAPTER 4

STAN ANDINO

It was raining cats and dogs as Stan drove home. The storm, which had been waiting in bloated clouds all day, had finally been unleashed.

Menopause. The word went back and forth in his head in time with the windscreen wipers.

At least it wasn't serious. He'd let his imagination run away with him.

Almost convinced himself Carmen was having an affair.

Just forming *that* word in his head left Stan's mouth dry and his gums prickling. From the day twenty-four years earlier when Carmen had sat down next to him on the Contiki Tours' bus, he'd been waiting for his luck to run out. As if it was too good to be true that a vivacious and seriously switched-on girl would fall for him.

Only his mother had seemed unsurprised. But that was Greek mothers for you.

'Stan, he is very special boy. Very special. Good you catch him now, Caramel, before the other girls, no?'

'Ma, stop! And her name is Carmen.'

His mother shrugged. 'Why I must stop? Is the truth. You are hot property, Stanley Andino.'

Stan pulled into the driveway of their simple brick and plaster bungalow, built in the sixties, no architect in sight.

The gutters were spewing water, as if crying uncontrollably. Carmen had been nagging him for months to get up on the roof and clear them.

—girl, are you happy in this—

He pulled up the handbrake and switched off the ignition, unintentionally killing Lady Gaga. He turned the ignition back on, but there was a delay before the song resumed, and by then he'd popped out of the mood. He switched off the car again, killing the headlights and dropping darkness over the house.

There were no lights on inside, which was odd. And Carmen usually left the porch light on for him if he was going to be late.

A flash of lightning brought the bungalow to life in a gasp of blue. Then everything went black again.

Stan rummaged blindly in the back for a brolly. Why was there never one in the car when he needed it?

Despite no umbrella, he was glad for the rain. It was a welcome reprieve from the relentless block of heat that had stretched across the month – day after day, temperatures in the thirties. It had left people on edge, as if the seemingly unending summer had somehow been a mistake and there would be a price to pay besides the restless nights. So much sunshine felt like a threat. *Don't enjoy yourself too much…*

He opened the car door and, canopying his sweatshirt over his head, ran around to the passenger side to get the flowers he'd bought at an after-hours florist. Six long-stemmed ivory roses tied together with a hessian bow and secured with a pearl-headed pin. They'd cost a small fortune. More than an impoverished pottery teacher could afford anyway. And now they were about to get battered by oversized raindrops.

He made a dash for the garage door and tried unsuccessfully to roll it up with his spare hand, but it required both.

Carmen had got a quote for installing an automated garage door, but he'd resisted. There were other ways to spend the bank's money.

He felt a dart of irritation towards Austin. 'Buy her

flowers.' 'Thanks for picking up the tab.' 'A new garage door – no problem.' It was different on a doctor's income.

Stan stood dripping in the darkness of the garage – the air a suffocating mix of dust, lawnmower fuel, and weed spray – and tried to plump out the saturated hessian bow. The bouquet no longer looked expensive.

He made his way through the interconnecting door. 'Hiya! I'm home!'

The house was quiet and disappointingly devoid of dinner smells. Had Carmen succumbed to the boys' endless nagging and gotten takeaways? He switched on the hall light, the solitary bulb bringing the narrow corridor and worn paisley runner to sepia life. The door to the living room was shut.

'Hellooo!' he called out. 'This is your father and loving husband calling any live members of the Andino household to please present themselves.'

He moved down the hallway, his gaze taking in the framed family portrait of his grandparents in Greece three-quarters of a century ago. Both dressed in black. Neither smiling. It had been hanging on the wall for years and was so familiar it had become invisible. But now, his yaya's dark eyes held his gaze.

'Anybody home?'

'Don't come in!' Carmen shouted from behind the shut door. 'Not till I say so.'

'Okay, okay,' Stan said, smiling to himself. 'I've got a surprise for you, too. Just saying.'

Reuben put his head out of his bedroom door and pulled out an earphone. 'Hey, Dad.'

'How you going, Squirt?'

Leon's head appeared beside his brother's.

'And another body surfaces! Any more of you in there?'

It had taken Stan about ten days to tell the twins apart after they first came home. In the neonatal unit they'd been in clearly labelled incubators – REUBEN ANDINO. LEON ANDINO. But outside the Perspex breathing boxes, they were just indistinguishable shrivels of pink.

Eventually, he'd got better at recognising their little idiosyncrasies that subtly toyed with the identical-twin template; Leon tended to scrunch up his eyes to the light, and Reuben was a thumb-sucker.

Of course, now, at the age of thirteen, it was sometimes hard to believe they were even siblings, let alone identical. They couldn't have had more different personalities.

'Good day at school, guys?'

The boys glanced at each other, then Leon blurted out: 'Mum's been... She's, like, doing some seriously weird stuff, Dad.'

Stan frowned. Looked at the hallway door. It was never normally shut.

He swallowed, then passed the roses to Reuben, as if he was going to need both hands.

CHAPTER 5

STAN ANDINO

Stan winced as he stepped into the lounge, a strong chemical smell searing his nostrils. He scanned the room, which at first glance was empty. Then Carmen jumped up from where she'd been kneeling in front of the couch. 'What part of "Do not come in till I say so" don't you understand?'

Stan's eyes narrowed. His wife was naked, except for his black barbecuing apron.

Every minute detail of the scene registered on his retinas, like some all-seeing eye. The bucket of silvered foam. The industrial-size bottle of bleach, cap askew. The carpet disfigured by large, pale pockmarks. Carmen's pendulous breasts escaping from behind the black fabric. The kidney-shaped sponge he kept for cleaning the car, in her rubber-gloved hand. A dead moth upended on the windowsill. The cat backed into a corner.

'What's happened?'

'Now you've gone and spoilt the surprise,' Carmen said, pouting.

Stan moved towards the window. Forced it open. 'Jeez, how can you breathe in here?'

The cat shot across the room and dived through the gap.

'Oh, come on! It's not that bad.'

'Carmen, what on earth are you doing?' Stan's thoughts could find no anchor. Nothing about the scene made sense.

He turned. The boys were standing at the door, their eyes wide.

'Give us a minute, guys,' Stan said, trying to steady his voice.

As the twins backed obediently down the hall, he closed the door, then turned to his wife. 'Carmen, what are you doing to the carpet? And why in God's name are you naked?'

'It's not like you haven't seen all this before,' she said, with a snort.

'But… What are you doing?' he asked again, searching the room for some clue. For a bizarre moment he was looking for blood spatter, a chainsaw, a dismembered body.

'It's such a dark, depressing brown. We keep talking about getting new carpets. Talking. Always talking! You and I both know it's never going to happen. We can't afford to. So I'm taking matters into my own hands.'

'You're bleaching the entire carpet?' Stan said, trying to compute the scale of what his wife was undertaking.

'No, I thought I'd just do one corner of the room,' she said sarcastically. Then, with a smile, 'Of course I'll do the whole carpet.'

In that moment, as Carmen spoke in a calm, logical voice, Stan had never felt more alone, or more frightened.

'But what possessed you to embark on such DIY madness at this time of night? You didn't think that perhaps we should discuss it first, before you let loose with bleach in our lounge?' Anger surged through him. 'And you're… doing it naked because, what, you want to scare the kids?'

'Oh, don't be such a prude,' she said, flinging down the sponge. A spray of bleach bubbles landed on his jeans.

'I didn't want to discolour my clothes,' she said, as if the answer couldn't have been more obvious. 'Anyway, it won't do the boys any harm to see how real work gets done. They're too used to sitting around on their arses all day.'

It was Carmen's last comment that gave Stan his first clue and helped him interpret the uninterpretable. Carmen adored her sons. Would offer herself up as a sacrifice for them in a heartbeat. She'd never refer to them in this way. Not unless something was wrong. Very, very wrong.

As terrifying as the thought was, it was easier to deal with than trying to rationalise her actions within some normal domestic paradigm.

Stan grabbed a kitchen cloth and dabbed at his jeans. Already the bleach had leached speckles of colour from the denim. It must have been undiluted.

'Have you and the boys had dinner?'

She shook her head.

'Tell you what, why don't you call it a day?' he said slowly. 'I'll clean up here while you hop in a bath. We can finish the job together on the weekend.'

She opened her mouth as if to object.

'Go on. The kids must be starving. I'll make us some scrambled eggs.'

Carmen peeled off the pink gloves and flung them down. 'Kids, kids, kids! It's always about the kids.'

'I know,' he said, rolling his eyes collusively. 'Off you go, love.'

Stan stood motionless in the middle of the room until he heard the bath water running, then he pulled out his phone and, with trembling fingers, punched in the Lambs' home number. Tibbie picked up.

'It's Stan,' he said in a loud whisper. 'Sorry to disturb you guys at this hour. Could I have a quick word with Austin?'

'He's just this minute got in from a house-call, Stan. Can I get him to call you after he's had his dinner?'

'Look, I really need to talk with him now, if you don't mind.' He cupped his hand around the receiver; the bathroom door was ajar. 'It's sort of an emergency,' he whispered.

'Gosh. Okay. Just a minute.'

He heard her footsteps across the parquet floor. The woosh of the sliding door. Her distant voice. 'Austin, it's Stan.'

Lovely, long-suffering Tibbie, ever obliged to share her

husband with a village of patients. How many times over the years had she attended dinners and birthday parties and gallery openings on her own because Austin had been called away to deal with some heart attack, broken bone, or the impending birth of a baby? If Austin was the perfect, dedicated doctor, then Tibbie was, without doubt, the perfect doctor's wife. Uncomplaining. Gracious to a fault. Not to mention beautiful.

'He's coming now,' she said, a little out of breath. 'Is everything alright?'

He wanted to tell her about the craziness that was happening inside his house. But that would not have been fair on her, or Carmen. They were best friends.

'I just need… a word.'

'Here he is.'

'Stan, what's up?'

Stan could detect a hint of irritation behind Austin's unfailing civility. He closed his eyes. Swallowed.

'Just when you thought you were rid of me for the night,' he said, forcing a laugh. 'Listen, I'm sorry to ask this of you, but I need you to come over here as quickly as you can.'

CHAPTER 6

ELIOT BARD

When Eliot heard the doorbell ring, he buried his head under his pillow. Greeting visitors at 33b was his job. He was the one who got to let in Uncle Alan and Aunt Sally. And Roz, the once-a-month cleaning lady. His mum's stitch-and-bitch group, too. The one who signed for courier packages and parcels too big to put in the post-box. And the person who got to buy two packets of Girl Guide biscuits with the money left out in the small wooden bowl on the hallway table. He also knew to politely take pamphlets from Jehovah's witnesses, but never invite them in. Yes, he, Eliot Bard, was gatekeeper of the castle.

'This is a responsible job,' his mum always reminded him. 'Remember to harness your enthusiasm, Elli, like a well-trained steed. A runaway horse is no good to anyone.'

Eliot loved horses. His bedroom walls were covered with them – palominos, appaloosas, Scottish Clydesdales… Horses and red-haired superwomen. He had a life-size poster of Queen Medusa, and three smaller ones of Queen Mera, Lana Lang, and Kate Kane. Just recently, he'd also added Artemis Grace to his collection of red-headed warrior women.

The bell rang again.

He started to rock backwards and forwards on his bed, his eyes scrunched tight, his fingers rammed into his ears.

Time collapsed. Darkness took over. Purple and green

ripples spread behind his eyelids like fireworks dissolving into a night sky.

Someone's hand gripped Eliot's shoulder. He squealed. Then came the warm, sweet smell of his mum.

He flicked open his eyes.

'Eliot, what's wrong? Why didn't you come and open the door?'

He looked up. Shook his head.

'I had to use the key behind the birdbath.'

'Sorry.'

She sat down beside him. 'What's up?'

He craned his neck to look past her through his open bedroom door.

'Eliot?' She was staring at his bloodied knees and muddy shoes. He was going to get into trouble for not taking them off before coming inside.

'Look at me.' Her voice was like fishing line wound too tightly around its reel.

Eliot liked fishing, but not the bit where you had to stick a knife into the fish's brain, just behind the eye.

He stared at the floor, fingering an outcrop of bristly hairs on his cheek that he must have missed when he'd shaved on Monday.

'At me, please,' his mum said.

His eyes crept up.

'Did something happen on your walk?'

She always knew everything.

He gave a shallow nod.

She started to rub his back in slow, smooth circles. 'There are two police officers here who would like to ask you a few questions. They arrived just as I was pulling in.'

Police. Eliot began rocking again.

'No, Eliot!' his mum said firmly. 'Remember, the police help us. Firefighters, too.'

He looked at her warily.

'Who else?'

'Ambulance drivers!' he blurted out. 'And teachers. And doctors. And—'

'That's right. Doctors and nurses and firefighters and the police. Now, let's go into the lounge and say hello, shall we?'

She stood up and put out her hand.

Two strangers were standing in the lounge, their back to the door. A man and a woman. Only the woman was dressed in uniform, but both wore padded blue vests. They turned.

'Eliot, this is—'

'Ramesh Bandara,' said the tall, dark-skinned man, stretching out his hand in greeting. He had a thin scar running from his lip into his left nostril, which made his mouth look flat and his smile sort of square.

Eliot ran a finger along his own lip and up into his nostril.

His mum yanked down his hand.

'DC Hilary Stark,' said the woman officer. She had a flat body, like a paper doll, and a skew blonde fringe.

Stark. She was nothing like Tony Stark, Iron Man's alter ego.

'Please have a seat,' his mum said. 'I'll put on the jug.'

'Not on our account,' Ramesh Bandara said, sitting down and spreading his legs manly wide. 'We're fine, thank you.'

Eliot copied him, spreading his legs wide, too, while keeping hold of his mum's hand.

'Is that to stop bullets?' Eliot asked, pointing at the woman's bolstered vest.

'Knives,' she said.

'What about guns and stuff?'

'We can insert ceramic plates in here,' the man said, pulling at the top of his vest. 'But they're pretty heavy to wear around all day.'

He was definitely more friend than foe. Eliot wasn't sure about the Hilary woman. Her voice was hard and splintery like the old-fashioned school desk his mum had stored in the garage.

'How come you're not wearing a uniform?'

'Eliot, that's enough questions,' his mum interrupted.

'It's fine,' Ramesh Bandara said, wobbling his head from side to side. 'I'm a detective sergeant. We don't often wear uniforms in CIB. Whereas Detective Constable Stark is in training to be a detective, so she's still a part of the uniformed division.'

'Hey, you've got different-coloured eyes,' Eliot blurted out. One of the policewoman's eyes was blue, the other brown.

'Eliot!'

Detective Bandara leant forward. 'If it's okay with you, we'd like to ask you a few questions about your walk to the beach this morning.'

Eliot opened his eyes wide.

'Let's start with your age. How old are you?'

'Twenty-one! My birthday is on the sixth of February, which is Waitangi Day, which means my mum will always be home from work, because Waitangi Day is a public holiday and always will be, unless New Zealand turns communist, or into a totalitarian state, or something like that. Next year my mum's going to make me an ice-cream cake. Hey, Mum?'

She nodded.

The detective smiled as he scribbled in his notebook. He looked up. 'Want to know something pretty cool?'

He was obviously a good toothbrusher; he had super-white teeth.

'The sixth of February is my birthday, too.'

'No way! He's got the same birthday as me, Mum. That's crazy wild.'

'Virtual high-five,' Ramesh Bandara said, putting his hand in the air.

Eliot did the same, grinning widely. 'Virtual high-five.'

'Do you walk to the beach often?' Hilary Stark asked, cutting into the fun with her one-level voice.

Eliot swallowed his grin. He looked at his mum.

'Mondays, Wednesdays and Fridays,' she said, answering for him. 'He likes to explore the rock pools at low tide. Collect treasure.'

'Wanna see my collection?' Eliot said, jumping up off the couch.

Stark put up her hand. Shook her head.

'Maybe later,' Ramesh Bandara added. 'Now, Eliot, can you tell us what you told the men you met on the pathway this morning?'

Eliot turned to his mum.

'It's alright, my boy.'

He looked back at the policeman, while trying to block out the woman with his hand.

'The two runners?' the detective prompted.

Eliot's eyelids started twitching as the events of the morning burst into his head.

'You told them something?'

'Hmm.'

There were fly spots on the ceiling. His mum hated fly spots. Pesky things pooing upside down. It would be hard to poo upside down, he thought, imagining himself doing a handstand and—

'Eliot?'

'I told them... I told them... that she was down there.'

'Who?' Hilary Stark asked, sitting forward.

Eliot frowned, trying to make her small by looking at her through a slit between his thumb and forefinger.

'Who was down there?' she persisted.

'The lady.'

'Which lady?'

'The one under the water.'

He started rocking.

His mum pulled his head against her shoulder. 'Oh, you poor baby.'

Eliot whimpered, trying to sweep away the picture that had grown from thumbnail to full-size in his head. He jerked out of his mum's hold.

'She looked like a red sea urchin.' He flapped his hands. 'Her hair swishing in the waves.'

Eliot felt his mum's body stiffen.

'You must have been quite a long way around from the beach to spot her,' Stark said. 'Do you always walk so far around?'

He glanced at his mum out of the corner of his eye, all the while shaking his head.

'The tide would have been coming in.'

'I thought she was treasure.'

'Treasure?'

'She had on this ginormous bracelet.' Eliot turned, spreading his thumb and forefinger wide. 'It was, like, this big, Mum.'

His mum's breathing had gone all strange, as if she'd trapped it inside a box. It sounded like it wanted to be louder, but she was holding down the lid.

'You must have been very close to see her bracelet,' Stark persisted.

Eliot decided he didn't like her.

'I'm a real good spotter. Mr McDougal calls me eagle-eye.'

Then the lady with long red hair was there, right in front of him. He shut his eyes.

'How far away were you?' the policewoman asked. 'As far as the dining-room table? More?'

'It was sparkling in the sun. So, I went closer.'

'But it was raining,' Hilary Stark said.

'Only for a bit, silly.'

'Eliot!' his mum said sternly.

'Well, it's true,' he protested. 'The rain was just in the beginning. Then the sun poked through. Toad-in-the-hole sort of sunshine.'

'Roughly what time was this?' asked the proper detective.

'10.05 am.'

'That's pretty exact.'

'Eliot never makes mistakes with time,' his mum said. 'Time, dates, numbers. He's a stickler for detail. Remembers things most of us wouldn't. He's very observant, too.'

'Yeah. I'm really good at remembering stuff. Like Mum wore her black and white spotty dress on my ninth birthday. Didn't you, Mum? And that was *twelve* years ago! And there were exactly 322 different Christmas decorations at the pop-up Christmas shop last year. And—'

CHAPTER 7

STAN ANDINO

Stan stared straight ahead. The space had been designed to trick a person into feeling at ease – the pastel hues, expensive coffee machine in the corner, thick-piled carpet, the bowl of assorted chocolates on the table. But none of it was working; Stan sat rigidly in the only straight-backed chair in the room, gripping the armrests as if on a turbulent flight. Even the *Classic Car* magazine couldn't tempt him.

He usually enjoyed people-watching, his sculptor's eye fascinated by the infinite variations of the human visage. And what better place to observe the human form than in a medical waiting room – a person's mouse-curled ears, sharp nostrils, collapsed-parachute jowls. But not today. He was tired. Really tired.

After what felt like forever, the door swung open and out shuffled Carmen, his lovely wife a decade older in just seven days. Same, but different.

Her impish haircut and luscious dark brows. Her cute, cubed toes peeping out from her sandals. Her otter eyes. Same. But her gaze disconcertingly vacant, as if she'd just endured electric shock therapy.

Electric shock therapy. Stan tried to banish the thought that had crossed his mind a few times over the previous week. Was it even something doctors still did? Could it help?

'We'll be in touch with your doctor as soon as the radiologist has reviewed the scan,' the radiographer said, her voice calm and warm, her face giving nothing away. 'Carmen might be a little sleepy; we gave her a sedative to keep her still, while in the scanner.'

'Thank you,' Stan said, lingering in the woman's kindness.

'Rachel Barry,' a voice called out over the PA.

A heavily pregnant woman heaved herself up.

And just like that, the busyness of other people's lives resumed around them.

Stan led Carmen to the front desk.

'That will be one thousand and thirty dollars,' the receptionist said, her casual tone at odds with the exorbitant sum.

'One thousand and thirty!' Stan repeated. 'Bloody hell!'

The woman looked up sharply.

'We have insurance,' Carmen said robotically.

'Yes, of course,' Stan said. 'We have medical insurance.'

'Because you didn't get prior approval,' the receptionist went on, addressing only Carmen, as if Stan was suddenly invisible, 'you'll need to pay the full amount now and claim it back from your insurer afterwards.'

'Right.' Carmen turned to Stan. 'Did you bring your wallet?'

Stan fumbled in his back pocket.

Carmen took it from him and pulled out two credit cards.

'Put half on each,' she said.

'All done,' the woman said, with the first flicker of a smile.

'Talk about up herself!' Stan muttered, once they were outside. 'Anyone would think she was the bloody Queen of Sheba.'

'She's just doing her job,' Carmen said.

Stan rubbed his chin, trying to make sense of his confusion. Beside him stood his wife – sensible, unruffled, in charge.

They decided to grab a bite in the café abutting the radiology suite; neither of them had had breakfast yet.

Stan ordered a mince-and-cheese pie, Carmen a pottle of fruit salad topped with granola.

He welled up watching her eat. The ordinariness of the activity. What had once been commonplace, now felt precious. In that moment, he loved her so much.

They were driving home when his mobile rang. Stan reached into his pocket.

Carmen grabbed the wheel. 'Pull over, Stan!'

'It's fine,' he said, pressing the speaker button. His phone fell into the footwell.

'Stan, it's Gwen from Austin Lamb's rooms.' The woman's voice filled the car.

Stan slowed.

'Austin was wondering whether you and Carmen would be able to come down to the rooms later today. He suggested about five-thirty?'

'That was quick,' said Stan, pulling over and retrieving his phone. It had been less than an hour since they'd left the radiology suite.

He felt hopeful. Reporting on an unremarkable scan surely took less time than if there'd been something serious to document.

A flash of doubt niggled at this logic, but his optimism would not be quashed. Normal, sane Carmen was sitting beside him.

He let out a sigh, the previous week already losing some of its turgidity. Had there been something structurally wrong with Carmen's brain, surely she would not have bounced back so easily? One of the possible diagnoses Austin had posited – Carmen's dipping hormones precipitating a psychotic episode – now seemed the most plausible explanation.

Stan was no doctor, but his wife's response to the antipsychotics had been dramatic. Miraculous even. He was just grateful they were living in the twenty-first century, where there were drugs to deal with such anomalies. A psychotic episode precipitated by menopause felt like something to be happy about. Even grateful for. Certainly when pitched against anything more sinister.

He shook his head, musing on how easy it was to reframe one's outlook.

The remainder of the day completed the reinstallation of normality. Carmen took a short nap before preparing macaroni cheese for the boys. She helped Leon with his Maths homework, revised an article due for the magazine, and spoke with her editor about getting an extension on another feature. Then, at five o'clock, she and Stan made their way through rush-hour traffic to Austin's practice.

CHAPTER 8

CARMEN ANDINO

The waiting room was empty, except for a locum nurse tidying the toybox. How many times had Carmen been there over the years, to the rundown cottage Austin had converted into medical rooms on his return from a lucrative stint in Saskatoon as a new graduate? The polished wooden floors, leafy pot plants, the cork board connecting a community with news.

Austin's door stood ajar. Through the gap Carmen could see her friend hunched over his keyboard.

'Go on in,' the nurse said to her and Stan. 'Doctor's last patient cancelled.'

Carmen knocked. Austin double-clicked his mouse and jumped up.

'Hi!' he said, coming around from his desk and wrapping Carmen in a tight hug. 'And how's my girl bearing up?'

'Thick fog and poor visibility. But other than a headache you could mistake for a bad ski-report, can't complain.'

She and Stan had skied only once together, the entire exercise proving a costly disaster for the uncommitted beginners. Because of the expensive outlay for accommodation, ski hire, and a week-long lift pass, Stan had insisted they go up the mountain every day, despite appalling weather. It was an experience Carmen vowed never to repeat.

'Take a seat, guys,' Austin said, closing the door behind them.

Carmen looked around the room she knew so well. The row of suspended silver balls, which, when set off, knocked against each other ad infinitum. The portrait of Tibbie taken on a trip to India, her auburn tresses blending in with exotic Jaipur. The crayon scribbles from adoring little patients taped neatly to the wall... Austin would have made a great dad. It was such a pity he and Tibbie had never had children.

'You had the MRI this morning.'

'Yup,' Stan said. 'For the price of a small car.'

'You've got insurance, right?' Austin asked, his brow furrowing in concern.

'Yes, but—'

'Stan, it's not important,' Carmen interjected irritably. 'We'll get the money back.'

'According to the high goddess of all receptionists,' Stan continued, setting off the silver balls, 'you have to apply for retrospective approval,' he said, mimicking the woman's voice. *Click. Click. Click.*

Carmen swiped at the silver balls, bringing them to a stop. 'There's a toybox outside if you want to play, Stan.'

Austin's face darkened. He slipped his hands between his knees. 'I'm afraid, guys, I don't have good news.'

'I knew it!' Stan said. 'Bloody insurers. What do we pay outrageous premiums for if when we need them they decline? I mean how—'

'Carmen.' Austin's eyes were glistening, and the tip of his nose had turned red.

A sense of unease burrowed into her.

'I really wish I didn't have to tell you this.'

Time slowed.

Austin took her hands in his. 'The scan shows you have a tumour in your brain.'

His words swung into the space like a demolition ball.

Carmen sank back in her chair.

The steriliser in the corner of the room crackled and creaked through a heat cycle. A lone car horn punched its way in through the open window. The Venetian blinds slapped against the sill.

'Actually, a few tumours.'

Carmen freed a shaking hand. Put it to her mouth. Dropped it to the desk. 'A few?'

Austin nodded. 'One large tumour and several smaller ones.'

Stan grabbed Carmen's free hand, linking the three of them like a fragile chain of paper dolls.

The ticking of the antique clock on the back wall counted out the events of the past few weeks. The police arriving to assist ambulance officers in taking her to hospital. Nosy neighbours on the footpath, whispering, pointing, ignoring her pleas. Strong hands holding her down. The door that required one code to get in and another to get out. The starched, strange-smelling sheets. The fog.

Her twin boys visiting with careful smiles, fear and confusion peering out from behind kind eyes. The door with the code opening. Home. Her own duvet. Sleep.

All this now seemed so insignificant when held up against the goliath of cancer.

For a moment, Carmen felt vindicated. She was not mad, after all. There was a tumour in her brain. A tumour!

She extricated her hands and placed them over her head, as if expecting it to feel different.

'Is this a death sentence, Austin?'

For the first time that she could recall, her suave, sage friend looked flummoxed.

'I'm referring you to one of the best oncology teams in the country, Carmen. There have been exciting new advances in the treatment of brain tumours. It's going to be a hard road, but Tibbie and I will be with you both every step of the way. Whatever time of day or night. Whatever you need.' He told them that the biggest tumour was in her frontal lobe, 'the centre for personality and emotion'. Mood swings could be expected. Confusion, too. Headaches, an altered sense of smell and taste, anxiety, depression, disinhibition. All possible. The risk of seizures, too.

'First step, if it's feasible, is to remove all, or as much of, the biggest tumour as possible. This will also allow us to identify the tumour type, which will help direct the treatment plan. We could be dealing with metastases from the melanoma on your thigh I removed four years back. Or there might be another primary altogether. A full body scan will help answer that.'

Aside from surgery, there were medications to lower the pressure on her brain. Drugs to reduce the risk of fitting. Radiotherapy and chemotherapy to shrink the growth. Possibly immunotherapy to boost her own defences... All would become clearer once a diagnosis had been made. 'One step at a time. One day at a time.'

Carmen was reeling. Something had slipped into her brain when no-one was watching. Something evil and malicious, which did not need a door code to get in. And now, like malware installed on a computer, it was poised to disrupt her life and that of her precious family.

A phone dinged.

Austin opened his top drawer and pulled out his mobile to read what must have been a text message.

'Sorry,' he said, looking up sheepishly. 'Just need to send a quick reply.'

A dart of anger shot through Carmen. She couldn't remember Austin ever answering his phone during a consultation before.

'Just some important results needing urgent follow up,' he said, putting his phone away again.

'Don't let us get in the way of something important,' she sniped.

'Now, where was I?' Austin said, floundering a little.

'The referral,' Stan prompted.

'Yes! The referral. The whole process is going to be a lot easier with you having health insurance. There should be no unnecessary delays. I've taken the liberty of getting Gwen to book you an urgent appointment with Ngaire Bell this Friday. She's a top oncologist. Her rooms are in Remuera.'

Carmen's head felt heavy. Heavier than when she'd walked in. There was a cancer growing inside her brain.

'You'll be feeling pretty shell-shocked, I'm sure. However, once it all starts to sink in, you will have questions. And when you do, I'll be here.'

Carmen couldn't think of a single question. Couldn't pin down a single thought.

'Thank you, Austin,' Stan said, standing up and positioning himself behind Carmen, his hands resting lightly on her shoulders.

Thank you seemed the wrong thing to say.

The waiting room felt foreign and desolate, as if there'd been a silent apocalypse while they'd been holed up inside Austin's office.

'Before I forget,' he said, opening the front door for them. 'Tibbie's got dinner sorted. She'll be dropping it around to yours shortly.'

'Hope it's not chicken,' Carmen said, blowing her nose. 'Because we had chicken last night.'

Stan nudged her in the ribs.

The humidity of the evening came as a surprise after the air-conditioned coolness. The temperature outside was more real. More aligned with the news.

Stan opened the car door for Carmen, and she sank into the springless seat. The smell of a banana skin that had been macerating on the dashboard was even more pungent for the heat. But Carmen didn't have the energy to berate Stan. What was the point?

He climbed into the driver's seat and they both sat there in silence, staring at the sign on the wall in front of them. *5-minute-drop-off zone.*

The letters blurred. Carmen blinked. She was going to die. The twins were just thirteen. She wasn't going to be there for their final-year ball, or to see them graduate. They would become professionals, lovers, husbands, fathers, without her. She was going to leave them and their bumbling, kind, kid-of-a-father. How would they cope? How could they cope?

'That's Tibbie for you,' she said finally, flicking her forefinger with her thumb. 'Already muscling in on the tragedy with offers of her pretentious cooking.'

Stan turned to her, tears in his eyes. 'No.' He shook his head. 'How can you say that?'

She sucked in her lips. 'I'm not even in the ground yet and already she's making a move on you.'

CHAPTER 9

ELIOT BARD

Eliot's mum had made his favourite dinner – nachos. He'd set the table out on the deck from where they could see a sliver of the sea. That's what his mum called it. A sliver of sea. Eliot loved the sound of those words. Sometimes he would say them over and over, faster and faster, until nothing but gibberish came out.

Houses with a sea view were super-expensive. His mum would never have been able to afford one. But then, the previous winter, a big old Norfolk pine in the garden on the other side of the street blew down, opening a spyhole of blue. In just one night the value of their house went up by thousands.

'I like Ramesh,' Eliot said, spraying speckles of mince across the table.

'Don't talk with your mouth full,' his mum growled, as she leant over and wiped his face with a napkin.

He pulled away. 'Stop it, Ma. I'm a man now.'

'You are. Sorry.' She took a gulp of wine. 'Yes, Detective Bandara seems nice enough.'

'What will he do with the red lady?'

His mum lowered her fork. 'Was there a lot of blood?'

He shook his head.

His mum's cheek started to twitch. 'Then why do you keep calling her red?'

Eliot began grinding his teeth and making patterns in the mince with his fork.

'Eliot?'

'Cause of her red hair, silly.'

The pink in his mother's cheeks drained away like water down a plughole, making the mole on her temple stand out like a giant fly spot. She used to have long brown hair, but then she cut it off, because she said women her age didn't suit long hair. Eliot was so mad with her he didn't talk to her for two whole days. He was not a fan of the short and spiky look. But he was used to it now. She'd let it grow a bit and looked less like a puffer fish.

'What will Ramesh do with her?'

His mother reached for her glass again. 'Well, the woman's family will probably arrange a funeral.'

'And they'll talk about all the things that made her special, hey? Like we did at Gran's funeral. How she baked the best Eccles cakes ever and could beat anyone at swing ball.'

His mum smiled slowly. 'Yes, they'll mention all her special qualities. And afterwards, they'll probably bury her somewhere pretty.'

'Or burn her, hey?'

'Don't say "hey"! I've told you a thousand times.'

Eliot put his knife and fork together. He wasn't hungry anymore.

'Sorry,' his mum said, stretching her hand across the table. 'I don't mean to be cranky. I'm just a bit tired.'

'Is it your moody time of the month?'

She laughed. 'No, it is not!'

'What will they say at my funeral, Mum?'

'Oh, Eliot, don't think about an awful thing like that. You're going to live for a long, long time.'

'That I was great with numbers. And super-friendly. And that I loved treasure more than anything. Treasure and horses and—'

'And that you are a whizz with the vacuum cleaner,' she said quickly.

'*Was* a whizz with the vacuum cleaner. Past tense. I'll be dead, remember.'

His mum got up and cleared away the dishes.

'And that I was the fastest dishwasher unpacker.'

She was making a real racket scraping their plates into the bin.

'What will happen to the bracelet, Mum?'

'What bracelet?'

'You weren't using your listening ears when I told the detective about the lady's big bracelet, were you?'

His mum scooped the leftover mince into a Tupperware.

'Will it go in her tomb, too, like a pharaoh's treasure?'

'I don't know.'

'Are you angry with me?'

'Of course not!' She turned on the tap full blast and water sprayed all over her. 'Shit! I mean, flip!'

Eliot felt muddled.

'I'm just sad for the woman's family, those who've lost her,' his mum said, trying to smile.

'She didn't get lost. She fell off the cliff. That's what Ramesh said.'

His mum spun around. 'And that is why I do not want you going on the cliff track again. Do you hear me? No more ferreting in the bushes up there. I've told you before to take Browns Bay Road down to the beach. It's only ten or fifteen minutes longer.'

Eliot tugged at his eyebrow hairs.

'You were up there before you went down to the beach today, weren't you? On the cliffs.'

He scrunched up his nose. Released. Scrunched. Released.

'Eliot?'

He shook his head, then nodded. 'But only on the path. I never went on the other side of the barrier. Promise.'

'Eliot, I want you to—'

'Can I have peanut-butter ice-cream tonight?'

'No, you cannot.'

His mum was angry with him. Even if she said she wasn't, she was. He could tell.

CHAPTER 10

STAN ANDINO

Stan woke with a start. His whole body ached. He'd been sleeping across two hospital chairs. His scalp was itchy. A baby was crying.

He sat up and scratched his head.

A woman in a turquoise dressing gown sloped past, a newborn propped against her shoulder.

In an instant Stan had rewound thirteen years and was again holding Reuben against his chest while Carmen tried to express milk. How terrifying that time had been for Stan and Carmen. How bleak and hard.

Reuben. A nervous wrinkle of skin with such a high-pitched cry. Poor thing, abruptly separated from his brother with whom he'd shared a womb for just over seven months. Leon, still in an incubator, had seemed less fazed by the separation.

Who would have thought that such a tiny human being would grow into a kid who played guitar, was fastest in his year in the hundred-metre sprint, and could put back four jam sandwiches without even a burp? Stan smiled to himself. Despite all their first-time-parents-of-prem-twins anxieties, things had worked out. Neither Reuben nor Leon was going to become a rocket scientist, but that probably had less to do with their premature birth than their genes.

He thought about that first round of IVF. The excitement of

a plan, the START DAY ringed in red. In retrospect, it would have been better to ring it in ballpoint blue or black. Red was just tempting fate. Almost inviting Carmen's monthly bleed.

He and Carm had been feeling buoyant. After all the trying, all the waiting, all the dreams trickling out of Carmen each calendar month – finally, something constructive. Hope underwritten by science.

But IVF only proved a new sort of hell, neither of them prepared for the havoc hormones would wreak on poor Carmen. Nor the devastation and grief that would accompany her period, which arrived each time as punctually as one of Mussolini's trains. The fall somehow felt greater coming from the perch of a pharmaceutical promise.

They could only afford two rounds. Or rather it was all Carmen's parents could afford. Twice the devastation. Twice the grief. Twice the guilt. As if Stan and Carmen were somehow to blame for wasting their two big-ticket chances and Geoff and Pam's retirement savings.

Richard, Carmen's brother, paid for one further round, but by then Stan was over it. To him it was just another turn at spinning the wheel when the odds were so clearly stacked against them.

They never saw it coming when the sonographer picked up the first faint *whoosh-whoosh*. Then her bemused expression as she tilted the probe. Two heartbeats! Talk about hitting the jackpot. Billionaires overnight.

Stan ran his hands through his hair and took a sip of cold coffee.

For all the doubts that forever played on shuffle in his head, he'd managed to secure a wonderful wife and become the father of two beautiful boys. Good things could happen to him. Had happened to him.

The neurosurgeon now looked more like a surgeon in his theatre greens than he had dressed in a business suit and floral tie.

'We managed to remove a significant amount of the largest tumour,' he said, rubbing his eyes. 'Unfortunately, as I suspected, we were not able to remove it all. Saying that, we now have tissue to confirm the tumour type, which will help us tailor Carmen's treatment.' He pulled off his theatre hat, exposing sandy blond hair plastered to his scalp. 'By debulking the tumour, we've reduced some of the pressure on your wife's brain, which should alleviate some of her symptoms.'

The man had a firm handshake. Warm and manly.

He pulled Stan towards him, patting him on the shoulder with his other hand.

The gesture felt too familiar; they were practically strangers.

In another way, it felt strangely formal, considering the man had just held Carmen's life in his hands.

'She'll be in Intensive Care for a few days. Standard in these sorts of cases. Just give the team an hour or so to get her settled, then you can pop up and see her.'

When Stan slipped through the silent swing doors of ICU, he found Carmen in a corner bed, her head swathed in a thick white bandage, her body plugged into a multitude of monitors.

He kissed her forehead.

She smelt strange. Different. Of antiseptic. Hospital. Something else, too. Freshly disturbed cancer, perhaps?

'I love you,' he whispered.

Her eyes remained shut and her breathing was oblivion deep.

'Dad!'

Stan was feeding coins into the coffee machine in the hospital corridor when Reuben and Leon emerged from the lift, Tibbie in their wake.

'Ssh,' Stan said, putting a finger to his mouth, as the boys crushed him in an urgent hug.

'Can we see her? Can we?'

'Yes, but you have to be dead quiet.' He gulped. Wrong word to use. 'There are very sick people here.'

'How is she?' Tibbie asked, as they walked towards ICU. She was wearing a tourmaline silk top, which reflected the colour of her eyes and offset the flush in her cheeks.

He nodded. Turned away from the twins. Gave a half-hiccup, half-cry. 'Doing okay, all things considered.'

She slipped an arm around him. Her hair smelt of caramelised sugar and cinnamon. She must have been baking.

'If anyone can pull through, it's Carmen. She's a fighter, Stan.'

He closed his eyes. 'I hope so.'

Tibbie turned, converting her side-on hug into a proper one. He could feel her breasts up against him. He felt a shot of shame for the intrusion of this thought.

Leon yanked at his arm. 'Can we go in?'

'There are chicken enchiladas to warm up when you get home,' Tibbie said. 'I've given the boys instructions.'

'Not chicken again!' Stan said, rolling his eyes.

Tibbie laughed. 'Poor love.'

As Stan expected he would, Austin had told her about Carmen's embarrassing comment at the practice.

'But seriously, thank you, for everything.'

She swotted away his gratitude, her eyes filling with tears.

'Try to get some sleep tonight,' she said, stepping away. 'Oh, and Austin said to tell you he'll stop in to see Carmen after work.'

CHAPTER 11

CARMEN ANDINO

The weeks following surgery were a blur marked by small milestones, like road signs spearing a thick fog.

Carmen was discharged home. Her surgical scar became infected. District nurses arrived every morning to clean and dress it. The primary tumour was confirmed to be a melanoma. A treatment plan was proposed: wholebrain radiation plus focused stereotactic radiation.

Geoff and Pam, Carmen's parents, travelled up from the South Island to be closer, but to Stan's relief they stayed with friends.

Stan's mum, who was on an extended holiday in Greece – something that had been in the planning for three years – called most days. 'You want me to come home, Stanley? Really, I can be coming now now. Just say one word and I am here yesterday!'

A tsunami of friends and colleagues rotated through the house with cards and flowers and food. Meals were jammed into the tiny freezer, and flowers into any container that resembled a vase. Cards reiterated the same sentiments: *Get Well. We Love you. Kia kaha.* Richard, Carmen's brother, paid for a weekly cleaner, a treat they would have celebrated under different circumstances. Tibbie organised a lift-scheme to get the boys to and from school and sporting commitments.

And Austin coordinated the various specialist appointments, blood tests and prescriptions, while helping Carmen and Stan interpret mind-boggling medical speak.

'You okay?' Stan asked Carmen, as they drove over the harbour bridge on the first day of her treatment.

She nodded.

'In a bizarre way, this reminds me of our first round of IVF,' he said. 'The excitement of finally doing something constructive. Sort of like going into battle, instead of sitting around waiting for the enemy to appear.'

Carmen chewed her lip. If Stan couldn't see that IVF was about giving life, while radiotherapy was about holding back death, then she couldn't be bothered to enlighten him. Right now, everything about Stan irritated her. His shaggy head of hair and dull brown beard. His creased clothes, despite his best ironing efforts. His small paunch and ridiculously robust health. His anxious energy, which was something new for him; he'd always been the laid-back one. Also, his excessive gratitude every time Tibbie did them even the smallest favour. Although that was no great surprise; he'd never been very good at disguising his soft spot for her best friend.

'You know what pisses me off the most?' Carmen said.

'What?'

'Not being allowed to drive.'

There were so many other things that should have bothered her more.

'Just think of me as your chauffeur,' Stan said, smiling uncertainly. 'You get to call the shots.' He held his hand to his head in a salute. 'At your service, ma'am.'

She was already the one calling the shots; Stan was most definitely the weaker of the two of them right now. In the past he'd always been an antidote to her hype. A no-worries, things-will-work-out kind of guy. But the past few weeks had seen him relying on her more and more for strength, direction, hope. She was looking down the barrel at death and yet he was the one falling to pieces.

'What's the first thing that came into your head when Ngaire Bell said I couldn't drive for three years?' she said.

He shrugged. 'I don't know. What?'

'You must have thought something.'

'I guess, I was trying to work out the logistics of kids lifts, work, that sort of thing. What about you?'

'I thought, *what you really mean is, no driving ever again.*'

Stan's face collapsed. She felt a twinge of guilt ramming home this reality. But it was time he caught up with the play. He'd been beguiled by the illusion of hope. Distracted by the momentum and white noise of each day. Well, he needed to face the truth. Her truth. She had metastases in her brain. Her expiry date was no longer some universal vagary. The homestretch had been logged.

'That's what it amounts to, right? I mean, my life expectancy is most likely less than that.'

They drove the rest of the way in silence.

The previous week he'd left the room when the radiotherapists were moulding a treatment mask to her face. He couldn't handle watching them drape the webbed piece of plastic over her, as they created the device that would lock her head in position for each treatment. He told her it reminded him of *The Man in the Iron Mask.*

It was frightening enough having something foreign growing inside of her, without Stan being so melodramatic.

The malware in her head was randomly resizing her thoughts, reconfiguring her perceptions, altering colour, depth and contrast. It deleted and amplified on a whim. She was her brain. Any change to the convoluted orb inside her skull changed who she was. Changed Carmen.

'Take it off! I can't breathe.'

'Sit tight, Carmen. I'm unlatching it,' said the nurse, calmly lifting it away.

Two heads. One perfect plastic shell. The other, chockful of bad brain.

Carmen sat up. Ran her hands through her hair. 'Sorry.

I'm claustrophobic. Remember the Yucatan pyramids, Stan? Stan?'

He'd done a runner again.

When he came back in, he looked pasty and grim, like a prisoner forced to watch punishment being meted out on a fellow inmate.

Carmen kept her breathing measured second time round as they lined her up with the laser beams. In the rifleman's sight… 'Nice and still now.'

No bang or explosion or recoil. No shells dropping to the ground. Just some background buzzing, masked by the music in her ears.

Thirty-nine grays of radiation delivered in ten-minute doses over three weeks. Whole-brain radiation with hippocampal sparing, plus stereotactic radiation to target individual tumours.

The downside of such global treatment, Ngaire Bell told her, was the impact on normal brain functioning. 'Some of the more detrimental side-effects can manifest months or even years down the line.'

Years? That was being optimistic, thought Carmen.

CHAPTER 12

ELIOT BARD

Eliot finished his muesli, rinsed his bowl, and headed for the bathroom to brush his teeth. His mind was all over the place as he squeezed a strip of mint toothpaste onto his electric toothbrush.

He activated the timer – thirty seconds for each quadrant, two minutes all up – and turned on the toothbrush. Toothpaste sprayed all over the mirror.

'Stupid!' he shouted, rubbing the splatter off with his sleeve, but only making things worse. Now there was a big fat smudge interfering with the reflection of his ghost-long face and thicket of blond hair.

He squinted at the picture of his favourite superwoman pasted to the top right corner of the mirror. There was a blob of green toothpaste on her breast. He moved a hand towards her, then froze. Shut his eyes tight. Tighter. But the dead lady with long red hair was there again, swimming in front of his lids. He opened his eyes super-wide and stared at himself in the mirror, his nostrils flaring. Then he was tearing down Kate Kane and throwing her in the bin.

He backed out of the bathroom, hurried down the hall, and grabbed his backpack off the hook.

As he opened the front door, he heard the toothbrush timer beep in the bathroom.

He hovered, chewing his lip. He didn't want his teeth to rot, become loose in his gums, and fall out, but… He slammed the door behind him and headed over to Mr McDougal's via the shortcut behind the rubbish bins.

Every Tuesday and Thursday Eliot helped out their elderly neighbour and got fifteen dollars for his efforts. He worked mostly in the garden, but sometimes did other jobs for the old man, like cleaning his Venetian blinds and sweeping leaves off the back deck. Fifteen dollars and morning tea. Mr Zhao from the bakery down the road usually gave Mr McDougal leftovers from the previous day's produce at half-price. Best were the cheese scones which, if rewarmed in the microwave, tasted as if they'd just been baked.

Sometimes, for a treat, Mr McDougal bought sweet buns topped with bright pink icing. Eliot was not meant to eat sugar, but Mr McDougal said that, once in a while, rules could be broken. Even Eliot's mum allowed him ice-cream every now and then. Ice-cream plus an extra dose of insulin.

'Top of the morning!' said Mr McDougal, opening his front door. Eliot didn't know what 'top of the morning' meant. The old man said it every time, like a toy in a toyshop with only one button.

Mr McDougal was over ninety years old, but as sharp as a tack, according to Eliot's mum. He was taller than Eliot, which was saying something, because Eliot was six foot two. However, the old man looked shorter because he stooped like *The BFG*. He had crusty skin and a droopy eye, which leaked like a tap with a perished washer. Mr McDougal's own words.

His garden was ramshackle. Eliot liked that word. Ramshackle. There was always something to be done – weeding, watering, digging in compost, mowing the lawn. The lawnmower was seriously temperamental, though, and sometimes Eliot and Mr McDougal would spend an entire morning tinkering with it, trying to make it work. Tinkering. Another favourite word.

Eliot didn't mind how long it took to fix the mower,

because Mr McDougal always had some story to tell about his time fighting communist guerrillas in the Malayan jungles.

'And how are we today?' he asked, inviting Eliot in.

Eliot didn't feel like talking, nor did he feel like listening to another military adventure. Luckily for him, the phone started to ring.

Mr McDougal picked up, rolled his eyes, then covered the mouthpiece. 'It's Pauline,' he said in a low voice. 'This won't be quick. Perhaps you can start by weeding the veggie patch.'

Pauline was Mr McDougal's super-bossy daughter.

An hour later, he came outside with a tea tray.

'You striking for better pay, boy?' he said, eyeing the barely touched bed of weeds.

Eliot frowned.

'Unwell?'

Eliot shook his head.

'Had enough breakfast?'

Eliot nodded.

'Perhaps some ginger beer and a spinach muffin might reboot the system?'

Eliot shrugged.

Usually, Eliot loved Mr McDougal's homemade ginger beer, which he stored in corked bottles in his cellar. But today Eliot had a sore stomach. As the old man lowered the tray, ginger beer sloshed all over the muffins.

'Blasted tremor! Anyone would think I'd been drinking.'

Eliot grabbed his muffin before it went all soggy.

'What's up, then?' McDougal said, slumping into his garden chair and nearly toppling over.

Eliot looked down at his own feet.

There was a long space with no words.

'Out with it, young man.'

Eliot could feel his heart thumping in his throat. Even though he knew his heart lived in his chest, it occasionally tried to climb out of his body through his throat. It had never succeeded, which was just as well, or else he would be dead.

Dead.

'There was a dead lady in the water.'

Mr McDougal lowered his glass and leant forward.

'I beg your pardon?'

Eliot nodded. 'There was a dead lady in the water at the bottom of the cliff.'

'I see. Did you tell your mum?'

Eliot nodded. 'The police came and everything.'

'The police? To your house?'

'Ramesh and Hilary,' Eliot said, slicing his hand across his forehead to depict the policewoman's skew fringe. 'They were wearing stab-proof vests. They didn't have the ceramic plates inside, though, which make them bulletproof.'

'My, my. And why did they come to your house?'

'Cause I told the man in yellow and grey about her. There was also a man in stretchy black. He had lots of little teeth in his mouth. I didn't like him much.'

Mr McDougal snorted. 'I'm not surprised. In my day, a man wouldn't have been seen dead in stretchy black.'

Dead. That word again, pricking the inside of Eliot's head.

'She had long red hair and a big brass bracelet,' he said breathlessly.

'Red hair?' Mr McDougal said, spraying little pieces of muffin everywhere.

Eliot's eyes darted around the garden looking for somewhere safe to land.

'Well, that's quite a thing.'

'Quite a thing,' Eliot repeated.

Later that day, after he'd got home, Eliot heard his mum talking to Mr McDougal on the phone.

'I'm so sorry, Terrance. Hope you didn't pay him the full fifteen. Yes, you might be right. Good idea. I'll see if I can get him an appointment.'

His mum replaced the receiver, then picked it up again and dialled.

'Gwen, Andrea Bard here. Good, good. Thank you. I

was hoping to get Eliot in to see Austin tomorrow... Oh. Goodness! Right. No. Of course. I'll... I'll ring again next week. Nothing urgent. Hope everything is alright.'

Eliot darted back to his bedroom.

'Bare feet!' he shouted, as his mum padded up the hallway. It was a game they played, guessing which shoes the other was wearing just from the sound they made coming up the hall.

'Point to you,' his mum said, appearing in the doorway. She was frowning.

Eliot took out a pen from his drawer and added a point on the chart under his name. He was leading this week, seven to five.

'That's odd,' his mum said, chewing her pinkie nail. 'I just rang Austin's rooms. Thought it might help for you to have a chat with him about your scary experience yesterday. But his receptionist said that the practice is closed for the rest of the week. Something about a family emergency.'

Family. Eliot wished Austin Lamb could be part of his family. He wished Austin could be his dad. He kind of was, in a way, considering he'd delivered Eliot when he was born and had known him for his whole life.

Still. It was different. Different to seeing him every day and building Lego castles together and going horse-riding, and all that sort of stuff. Different to Austin being married to his mum. His mum would like that. She was always happy when Austin was around. And always wore lipstick, too.

CHAPTER 13

STAN ANDINO

The routine of Carmen's treatment imposed a comforting order on the Andinos' lives. There was security in having the same shape to each day. Stan did his best to keep going with his morning classes at the Arts Centre and some of the evening ones, too. However, he was forced to cancel his afternoon commitments.

Carmen also continued to work where possible, tackling articles for the magazine with superwoman gusto, and writing wherever she could – in bed, the car, in waiting rooms.

Her freelancing had always brought in more money than Stan's work, except for when he put on an exhibition – but he hadn't exhibited in over three years. And though Stan couldn't bear the thought of his wife working when she should have been focusing on getting well, he rationalised that it was an important distraction for her.

The reality, their reality, was that finances were tight and there was only so much charity a man could respectably accept from his brother-in-law. Richard made no bones about the fact that he thought Carmen had married a loser, and he had the annoying habit of swooping in like some knight in shining armour to save the day. Stan did not want to give him any cause to feel compelled to intervene once again.

It was the specialist, Ngaire Bell, who finally put a stop to it.

'Carmen,' she said, as they sat in her suite one afternoon, 'I usually suggest to people to keep working for as long as they feel able. But my sense is that you might take such advice too far.' She looked over to Stan for corroboration. 'You are not someone who likes to be idle. Nor, I suspect, are you easily able to moderate commitments. Your reserves are low right now and your brain needs all the rest it can get. Rest and routine. Not deadlines and stressors.'

Stan nodded supportively, while inwardly panicking.

'Some daily exercise,' Bell went on. 'Small, regular meals and unbroken stretches of sleep.'

Sleep. Ha! The high-dose steroid regime Carmen was on kept her brain spinning long into each night. Stan couldn't remember the last time they'd slept through. As for small, regular meals. Really? The steroids had given Carmen the appetite of a horse.

They drove home from the appointment in silence, both locked in their own thoughts. Stan could feel the cancer starting to alter their orbits. At first it had been almost imperceptible as they'd tackled the challenges together. But a divergence in their paths was becoming more obvious, the overlap in their projected lives less clear.

Carmen would see being forced to give up work as yet another subtraction from her life. Whereas Stan, as much as he hated to admit it, and as callous as it might have seemed, saw it as a subtraction from their bank balance.

As they pulled into their driveway, Tibbie's silver Audi followed them in.

She was dropping the boys home from school.

'How's my beautiful friend?' she said as she got out of her car, her thick, auburn ponytail swinging from side to side.

'Good, good,' Carmen said briskly, ruffling Reuben's hair affectionately, as he came up alongside her. Then she turned and walked into the house.

'Sorry, Tippy,' Stan said, using his affectionate nickname for her. 'She doesn't mean it. It's been a tough day.'

'Please don't apologise,' Tibbie said emphatically. 'Remember my mum after the accident? How the head injury changed her? You, for one, were demoted overnight from being her favourite fellow to *that Greek good-for-nothing.*'

Stan forced a laugh.

'The specialist has just told her she has to give up work.'

'Oh no! Her work means everything to her.'

'The thing is,' Stan said, kicking at the grass edging, 'she needs to rest her brain. Not tax it. Otherwise, we'll be in for a crash-and-burn scenario.'

'Good luck with that,' Tibbie said. 'You and I both know that short of stapling Carmen's feet to the ground...'

'Tell me about it. Though Bell reckons Carmen soon won't have the energy for it anyway. Overwhelming fatigue is apparently a common side-effect of the cancer and the treatment.'

Tibbie's shoulders slumped forward, her whole body registering her dismay. 'Poor love.'

'I mean, work gives her a purpose,' Stan said. 'She'll go spare sitting around all day. I—' He hesitated, hovering on the brink of something else.

'What?'

'Nothing.'

She held his gaze. The way Tibbie engaged with a person was such an endearing trait. She never failed to make him feel listened to. Heard.

'We're pretty much in the red right now,' he blurted out. 'And I'm not sure what I'm going to do.' He felt grubby mentioning money at a time like this, but it was hard to remain noble when the wolf was at the door.

'Oh, Stan.' She put a hand on his arm. 'This is the last thing you need to be worrying about right now.' Her hand was cool against his skin.

'Things have a way of working out,' he said, ashamed for

having shared something so private and selfish. 'I can extend our mortgage, I'm sure. That's if I can handle our prat of a bank manager and his bloody condescending attitude.'

'Listen,' Tibbie said, 'I've got some of what my mum left me in a call account.'

Stan shook his head vehemently. 'Never! I couldn't. But thanks all the same.'

'Don't be silly, Stan. It's there. You can pay me back when this is all over. If I can't help my best friends, how sad is that? I mean, we're practically siblings.'

Siblings. Stan had imagined Tibbie in several other scenarios, though never as a sibling.

'It'll just be a loan,' she said, picking a thread off his shirt. 'You can pay it back with interest if that makes you feel better.'

She glanced over Stan's shoulder, then quickly dropped her hand.

He turned.

Carmen was standing at the window, half-shielded by the curtain.

'You better go in,' Tibbie said, stepping back. 'Just text me your bank account details when you get a moment.'

Stan chewed his lip. 'Carmen and I have a joint account. She'll kill me if she finds out I've accepted money from you.'

'Stan, it's a loan. That's all. Open a separate account if that'll make things easier. I can lend you some cash in the meantime, to tide you over.'

He stared at the ground, feeling so tacky for his silence.

'Sorted,' Tibbie said, opening her car door. 'I'll get onto it ASAP. Now tick that off your list.'

CHAPTER 14

TIBBIE LAMB

It was Tibbie's idea. She'd conspired with the Andino twins to introduce a bit of fun into what was a very challenging time for the family. The boys had been buzzing with excitement all week. Stan and Austin were both on board, too. The only person who didn't know a thing about it, until she opened her front door, was Carmen.

'Surprise!' Tibbie and Austin cried.

'Hiya,' Carmen said, looking nonplussed at her glammed-up friends on her doorstep. She was in baggy trackpants and her faded green sweatshirt.

'It's Saturday night!' Tibbie said, flicking her arms wide, as if the compere in some glamorous TV show. 'First Saturday of the month.'

Carmen looked her up and down.

'And that means?' Tibbie continued, feeling suddenly overdressed. 'Date night!'

As if on cue, Leon and Reuben appeared behind their mum, looking very dapper and grown-up in long pants, white-collared school shirts, and school ties.

'Welcome to Chez Andino,' Leon said, stepping forward. 'Can I take your coat, ma'am.'

'Why, thank you,' Tibbie said, slipping off the silk coat she'd bought in Japan. It was one of her favourites – a real eye-catcher, with vibrant flower motifs embroidered onto a liquorice-black background.

Austin handed Reuben one of the baskets he was carrying and leant in to give Carmen a kiss.

'How's my gorgeous Carmen?'

'What are you all up to?' she said, with a slightly baffled giggle.

Austin pointed to Tibbie and the twins. 'Credit entirely to this trio.'

'If you'll follow me, please,' Reuben said, blushing as he led them towards the lounge.

Stan was in the dining room, frantically putting the final touches to the table. There were candles, napkins folded like they used to do in restaurants in the eighties, and Air Supply playing in the background.

Tibbie felt a rush of excitement. 'Time to get our monthly Saturday nights back on track, don't you think?' she said, coming up behind Carmen and enveloping her in a hug.

'Don't I feel out of place?' Carmen said, turning to face Tibbie. 'You in your glad rags and all.'

Tibbie wished she'd worn something a little less fancy. 'Then it's time to get you suitably kitted out for the occasion, girl,' she said, grabbing Carmen's hand and trying to twirl her.

'Thanks, but I can dress myself,' Carmen said, freeing her hand and disappearing down the corridor.

Reuben and Leon hovered. Tibbie could see their fragile enthusiasm wavering.

She pulled on a smile and gave them the thumbs-up. 'Great job, guys! You both look awesome.'

Reuben gave a lopsided smile.

'Now into that kitchen,' Tibbie said, in a faux-stern voice. 'Each course has instructions for the final prep. Which of you is the wine waiter?'

Leon raised his hand.

'I should have known!' Tibbie said with a chortle. 'I've made up a non-alcoholic cocktail to serve first, okay? There's some for both of you, too. And when it comes to the wine, remember, just half-glasses for us all. And that's adults only, Mr Wine Waiter.'

Austin was showing Stan a photograph of the new Mercedes coupe he had on order, when Carmen reappeared in the doorway.

She was wearing silver heels and a floral summer dress Tibbie recognised from maybe a decade earlier. It didn't fit Carmen as well as it once had, the ruching around her waist stretched and distorting the fall of faded fabric.

Carmen had left the top four or five buttons undone, putting her cleavage very much on show, and she'd circled her eyes heavily with black kohl.

Tibbie's chest constricted, strings of sadness pulling tightly around her. It was the eyeliner. The way it gave Carmen an almost clown-like appearance.

Of all the times for it to dawn on her that she was going to lose her best friend. Not when she and Carmen were snuggled up in a beanbag, talking through the terrifying diagnosis. Not when she was waiting by the phone for Carmen to come out of surgery. Not when Carmen couldn't keep her food down for five days straight. But now, as her friend of almost a quarter of a century stood in the doorway in high heels, a dress she'd long outgrown, and her eyes bizarrely ringed in black.

'Now, we're talking!' Tibbie said. 'You look… lovely.'

Carmen seemed to buy into the evening, and for a while it felt as if the make-believe was working. As the four of them sat around the table eating their pear and blue cheese starter with toasted walnuts on top, they could have been in some cosy Auckland restaurant, the men talking cars, and Carmen commenting like a true journalist on some parliamentary gaffe.

But as Tibbie looked on and listened to Carmen, she felt strangely alone in the friendship. As if all the little changes that had crept into their relationship over the past months were kept on a running tab, and now, out of the blue, had been tallied.

'That was pretty darned delicious,' Stan said, leaning back so that Reuben could clear away his plate. 'And my sons doing all the work!'

'Don't get used to it, Dad,' Reuben said, punching his father affectionately on the arm.

'Do you hire out your waiters?' Austin asked, a twinkle in his eye.

Carmen shook her head. 'Too expensive.' Then, in what seemed like an afterthought, 'Pity you guys don't have your own.'

Tibbie glanced across at Austin. She saw his Adam's apple move up and then down his throat as he swallowed the barb.

No matter how many years had elapsed, or how long they had lived with the reality, the topic of children, or rather their lack of them, had the power to sting Austin and their marriage as sharply as a blue-bottle on an unsuspecting foot. It was one argument that had cycled on repeat for years, the topic like a recurring bad dream, until she'd finally promised to come off the pill.

And Carmen knew that! Knew the anguish childlessness had imported into Tibbie and Austin's relationship. After all, there was very little the two women did not share.

The cruelty of Carmen's comment ricocheted around the room.

'But I guess it would have been nothing short of a miracle,' Carmen added, pulling out a piece of walnut from between her teeth, 'considering how effective the copper coil is.'

'Carmen!' Tibbie said, flushing. 'What a... bizarre and awful thing to say.' She felt the prick of tears. Closed her eyes, trying to stop them. She did not want the evening to deteriorate. Most especially not for the boys, who hung there on the periphery of the room like overgrown puppets deserted by their puppet master.

She pushed her chair back. Tried to smile. 'I'd better see if that pasta bake is ready.'

CHAPTER 15

AUSTIN LAMB

Carmen was making her way through the jar of jellybeans on Austin's desk while he skimmed through the latest update from her specialists.

'Maybe that's enough now, hon,' Stan said tentatively.

Carmen swatted away his hand. 'I'm hungry, damn you!'

'The steroids won't be helping,' Austin said, looking up over his reading glasses. 'They can really ramp up a person's appetite.'

'No kidding,' muttered Stan.

'Stan just wants me to be thinner,' Carmen said, her mouth full and leaking garish colours. 'If he had his way, he'd starve me till I looked more like Tibbie.'

Stan flushed. 'How can you say that?'

Carmen gave a supercilious toss of her head. 'Don't look so wounded. I mean it's no secret you've always thought Tibbie gorgeous. Am I right, Austin? Am I? Do you remember the time when—'

'Hey, enough squabbling, guys,' Austin said, putting up a hand.

The window of respite after Carmen's surgery was definitely closing; she was becoming increasingly unpredictable again. Austin had spoken to Stan and the boys about all the possible behaviours Carmen might exhibit, what with high-dose steroids and whole-brain irradiation thrown into the mix. Emotional yoyo-ing, paranoia, crushing tiredness, a ramped-up appetite, sexual inappropriateness, aggression, confusion, loss of memory…

'Your mum might behave strangely at times. It's hard to know what to expect. Every person is different in the way their brain responds.'

What made it even harder, he told them, was that the symptoms could fluctuate over time. Melanoma metastases in particular had a habit of bleeding, which could further aggravate symptoms.

Austin believed in being upfront and honest. There was no point pretending. Kids especially could always tell when you weren't being frank. It was one thing to hear about these things in textbook talk, though, and quite another to live through them. Each day had become like some evil lucky-dip for the Andinos. Outbursts and raging, interspersed with pockets of kindness and love. Devastated by their mother's ever-changing personality, the twins had started to grow wary of her. Especially Leon, who seemed distrustful of any affection she might show, knowing that it was unlikely to endure.

Austin tried to remind them that it was the tumours talking. That their mum couldn't help herself and still loved them dearly. But it became harder and harder to keep their empathy engaged; the Carmen they'd known and loved was making an appearance less and less often.

It was hard for Austin, too. In all his years of practice, he'd never felt quite so conflicted as he tried to balance his role as Carmen's doctor with that of being one of her most longstanding friends. His duty was to preserve her life. However, when he put on his 'best mate' cap, he found himself wishing the inevitable would come more quickly, to minimise the fallout and suffering for everyone.

He and her specialists did everything they could to keep Carmen on track, which mostly came down to manipulating her medication. But weighing up side-effects with benefits sometimes seemed an impossible task.

'Bell recommends you stick to a very regular routine,' Austin said, looking up from the latest letter. 'Maintain and reinforce the familiar.'

'Yup,' Stan said, chewing his thumbnail.

'Stop fidgeting!' Carmen growled.

'She's suggested a gentle exercise programme to counteract the muscle weakness from the steroids.'

'We played a few rounds of golf last week,' Stan volunteered, 'but that didn't really work out.'

'What did you expect?' Carmen said, turning back to Austin. 'He spent half the bloody morning in the bunkers.'

'How about something simpler?' Austin suggested, glancing up at the Victorian clock. It had been keeping superb time since he'd serviced it. Over the ticking, he could hear the low hum of a packed waiting room. 'A daily walk, perhaps?'

'Good idea,' Stan said, taking the cue and moving to the edge of his chair. 'C'mon, love, we've wasted enough of this good man's time today.'

Austin pretended to protest; however, he did nothing to hinder their departure.

Carmen harrumphed to the door.

She reached for the door handle. Her hand missed it and she pulled at air. She tried again, but once more misjudged the distance.

Her face went blank and her handbag slid off her shoulder, spilling its contents across the room.

Carmen gave a small, high-pitched cry as she went down, then she was frothing at the mouth, her body jerking and flailing.

Half an hour later Carmen lay in a groggy doze in the recovery position on Austin's office floor while he finished putting seven stitches in her forehead. He dabbed the wound, inserted the needle, flicked his wrist, captured the curve of steel, drew the nylon through, tied a knot. Dabbed, inserted, flicked… General Practice involved a lot of talking; however, he really came into his own when he was using his hands. He loved this practical side to his work. After all, he'd once wanted to be a plastic surgeon.

Performing finicky procedures – removal of skin lesions, ingrown toenails, that sort of thing – suited his attention to detail. It was why he so enjoyed restoring antique clocks. Who would have thought, considering the manual-labourer hands he'd inherited from his good-for-nothing father? However, Austin had overcome his genes and his predestined state-house trajectory. He'd trained his squat fingers to be deft and nimble, not unlike the way a heavy person might learn to navigate the dancefloor with skilled light-footedness.

'All done,' he said, still kneeling beside Carmen as he peeled off his gloves. He peered under his plinth. 'Amazing what you get to see from this vantage point,' he said, taking in the clumps of dust, a syringe cap, ball-point pen. 'Oh look, there's—'

'Where am I?' Carmen said, trying to sit up.

Austin sat back on his haunches. 'Hello, you,' he said smiling. 'Remember me?'

CHAPTER 16

STAN ANDINO

Stan, Carmen and the kids sat in front of the TV with their dinner. Lasagne. Again. The universal offering of comfort. There were still four containers in the freezer, all from well-meaning friends. Not that Stan was complaining.

Graham Norton was on, and the TV audience was in hysterics. But the mood in the Andino house was less jovial, the gauze patch taped to Carmen's temple a sobering reminder that all was not right.

Stan mused at how much easier it was to feel sympathy for someone when there was an outward manifestation of their illness. The person with a plaster cast got more attention than the person suffering from diabetes or depression. A square of white gauze taped to his wife's face evoked more sympathy than the abstract diagnosis of brain cancer.

When faced with some of Carmen's behaviour, Stan hadn't always found it easy to forgive her accountability. It distressed him to think that it only took a piece of gauze to reboot his compassion.

Reuben got up to pour himself a glass of water.

'Get me another wine, will you, Reu?' Carmen said, holding out her glass.

Reuben glanced at his dad.

'Carmen, love,' Stan began reluctantly, 'you know what

Austin said about alcohol. About it lowering the threshold for seizures. Especially after what happened today. I'll limit myself to one glass, too. How about it?'

'Bloody hell! Is there nothing I can do anymore? I'm an adult, for fuck's sake. A.D.U.L.T!'

'Well, start acting like one then!' Stan snapped. 'You had a massive fit today, in case you forgot.'

Carmen looked surprised and wounded by his outburst. As if she'd forgotten about what had happened in Austin's rooms.

'If you think this is only hard for you, think again!' Stan continued.

He should have stopped there, but it was a relief to vent, like biting down on a sore tooth. A relief to vocalise what was essentially taboo – demonising a patient with cancer.

The room was quiet, except for Leon chewing and Reuben breathing and the audience laughing as Graham Norton tipped his guest over in the big red chair.

Carmen had cancer. She was dying. And here he was bellowing like some big bully. What sort of monster was he?

The landline started to ring.

Carmen leapt up and disappeared down the hallway.

Leon muted the TV and the three of them sat in anxious silence straining to hear who she was talking to and what random direction the evening might take.

She was chatting comfortably. They heard her laugh. The twins' tight postures relaxed.

'Who was that?' Stan asked casually when Carmen plonked herself back down in the spare armchair, pointedly avoiding her previous position beside him on the couch.

'Tibbie.'

'Oh, nice. What did she want?'

Carmen sighed, as if it was a chore to fill in the gaps.

'Ma?' persisted Reuben, ever the mediator.

'She's keen to get in training for El Camino,' Carmen said, looking only at Reuben and not meeting Stan's eye. 'It's a walk across Spain. She and Austin are planning to do it next year. She's asked me to be her training buddy. Help keep her committed.'

'That's cool, Mum!'

Stan released an internal sigh. Clever, generous Tibbie.

'You keen?' Stan asked, doing his best to sound offhand and not give Carmen any reason to push back.

'Well, it's not like I've got anything else on.'

The plan, she told them, was to do an hour-long loop every weekday, taking in some of the coastal path between Murrays Bay and Browns Bay.

'We'll meet at nine every morning at the top of the road.'

An hour sounded like a lot to Stan. What's more, the coastal walkway had steep stairs on its return from Browns Bay. But the last thing he wanted to do was quash the idea. Anyway, Tibbie was sensible. She'd make sure Carmen didn't overdo it.

CHAPTER 17

ELIOT BARD

Eliot heard a key in the front door. He glanced at his watch. 1.27 pm. It couldn't be her. Too early. He grabbed the snooker stick from under his bed and positioned himself behind the cupboard. Sunlight swept down the corridor. His breathing picked up.

The quick click of heels.

He frowned. It didn't fit. Couldn't be.

'Brown courts,' he whispered.

Then there she was, standing in his doorway. His mum, wearing her brown court shoes.

'Point to me!'

But she wasn't smiling; her face was tight, especially on the right, as if someone had tightened the screws unevenly.

'How come you home early, Mum?'

She opened her mouth to answer, then stopped. Looked around. 'What have you done, Elli?'

He shrugged. 'Didn't like them anymore.'

She looked down at the rubbish bin overflowing with crumpled superwomen. He'd only left his horse posters up.

She didn't say anything for the longest time, then in her super-serious voice, 'Eliot, I want you to put on your corduroys and blue jumper.'

'Why?'

'We need to go down to the police station.'

He opened his eyes. Wide. Wider. Wider still.

Again. Small eyes. Big eyes. Bigger.

'Stop that, Elli!'

Small. Big. Bigger.

'Eliot! We're going to see Detective Bandara. You liked him.'

'And Hilaaaary,' Eliot said, mimicking the low, expressionless voice of Ramesh Bandara's colleague.

'Do you want to take in a few shells from your collection to show him?'

'Which ones?' Eliot said, darting over to his desk. He picked up a turritella. The Atlantic triton. An ormer.

'That's enough. Put them in a shoebox and get changed. I want to get there before the afternoon school traffic begins.'

Eliot sat in the front seat of his mum's yellow Ford Fiesta, balancing the box of shells on his knee. His stomach hurt and his chewed cheek was throbbing. His mum shoved a relaxation tape into the tape deck. One with pan flutes and sounds of the sea. Her car was probably the last car in the whole world to have a tape deck. Even CD players had nearly been phased out.

He started rocking backwards and forwards against the seatbelt.

'There's nothing to be worried about. The detective just wants to ask you a few more questions about Wednesday morning.'

'Why?'

'I guess he's being thorough. Like you are when you double-check under your bed at night.'

'Triple-check.'

She nodded.

'I don't like police stations.'

'I know, but Detective Bandara needs your help.'

Eliot did not want to help. Not if that Hilary woman was going to be there, too.

'You'll be like an extra detective.'

He stuck his forefinger in his left ear and jiggled it. It was the only way to stop the itch in the back of his throat.

He'd been to the police station before. Two years ago. Seven hundred and eighty-five days ago to be exact. He could already smell the disinfectant in the waiting room. Feel the air conditioner printing cold sheets of air. See the face of that stupid Detective Slater with his silver-thin eyebrows and shaver's rash. The rash that turned bright pink when he told Eliot that if he ever hassled the girl with freckles again, charges would be laid. The man didn't understand that Eliot had simply stopped the girl to tell her he had the exact same backpack as her. It was the one his mum had bought him when she went to Thailand with work, and he stayed with Mr McDougal for ten days. It was only when Eliot asked the girl if he could touch her red hair that she got upset. Then he had to grab her wrists to calm her down, just like his mum did when he got in a tizzy.

Eliot hadn't meant to hurt her. He just didn't know his own strength. That's what his mum always said. It pleased him when she said that. Not that he'd hurt the girl. But that he was strong.

Ramesh Bandara shook his mum's hand. He had big man hands. Eliot spread his fingers wide, trying to make his hands look bigger, but his fingers still looked like piddly ice-cream sticks. Mrs Rhoden, his piano teacher, said he was lucky to have such long fingers. 'The best concert pianists do.' But Eliot would have preferred proper man hands, like Detective Bandara.

'How are you doing, Eliot?'

Eliot looked at the floor.

His mum nudged him. 'Eyes, Eliot.'

He looked up, then back at the floor.

'What have you got in the box?'

'Shells. From my collection. Wanna see?'

'Want to,' his mother corrected.

'Sure,' the detective said, pointing to the table.

As Eliot lifted off the lid, the door behind them opened.

'Apologies. I got caught up with a client.'

Eliot swung round. 'It's Mr Younger, Mum!'

Mr Younger lived in the big white house at the end of their street. The one with a mechanised turning circle in front of the garage.

'Thank you for coming, Derrick,' his mum said, turning to Ramesh Bandara. 'Detective, this is our lawyer, Derrick Younger.'

Mr Younger walked into the room, followed by DC Hilary Stark.

Eliot's heart climbed into his throat, like it was making ready for a getaway.

CHAPTER 18

CARMEN ANDINO

Carmen pulled back the curtain carefully and watched him reverse down the driveway.

Her mouth was dry. Her right eye twitched.

After pausing at the end of the driveway, he swung out into the road, corrected, then pulled away.

She sucked in a shaky breath. Her entire body was trembling. She didn't have long. Three hours at most.

She opened her hand. The number had smudged and was barely legible. She reached for her phone. It was not in her back pocket.

She cast around the room. Where had she left it?

She stopped. Tilted her head towards the window. Was that the sound of his car slowing?

Carmen peered carefully around the curtain again, then rammed herself up against the wall, her heart and lungs going like crazy pistons out of sync.

He'd pulled up by the kerb further down the road! Had he spotted her spying on him?

She tried to centre her thoughts. If he came back now, saw that she hadn't touched her breakfast, he'd realise she was onto him.

She wondered whether she should tip some of her porridge into the bin. Make it look like she'd eaten at least some… but there wasn't time. And she'd put a new bin liner in only that morning. A clump of porridge would be obvious. She was as good as dead.

She dropped to the floor, scrambled under the bed, and wedged herself between the carpet and quenelles of mattress poking through the bedsprings.

The house started to shudder as the washing machine went into a spin cycle.

Carmen strained to hear over the racket for the sound of a car door closing, feet on the path, footsteps on the stairs, the creak of the front door, his pretend-sweet voice, '*Carmen*?'

Why had she left it so late? She'd been suspicious for a while, waking every morning with a dull, heavy head and a strange metallic taste in her mouth. If those weren't signs...

The thing was, he'd kept allaying her fears, pretending to be all loving and caring and concerned. And she'd kept falling for it. Stupid, stupid woman!

It had taken all her willpower not to eat breakfast that morning. She'd been ravenous but told him she wanted to shower first.

Another sound rose above the laundry's high-pitched whine. The growl and splutter of the Volvo's engine.

Carmen lay there, breathing in the dank smell of carpet as the washing machine wound down to naught. Then a *click* as the machine door disengaged.

Minutes passed before she allowed herself to crawl out from her hiding place. She pulled herself up to the window ledge and peered out.

He'd gone.

She crouched there for a time, as if trapped in a motionless nightmare, then her legs began to work.

She ran down the corridor. Found her phone on the console table. Punched in the passcode.

The screen vibrated.

She tried again.

And again.

The tenth of July *was* her birthday. Wasn't it?

That's when it dawned on her. He must have tampered with her phone. Changed the code.

Carmen grabbed the landline. It was dead! He'd outwitted her at every step.

She slammed the receiver into its cradle. Picked it up again. Nothing.

The walls of the hallway started closing in.

She tried one more time. Then came the sweet drone of the dialling tone. Relief spread through her. She opened her palm. Dialled the sweat-smudged number.

Two beeps, some static, then a woman's voice. 'Allstate, this is Bree speaking.'

Carmen closed her eyes. 'Bree, you've got to help me.'

'Can you speak up please, ma'am? I can't hear you very well.'

'He's trying to kill me,' Carmen said in an urgent whisper. 'For the money!' She was feeling lightheaded. Dizzy. 'Hurry. I don't have much time.'

Then black spots started crowding her vision.

CHAPTER 19

STAN ANDINO

'What can I say?' Stan said, driving the heel of his palm into his forehead. 'It's unbelievable. Ludicrous. Embarrassing.'

The policeman, probably half Stan's age, put a reassuring hand on his back. Stan wanted to succumb to it, to the certainty and strength of this young stranger. For the first time he wished his mum would cut her stay in Greece short. Wished his dad was still alive. Wished he could just be a child again and let the adults sort things out.

'A life insurance company in Canada, of all things! I mean, how the hell did Carmen even get their number?'

'It sounds like you've a lot on your plate right now, sir. I'm just glad this has had a satisfactory ending. If you know what I mean.'

Yes, Stan knew what he meant. Satisfactory in that some random insurance company in New Brunswick, Canada, had received an alarming call just before closing, that a woman was terrified her husband was trying to poison her. They'd contacted the Canadian police, who had traced the call to Auckland. The New Zealand police had tracked the call to the Andinos' home. There they'd found Carmen hiding in her bedroom cupboard under a pile of jumpers, claiming her husband wanted her dead, so that he could claim on her life insurance.

'Which ward is she on?' Stan asked, searching for a pen amongst the pieces of unfired pottery, opened envelopes, and old sandwich wrappers. His hands were still covered in clay; the policeman had arrived in the middle of a class.

'We left her at the emergency department. I believe she was admitted under the psych team.'

Carmen's six-day hospital stay proved a much-needed respite for Stan and the boys. As guilty as he felt, it was so much easier to visit his sick wife in hospital, shower her with love and affection, and then leave. He baked Greek *kourabiedes* for the boys, played games with them on their Xboxes, and slept right through for four nights in a row.

Although the house felt empty, Stan found himself inserting memories of *before* into the space. He fantasised that Carmen had just popped into the office for a meeting and would be back on the five o'clock bus, the jangle of her silver bracelets announcing her arrival. Then, over a cup of tea, she would natter on about how many words her editor had slashed, or which new intern had the office all aflutter...

Carmen had always had an aura of energy about her. It's what had so appealed to Stan – her vitality and enthusiasm, the way she spoke with her hands, laid her palms over her heart when talking about something emotional, the fire and shine in her eyes when she was angry. She was more Greek than any of his Greek relatives. But right now Stan was relishing the quiet and space, his carefully chosen memories providing more than enough of Carmen's energy.

Her stay in hospital afforded the family a chance to recover, and by the time she was discharged home, everyone felt refreshed, renewed, stronger. Carmen, too. And once more they all eased into a new normality.

A couple of weeks later, as Stan was about to introduce a bunch of new students to the techniques of throwing clay, there was a power outage. Despite the studio having loads of natural light from its large picture windows, the class had to be canned because most of the pottery wheels were electric.

Estimated time till restoration three hours. It was not worth hanging around, so Stan headed home.

He was driving up Beach Road when he spotted her, half-walking, half-running, in lime green trainers and black leggings, her auburn ponytail popping out the back of her cap. Stan would have recognised that ponytail anywhere.

He glanced at the car clock: 9.34 am. Smack bang in the middle of the time Tibbie and Carmen usually took their morning walk.

He drew up alongside her and lowered the passenger window. 'A very good morning to you, Mrs Lamb.'

Tibbie swung around, her face flushed. 'Oh, Stan. Hi.'

'Hope you didn't think I was some kerb-crawler,' he said, with a chuckle.

She flashed a smile, but remained where she was, not moving any closer to the car.

'So, what have you done with my lovely wife?'

Tibbie's face darkened. She rubbed the back of her neck. 'I'm sorry,' she said, avoiding his gaze, 'but I had to bail on her today.'

A brick of dread landed in Stan's belly. 'She's not been abusive to you again, has she?'

Stan was staggered by how much of Carmen's rudeness Tibbie put up with. Her empathy and tolerance left Stan feeling seriously lacking at times.

'Gosh, no! Not at all,' Tibbie said with a quick, reassuring smile. However, she didn't elaborate and seemed impatient for Stan to release her from the conversation.

He turned off the engine and leant across the passenger seat. 'I've been meaning to thank you for making time to walk with her every day. You've got so much on your plate already.'

Tibbie hadn't worked in a very long time. Not for a salary, that is. In the early years she'd been an assistant to some high-flying interior designer, while supporting Austin through his med-school years. But she'd stopped soon after he graduated and began earning a decent wage. Now she headed several charity boards, helped out at the local hospice, and was heavily involved in fundraising for an alcohol and drug rehabilitation centre. Very occasionally, she also covered for Austin's receptionist, Gwen.

The reality was that Tibbie was wealthy in her own right, even without Austin's income. Old money.

'It's really given her a focus,' Stan continued. 'Otherwise, she'd be at a loose end for much of the day. And it's freed me up for my morning classes. So, thanks, Tippy.'

Tippy was a nickname he'd coined for her one evening some years back when the four of them were holidaying in Fiji. Tibbie had had one too many tropical cocktails, which was unusual for her; she rarely drank. Easily enough done, though, what with fruit juice and coconut cream masking the heavy hitters. Anyway, Tibbie could not stop giggling, her silliness endearing and infectious. She kept saying: 'I think I'm a little bit tippy.' She meant tipsy, of course. But the nickname stuck. Stan saw it as a gentle goad, encouraging the ever-gracious and in-control Tibbie to let her hair down more often. It made him sad to think that inside of her, held tightly under wraps, was this beautiful, carefree magic.

She gave him a small smile. 'My pleasure.' But her words hung there, oddly flat and lifeless. She seemed distracted.

'Can I give you a lift? Where you headed?'

'Austin left his phone at home. I'm just dropping it in at the rooms,' she said. But before Stan could repeat his offer of a lift, she added, 'I need the exercise.'

She managed another smile, although it was clear that politeness was pulling the strings.

Stan's head filled with doubts. Tibbie was probably feeling taken for granted, what with all the lifts and meals and walks and the money. The money! Other than via a brief text, he hadn't yet thanked her properly for the loan. And it wasn't that the chaos of his life had seen it slip his mind. On the contrary, Tibbie's generosity had very much been on his mind ever since.

It had been mortifying having to admit to her of all people that he couldn't provide properly for his family, especially in a time of crisis.

Then, to be handed a supermarket bag one afternoon when she was dropping off the boys, filled with a stash of rubber-band-bound bills camouflaged by groceries... How did a person even go about drawing that amount of cash? Stan had felt like such a lowlife.

And when, a few days later, a transfer of thirty thousand showed up in his newly opened bank account, his shame shot off the charts. Threading through his mortification, though, was something else, too. Such a generous gesture was clearly a measure of Tibbie's affection for him, and he was touched and flattered by just how deeply she clearly cared about him. But it had been next to impossible to get her alone to thank her, what with either Carmen or Austin inevitably around, too.

'You must think me so rude,' he said, leaning further across the passenger seat so that he didn't have to shout. 'I haven't had a proper chance to thank you for the loan. Truth is, I've been seriously embarrassed about it. Wanted to give it back. But look, hey, it's been a lifesaver. Honestly. I can't tell you. And with me being able to work a bit more, I am hoping to be able to repay it pretty—'

'Stan, there's no hurry.'

He was glad she stopped him. He didn't need to be digging himself a hole. There was no way he could think of getting the money back to her anytime soon. An invoice for the boys' school camp had just arrived, the rates were due, and the car needed a new warrant. He knew he had a bad habit of promising to do things he couldn't deliver on, creating false expectations.

He cleared his throat. 'You're an amazing woman, Tippy. I hope Austin knows how lucky he is.'

Her mouth quivered. She looked like she might cry.

Stan was emboldened by her show of emotion. 'Had I met you first, I'd have been in there like a shot. But I think you already know that.'

Tibbie's face collapsed. 'Stan, I'm going to pretend you didn't just say that.' She shook her head. 'Your wife, my best friend, is *dying,* and you come out with this!'

He opened his mouth.

'No, stop! Just stop. Please. Anyway, I have to go,' she said and took off up the hill.

Stan remained there, leaning across the seat, his body pitched towards nothing.

The sun ducked behind a cloud, extinguishing the thin band of light filtering through the branches above, and burying the car in gloom. The pōhutukawa had long been denuded of its crimson blooms, and summer was a fading memory.

What had he been thinking? Tibbie and Austin were as close to perfect as a couple could get. Wealthy, beautiful, popular people, who pursued caring, philanthropic professions. It was hard not to feel very average beside them, and years of friendship had done little to assuage this truth. Nevertheless, there was no need for Tibbie to have been so blunt. It was the curtest she'd ever been with him. He was really just paying her a compliment.

In Fiji she had most definitely been flirting. No two ways about it. He and Carmen had had a big row about it afterwards. Sure, the cocktails might have been talking. But still. Alcohol only lowered inhibitions. It didn't make a person think differently.

He started the car and pulled out onto the road, not bothering to wave when he passed her.

When he arrived home, Stan sat in the car brooding. Ahead of him stood the house he and Carmen had lived in for most of their married life. The lawn was peppered with weeds. Leggy blades of grass licked mould-blackened bricks. The unravelling went on – a listing letterbox, dead-dry hydrangeas, sagging roof guttering, the cracked porch tiles. He felt as if he was seeing it all for the first time. The summation of their lives. The disintegration.

He climbed out of the car and slammed the door.

Material things were not important in the scheme of things. Not when your wife was battling brain cancer.

He let himself in and found Carmen in the laundry, sorting washing. She turned her head and smiled. 'You're home early.'

He came up behind her and wrapped his arms around her. 'We had a power cut, so I skived off.'

Regrowth on the square of her skull that had been opened like a trapdoor no longer prickled, and the downy strip of new baby hair caressed his cheek.

'I missed you this morning,' he said, not letting go.

'Oh, you big softie.'

He nuzzled into her neck. 'You smell nice.'

'Last few drops of Dior. I'll have to ask Richard to get me some more next time he comes through Duty Free.'

The mention of Carmen's brother almost snuffed out Stan's erection. But then, the fact that Carmen was projecting herself into the future was an aphrodisiac in itself, nulling out the Richard negative.

'Stan Andino, you horny boy,' she said, spinning around in his arms and kissing him on the lips.

He pulled her in to him, feeling the fullness of her breasts against his chest. She was at least two cup sizes bigger than Tibbie. And when she was pregnant, her breasts had been even bigger.

He slipped his hand up her skirt and hooked his fingers under her panty elastic.

'What, here? In the laundry?'

'And why not?' he said, hoisting her carefully onto the drier.

There was a restrained urgency to their lovemaking. It was the first time since the diagnosis. The first time in two-and-a-half months. They'd survived one round of radiotherapy, Carmen's medication regime had been adjusted, and she was... well, in the past week she'd been doing okay. Finally, the stars had aligned for long enough that she could break through the fug of drugs and fatigue and frightening fictions to fuel her love which, like a pilot light, had never quite gone out. And for Stan to feel a little reckless and not completely consumed by thoughts of her fragility.

Afterwards, they took a shower together like young lovers.

Carmen was lathering her hair with shampoo when she let out a low, anguished moan.

'What's wrong? Where's it sore?'

She was looking down, her face contorted.

In her hands was a clump of her hair.

Stan felt a wave of nausea. There was something about seeing a handful of human hair.

Then Carmen was sobbing, her tears mingling with the warm water raining down on her.

'Oh, Carmen. My poor, poor Carmen.'

What else could he say? Bell had warned them that hair loss would not be immediate, but usually occurred towards the end of the radiation cycle, or soon after. Carmen had completed the first course of treatment, full head of hair intact (bar the cricket pitch they'd mowed for the op). Had she thought that by some stroke of luck she'd be spared?

'I love you, hair or no hair.'

'I don't want to lose my hair, Stan. It's not fair. Not fair! Now I'm going to look even more pathetic next to Tibbie with her flaming mane.'

The comment hung there uneasily between them.

After their shower, and with Carmen less agitated, they lay down for a nap, their bodies fitting with ease around each other's familiar contours. It felt like a sneaky thing to do, napping in the middle of a weekday; however, nothing in their life was normal anymore.

'I'm sorry you missed out on your walk with Tibbie,' Stan said, as he was drifting off.

'No, I didn't,' Carmen said, pulling the blanket off him as she covered herself. 'It was pleasant enough.'

CHAPTER 20

ELIOT BARD

Eliot watched Ramesh Bandara examine the last of the shells in the shoebox. The turritella was the least remarkable of the three he'd brought in. At home he had more than a hundred of them, and together they were something special – a town of turrets. He loved running his forefinger and thumb down the slim cones. It felt weird.

'Kingdom: Animalia. Class: Gastropoda. Order: Neotaenioglossa, Family: Turritellidae.'

The detective nodded, sliding his forefinger down the shell.

'Cool feeling, hey?' Eliot said.

'Thank you for bringing them in, Eliot,' Bandara said, putting the shell carefully back in the box. 'Fun fact. I've got a fossilised piece of turritella at home. It's called Turritella Agate.'

'No, you haven't,' Eliot said, shaking his head. 'Common mistake you just made there, Detective. Everyone thinks the agate is made up of fossilised *sea* snails. But the guy who named the gemstone got it all wrong; it's the fossils of *freshwater* snails you see in cross-section. Not these.'

Eliot's mum put a hand on his arm. It was her secret language for 'calm down', 'think before you speak', 'not now'.

'Don't worry, you're not the only one to get it wrong,'

Eliot said. 'Anyway, how come you got some? It's mainly found in Wyoming.'

'You do know your shells.'

'Yes, I do,' Eliot said, putting the lid back on the box.

The detective was watching him with super-focused eyes. Watching Eliot's hands. It made him feel weird. He slipped them under the table, out of sight.

'Down to business then.'

'Can I see it sometime?' Eliot asked.

'See...?'

'The agate, because—'

'Eliot,' his mum interrupted. 'Mr Younger and Detective Bandara are busy people.'

Eliot turned around; he'd forgotten Mr Younger and the Hilary woman, DC Stark, were also in the room.

'Don't worry on account of me. I'm in no hurry,' Mr Younger said with a quick up-down smile.

The detective picked up a pen and repositioned his notepad at an angle.

'Ha! You're left-handed, too,' Eliot blurted out. 'I also have to turn the paper to stop my hand from smudging my writing.'

'Not a bad detective,' Bandara said, with a smile. 'Not bad at all.'

Eliot grinned. That was what he was going to be when he got older. He'd just decided. He was going to be a detective.

'Can we go over Wednesday morning again,' Bandara said, 'and perhaps you can tell me once more how you discovered the woman in the water.'

Eliot screwed up his eyes. He did not want to talk about all that. Shells were much more fun.

'Let's begin at the beginning.'

That was a silly thing to say, thought Eliot. Where else would you begin? Start at the start. End at the end. Start at the end. End at the start.

'Eliot?'

His heart was doing it's thumping-up-the-throat business again.

'Elli usually has his breakfast before I leave for work,' his mum said. 'Around seven-thirty.'

'Eliot needs to tell us in his own words,' Hilary Stark said, her voice school-principal serious.

Eliot looked down at the carpet, which was police-blue with speckles of maroon. It would take a long time to count all the speckles. Less time, though, than the grains of sand on Browns Bay beach.

'Off you go then, Detective Bard,' his mum whispered.

'I had a plate of Mum's homemade muesli. It's much healthier than the supermarket brand and has loads of roughage. Roughage helps carry cholesterol away. The bad cholesterol, that is. Sort of like a rubbish truck. That's what Dr Lamb says. But roughage also makes you poo more.'

Ramesh Bandara's dark brown eyes flicked wider. 'Dr Austin Lamb? Is he your doctor?'

'Yup. Best doctor this side of the moon. And my best, best friend. Hey, Mum? He delivered me with forceps, which are like these giant pliers. The cord was wrapped twice around my neck. I nearly died. Ask her.' He pointed to his mum.

She nodded.

'So you also knew Dr Lamb's wife?' Bandara said.

Eliot tossed his head from side to side. 'Sort of—'

'We've met a handful of times over the years,' his mum said coolly. 'When she's covered for Gwen at receptio—' She stopped. Put a hand to her mouth. 'It's not…'

Bandara nodded.

'What, Mum? What?'

'The deceased, whom Eliot discovered on Monday morning, was Dr Lamb's spouse,' the detective said slowly. 'Mrs Tibbie Lamb.'

Eliot frowned as he tried to catch up with the detective's dictionary-fancy words – deceased, spouse, Dr Lamb… The room started to spin. He gripped his chair. Faster and faster.

Long strands of silky red hair were twisting around him like he was the stick at the centre of a giant cloud of red candyfloss.

Soon he was buried so deep he couldn't breathe.

He stood up, stumbled, then everything went black.

CHAPTER 21

STAN ANDINO

A fortnight had elapsed since Stan had stopped to talk to Tibbie on the side of the road. A fortnight since their uncomfortable interaction. He'd started taking a slightly different route home to avoid any chance of seeing her. And it seemed she was also trying to avoid him, dropping off the boys at the end of the driveway and sending in meals or messages with them.

He turned carefully into his street. The driver behind him hooted, gesticulated, then overtook.

Auckland drivers were so bloody impatient! Didn't people realise that at any moment something could happen to rip the core right out of their lives? A wife might discover she had a tumour growing inside her head and be forced to hand over her car keys and her kindness. A family's bank account might grind down to nought, then settle in the red, like a footprint in cooling concrete. Two bright boys might go quiet, cry at night, fight at school, bully, be bullied. A father might find himself so desperate, he'd do anything to save his family. Anything. Then all the small issues that had previously occupied centre court would suddenly seem insignificant. Completely insignificant.

He slowed, eased over the first speed bump, coasted to the next, slowed, eased over it. He couldn't risk his students' work toppling over, even though he'd packed the pieces into the boot with great care. Hours of love and labour had gone into them, and he'd been charged with delivering them to the foundry the following day. He'd already dropped off the biggest bust that morning.

He indicated, turned into his driveway, then braked sharply. There was a car in his parking spot. A police car.

Stan shivered as all the tiny vessels in his skin shrank away from the day, taking the afternoon warmth with them.

He swept his tongue over his gums, reversed back onto the road, and parked on the street. It took three goes to align his car close enough to the kerb without graunching the wheels. Not that the rims of the old Volvo were precious. The car was already second-hand when he'd bought it thirteen years back and bore the scars of many a skirmish since then. Carmen had wanted a safe family vehicle after the boys were born. She'd done her research. Volvos topped her list.

Stan made his way across the front lawn, flinching as he crunched a snail underfoot. Up the steps. Through the front door, spiderwebs matting the corners like some Halloween window display. Down the corridor.

Voices were coming from the lounge. And the sound of someone sobbing.

Stan hurried towards the room that, ever since the bleached-carpet night, filled him with dread. The night that had sliced his life into *Before* and *After*. Ever since then, the room, with its seventies' orange curtains, bleach-blemished carpet, and expensive Swedish coffee table (a gift from Richard, of course), had harboured something insidious and malevolent, like a piece of furniture riddled with borer.

Men's cologne, a metallic, spicy smell, wove through the smell of bleach that still lived inside the room.

A smooth-skinned Indian man was standing in the middle of the room. He looked maybe in his late thirties.

Carmen was hunched on the couch beside a young policewoman.

'Stan!' Carmen cried, as he walked in. Her eyes were red and puffy.

He dropped his satchel, searching for some clue to pre-empt the shock he knew was coming.

'Mr Andino?' the policeman said, stretching out a hand. He had a strong, suave presence and an open face. 'DS Bandara, and this is my colleague, DC Stark.'

'What's going on? Are the boys okay?' Both Leon and Reuben were away on school camp, doing the Tongariro Crossing.

'It's Tibbie!' Carmen cried.

'What about her?'

'She's dead.'

Stan swayed unsteadily. 'What?'

Carmen nodded. 'Tibbie's dead.'

Stan sank down onto the couch, squashing in beside the policewoman. She shuffled forward and stood up, letting Stan spill into the space next to Carmen.

'You alright, sir?'

'She can't be.'

'She fell off the cliff,' Carmen said, taking a gulp of air, 'at Browns Bay. This morning.'

'The deceased was discovered by a walker,' the policeman said. 'She appears to have fallen onto the rocks below.'

'I… How? I mean… was there—'

'It is our understanding,' the policewoman said, 'that Mrs Andino was likely the last person to see Mrs Lamb alive.'

Carmen nodded, her hands trembling.

'We are trying to reconstruct the deceased's final movements and were hoping your wife might be able to assist us,' DS Bandara said. He had a slightly flattened band of skin below his nose from a repaired harelip.

Stan hauled himself out of the dip in the couch. 'My wife is not well. She cannot be answering questions when she's had a shock like this. She has brain cancer.'

The detective's expression softened. 'Dr Lamb did mention it. And we don't want to create any unnecessary stress, I assure you. But as you will understand, the first hours after such an incident are crucial.' He wiped his hands down his trousers and looked at Carmen. 'Perhaps you would like a glass of water before we begin?'

'I'll make tea,' Stan said, pulling himself up and escaping the room.

The police interview didn't last long; Carmen's answers were too disjointed and confused. All they managed to establish was that Carmen and Tibbie had taken their regular morning walk.

'Nine to ten. Yes, nine to... Hang on. We walked earlier because Tibbie had something on after. An appointment. So, we met at nine. Poor Tibs. I just can't believe she's gone.'

'Didn't you say nine is the time you usually meet up?' the policewoman said.

'Yes.'

'What time did you meet up today, then?'

Carmen looked scared, as if she realised her thoughts did not add up. 'Nine.'

'Carm, love, you and Tibs usually walk at nine.'

'That's what I just said!'

And no, she had not noticed anything particularly untoward about her best friend's mood or behaviour. 'She's always a little aloof.'

'Aloof? Tibbie?'

'Yes, Stan! Aloof. I mean, she took her own life without confiding in me, and I'm her best friend. You can't get more aloof than that... Shit! I can't believe it. Poor, poor Tibs.'

'We have not yet ascertained how Mrs Lamb died,' DS Bandara said, rubbing his chin.

Carmen then told them that she and Tibbie had only done a part of their usual walk. 'She walked with me to Masterton Road, where we parted ways.'

'So, in fact, you did not meet up any earlier than usual? You simply had a shorter walk?'

'All these questions! What does it matter anyway? She's dead!' Carmen said, grabbing her head as if it were about to fall off her shoulders. 'Trust Tibbie to beat me to the goalpost.'

She started to cry again, and the police finally took their leave.

Carmen had been crying for fifty minutes solid when Stan managed to get hold of Ngaire Bell. The specialist emailed through a prescription to the local pharmacy, and Stan made an emergency dash to collect it.

An hour later, dosed up on a strong sedative, Carmen finally fell asleep. Stan waited a while to be sure she was unrousable, then tiptoed out of the house, locking the door behind him. If Carmen woke to find no-one at home it would be a disaster, but he had to see Austin.

CHAPTER 22

STAN ANDINO

There were cars parked on either side of the road, a white Jag was in the driveway behind Tibbie's silver Audi, and another was parked on Austin's front lawn. Stan didn't dare follow suit; he knew how particular Austin was about his turf.

He found a space further up the road and was a little out of breath by the time he knocked tentatively on his friend's front door. Somehow, ringing the bell did not feel right under the circumstances.

Vicky, one of the Lambs' neighbours, let him in, her efficient and subdued manner suggesting she'd been in training for a crisis just such as this.

'Come in, Stan,' she said quietly, scooping back her hair.

Stan's heart hiccupped as he made his way through the villa. Tibbie was not going to come gliding through a doorway to greet him.

There was a cluster of people in the more formal of the two lounges, their conversations dialled down to a faint hum, like some expensive dishwasher.

Heads turned as Stan stepped into the room. His cheeks felt hot.

There were a few familiar faces – Milton and Denise Hogan, Cliff King, Vicky... He didn't recognise the others. Despite twenty-plus years of friendship, the Lambs had kept

Stan and Carmen slightly separate from the rest of their friends. Stan always suspected he was the reason they weren't integrated with the rest of the Lambs' social circle.

'Stan,' Austin said, standing up, his register caught somewhere between a boy's breaking pitch and its usual depth. The poor man looked bewildered and exhausted.

Stan stumbled into a clumsy hug. 'Jeez, Austin. I can't… I just don't know what to say. I'm so sorry, mate.'

Austin stepped out of the embrace and dusted down his shirt. There was dried clay on Stan's sleeves. 'You've met Lorna and Eric? Tibbie's aunt and uncle.'

'Carmen's husband,' the old woman hissed into her husband's ear.

There was something about the way she said Carmen's name that left Stan uneasy.

'Please, don't get up,' Stan said, as the old man tried to lever himself out of his chair. 'I'm not staying.' He turned back to Austin. 'I just wanted to stop by to say… to say that if there's anything I can do…' His voice lost its power.

Lorna nodded and began to cry quietly, her helmet of grey hair all a-tremor.

'Can't I get you something to drink, Stan?' It was Vicky. 'Tea, or something stronger? There's wine open. Whisky. A gin?'

Having thrown up his lunch on the way over, Stan did not trust himself to imbibe anything.

'Nothing, thank you. Really. I'm not staying.' He turned back to Austin. 'Carmen is alone at home.'

It almost felt wrong mentioning Carmen, when Austin had just lost Tibbie. 'We can talk tomorrow,' he mumbled. 'Or whenever. I just wanted to tell you I'm here for you, buddy.' His words sounded clunky and contrived.

'I'll see you out,' Austin said, ushering Stan into the corridor, his eagerness suggesting he was grateful for the chance to escape.

'I can't get my head around it,' Stan said, turning to his

friend at the door. 'Tibbie. I mean she was the last person in the world I'd have picked to take her own life.'

His words sucked up all the oxygen in the room.

Austin was staring at him.

Stan wished he could take them back. They sounded wrong articulated out loud.

He bumbled on. 'I mean, was she depressed again?' Stan caught himself. He couldn't remember if he was meant to know or not.

Tibbie had suffered from depression years back, following the death of her brother from an overdose. It was not common knowledge, and Tibbie's unfailing composure made it nigh-impossible for others to guess. Stan only knew because of how close Carmen and Tibbie were. Apparently, she'd responded well to antidepressants and had not suffered another episode in the nineteen years since.

'I think I of all people would have recognised the signs,' Austin said briskly.

Stan nodded vigorously, drowning in his faux pas.

'But *if* she jumped, then clearly she was,' Austin added coldly.

He picked up a framed photograph off the console table – Tibbie leaping into the sky against a Scottish-Highlands backdrop – her flight of hair, star-stretched limbs, and beaming face all joy and fun.

Austin shook his head, an odd, strangled sound escaping his throat. 'But you knew our Tibs. Ever in control. I mean, there could have been a volcano erupting inside of her for all any of us knew. Even after all this time there were still some doors she kept very firmly shut.'

It was disconcerting to hear Austin portray Tibbie's self-control as more flaw than admirable quality. Disconcerting to have Austin leave a smudge on the perfect picture Stan held in his head.

He reached for the door. 'If I could, I'd delete 2019 – the whole goddamned year – and reinstall it.'

'I'll second that,' Austin said.

Stan stepped out into the airless evening. 'Any idea yet of when the funeral will be?'

Austin kicked absentmindedly at the skirting board. 'We're waiting on a postmortem, which was meant to be today, but then got pushed back. So, the short answer is no. I imagine we're looking at next week at the earliest. Janice arrives tomorrow.'

Janice. Stan felt a cold twist of anxiety. Tibbie's sister lived in Sydney. The siblings could not have been more unalike.

Stan's car drove him home, and it wasn't until he'd switched off the ignition that he realised he had no recollection of the journey; his mind had been navigating very different scenery: A wind-sucked cry. Flesh splitting. Bones breaking. Waves crashing. A stainless-steel scalpel slicing, prying... answering.

CHAPTER 23

ELIOT BARD

Eliot thrashed around, trying to propel himself towards the porthole of light, but his body wouldn't work; the water was too heavy.

Something punctured his soft, shrivelled skin. A hairclip. As he cried out, the last pocket of air escaped his mouth. Water rushed in, filling his lungs and splitting the fine lining surrounding them.

He knew then, in the tangle of arms and legs, that he was going to die.

Everything dimmed.

Slowed.

Thickened.

Clouds of darkness coalesced into shapes.

A lampshade. Desk. The droop of his dressing-gown.

He sat up, gasping.

He was at home. In bed.

Stupid dream! He'd drowned three times already that week.

He winced as he swung his legs over the side of the bed, his hip still hurting from when he'd fallen off the chair at the police station.

The lump on the back of his head was smaller now. More the size of a ping-pong ball. He was lucky he hadn't broken a bone or injured himself more seriously. That's what his mum said.

It was the first time ever he'd properly fainted. He'd had near-misses before. 'Absences' was what Austin called them. But at the police station it had been different. A complete power outage. Kaboom!

The floorboards creaked as he padded to the toilet for a pee. Hearing his mum stir, he put his head around her door and squinted into the darkness, half hoping he'd woken her. Her silhouette was still. Eliot crept around to her side of the bed and leant in close, just to double-check. She smelt pink and warm. He loved his mum's smell. Suddenly the whites of her eyes spun open like flying saucers. She screamed. Eliot jerked backwards.

'Eliot! You gave me such a fright! I thought...' She was panting. 'What are you doing up? What time is it?'

He couldn't find any words, like when he only got vowels in Scrabble.

'Bad dream again?'

He nodded.

'C'mon, let's go and warm you some milk,' she said with a sigh, sliding her feet into her slippers.

The one good thing about having a bad dream was getting to be up late with his mum when everyone else in New Zealand was asleep. Well, not everyone, but a lot of people.

In the silent darkness, the house felt strong, like a fortress. And his mum, all sleepy and slow, was less distracted and more his mum.

After he'd finished his milk, she lay next to him until he fell asleep. Or rather, until he pretended he'd fallen asleep. He could never nod off while she was there, the weight of her body on top of the covers pulling the sheet too tightly over him like kitchen wrap. So, he just lay there, superstill, until she went back to her room.

After she'd gone, he monitored the fluorescent numbers on his alarm clock as they crept forward. 2:43. 2:56. 3:01.

Twenty minutes passed before he decided it was safe.

He reached under his bed for his torch and shone it into the tissue box on his bedside table.

Nothing, except the circle of blue torchlight on the base of the box once he'd pulled aside the tissues.

His gums tingled. Where was it?

He shook the box. The tissues thudded softly against the cardboard. No other sound.

He began to pull them out, one by one, flinging them into the air. All dud parachutes.

Then something solid spun through the darkness and landed on his bed with a *thwip*.

He breathed out; it was the tortoise-shell hairclip.

Eliot ran his forefinger in a calm oval glide across the brown splodges trapped inside the amber gel. His best treasure ever.

But he couldn't keep it. Not now. Not after everything that had happened.

He stroked it for one last time, before wrapping it in several layers of tissue, securing it with a rubber band, and burying it back in the box. Then he stuffed a handful of crumpled tissues on top of it and slid the box under his bed.

'Up you get, lazy bones.'

His mum had opened his curtains and the daylight was squint-bright.

He groaned, pulling the duvet over his head.

'This is what happens after midnight meanderings; you don't want to get up. Well, I could do with a sleep-in, too, let me tell you.'

Eliot grumbled under his breath, though it was pointless arguing; his mum never let him stay in bed late on a weekday.

'You need to get in practice for when you one day have a real job,' she always said. 'I won't have you staying in bed till goodness-knows what hour, then loafing around all day.'

She told him she'd made scrambled eggs for breakfast. Her voice trailed off.

Eliot peered out from under the duvet. She was looking at the superwoman posters he'd put back up on his walls.

'Glad I didn't empty your bin, then,' she said with a slow smile. 'I didn't think you really wanted to throw away your favourite ladies.'

The rescued posters looked pretty munted; most of them had lost their smooth, just-out-of-the-shop sheen. Medusa looked particularly bad, with a tear through her right eye. But it was the ones he'd cut out of magazines that had fared the worst; the paper too flimsy to tolerate rough handling.

He wasn't overly fussed. It felt good to have the superwomen back in his life.

He just wished he could give Dr Lamb's wife her life back, too.

CHAPTER 24

REUBEN ANDINO

Mrs Tan, Reuben's outdoor ed teacher, dropped him home from camp. Leon was still on the road. His group had stopped in Te Awamutu for lunch.

Reuben crept into his parents' room. It was hot and stuffy and smelt of sour sweat, like a boys' locker room. His mum was lying across the bed on her back, snoring loudly, her pale belly exposed where her pyjama top had ridden up. He would never be able to fall asleep on his back like that; he liked to curl into his pillow, with his back to the world.

He crept around to the other side of the bed and opened the long, narrow window above her. He thought about covering her with a loose sheet. She used to do that for him and Leon when they were small, but he didn't want to risk waking her. Her brain needed lots of rest.

He stood there for a moment, taking in all the changes that over the past few months added up to a different mum. Her face, which had once narrowed to a pixie point, was all puffy and spongy like bread dough. And her Halle Berry hair (he was with her the time she showed her hairdresser a photograph and said 'I want to look like her') had become a crazy paving of pale scalp and prickly brown bristles. Her arms were bruised and punctured from all the needles, and her fingernails, which she always used to keep brightly painted, were ridged and chewed. There was also a nasty red scratch across her belly. He wondered how she'd gotten that.

He wiped his nose on his shirt sleeve. He'd missed her. Missed her so much. But the missing reached beyond the few days he'd been away on camp. He missed his mum. His old mum. When he left school, he was going to become a doctor and learn how to make people with brain cancer better.

A loud whisper startled him. He spun round.

His dad was standing in the doorway, signalling to him.

'Hey, kiddo, when did you get home?' his dad whispered, closing the bedroom door quietly behind them. 'I wasn't expecting you till later.'

'Caught a ride with Mrs Tan,' Reuben said, following his dad down the corridor. 'She didn't stop for lunch; had to get back for some family thing. Leon's coming on the bus.'

'So how was it? Pretty awesome, I'll bet.'

Reuben shrugged.

'Were you warm enough?'

'Yeah.'

'It sounded like you had good weather for the crossing.'

Reuben nodded.

'I was just about to make some lunch. Come on, I'll make us a toasted sammie. Tuna mayo?'

'Okay.'

Reuben hoisted himself onto the bench.

'How did sharing a tent with Collin work out?' his dad asked, peering into the fridge.

'He's a dick.'

His dad kept staring into the open fridge, despite the irritating *close-the-door* beeps.

'Who? Collin?'

'A stupid, fucking dick.'

His dad shut the fridge door. 'Please don't use that sort of language.'

'Mum does.'

His dad opened his mouth. Closed it. The light on the

sandwich press had turned green and he hadn't even opened the can of tuna yet.

'That's different, and you know it is. She never used to.'

Reuben looked at the floor. 'Whatever.'

'Anyway, why's Collin a dick?'

'He said Mum is mental. That she threatened to kill April Edelman's dog if it didn't stop yapping. Said his mother's forbidden him from coming over here anymore.'

A tear ran down his cheek. He was crying like a stupid baby.

'Oh, jeez,' his dad said, grabbing him in a hug.

Reuben held himself rigid. He was too old for hugs. They didn't help anyway. And he didn't want his dad's stupid words either. What good were they? He didn't want to think or go to school or do anything anymore. Just disappear. Burn blue like gas in a Bunsen burner. Poof!

'Listen, Reub…'

Reuben hung forward, his eyes stuck to the floor.

His dad lifted his chin.

He pulled away.

'This is a tough time for you, I know. I wish I could make it better, but it's the hand we've been dealt. We have to cope as best we can and just hope Mum gets better.'

Tears were leaking out of his dad's eyes, too.

'It's hard enough for us to get our heads around. Imagine how it is for others, like Collin and his airhead of a mother.'

Reuben snorted. Collin's mother was an airhead.

'But seriously, boy, you've got to let those sorts of comments wash over you. People can be cruel. Your mum is really sick right now. She's battling for her life.'

Reuben felt his innards yank tight. He wanted to go back in and wake his mum up and give her a hug and never let go.

'When this is all over, we'll have one hell of a holiday. You, Leon, Mum and me. How about it?'

Reuben blinked slowly.

'I'm thinking Fiji,' his dad continued. 'Or Rarotonga.'

Reuben felt a flicker of excitement. But the idea fizzled like a dying sparkler. 'We can't afford it.'

His dad's back was turned to him as he closed the lid of the sandwich toaster.

'Dad?'

'What?'

'We can't afford it, can we?'

'You wait and see,' his dad said, licking mayo off his fingers. 'I may just have a plan.'

CHAPTER 25

STAN ANDINO

Stan and Carmen sat motionless in the car, neither making a move to get out. At that moment, Stan loved her with every cell in his body. They'd driven home from the police station in silence. The quiet was unusual; Carmen had been speaking really loudly of late, as if she'd lost the ability to modulate her volume.

Unusual. Ha! What was usual? Stan didn't know anymore. There was nothing usual left in his life. No land in sight he recognised.

What was he to do? The Andino family, his reason for getting up every morning, was under threat. He'd fight to the death to protect it. Do whatever it took. Whatever.

And yet, weaving through this passion and conviction was resentment, too. Towards Carmen for landing them in this situation in the first place. If she hadn't got sick, none of this would have happened. Their lives would be trucking along – Saturday sports, school prize-givings, bohemian pottery students…

He bit his lip as he thought back to that dark brown freckle that had appeared on her thigh at the end of summer four years back. How many times he'd told her to go and get it checked. And how many times she'd ignored him. His indestructible, invincible wife!

'I don't like the look of that,' Austin had said, when Carmen finally heeded Stan's nagging. 'I think we should take it off.'

Little did they know what a small brown spot no bigger than a business-shirt button would mean.

'My funny freckle' was how Carmen used to refer to it. Turns out there was nothing funny about it at all.

If only she'd taken better care of herself, used sun protection, got the damned thing checked sooner.

'Maybe I did it.'

Stan swung round in his seat. 'What are you saying, Carm?'

He turned on the ignition and closed her window.

'Maybe I did push her, like the detectives are implying. I mean, it's not rocket science why they're going at me so hard. Even I realise I'm a suspect in Tibbie's death.'

Stan opened the car door just in time and vomited onto the stippled grey concrete. He stayed there, leaning out of the car, threads of saliva hanging from his mouth.

'That's what all this amounts to, isn't it?' she said, seemingly oblivious to his state.

Stan wiped his mouth on his sleeve and closed the door. 'Carmen, we cannot be having this conversation. Tibbie took her own life. You hear me? That's it. Perhaps we could have helped more. Been more observant of her mood. But we had other things on our mind. Right?'

It had been a strained, supposedly informal chat at the police station. Ramesh Bandara's manner tempered by an obvious awareness that he was questioning a woman who in all likelihood was going to die within the year.

The same couldn't be said for the trainee detective, Hilary Stark, who emphasised that Carmen's behaviour had, according to several sources, grown increasingly erratic and aggressive over the past months. There was the supermarket incident; the altercation with their neighbour one down. The threat to April Edelman's dog. Carmen's increasing paranoia that Tibbie was 'making a move' on Stan. Her accusations of poisoning. Only

Austin could have supplied this 'inside information' in such a comprehensive bundle. After all, only he, Carmen's doctor and long-time friend, had been privy to all the dramas.

Stan couldn't help but feel betrayed. Austin had pretty much thrown Carmen under the bus. What about patient confidentiality? In what capacity had Austin reported Carmen's behaviour? Surely there were laws to protect patients?

Of course, Stan knew it was complicated. It was not just about Austin being Carmen's doctor and friend. They were talking about the death of Austin's wife. It was such a bloody mess. However, Stan would sue if he had to. Sue Austin for breach of his oath, or whatever it was called.

He stopped himself. His mind was getting away on him. It was Austin they were talking about. Austin! Their best friend for more than two decades.

'You would never have done something like that, Carmen. It's not in your nature,' Stan said. 'You are not some monster, just because you have a brain tumour.' He gently cupped her chin and turned her face towards him. 'What's more, you have no recollection of doing anything,' he said, carefully enunciating each word. 'Your brain wouldn't completely wipe the memory.'

As he said it, Stan thought about the time Tibbie had cancelled on Carmen, yet Carmen had later insisted they had gone for a walk.

What was he going to tell Reuben and Leon? They didn't even know about Tibbie's death yet. Or maybe they did. Perhaps he was being naïve to think that word hadn't got to them yet. He could only hope that because they'd been away on school camp, the kids had been kept in the dark.

What was he meant to do? Keeping Carmen alive had been his priority. But now everything had suddenly changed.

Should he be scrambling to hire a lawyer to defend her? Or should he rather be focused on mitigating the fallout for the family? Surely they wouldn't send a woman with brain cancer to jail?

He was jumping the gun. Carmen had not yet been charged

with anything. All the police were going on was supposition. Nothing more. Nothing they were letting on anyway. He wondered if they knew more.

He rubbed his palm over his mouth. Bandara had told them not to leave town. Ha! Really? Like in some movie. Where would they go? As if he was going to bundle Carmen and the kids into the car and speed off into the sunset.

'You should not be in contact with Dr Lamb either,' DS Bandara had added.

That was one step too far. 'He's Carmen's doctor, for God's sake!'

'We are talking about the death of Dr Lamb's wife,' the female constable said.

'It would be prudent to look for another physician in the interim,' Bandara continued, more gently. 'Besides the conflict of interests, I'd imagine Dr Lamb is unlikely to return to work for a few weeks. And you will be needing more immediate care, won't you?'

Stan now stared at the weathered garage door. How had their life unravelled to this?

Carmen put a hand on his lap.

He looked down at it with surprise, as if a baby falcon had landed on his leg.

He wanted to respond to it. Pull her in. Lose himself in her affection, in the protection of being a couple. In the normalness of *Before*. But that life no longer felt recent or real. Had it ever even existed?

Her fingers looked so stubby now that her nails had been chewed. Once upon a time she'd never have been seen dead without them perfectly manicured – not an uncommon trait in short women, as if, like a pair of heels, painted fingernails extended the frugal measure of a small frame.

DC Stark had taken a photograph of them. Of Carmen's hands.

Stan climbed out the car, letting his wife's hand fall to the seat.

CHAPTER 26

LEON ANDINO

Oil trickled down Leon's chin. He wiped his arm across his mouth. The afternoon had turned out surprisingly well. Fast food was something his parents were insanely strict about. Mostly his mum. She'd read this book about big guys in the fast-food industry, with dubious ethics and one goal only – to make a profit. As a result, she was anti all the usual fast-food suspects, though stopped short of forbidding them outright. The upshot was that burgers and fried chicken had taken on the status of an illicit currency in the Andino household. Leon would pretty much sell out his brother for a Big Mac, if push came to shove.

As it turned out, he didn't have to. His dad picked them up from school and said the most random thing ever. 'How about a cheeseburger?'

'Far out, Dad!' Leon cried, punching the seat in excitement. 'You're the best!'

Reuben was more suspicious. 'How come?'

'Just because. I reckon we need more just-because moments, don't you?'

All three of them ordered 'the works'; however, their dad still hadn't touched his by the time he and his brother had almost finished theirs.

Leon wolfed down the last of his, hoping to get first dibs on his dad's.

'Close your mouth,' Reuben growled. 'You eat like a pig.'

'You *are* a pig.'

'Boys, please!'

Leon took a swig of milkshake, held his breath, then let out a gigantic burp.

Reuben and his dad burst out laughing.

Leon repeated the trick. It was cool to be a team.

'Hey, guys,' their dad finally said, fiddling with a soggy fry. 'I wanted to talk to you about something.'

Reuben began scratching his already raw knuckles. He had seriously bad eczema and his skin was as scaly as a dinosaur's.

'Don't scratch, Reub,' their dad said, putting his hand over Reuben's. 'It'll only make it worse. Are you still using the cream Austin prescribed?'

Reuben had suffered from eczema since he was a baby, but lately it had gotten real bad. There were angry patches on his neck, under his arms, over his chest, and on the backs of his hands. His whole body was one raw, red itch. Austin said stress was the culprit. The stress of their mum having brain cancer.

'Yeah, Reub!' Leon taunted. 'Are you moisturising your hands, honey?'

'Shut up,' Reuben said, shoving his brother.

Leon returned the favour.

'Cut that out, right now!'

Kids at the table one along turned and stared. Leon gave them the finger.

'Leon, for God's sake, what's got into you?' his dad hissed. 'And you're in school uniform.'

He opened his mouth to respond, but his dad beat him to it.

'Enough, okay? Enough.'

It was the way his dad said it that made him stop. He sounded sort of desperate.

'I'm afraid I've got some… some very sad news to share with you both.'

Reuben switched from rubbing his knuckles to shredding his paper napkin.

'It's about Tibbie.'

Instantly, he had their attention. They loved Tibbie. She was like their honorary aunt. Right from when they were small, she'd spoil them something wicked. If their mum and dad went there for dinner, she'd make up the spare room for him and Reub. They got to eat Kohu Road ice-cream (super-expensive) and read comics from Austin's Asterix and Tintin collections.

Even now she was still cool. When she picked them up from school a few weeks back, one of Leon's classmates mistook her for his mum.

'You've got a shit-hot mother.'

Leon didn't bother setting him straight.

'Tibbie died last Wednesday,' their dad said slowly.

All the other noise in the place disappeared, like dishwater down a drain, until there was nothing but their dad's words caught in the steel strainer. Words that did not make any sense. That could have come from some stupid English lit test. *Was Desdemona's death foreshadowed? Are there examples of this device used elsewhere in the text?*

'For real?' But he already knew the answer. His dad's face said it all.

'How?'

'She fell off the cliffs at Browns Bay.'

The noise in the fast-food joint came back on full force. His dad's eyelid twitched. A baby in a highchair squawked. An oven timer beeped.

'Did she kill herself?'

Trust Reuben to say something like that!

Their dad cracked his knuckles. 'We don't know. It's one possibility the police are looking into.'

'Police?' Reuben's face went milk-white.

'They always get involved in an unexplained death. Which is why they're also—'

'That's mental, man,' Leon said, taking another sip of milkshake.

Reuben let out an old-man sigh. 'So much horrible stuff keeps happening, Dad.'

'I know, son,' he said, slumping back in his seat.

He looked like he'd run out of fuel. Like there might have been other stuff he wanted to tell them, but his engine was properly caput.

CHAPTER 27

ELIOT BARD

'Lousy weather out there,' Mr McDougal said, closing the door behind Eliot.

Eliot shook the raindrops out of his hair.

'Thought we might focus on indoor tasks today,' Mr McDougal said, shuffling down the corridor. 'Don't want you catching your death.'

Eliot sloped after him. 'It's just water, Mr McDougal. I won't melt.'

Mr McDougal rolled back his lips. His dentures made an annoying clicking sound. 'No, no. Your mother would not be very happy if I sent you home sick.'

'She won't mind,' Eliot said, flicking his temple with his finger till it hurt. 'I mean, I won't get sick, so she won't mind.'

The old man shook his already shaky head. He reminded Eliot of one of those retro bobbing cows people kept on their dashboards.

'Give me your jacket. I'll hang it up in the hot-water cupboard. It'll dry off in no time.'

'Nah, it's fine,' Eliot said, pulling the unzipped gap closed.

Mr McDougal frowned. 'You surely not going to stay in that all morning?

I've got the heater on in the spare room.'

'I need a pee,' Eliot said, stepping around his neighbour.

'Right you are then.'

Once Eliot had locked the toilet door, he dug a hand into his jacket pocket.

He sucked in a back-to-front sigh. Still there!

Quickly, he pulled out the soft bundle and stuffed it into the back pocket of his jeans, then turned and looked over his shoulder at himself in the mirror. The thing barely made a bulge.

He flushed the toilet, ran the tap, then opened the door. Mr McDougal was where he'd left him, standing in the corridor like a TV show on pause.

Eliot handed him his jacket.

'I think you can put it in the hot-water cupboard yourself, young man,' Mr McDougal said, gruffly. 'You'll find a wire coat hanger inside.'

Eliot did as he was ordered and followed the major into the spare room, which was super-hot and smelt of old man.

'Pauline has been threatening to come and sort this space out if I don't.'

Eliot slumped down in the armchair. Why did Mr McDougal's daughter always have to be so bossy?

'It's not her room,' Eliot grumbled.

Mr McDougal hauled his trousers higher. The hems were frayed and grubby. 'She says if I don't do it, it'll be left to her to sort out when I'm gone.'

'Then… then *she* should help! She's your daughter.'

'Wouldn't hear of it,' Mr McDougal said, drawing his bushy eyebrows together. 'She'd take it all to the tip, I guarantee you. Doesn't appreciate my treasure, does my dear Pauline.'

Treasure. Eliot's innards tightened.

'Women,' the old man said, shaking his head. 'They get very worked up about tidiness.'

Eliot nodded; his mum was a case in point.

'Mind you, when I was in the army, we had to keep our dorms spic and span. Night before inspection we'd iron our beds and sleep on the floor. Once—'

Eliot's mind drifted off. How was he going to do what he needed to do with Mr McDougal insisting they stay inside? He pulled irritably at his left ear. The weather was scuppering his plan.

'—according to the date, then I can go through them easily and decide which ones to keep.'

Eliot landed back in the room.

'Where is your mind, Eliot Bard? You're away with the fairies today.'

'Fairies aren't real.'

Mr McDougal was perched on a stool-high pile of newspapers. 'I was saying to sort these cuttings according to their date, then I'll make a final call on them.'

'That's double-handling,' Eliot said, clearing a space for himself on the floor; there was no room on the bed. 'Mum says you should deal to things just once and not procrastinate. She says it wastes a lot of time and energy to move things from one place to another. Better to sort stuff straight-off.'

'Procrastinate. Hmmph! You're starting to sound like my Lani,' Mr McDougal said, with a yellow smile. His teeth needed to be put in a glass with one of those fizzy tablets.

Eliot felt bad for reminding Mr McDougal about his dead wife. It was a few years ago now that she'd died. Eliot remembered the day well. Arriving home from school to a bright yellow ambulance in the McDougals' driveway. Apparently, Mrs McDougal had been collecting fallen feijoas at the bottom of the garden when she keeled over. His mum said that was the way she wanted to go. With her shoes on.

A few days later, his mum sent Eliot round with a meal for Mr McDougal. Eliot got quite a fright when he found Mr McDougal and his daughter Pauline sitting in the lounge next to Lani McDougal. She was in a casket, with the lid open. Her feet were covered, so Eliot didn't get to see what shoes she was wearing when she died.

'Why do you keep so many pieces of old newspaper?' he

asked, opening out one of the cuttings. It was disintegrating along the crease line.

'Look at that, will you!' Mr McDougal said, straightening his glasses and carefully taking it off Eliot. His lenses were dulled by greasy fingerprints. '1976. Well, I never. How time flies.' He scanned the article. *'Rapturous welcome as athletes bring home four medals*. If the truth be told, it was not our proudest moment. Not when you consider twenty-nine nations boycotted the games because of our sporting ties with South Africa.'

Eliot scratched his neck irritably.

'You know about apartheid, don't you?'

Eliot shook his head, then immediately wished he hadn't. He'd just given Mr McDougal an invitation to launch into another history lesson. 'My, you are a fidgeter today, boy,' Mr McDougal said, stopping his story. 'Got ants in your pants or what?'

'It's stopped raining. I think I should go tackle those weeds in the veggie garden before they get away on us.'

Mr McDougal gave Eliot a quizzical stare. 'Rightio then, you eager beaver, you. But first, put the kettle on. Must be time for a cuppa.'

Eliot harrumphed down the corridor.

'There are some sugar-free pancakes in the tin on top of the microwave,' McDougal called after him.

Eliot pulled out the tray that lived beside the cooker. Sugar bowl. Teapot. Milk jug. Strainer. Side plates. He knew his way around Mr McDougal's kitchen like it was his own.

'How many spoons of tea did you put in?' the old man asked, as he poured the pale brown liquid into Eliot's mug.

'One.'

'Thought so. It's as weak as cat's pee.'

Eliot shrugged and poured loads of milk into his, so that he could drink it down fast. But it was pointless, because he still had to wait for Mr McDougal to finish his, and he took forever.

Eliot didn't really feel like it, but he ate another pancake just to pass the time. It was dry and sucked up all the spit in his mouth.

Finally, Mr McDougal was done. Eliot rinsed the dishes, put them on the drying rack, and escaped into the garden.

It was a relief to get outside.

He pulled on his gardening gloves and picked up the old kitchen knife Mr McDougal kept for weeding. Then he was driving the rusty blade into the thigh-high box of soil, unearthing several clumps of weed as he dug a hole as deep as the container. With shaking hands, he took the tissue-wrapped parcel from his back pocket, dropped it into the hole, and covered it up with soil.

Eliot glanced over his shoulder before hurriedly carving an X into the plank bordering the bed. A permanent mark, which could not be washed away with the next downpour, nor bleached invisible by the sun.

As he straightened, wiping his muddy hands on his jeans, someone behind him sneezed.

Eliot spun round. Mr McDougal was standing beside the old wine barrel, a clump of parsley in his hand.

'For tonight's stew,' he said, his eyes latching onto Eliot's.

CHAPTER 28

AUSTIN LAMB

Austin closed his eyes when he heard the doorbell ring. It had been relentless, the stream of people arriving to express their condolences. Not only friends and relatives, but patients, too. Clearly his wife's death was considered an exception to the unspoken rule of not bothering the doctor at home.

He'd never been a fan of spontaneous drop-ins. The science of his brain favoured order, preparation, predictability. There was a messiness in the unrehearsed and uncertain. He felt exhausted by all the outpouring of emotions. More exhausted than he'd ever felt after a forty-eight-hour shift as a junior doctor.

The previous week had thrown his life into disarray in a way he could never have imagined, unearthing memories of his chaotic childhood. Would his father stumble home drunk, fists flying? Would his mother spend their entire benefit on a four-hundred-bulb set of outdoor fairy lights from the US? Would the creak of his bedroom door announce some random adult visitor? Were they going to move house again, change suburb, change school? Would he have to try and make new friends again?

He hadn't allowed his head to go back there for years. That time belonged to some other Austin. But now, all of a sudden, it felt very recent, very real, and very raw.

So much for the healing passage of time.

As a child he'd never thought it possible to escape the quagmire that was his family. It was not an option he ever entertained, despite catching glimpses of other kids' 'normal' lives. Then Mr Takashima came along. He was Austin's teacher for two terms only. Not even a full school year. But enough time to show Austin a different horizon. Enough time to instil in him the belief that life above water level was possible.

Mr Takashima's classes were about a strict, stable routine balanced with some freedom and fun.

Austin had never lived within the secure walls of structure before, and the predictability of those two terms settled the angst which had fermented for so long at the bottom of his belly.

He could clearly remember the day he bumped into Mr Takashima and his wife on Queen Street.

'This is Austin, my star pupil.'

Mrs Takashima smiled widely. She was the most beautiful woman Austin had ever seen, her hair the swish-and-settle of black silk, her teeth all white symmetry.

'I've heard a lot about you, Austin. I hear you have a bright future ahead of you.'

A bright future. Said with such certainty.

Mr Takashima nodded. 'Wouldn't be surprised if this good fellow is the first person to set foot on Mars, or becomes the next best brain surgeon. Something stellar like that.'

Austin sat back now in his leather chair and looked around his study. It was a microcosm of the life he'd so carefully curated. The awards and qualifications garnered over the years. The trio of photographs taken as he crossed the finish line at the London Marathon. The large sash windows leading the eye into a lush, leafy garden. The pendulum clock made from cherrywood and oak, which he'd meticulously restored. The shelves lined with books – medical texts on the left, others on the right – spines aligned, and titles alphabetically ordered.

He sighed. The room was his Shala, his meditational retreat. A space that echoed Mr Takashima's words. Bright future. Bright future. Bright future. It showcased the sanctity and order of Austin's life. A space that could never be sullied because no-one else was allowed inside. He had not even liked Tibbie to intrude, something she'd graciously respected.

Stan's voice in the hallway popped Austin out of his reverie.

'Janice! I didn't expect—'

'Didn't expect what? Me to come over for my sister's funeral?'

Austin closed his eyes and rubbed his forehead. He couldn't face Stan. Not today. He'd leave Janice to deal with him.

Janice had been 'helping' with preparations for the funeral, filtering visitors, warming meals, things like that. But for all her efforts, Austin found life more challenging with his sister-in-law around, her belligerent temperament and unfocused energy contaminating the already difficult days.

The sisters could not have been more different. If Tibbie had been gracious, loyal and constant, Janice drifted through partners, friends and jobs. She'd done stints in real estate, reception (at a brothel), retail, massage therapy, telemarketing… even tarot card reading. And despite her receiving a significant inheritance almost two years back now (as had Tibbie), her trajectory remained relatively unchanged. Within months of coming into the money, she'd squandered a significant portion on some hairbrained weight-loss franchise that went belly-up. ('Excuse the pun' is what Austin always said, when relating the story to friends.)

When Janice had followed her lover to Sydney twelve years ago, Austin and Tibbie welcomed the distance it inserted between them and Janice's inevitable dramas. That said, Tibbie never neglected her familial duties, loyally visiting her sister at least once a year. They rarely heard from Janice in between these visits, unless of course she needed money.

'Good to see you,' Austin heard Stan mumble. 'Just wish it wasn't under such awful circumstances.'

'You should not be here, Stan,' Janice said, her Australian twang more noticeable from a distance.

'I know, but I really need to see Austin. Something like this should not get between us.'

'Something like what? A little murder? Really?'

'Look, I know how messed-up it all seems.'

Stan clearly wasn't going to go away easily, and by the sound of it, Janice was only making a difficult situation worse.

'Who is it?' Austin asked, feigning ignorance as he emerged from his study.

Stan was on the doorstep, pale, unshaven, with dark shadows under his eyes.

'I was just suggesting he leave,' Janice said, interposing herself between the two men. She was dressed in orange leggings and a low-cut leopard-print sweatshirt, the top of her crimson bra visible.

'Can we talk?' Stan implored, looking past her. 'Just for a minute.'

Austin tilted his head, beckoning him inside.

Janice glared at Stan as he crossed the threshold.

Austin hesitated, then invited Stan into his study. Stan, of all people, allowed into his sacred space! But it was the only place they could escape Janice, and Austin needed the energy and order of the room to protect against the chaos Stan would inevitably import.

'Have a seat,' he said, closing the door behind them.

He felt an injection of satisfaction as Stan took in the room and all the success it documented.

Oddly, it felt like a first consultation, not a chat between friends who'd known each other for years. A foreignness had wedged itself in the space between them.

Stan perched on the edge of a chair. 'Don't think I've ever been in here,' he said. It felt like an accusation.

'Want a drink?' Austin asked, walking over to the crystal decanter he kept on a silver tray – the arrangement was right out of *Dallas*, the soap opera he used to watch as a kid. JR Ewing, a powerful and wealthy businessman had a drinks trolley in his office, the stiff stuff ever available to celebrate big deals, calm crises, and lubricate difficult discussions. Whisky, the sophisticated mediator.

'Cheers. I could really do with one.'

Austin poured him a double measure.

'Great photos,' Stan said, looking at the London Marathon trio.

'Thanks.'

'I believe the funeral is this Friday,' Stan said, hurrying to fill the pause. 'I just wanted to double-check you're okay with me being there. Carmen won't be, of course. She'd very much like to, but fully understands with all that's going down. The last thing she'd… we'd want to do is add to your distress.'

Austin cleared his throat. 'Sure.'

'It's just I couldn't imagine not being there to farewell Tippy. And being there for you, too.'

Tippy. Stan's nickname for Tibbie had always annoyed Austin, as if Stan and his wife shared some sort of exclusive intimacy. Tibbie was already a nickname in itself. The diminutive for Elizabeth. Was that not good enough for Stan?

He caught himself. Tibbie was no longer his wife. She was dead.

'It may not even go ahead on Friday,' Austin said, putting his glass down abruptly. 'We're still waiting on a second pathologist's review of—' He stopped himself. 'We should know by later tonight.'

'A review of?'

'Stan, I really cannot be talking to you about this. You should know that.'

'No, no. Of course. It's just that I don't know what to think. Or say. And it must be hard for you to be objective, too. For both of us to be. The thing is, the police have kept Carmen and me in the dark. We don't know what's going down. Whether they are really considering her as a suspect, or whether…' His chin was trembling. It was embarrassing and awkward for them both.

Austin passed him a hanky.

'Sorry,' Stan said, blowing his nose. 'It's you who needs comforting. But it's just... Look, I've got to be honest: we're struggling, Austin. I... I don't know what to think.'

'I wish I could offer you some reassurance,' Austin said, feeling oddly detached from the Andino melodramas, the sentiment quite sudden, as if some data plan had just expired. 'The truth is, I'm just trying to cope myself right now. On one level, I understand Carmen is not the Carmen we've always known, and through no fault of her own. She has organic brain disease. But I've lost my wife. And I can't help thinking I should have done more to keep her safe from... well, from Carmen. I should have understood the risks. Anyway, as I say, this is really not appropriate for us to be talking like this.'

Stan's face collapsed, his eyes dying right there. It was hard to watch.

'If she... I mean, if she did it, it's not like we'd try to avoid conviction.'

How quickly the guy was adjusting to the new goalposts.

'Jeez, you're my, our, best friend, Austin. But, I mean, can you tell me – would she be held culpable of murder, with a brain tumour? You talk of organic brain disease. It sounds so clinical. So scientific. Would it be... ?'

Austin couldn't take any more. This had been a bad idea.

He got up and moved towards the door. 'My understanding is that Carmen is just one line of inquiry. The police are considering a number of possibilities.'

Stan opened his mouth to reply.

'I think we should leave things there.' He reached for the door handle.

'What makes the police think it wasn't suicide anyway?' Stan persisted, scrambling for time.

Austin clenched his jaw. 'You're not hearing me, Stan. You need to leave, my friend.'

Janice was still in the corridor when Austin opened the door. She'd almost certainly been eavesdropping.

CHAPTER 29

ANDREA BARD

Eliot stood stiffly as she did up his top button. He hated wearing a shirt with a collar. Especially with the top button done up. She knew it reminded him of school, a period in their lives neither was in a hurry to revisit. However, certain occasions demanded a collared shirt, and this was one of them. She would not have anyone pass judgement on her boy, nor her parenting.

Being a solo mum was hard enough, without having a kid like Eliot. She wouldn't have swapped him for the world, but there was no denying that having Eliot for a son was a challenge. Andrea Bard lived in a permanent state of self-doubt. It was hard knowing whether the roadblocks she encountered were things every parent experienced, or whether they were a manifestation of Eliot's fatherless upbringing. Then again, perhaps they were peculiar to him because of his unique genetic makeup. It was impossible to know.

One concern that hovered at the back of every day was what would happen to him once she was no longer around. And because of it, she found herself swinging from being overly strict, as a way of preparing him for independent living, to being far too lenient, out of guilt and love.

When Eliot was diagnosed with Type 1 diabetes at age eleven, it was less traumatic for Andrea than it might have been. Diabetes was a diagnosis she could face head-on and manage. There were documented signs and symptoms, treatments available, guidelines and expected outcomes. It was the other vague, obscure non-diagnosis she found so much harder. Eliot had learning difficulties in some areas, while exhibiting extraordinary ability in others. He was overly trusting and gullible at times, yet also displayed remarkable empathy and insight beyond his years. He was obsessed with horses, treasure and auburn-haired women, believed in superpowers, and engaged in a series of daily rituals to keep calm. Yet he also astounded her with his common sense and practical approach to life. He was unaware of his strength and unwittingly broke things, but he had a huge heart and would never intentionally hurt a flea.

Labels such as 'on the spectrum' and 'Asperger syndrome' were bandied about by specialists; however, no single diagnosis was ever formally committed to. In retrospect, this was probably a good thing; at least Eliot's potential was not automatically foreclosed. Nonetheless, the vagueness did not make for easy living. It meant that any expectations she had of her son were grounded in nothing more than anecdote and hope.

Sometimes she found herself fixating on whether his birth was to blame; he'd come in such a hurry, the cord wrapped twice around his neck. With no time to get to the hospital, Austin Lamb, the new, young doctor on the block, had been forced to deliver Eliot at home. Austin Lamb. She and Eliot had been so fortunate to have him in their life.

Other times, she wondered whether Eliot was the way he was because of the genes he'd inherited from the man who'd passed through her life one night.

Whatever the reason, all Andrea Bard knew for certain was that she loved her son more than anything in the world and would do everything in her power to keep him safe.

'Now what have you gone and spilt down your front?'

Eliot squinted at the blob of toothpaste on his shirt.

'Come here!' she said irritably, dampening a corner of

kitchen cloth and rubbing roughly at the mark. 'We're late enough as it is. The place is going to be packed.'

And she was right. By the time they arrived, cars were lining the roads two blocks back from the church.

They finally found a parking space only her small car could squeeze into.

'Told you so,' she said, as they scurried along the pavement. 'Austin is such a significant member of our community.'

It was no wonder he was so loved and supported by his community. He was a remarkable person. Someone who saw the practice of medicine as a vocation. That he'd insisted on covering the bills for any private specialists Eliot needed to see over the years (specialists she would not have ordinarily been able to afford) was a measure of the man. A measure of his care.

'Hurry up and stop dawdling, will you?'

As they rounded the corner, they encountered the first cluster of people. Men in dark suits. Women in heels.

Heads turned, eyes appraising, evaluating, judging.

Andrea smoothed her skirt and adjusted her hair. 'C'mon, love.'

Eliot stopped abruptly and stared at the long black hearse. Then he was hitting his head with his fist.

Andrea pulled his hand down by his side. 'None of that today,' she whispered. 'On the way home, I'll stop at the supermarket, and we can buy a tub of peanut-butter ice-cream. How about it?'

'Hello there, lovely.' A woman wearing a fitted tan dress and a necklace of engorged white beads tottered towards them.

'Abby,' Andrea said, forcing a smile.

'This isn't young Eliot, surely?'

Andrea nodded. 'Eliot, do you remember Abby Manderson?'

He shook his head.

'To think you and my Adam used to toddle around together in nappies. How tall are you now?'

'Six foot two,' Eliot said, pulling his shoulders back.

'Hmm, Adam's about that.'

'What's he up to these days?' Andrea asked.

'Oh, in Dunedin studying law and girls,' she said with a sardonic grin. 'Changes his girlfriends more frequently than his underpants.'

Eliot let out a spluttering guffaw.

'Terrible business this thing with Tibbie, isn't it?' Abby Manderson said, dropping her voice to a whisper.

'Yes. Really awful. I—'

Abby waved to someone behind Andrea. 'Anyway, lovely to see you both,' she said, winking at Eliot and manoeuvring past them.

'How do you know *her*?' Eliot asked.

'We were in the same antenatal group, you and her darling Adam.'

'Darling Adam!' Eliot said, giggling. 'He changes his girlfriends more often than his underpants.'

'Not so loud, Elli.'

The church was chock-a-block, and just when it looked like they were going to have to stand, a boy in a navy-blue blazer directed them to two spare seats up at the front.

Andrea reluctantly followed the lad down the aisle, Eliot at her side. She knew how much he hated being the centre of attention.

They were shown to seats just a few along from the detective, Ramesh Bandara.

Sitting down, Andrea realised that she and Eliot were also just feet away from Tibbie Lamb's casket – a shiny mahogany box topped with lilies, roses, lisianthus and baby's breath.

Eliot started grinding his teeth.

Andrea put a finger to her lips.

He stopped the teeth grinding, but started rocking, the weight of his body juddering the entire pew.

'Eliot!'

Harder. Faster. Thump. Thump. Thump.

This was not going to work. Andrea stood up and grabbed his hand. 'Sorry. Excuse me. Sorry. Can we get past, please?'

Determined not to have to walk back down the length of the church, she wrestled with the fire escape door, and finally they burst out into the sunshine. 'Sorry, Mum,' Eliot said, his eyes fixed on the ground as they made their way back to the car.

'It's not your fault,' she said, her face burning hot, her temples throbbing. 'I should never have brought you.'

They drove home in silence. She knew Eliot would be churning; he hated disappointing her.

As they turned into their driveway, Eliot blurted out: 'The peanut-butter ice-cream! You forgot, Mum.'

Andrea tilted her head in apology. 'What about I make you a hot chocolate instead? It's not really ice-cream weather anyway.'

'You promised!'

Grinding the gears, she put the car in reverse, and they shot back up the driveway.

Near the top she slammed her foot on the brake; Terrance McDougal was standing in the middle of their path, right behind the car.

'Gosh, Terrance, I nearly ran you over,' she said, winding down the window. 'Everything alright?'

'You heading out again?' he said, looking puzzled.

'We forgot to pick up something at the shops. Can I get you anything while we're out?'

He peered into the car. 'Ah, you've got young Eliot with you. Tell you what, perhaps you could pop in for a wee chat when you get back.'

Andrea hesitated. There was something about the old man's demeanour that sent a dart of worry through her. She pulled up the handbrake. 'Elli, why don't take my purse and go buy yourself a cone at the dairy.'

Elliot's eyes grew round. 'A cone!''

She almost never allowed him to buy individual ice-creams. Two-litre tubs from the supermarket were far more economical.

'Just the one now,' she said. 'And remember, you'll need to check your sugars in an hour.'

'I know, I know,' he said, taking her purse out of her bag. 'Thanks, Ma!' Then he was run-walking down the road.

Andrea beckoned to her neighbour. 'Hop in, Terrance. We can talk in the car.'

CHAPTER 30

RAMESH BANDARA

'Black with one sugar, please.'

'Sugar's over there,' the woman behind the counter said, pouring tea from a huge aluminium teapot.

Ramesh watched Stan Andino scoop two heaped teaspoons of sugar into his cup, cast around guiltily, then add another spoonful. Sugar was clearly the new tobacco.

Andino made his way over to the table of eats, shoved a piece of citrus slice into his mouth, hovered, put two asparagus rolls on a plate, then navigated his way to the periphery of the room.

Ramesh always valued the opportunity to observe people when they weren't aware they were being watched. It was fascinating, the clues a person gave away.

He'd fine-tuned his powers of observation at school. One of the benefits of being assigned to the margins as an immigrant kid with brown skin and a repaired harelip.

His masterful bowling, thanks to practising with his dad every weekend, eventually saw him selected for the top cricket team, and with that came an automatic invitation to the 'cool club'. So long as he left his Sri Lankan culture and accent at home each morning, and disposed of the contents of his lunchbox en route to school.

But that was only in senior school, and by then he'd already had hours of practice studying playground dynamics from the safety of the bench behind the tuck shop.

'Mr Andino.'

Stan turned, flushed, his mouth still full. 'Detective,' he managed.

'Nice service.'

Andino nodded.

'How is your wife?'

Stan Andino cleared his throat. Shrugged.

'Actually, have you got a minute?' Ramesh said, tilting his head towards the door.

The two men stepped out into the cloudless afternoon. It was one of those June days when the sky was an upside-down ocean and the air glassthin and brisk.

'Something's come up and I was wondering whether you would mind popping down to the station to have a chat?'

'What, now?'

'On your way home, perhaps?'

Andino's face tightened, his expression incongruent with his benign, teddy-bear appearance. 'Jeez, you guys are relentless. Is no occasion sacred?'

Ramesh opened his hands in apology.

'Can it wait till tomorrow? Carmen's at home and... I'm assuming you want to talk with her, too?'

'No, no. Just you. It shouldn't take long.'

'Can we talk here?'

Ramesh shook his head. 'Afraid not. How about three-thirty down at the station?'

'Fine,' Andino said, ditching his asparagus rolls and half-drunk cup of tea on a concrete ledge, and heading back into the hall.

Ramesh took a bite of one of Andino's deserted asparagus rolls, then followed at a distance.

Was he heading down a dead-end? Tibbie Lamb might well have taken her own life. Even her husband had conceded that suicide was possible. She was, he said, a very private person who had suffered a bout of depression some years back, after losing her brother to a drug overdose.

Not that responding to the loss of a loved one with deep sadness necessarily signalled a tendency to depression. Not to Ramesh anyway, but then he was no doctor and probably more than a bit biased.

His boss was certainly in favour of the suicide conclusion and had assigned the case low priority. 'From what I gather, Bandara, there's nothing sinister in the initial findings. No evidence of sexual assault or robbery. No sign of a struggle. All you have are a few people suggesting that suicide was *out of character*. How often is it *in character*?'

He had a point. Depression was a demon often battled alone from behind the pretense of an untroubled life.

'Family and friends see suicide as a poor reflection on themselves,' his boss added. 'As if they should have been able to predict and thereby prevent it. Understandably, they'd prefer you to find a more "acceptable" explanation for the death. One which leaves behind fewer questions.'

And once the big guy had made up his mind…

'I'm happy to give you a week,' he'd said. 'You and Stark. But with two other homicide investigations underway, I can't justify a bigger team. Sorry.' Ramesh understood the pressures the department was under; however, he could not let that influence his process. He'd ignored his instinct in the past, to his peril. The Russo murders were a case in point.

Assume foul play until proven otherwise was the dictum his forensic pathologist father had drummed into him. And while it might have sounded cynical and overly suspicious, Ramesh had been in the game long enough to appreciate the wisdom of his late father's words.

That the initial management of the Lamb case verged on incompetent hadn't helped, and Ramesh felt a responsibility to be all the more rigorous because of it.

Anxious to get the deceased's body out of the incoming

surf, the first responders had moved it quite a distance from where it was first found. The on-call pathologist was notified, but because she was busy at another crime, the initial scene examination had been left to forensic scientists.

Ramesh had nothing against forensic scientists. His frustrations were directed more at a system which had suffered so many cutbacks that poor procedure and bungled management of crime scenes were more the norm than the exception.

Ha! He was starting to sound just like his father.

Back in his dad's day, the pathologist was one of the first people on the scene of a suspected suicide and would be the person to oversee the scene and body examination, police photography, and upliftment to the mortuary. Prompt evaluation of the corpse was a priority, and postmortems were rarely delayed, even if this meant getting the coroner's blessing after a postmortem was already underway. This ensured vital evidence was not undermined by the passage of time. Which is exactly what had happened in the Lamb case.

At Tibbie Lamb's postmortem, symmetrical bruising resembling human hands had been noted on her upper arms. The 'thumbmarks' were imprinted on the fronts of her arms, suggesting someone had gripped her from behind with some force. That the bruising was more pronounced on the left suggested the assailant might have been left-handed.

Much to Ramesh's annoyance, the bruises were missed at the initial scene examination, hidden as they were under Tibbie Lamb's sleeves. This oversight was further compounded by a delayed postmortem. By the time the corpse was finally undressed and the bruises noted, at least twenty-four hours had elapsed, significantly reducing the information they could yield. Ramesh knew that the grip marks, being bruises of the skin, would have continued to spread after death, losing both definition and shape with time. That no photograph had been taken at the scene with a scale in place made any extrapolation difficult. All that could be confidently concluded was that the bruises resembled a pair of adult hands large enough to encircle the deceased's upper arms. That the fingers were squat was even too much to deduce, the width possibly just a feature of cutaneous spread. Of course, the grip marks might have had nothing to do with Tibbie Lamb's death anyway.

Ramesh thought back to one of the many cases his father had told him about when he was a kid.

'It was only because of the astuteness of the savvy young detective first on the scene, Ramesh, that we got to send the killer down.'

Apparently, within minutes of arriving at the scene of a homicide, a rookie detective had taken photographs of the deceased's injuries.

'Poor woman had been stabbed and then stomped on.'

His father performed the postmortem within hours of the body being found. *'Five hours at most.'* However, the markings had already started to spread and were no longer definitive.

'Now this is where it gets interesting, son.'

In his mind's eye, Ramesh could see his father shaking a finger to underline the lesson of it all, as a young Ramesh waited for the climax to the story.

'A review of that young policeman's first photographs showed with the utmost clarity a boot print that proved to be identical to that of a boot belonging to the prime suspect. Enough proof to convict!'

'You'll give the boy nightmares, Vidu!' Ramesh's mother always complained. But the blood and gore didn't bother Ramesh. He was enthralled by the tales that his father brought back from the morgue, ever fascinated by the puzzles his dad seemed to solve with his scalpel and super-sharp wit.

As he revisited the memory, Ramesh felt pride for his father all over again. He would have been seventy-four now. An upright man, who always had a twinkle in his eye, despite the stresses of shepherding his family out of war-torn Sri Lanka, negotiating the prejudices of a new country, and helping run the family home with his homesick wife.

Ramesh followed Stan Andino through the crowd of mourners towards the exit.

At the door to the foyer, he hung back, watching Andino sign the memorial book.

A woman emerged from the Ladies.

Ramesh recognised her from his recent visit to the Lambs' house – Janice Hyde, the deceased's buxom and brassy-blonde sister. She was dressed in a clingy purple dress and scuffed black stilettoes.

Ramesh was all for funerals not being overly sombre occasions, but the dress… It felt wrong.

She held her lower lip in a permanent pout, something he couldn't help feeling oddly titillated by. The woman was titillating in a cheap sort of way.

'Janice,' Stan Andino said, looking up.

The woman glanced down at the memorial book. 'So, you think you can write a few nice words, and everything will be hunky dory?' Then she turned and swept back into the main hall, past Ramesh, leaving him in a cloud of cloying fragrance.

When he looked back into the foyer, Stan Andino had gone.

CHAPTER 31

ELIOT BARD

Eliot decided he'd have a triple-scoop of ice-cream – chocolate-chip, boysenberry and hokey-pokey. His mum had said one cone, but she hadn't put a limit on the number of scoops.

The man in the dairy shook his head. 'Three scoops, that is too much. The ice-cream, it will fall over.'

Eliot reluctantly agreed to forgo the hokey-pokey.

The second disappointment came when the man put the scoops in the wrong order, with boysenberry on the bottom. This meant Eliot was forced to eat his favourite flavour first. He loved chocolate-chip nearly as much as peanut-butter ice-cream. Finding little flecks of chocolate was like finding treasure.

He dawdled down the road, savouring every lick, so that by the time he got home he only had the cone left to eat. He felt sort of bad about this. He didn't really mind sharing his ice-cream with his mum, but sometimes her 'just a taste' could be pretty ginormous.

'I'm back!'

The house was quiet and his mum's bedroom door closed. Eliot knocked – a strict mum rule.

'Just a minute.' Her voice sounded weird.

He waited.

After what seemed like forever, he knocked again.

'Eliot, I'll be out shortly! What do you want?'

He wondered if she was still angry with him about the funeral.

'I've got your purse.'

'Leave it on the benchtop.'

He couldn't do that. What if it went missing? He'd be responsible. His mum of all people knew that. *Never be lackadaisical about money.*

'Muuum.'

The door swung open. 'For goodness' sake, Eliot. What is it?'

Her mascara was smudged.

Eliot shoved the purse into her hand. 'You've been crying.'

She closed her eyes and sucked in a big breath.

'Do you need a supercharged Eliot Bard hug?'

She reversed into her room and sank down on her bed. 'Come here,' she said, patting the space beside her.

He sat down next to her. He didn't like it when she was sad.

'What flavour did you get?' she asked, with the same flat voice she used when asking about something like the outcome of a boxing match on TV.

'Chocolate-chip... and boysenberry. I wanted hokey-pokey, too, but the man said three scoops would topple over.'

She smiled and shook her head. 'Oh, Eliot, what am I going to do with you?'

'You said one cone, not one scoop.'

'I did. You're absolutely right. I did.'

They sat there together staring at the picture on her wall of a leopard lying in a tree. His mum had bought it at the Salvation Army op shop because the olive-green frame matched her bedspread.

He rested his head on her shoulder. Things had been all topsy-turvy lately.

'Just know, my boy, that whatever happens, I will be here for you.'

'Where?'

'Here.'

He sighed, releasing a puff of worry. 'You for me. Me for you,' he said.

'Yes. You for me. Me for you.'

She stood up and walked over to her chest of drawers.

He watched as she bent down and tried to yank open the bottom drawer. It only budged a bit.

'Bloody drawer!' she said, kicking it.

Eliot had never seen his mum kick a piece of furniture before. And she never, well, hardly ever, swore. He burst out laughing and ran over to kick the drawer, too.

'No. No. Stop it, Elli! Sit down, please.'

Things were getting very confusing.

His mum knelt on the carpet and pulled at the drawer again. This time she got it open all the way.

She sometimes hid presents in her bottom drawer. It was the first place he looked in the weeks leading up to his birthday.

He craned his neck as she slid a hand under the pile of jumpers and pulled out a small Ziplock bag.

Eliot's scalp went cold and the hairs on his arms stood to attention. His gaped at the wad of dirty tissue inside the plastic bag. Then he was running from the room.

Eliot's mum held his forehead as he continued to wretch over the toilet bowl.

Nothing left. His stomach was empty.

'Just wait while I fetch a facecloth.'

Eliot stared into the pan at the pinky-chocolaty stuff. What a waste of ice-cream.

'Sorry for wasting your money, Mum.'

'Don't be silly,' she said, wiping his mouth with a warm flannel.

She helped him up and started to unbutton his shirt. 'Let's get this off you.'

'I hate this shirt.'

'I know. You go and put on something more comfortable.'

Eliot glanced in the bathroom mirror. His chest was pale and pimply. He hated it. He hated everything. Everyone. Especially Mr McDougal for spilling the beans.

The only person he didn't hate was his mum.

'That's better,' she said, after he'd put on the zany green T-shirt he'd won as a spot prize at the church fun run.

'Would you like a glass of warm lemon water? It might help settle your tummy.'

He shook his head.

'Come sit down,' she said, pulling out a dining-room chair.

He slumped down next to her. It felt serious sitting at the table.

'I know how upsetting this is for you, Eliot, but we need to talk. Can we? Just you and me. Not for anyone else's ears?'

He looked at her, his blackest thoughts turning sepia brown.

He nodded.

She pulled out of her pocket the packet with the thing inside and laid it on the table.

He stared at it, like it was about to explode.

Then he was hitting his forehead with his fists.

'You and me. Just you and me, Eliot.'

He ran his tongue around his lips.

'We never lie to each other, do we?'

He shook his head.

'We've got that special truth bond, right?'

He nodded.

'So, I want you to tell me everything about this.'

She unsealed the packet, pulling out the wad of soil-stained white. Her long fingers unfolded the tissue. There, in the centre, like a bird in its nest...

'I didn't mean to, Ma! I didn't mean to, I swear.'

His mum's face pulled tight, but her voice stayed steady. 'Didn't mean to what?'

'Take it. I thought it was treasure.'

It was treasure, the smooth tortoise-shell oval hinged to a tiny gold clasp.

'Where did you find it?'

'On the rocks.'

'Did you take it out of the dead lady's hair?'

He shook his head so hard it felt like it might fall off his shoulders.

'Are you sure?'

Eliot's eyes grew wide. 'Strike me down dead if I tell a lie.'

'Then how did you get it?'

'It was lying on the rocks. Next to her. I didn't see her at first, until I'd picked it up. Well, like, something shiny caught my eye, so I went closer. It was the big bracelet. Then this sharp thing pricked my foot. I bent down and that's when I saw the clip and the lady and the shiny bracelet on her arm. But I never touched her or the bracelet. Promise. Promise. We can give it back.'

'Eliot, the lady is dead.'

Dead.

He could see the woman's red hair swishing over her pale, freckled face. And her eyes like two green marbles.

'Did you hurt her by mistake?'

Eliot scrunched up his nose, relaxed it, scrunched it up, relaxed it.

'Did you hurt the lady by mistake, Eliot?'

'No!' he shouted, blocking his ears.

She gently removed his hands. 'Are you absolutely sure?'

He nodded.

'Then why did you hide this in Terrance's garden?'

'I hate Mr McDougal.'

'Eliot, why did you hide it?'

'Stupid, stupid, old geezer.'

'Eliot, that's quite enough!'

He looked down at the floor, sulking.

'Why did you hide this?'

He mumbled.

'I can't hear you.'

'Cause of the police.'

'Yes?' she said, egging him on.

'Especially DC Hilary Stark,' he said, imitating the constable's flat voice. 'She'd be angry with me.'

His mum's shoulders dropped to their proper place. 'We need to tell them.'

Eliot started to whimper. 'You promised. You promised! You're a liar. You said just between you and me. You said.'

'They won't be angry if we tell them how it happened. But you will be in much more trouble if they find out you've been hiding it.'

Eliot scratched his head, trying to stop all the itching inside his brain.

'But first,' his mum said, 'I'm going to give Derrick Younger a call.'

CHAPTER 32

STAN ANDINO

As Ramesh Bandara logged the time and date of the interview, Stan found himself floating above the scene. The sequence of events felt movie-familiar – cautioned about the right to remain silent, the right to consult with a lawyer, that anything he said would be recorded and could be used in… He felt like he was starring in one of those Sunday night thrillers.

He'd declined the right to seek legal advice, because he hadn't been charged with anything, and therefore was not entitled to a free lawyer. As for hiring some high-powered suit, they charged by the minute. What's more, surely asking for a lawyer would only make him look guilty.

The thing that puzzled Stan was why the detectives were interviewing him alone. Perhaps they were hoping to elicit more without Carmen present. However, spouses were protected from testifying against each other, weren't they? He couldn't remember for sure. He'd seen an article about it in the papers recently.

Something has come up. Something has come up. Bandara's words bounced around in his head.

'Mr Andino, how would you best describe your relationship with Mrs Lamb?'

'Tibbie? I… What?'

'Can you please describe your relationship with Mrs Tibbie Lamb.'

The question came out of left field. Stan was reeling.

'She is… I mean, was, my, our, Carmen and my closest, most long-standing of friends.'

'If we could leave your wife out of things for the minute.'

'Leave her out?' Stan snapped, his voice rising, against his better judgement. 'What I'm saying inevitably involves her. I mean, I only got to know Tibbie through Carmen. They were best friends at school. I've known Tibbie for going on twenty-four years now. As long as I've known my wife.'

'And during that time was your relationship ever anything more than platonic?'

Stan frowned, his mind trying to find its way around the detective's words. 'What are you getting at?'

'Was your relationship with Mrs Lamb ever of a sexual nature?'

'Now look here!' Stan said, jumping up. Too quickly. The room started to spin. He sank down. 'Jeez, I'm married with two kids, for God's sake.'

'Just answer the question, Mr Andino.'

For a trainee, the policewoman had the confidence of someone well above her paygrade.

'No! Never.'

Bandara leant back in his chair. It creaked loudly. In another setting, thought Stan, he would have made an interesting model for a sculpture class. His generous forehead, handsome symmetry, marble-smooth skin, and then the small confusion of his flattened top lip.

The man had a quiet professionalism about him. Stan found him less intimidating than his female colleague, DC Stark, a toothpick of a woman with darting, different-coloured eyes that did not miss a trick.

'Were you and Mrs Lamb ever in business together?' Ramesh Bandara asked.

Stan opened his mouth. Closed it. Both detectives waited.

'No, we were not.'

'Are you aware that Mrs Lamb came into a significant inheritance early last year?'

The saliva in Stan's mouth dried up and his heartbeats started tripping over each another.

'I… I knew her mum died about eighteen months ago, if that's what you mean.' But that was not what they meant, was it? 'She suffered an awful head injury in a car accident. Was in hospital for months. Her personality changed completely. Not that she was a particularly nice person even before the accident. Never really gave Tibbie the time of day. Anyway, when she got pneumonia – some hospital superbug – it was a blessing really.' The words spilled out, all true, the back story bolstering him.

'Were you aware Mrs Lamb came into a significant inheritance?' Bandara's offsider asked again.

His throat tightened. 'She might have mentioned something once about inheriting some money. She wasn't the sort to brag.'

'Some money? Once.'

Jeez, she was like a pitbull.

'Yes, *some* money. People don't go into numbers. It's not done. And yes, once. Maybe a couple of months back. Spontaneously in conversation.'

'She and her sister Janice came into quite a substantial amount of money,' Bandara said.

Stan nodded, trying to look indifferent, while steadying his legs under the table.

Bandara paused. The detective's seemingly casual pauses were starting to feel more meticulous and purposeful.

Stan shifted in his seat. 'Look, I'm not sure what Janice has told you, but that woman has her own agenda. She's not a nice person. I don't want to say more than that, but she's had it in for me for a very long time.'

Stan had referred to both Tibbie's mother and sister as not being nice. Did he sound too critical? Would the police think that he was the one with the problem?

Bandara looked over Stan's shoulder into the middle distance, as if weighing up which of two roads to pursue. 'Was there a reason for Mrs Lamb sharing this information with you well over a year after the fact?'

'What information?'

'About her inheritance.'

Bandara's eyes now looked more tarry-black than brown.

'I think it was just something she said in passing. We were friends. Confidantes.'

'Confidantes.' Bandara folded in his top lip. 'Perhaps you can tell us why she transferred thirty thousand dollars into your personal bank account seven weeks ago?'

Stan's chest collapsed, as if he'd been shoved back into the hard metal chair.

'Without the knowledge of her husband. Or sister.'

Stan cleared his throat. Leant forward. 'It's... I... I assure you, it might look fishy, sound suspicious, but there was – there *is* – absolutely nothing untoward about it! Why should her sister need to know about it, anyway? Bloody vindictive woman. I bet she's the one who told you. Right? It was not her money. She's just a stirrer. Has sponged off her family and other people for as long as I can remember. Tibbie had the right to give away her money as and when she saw fit.'

Bandara and Stark were staring at him. Their expressions said it all.

'I... I think I'd like a lawyer.'

Bandara rubbed his forehead irritably. The hunter had just lost his prey down a rabbit hole.

Stan breathed. He was out of reach, for now anyway.

CHAPTER 33

STAN ANDINO

Carmen and Reuben were at the dining room table poring over Reuben's iPad when Stan walked in. Mother and son looked up in unison, their faces open and warm. Carmen was wearing a bright yellow headscarf twisted creatively into a double headband. She looked lovely.

For a blissful moment Stan was transported back to pre-tumour days.

Pre-tumour, pre-Tibbie's death, pre-this-fucked-up-life.

He rounded the table and grabbed them both in an urgent hug. Carmen smelt of lemons, reminding him of when she used to rinse her hair in lemon juice and then sit out in the sun to create 'natural highlights'.

The treatment was working. The tumours had shrunk. His wife and soulmate was pushing through the dry winter ground like a spring bulb.

'So?'

'So what?'

'How was it?' she asked.

'Can we talk later?' He didn't have the words or the energy. It would mean having to tell her about the money and… there was Reuben to consider, too.

'Did they read out my message?' she persisted.

He realised she was talking about the funeral. His day had moved on considerably since then.

'Sure,' he said, pulling away and moving towards the kitchen. He was no good at lying to her; she could always tell. 'Anyone for tea or a hot chocolate?'

'How come we didn't all go?' he heard Reuben ask.

'My immunity's pretty low at the minute,' Carmen said. Stan breathed. 'The church would have been a bed of bugs. Dad went as our representative.'

He switched on the kettle, then pulled out his phone and typed *legal aid* into the search bar.

Five minutes later he carried out a tray with three mugs of tea on it and a plate of digestive biscuits. There was nothing else in the tins; the baking from well-wishers had long since dried up. People led busy lives and sympathy had its limits. What's more, the grapevine had been busy. He could see it in people's eyes. It was common knowledge that Carmen had been the last person to see Tibbie alive and the police were investigating. Information like that had a way of killing off goodwill.

'Did you make me a hot chocolate, Dad?'

'What?'

'I asked for a hot chocolate.'

'Sorry, I must have misheard you. Can you cope with a cup of tea?'

Reuben rolled his eyes and scraped back his chair, bumping into Stan as he stormed past. 'Thanks for nothing.'

'Excuse me?' Stan bellowed, swinging around and grabbing Reuben by the arm. 'Who the hell do you think you're talking to?'

'Stan! Let him go.'

The rage in Stan's head was paused by Carmen's shouting, then smothered by the fear in his son's eyes. He was holding his son tightly, his fingers digging in.

Stan released his grip as if he'd just been shocked, but his fingerprints remained, rising up in discrete red circles on Reuben's pale skin.

'Oh God, I'm sorry. I'm so sorry,' he said, grabbing his car keys off the table and stumbling out of the house.

He careered along the suburban streets, not caring where he was going, so long as he was moving. Houses, shops, school.

He saw a flash of colour out of the corner of his eye and braked sharply. There was a thud as he screeched to a stop, just as a young woman pushing a pram stepped out onto a pedestrian crossing. In slow motion she turned, her face pinking with alarm.

'Sorry,' Stan mouthed. 'Sorry.'

He remained there, trapped in the nearly, what-if moment, until a car behind honked.

His life was spiralling out of control. He was losing it.

Stan drove on, cruising more cautiously through the dusk-dimmed streets. It had started to drizzle, and the rubber windscreen wipers clawed at the barely wet glass.

Something had slipped into his subconsciousness when he'd braked suddenly, and now, as a delayed reaction, it presented itself in colour.

The noise. A thud.

He pulled over, climbed out, and walked warily round to the back of the car, blood pulsing in his ears. He depressed the boot button, already knowing what he'd find.

The lid sprang open. Stan lifted it. There in the cavity was a crushed head. He leant in and picked up a perfect ear lobe. It disintegrated in his hands.

Stan fingered the dry clay of his student's broken sculpture. Kora had been working on it for months. It was unsalvageable.

He slammed the boot shut, climbed back in the car, and drove on, through Browns Bay, until he reached the beach.

It was largely deserted except for a young kite-surfer grappling with his black kite. Judging by the foam landing like dirty shampoo suds on the sand, there'd be gusts a-plenty to power his ride.

Stan parked. Got out. Crossed the short bridge over the inlet and scaled the stairs that led away from the water, two at a time, his chest burning with the exertion. Then he was following the path as it hugged the cliffs.

The metal barrier separating the path from the cliff face was interrupted by a small clump of bushes. A band of police tape hung across the gap, blocking off the thin, well-worn track that ran down through the flax.

Stan looked about, then lifted the plastic and skidded down the track into the clearing behind the bushes.

The dense ceiling of greenery blocked out most of the sky.

He moved towards the smooth, flat platform of rock jutting out over the water. Ahead, the ocean looked dark and menacing. An opaque sheet of rain far out at sea hid the horizon. Holding onto a thick pōhutakawa branch, he peered over the edge. High tide had swallowed the small strip of beach below.

He closed his eyes, his head filling with the sound of waves against the cliff face, and for a moment was lost in the memory of the last time he'd been there. It felt like a lifetime ago.

CHAPTER 34

RAMESH BANDARA

Ramesh sat at his desk eating a jam and sausage sandwich. It was dry without margarine. He hadn't done a shop in a while.

At least he was the one responsible for such mediocrity, and not some café. He'd got into the habit of buying his lunch at the very average eatery down the road.

Emily had been such a great cook. Her slow-cooked lamb, pea-andricotta pasta, her rhubarb crumble. He'd taken it all for granted until it wasn't there.

He missed those meals. Missed the anchoring ritual of sitting down at the table with the girls. Of coming home to a house filled with family.

While he hadn't married a Sri Lankan woman (much to his mother's initial disappointment), some of what had attracted him to Emily was that she came from a big farming family and valued the ceremony of sit-down meals and large family gatherings. She had a natural affinity for what had been important to him growing up. That she was a statistician to boot garnered her even more respect. As far as Ramesh was concerned, anyone who could love maths deserved high praise indeed.

As his parents got to know Emily, they fell in love with her, too. 'It was all in the horoscopes,' his mother would say, as if she'd always approved of the union. And when he and Emily split, it was his mum who could not stop crying.

He was in a sombre mood now. Morose is how Emily would have described it. Trapped under the weight of his thoughts.

He'd once again travelled back across calendars to *that* day. It seemed he was still able to spiral down to it, even if not as frequently as before.

It shouldn't have come as a surprise; revisiting the worst day in his life was almost the default destination when he was under stress. And although Tibbie Lamb's case had been deemed low priority, it was getting to him. He hadn't achieved the traction he'd hoped for, nor was he getting the backing he'd have liked from his boss.

'This is not some cosy murder mystery, Bandara, where the least likely person in the village turns out to be the culprit,' his boss had said, using a business card to dislodge something from between his teeth. 'You've got the quirky young lad with a supposedly superhuman memory. The woman with a brain tumour. Now, her financially strained husband. Soon the whole damned city will be under suspicion. You're all over the show, man. Give me something concrete.'

He'd slapped the desk with an open hand. 'Beyond reasonable doubt. You know the cost of a trial these days. You of all people understand that.'

This was the first case Bandara had headed since returning from his period of 'prescribed rest'. Prescribed rest. Ha! In his grandmother's day they were at least more honest. *Involutional melancholia. Mental breakdown. Admission to asylum.*

Society was supposedly more accepting these days. 'One in three people will suffer from depression at some time in their life,' his GP had told him. Sporting stars spoke publicly about their battle with the beast. Job applicants could no longer be penalised for 'coming clean'. You weren't even meant to ask about the big D in a job interview. Policemen, politicians and streetsweepers alike were all encouraged to admit their malaise without it impacting on their mana, their manhood, or their progress up the ladder. Stigma. What stigma?

Bandara knew that more rested on this case than him simply

getting to the bottom of Tibbie Lamb's death. It was also about proving himself again. Proving that he was up to the job and hadn't gone soft in the head. His credibility was on the line.

The email from Hilary Stark hadn't helped. An email, of all things, telling him that her transfer out of CIB to a community role had come through, with immediate effect. A transfer? First he knew of it.

Apparently, she'd decided to change career path and was ditching her detective training. She was moving over the bridge to Family Harm.

His boss confirmed the news. Told Ramesh he'd be replacing her with Ross Dwight.

Dwight! An arrogant clock-watcher, with no drive other than to pay his mortgage and bed as many women as possible.

Rationally, Ramesh knew Hilary's transfer wasn't about him. She'd had to have applied for the shift well before he'd even got back from leave. But to not bother telling him in person. That surprised him. And to email him only once she'd already moved on…

No doubt she was glad to see the back of CIB. He'd seen how her colleagues had treated her. She was different. Didn't fit in. Wasn't interested in all the horseplay that went on. Just the job at hand. That's why he'd liked her and valued working with her, albeit for such a short time. She had the makings of a good detective. Her single-mindedness and precision. Her inability to get riled. He was going to miss her.

His phone rang.

'Bandara speaking.'

'Eliot Bard and his lawyer are at the front desk to see you, sir.'

'Hello, Eliot. I hear you've something important to tell me?'

The twenty-one-year-old and his lawyer were seated across the desk from Ramesh. The lad was like a leggy grasshopper, his spindly limbs unable to keep still, his eyes springing about the room.

'Yes, you do, don't you?' Derrick Younger encouraged.

Apparently Younger was a friend of the family. Criminal cases not his specialty, civil more his line of work.

'I took this,' Eliot said, holding open his hand and dropping a soiled tissue onto the desk.

Ramesh leant forward and poked the bundle with his pen. Inside was a large tortoise-shell hairclip.

'It was lying on the rocks.' Eliot took a gulp of air. 'Near the dead lady.'

'I see,' Ramesh said, nodding slowly. 'You think it belonged to her?'

Before Eliot could answer, Younger interjected. 'That's not for him to speculate.'

Ramesh rubbed his temples. 'Why didn't you tell anyone about it until now?'

The boy shrugged.

'Eliot,' his lawyer prompted.

'Cause I thought I'd get into trouble.'

'Why did you think you'd get into trouble if you'd done nothing wrong?'

'Mum has this rule – I can only take something for my treasure collection if no-one else is anywhere near it. Like it's lying all alone. Then it's finders' keepers. Otherwise, I'm meant to ask people if it belongs to them.'

'And with the hairclip?'

'Someone was near it,' Eliot said breathlessly. 'I didn't know how to give it back. She was… dead. Scary dead. Then you and Hilary came to my house, and I knew I was in trouble. But I didn't mean to steal it. I promise. I was just keeping it safe for the lady.'

Ramesh smiled slowly. 'Thank you for bringing it in. I'm really glad you did. You've been very helpful.'

Eliot moved to the edge of his seat. 'Can we go now?'

'One last thing. Mr Younger said you told him that you took the cliff walkway on your way down to the beach that morning.'

Eliot looked at Mr Younger, who opened one of his hands as if to encourage Eliot on.

Eliot nodded warily.

'Can you remember seeing or hearing anything unusual on your walk that day? Someone in a hurry perhaps?'

Eliot was shaking his head, even before Ramesh had got out his last word.

'I just found the clip. That's all. I didn't mean to keep it.'

'Well, if you do remember anything, anything at all, will you please come in and tell me? Just like you did today. Even if you think it's not important. It might be really helpful.'

Eliot and Mr Younger stood up.

'Derrick, a quick word in private please,' said Ramesh.

CHAPTER 35

ELIOT BARD

'We're back!' Eliot cried, running down the corridor.

His mum was in the kitchen, still in her work clothes, unpacking groceries.

She dropped her hands and looked from Mr Younger to Eliot, then back to Mr Younger, her eyes wide with worry.

'Detective Bandara says I've been a huge help,' Eliot grinned. 'You would have been super-proud of me, Mum. Super-proud.'

She wrung her hands and smiled uncertainly. 'Would I now?'

'I'm going to train to be a detective, Mum. That's what I wanna be. One hundred percent.'

She lifted her eyebrows the way she did when she wasn't really listening. 'Got time for a cuppa, Derrick?'

'Unfortunately not,' he said, resting his briefcase on the benchtop. 'I have journal club starting at six and I'd like to pop home first.'

'So, it all went well?'

'He was great,' Mr Younger said, patting Eliot on the back. 'And what is the—'

'I don't think Eliot has anything more to worry about.'

His mum put a hand to her mouth.

'It is my understanding, Andrea, that Eliot is no longer of interest to the police.'

She sank down onto a chair, her body flopping like a damp dishcloth.

'Yes, I am!' Eliot said. 'Detective Bandara is very interested in me.'

'Quite right,' Mr Younger said quickly. 'What I meant was, in terms of the investigation into Mrs Lamb's demise.'

Eliot did not know what demise meant, but he got the drift. *Demise* sounded a lot like *dies*. 'Yup. He knows I'm not a thief. Just a treasure collector.'

Tears were trickling down his mum's cheeks.

'Don't cry, Mum. Why you crying?'

She wiped her face on her sleeve. 'Silly me. I'm just relieved.'

Mr Younger cleared his throat. 'I'll be on my way then.'

She jumped up. 'I'll see you out. Eliot, can you please unpack the dishwasher?'

Eliot knew that sort of job. A cunning ploy to get him out of the way.

'See you around then, Eliot,' Mr Younger said, slapping him on the back again. 'And well done today.'

Eliot slapped Mr Younger on the back. 'See you around, Derrick.'

His mum flashed him a disapproving glare. But it felt good to call Mr Younger by his first name, just like the detective had. After all, Eliot was planning on becoming a detective, too.

As soon as they'd left the room, he crept to the kitchen door to listen.

'I can't thank you enough.'

'Glad I could help. He's a good boy, Andrea.'

'I know, but it's good to hear it from someone else. Even though you think you know your child inside out, there's always the "what if". Especially with Elli. The way his brain works. We've had surprises in the past.'

CHAPTER 36

STAN ANDINO

Stan put his knife and fork together and pushed aside his plate.

'Recipe is from the weekend paper,' Carmen said, as if vouching for the meal's credentials.

'It's fine,' Stan said, eyeing the chicken breast slumped over a mound of mash and surrounded by a moat of sauce. 'Just too much.'

'Too much? You've hardly touched it.'

'I like it,' Reuben said quickly.

'Me too,' added Leon, elbows on the table, his knife and fork at ninety degrees.

Stan was in no mood for another Carmen showdown. For any of this. He wanted out. Out of this relentlessly bad dream. No book he'd read or TV series they'd binge-watched came close to depicting the day-to-day horror that was their lives.

He'd been to the Community Law Centre in the city that afternoon. Sat across from some fresh-faced woman called Joan, who looked too young and casual to be a lawyer. The suited student beside her seemed more the part.

Joan had summarised the situation, retelling Stan his own story. Carmen. The diagnosis. Her erratic behaviour. Their increasing debt.

Tibbie's money, which neither Austin Lamb nor Janice Hyde had any knowledge of. 'A sum intended to help you and your wife out of pressing financial difficulties, but which you failed to mention to anyone, even following the death of Mrs Lamb.'

Stan reiterated that it had been a no-strings-attached gift. Regardless, he'd been planning to pay it back. Was still planning to. Things had just spiralled out of control. Tibbie's death was initially presumed a suicide. Then Carmen came under suspicion, and it became too awkward to mention the money, what with Austin not knowing about it in the first place.

'I mean it was always intended to be something private between Tibbie and myself. Sure, others might find it hard to believe that she would give a friend thirty thousand dollars just like that, but it was different between us; we were almost like… siblings. I mean there's a paper trail, for Pete's sake! I'm not so stupid as to think her account wouldn't be checked after she died. She gifted it to me fair and square. And while I'm not the sort of person to accept financial help from others, I didn't want to offend her either. In my head it was always a loan. One I would pay—'

'Has the money been spent?'

'No!' Stan had said a bit too loudly. 'Not all of it. I've used some of it to pay off our credit cards and the kids' school camp and—'

Living expenses, power, groceries, fuel, fast-food… It was too embarrassing to vocalise, but they'd pretty much been surviving on it.

'How much is left?'

He wasn't sure exactly. Eighteen thousand. Twenty maybe. 'But look, I didn't kill her.'

Joan told him that they would need legal representation depending on whether the police had enough evidence to lay charges.

She turned to the student, in full tutor mode. 'Now, regarding Mr Andino's wife, if she were charged with murder, what defence options would be available to her?'

Murder. Hearing the word articulated out loud in such a matter-of-fact manner left Stan nauseous and lightheaded.

The student stopped typing. 'We would be best able to identify the weaknesses in the Crown case after disclosure,' he said, his words measured. 'But from what Mr Andino has told us about his wife, it sounds like a case to invoke the defence of insanity.'

Joan nodded and turned back to Stan. 'In other words, even if the prosecution can prove beyond reasonable doubt that your wife was there, carrying out the act that resulted in Mrs Lamb's death, she may not have had the requisite state of mind to understand her actions.'

'That's what I've been trying to get at,' Stan said, unable to temper his exasperation.

'However, the burden of proving insanity falls to the defence.'

'How hard can that be?' Stan said, jerking forwards. 'What with all the medical evidence.'

'It's not as easy as you'd think.' The lawyer scratched her shoulder with her pen. 'The defence would be required to prove that your wife's intellectual capacity was sufficiently compromised as a result of the tumours and treatment to render her *totally* incapable of comprehending the act.' She raised her forefinger. 'By your own account, your wife's mental state has been inconsistent. Indeed, it has fluctuated over time.'

'Even more reason to explain that she is unaccountable for her actions.'

Joan shook her head. 'Unlike in Britain and Australia, we do not have the defence of diminished or partial responsibility available to us.'

She turned to the student again. 'How would you approach this if you were defence counsel for Mrs Andino?'

Stan and Carmen's fate was being discussed like some academic teaching exercise. This was their lives being picked apart!

'First off, I'd speak to the medical professionals involved in Mrs Andino's treatment.'

'Correct. You would need a specialist to testify to the degree of brain-cell loss Mr Andino's wife has suffered. Look up *Blackwell v Chick*. An interesting case in terms of the challenges of quantifying a patient's cognitive decline. Also, *R v Shirkley,* for its relevance to the defence of insanity in a criminal case.'

The student resumed typing.

'What about me? My case?' Stan asked.

'Again, there is a significant gap, Mr Andino, between suspicion and the laying of a charge. The police have implied that you might have had a motive to murder Mrs Lamb. Although the money alone is a pretty weak one, considering, as you mention, the paper trail. They would need more. Or perhaps they already have more. Absence of an alibi, witnesses, et cetera.'

'Okay, okay,' Stan said trying to temper his panic.

'A defence lawyer cannot prepare a case until there is one, but we can certainly refer you on for legal assistance should that arise. Assuming you qualify for legal aid, the assistance would be free.'

She turned to the student. 'Anything else you'd like to add?'

The young fellow swept aside his dark fringe. 'Just that if there's something you haven't told us, anything which might impact the case, it is really important you do so.' He looked to his supervisor for corroboration.

'Absolutely. For a successful defence, Mr Andino, counsel will not want any surprises.'

Stan was still trying to digest all that had transpired that afternoon, while Carmen was more concerned about whether he was digesting the murdered chicken breast on his plate.

'At least someone appreciates that despite a jack-hammer headache, I spent an hour in the kitchen making dinner for my family,' Carmen said, glaring at him.

'Give me a break, Carmen.'

'Give *you* a break! That's rich. I'm the one with fucking brain cancer, in case you forgot.'

'How could I forget? How could I?' he shouted, thumping his fist on the table and toppling the salt cellar. 'When every second of every minute of every day is dominated by the fact.'

Both boys stopped eating.

Carmen opened her mouth. Closed it. Made a funny, warbled-hiccup sound in her throat. 'Sorry I didn't get better in one day, so that you could get on with your artistic pursuits sculpting naked women and musing about the human form.'

'Fuck you!'

'No, fuck you, Stan Andino. What a pity your poor Tippy died. Now whose shoulder can you cry on and whose breasts can you gawk at? But hang on, she was not the onl—'

Reuben scraped his chair back. 'Stop it!' he cried. 'I hate you both.' And he ran from the room.

Leon remained in his seat, flicking sauce off his plate with his fork.

'Cut that out,' Stan barked, then got up and also left the room.

He found Reuben face-down on his bed. He put a hand on his son's foot.

Reuben pulled away.

'I'm sorry, son. About everything.'

'Sorry. Sorry. Sorry. I'm sick of all your sorries.'

What more was there to say? Stan had always prided himself on being a good dad. On thinking his family was different. Special. But they'd crossed too many no-go lines. What was going to happen to them?

'Did you have an affair?' Reuben asked, his voice muffled by the pillow.

Stan felt the blood drain from his face. He pulled at his son's shoulder, trying to turn him over. 'Why would you think that?'

Reuben didn't budge. 'Sounds like Mum thinks you did.'

'Mum has—'

'I know, I know. She's not right in the head. Yeah, yeah.'

'Reuben, I love your mum with all my heart. I'd nev… Tibbie and I were just friends. Just like your mum and Austin are. Well… were friends. You must believe me.'

'You guys have a funny way of showing your love.'

'It's just stress, boy. There's such a lot going on right now, what with your mum's cancer and Tibbie's death and—'

'I wish Tibbie hadn't died. Everything's been bad since she died.'

'I know. But it's going to get better. I promise.'

Reuben turned over and searched Stan's eyes.

Stan looked away, unable to face the enquiry. He had to hold this family together, for his sons' sakes. Do anything and everything to ensure that at least he would be there to protect and guide them through the coming years. Carmen's future looked grim, regardless. It was awful to say it, but if she had to take the fall…

CHAPTER 37

ELIOT BARD

Eliot helped himself to a square of sugar-free chocolate. He didn't like the stuff, but he didn't want to offend Mr McDougal. They were sitting out on the back porch in a small rectangle of sunshine.

'After you've finished weeding the front bed,' McDougal said, shooing away a fly, 'I've got some silverbeet seedlings I'd like you to plant. One of the ladies from Probus gave me a whole tray.'

'One of the ladies from Probus,' Eliot said, tossing his head all hoitytoity. He and Mr McDougal were always joking about the single ladies jostling to be the next Mrs McDougal. 'Marcia du Toit?' Eliot loved saying the name du Toit.

'Not this time. They're from Sylvia. And she is very much still married to Phil.'

'Too bad,' Eliot said, trying to wink. He couldn't wink properly; both eyes always shut at the same time, unless he held one open with his fingers.

Eliot was friends with Mr McDougal again. He'd been wild at him for telling his mum about the hairclip in the veggie patch. But she'd said that it was only because the old man cared so much about Eliot that he'd intervened. 'He loves you like a grandson, Elli.'

Anyway, it had all worked out fine in the end.

Back in the garden, Eliot put in his earphones and turned up the music. Green Day. His favourite band. He liked the way the noise took over whatever was going on in his head. Today, though, his thoughts kept pushing through the music. They could be pretty persistent when they wanted to be.

If you do remember anything, anything at all, especially about your walk down to the beach, will you please come in and tell me? The detective's words kept arriving in his head.

Eliot wished he could think of something to help Ramesh Bandara. Something which would help solve all the questions the detective had about how Mrs Lamb died.

Eliot climbed back into that day.

A bowlful of muesli with warm milk, no sugar. Pack the dishwasher. Scrub the crusted casserole dish. Brush teeth. Vacuum. All the jobs his mum expected him to do to 'earn his keep'.

Then he put on his rainjacket, grabbed the backpack hanging by the door, and a plastic bag, so that the inside of his backpack wouldn't get all sandy from any treasure he found.

9.30 am clicking over to 9.31 am.

He pulled the green bin filled with garden clippings up the drive and onto the footpath, then put in his earphones and headed down the road.

His mum didn't like him to have music in his ears while he was walking.

She said it was dangerous. That he might not hear a car coming up behind him or reversing out of a driveway.

'Especially E-cars. They're incredibly quiet.'

But Eliot just felt like listening to music.

'Sometimes it's better to ask for forgiveness than permission' is what Mr McDougal once said when Eliot was in a quandary about his mum's many rules.

He compromised by keeping the volume down.

He stopped to pat the bouncy boxer that lived behind the gate of the house with bubbled-plaster walls. The dog always had a lot of love to give. Lots of drool, too.

He wiped the gob off onto his jeans and continued on past the cottage on the corner, the one being renovated. There was no one around to talk to, just the sound of someone hammering under the tight white plastic tent.

He walked down the hill, across the reserve and up the path, making a point of not looking into the windows of the houses on the side of the pathway, but out over the ocean instead. Once, when he'd walked this route with his mum, she'd said everyone deserved a bit of privacy, even if their houses were built right next to a public pathway.

Near the top he stopped to count the number of fishing boats out at sea – just two to add to his running tally of three-hundred and ninety-two. It was too drizzly to see further out.

No one else was on the walkway, probably because of the weather. The weatherman had said there was a cyclone passing west of the North Island which would bring heavy rain.

Then he was heading down the steps, careful not to stand on any cracks. If he did, he had to go back three steps, jump over one, then continue down.

At the bottom, he hid his shoes in the undergrowth before crossing the little bridge. He did this every single time. Eliot liked things to be the same.

The sand was firm and damp. Walking on it without sinking in made him feel like he was walking just above the ground, sort of like a hovercraft. He hated it when the sand was dry and grains burrowed between his toes, annoying his head.

He walked along at the foot of the cliffs, stepping carefully over the rocks, his eyes searching, searching. Always searching for treasure.

A shaving of sunlight slipped through a crack in the clouds, as if God had sliced open the sky with a letter opener. It landed on rocks out in front of him.

Something shimmered in the shallow water. Then a wave swept in, swallowing it.

Eliot moved carefully around the small rock pools to get closer.

He yelped as something sharp stabbed his water-soft foot. He looked down for the culprit. Barnacle or crab?

Neither. It was a tortoise-shell hairclip! The kind he could imagine a Norwegian princess wearing.

He grabbed it, just as another wave barged in.

The water swept back out.

Eliot stared... then he was backing away.

He stumbled. Fell into the water. Clambered back up, all the while still reversing.

When he was far enough away from the hair, the arms, the eyes, he turned and ran.

Back to the beginning. C'mon, Eliot, think!

Breakfast. A bowlful of muesli with warm milk, no sugar. Pack the dishwasher. Scrub the crusted casserole dish. Brush teeth. Vacuum...

Breakfast. A bowlful of muesli with warm milk, no sugar...

He could not think of anything more to help the detective.

CHAPTER 38

STAN ANDINO

The woman leant back further, her nectarine-sized breasts lifting as she did so. She had tiny areolas, each topped with a neat nub of flesh.

It fascinated Stan how women's breasts differed. Carmen's areolas were generous mauve discs that demanded attention, while her nipples were more nebulous.

The woman slid one leg further up the other, her foot flexed like a ballerina's.

'Is that comfortable?' Stan asked.

She nodded dreamily.

It wasn't right; the change in position had hidden her lush triangle of dark pubic hair.

'Down a fraction. That's better.'

He took photographs from several different positions around the room and then from behind each seated student – a safety net in case the model didn't pitch up for one of the eight classes. The photographs would also serve as templates for the students to work off after-hours.

His phone vibrated in his pocket.

He didn't usually look at messages during class, but what with everything that had been going on of late, he couldn't ignore it.

'Okay, guys, time to take the plunge. And remember, free

yourself from your inner policeman. Or policeperson, rather,' he added quickly. 'This stage is just about getting a feel for shape, form, a sense of movement. Finer details come later.'

He ducked out of the studio and into his office, closing the door behind him.

Hope your day's going well. Tippy.

Stan stared at his phone, his hand shaking.

Hope your day's going well. Tippy.

What was this? Some sort of sick joke? He was the only person who'd ever called Tibbie Tippy.

He looked at the number. ID withheld.

Someone knocked.

He rammed the phone into his pocket. 'Yup?' he called out, trying to steady his voice.

Morag put her head around the door.

He felt a dart of irritation. She was one of his more annoying students. It was her fake dependency that irritated him, the cloying queries camouflaging her hubris and bluster.

'Stan, can I get your advice?'

'Sure.' What kind of sicko would have sent such a text? 'What's up?'

'I was wondering about doing something kind of abstract. Sort of, like, well, maybe the female form in chains. To represent centuries of abuse. Like, I thought about putting the woman in shackles, have her grimacing.'

Stan nodded, trying to focus. 'It's good you're thinking outside the square, Morag. But these eight weeks are all about mastering the art of proportion and pose. Once you know the rules and have grasped them, you can knock yourself out breaking them. Overlay the physical with the abstract.'

'I mean, it would still be accurate. I'd really like to express more than—'

'Yup,' Stan said, flicking open his hands. 'I get it. Go for it.'

She hesitated in the doorway, clearly disconcerted by his impatience.

'And could you close the door behind you on your way out? Cheers.'

He pulled out his phone. Reread the text.

Someone was toying with him. Playing games. Perhaps trying to unnerve him. But why? What the fuck was he supposed to do about it? He should let the police know, even though he couldn't stand that Bandara guy. His fake nonchalance. His– He stopped. What if it was some sort of set-up by the police, just to see what he'd do? How he'd react? Then again, just maybe, Tibbie *had* sent the text and it had got lost somewhere in cyberspace, caught up in the tangled connections of some cell-phone tower. And now, weeks after her death, it had been released and finally found its way home.

Unlikely. Far-fetched.

Come to think of it, the reason Tibbie had blocked her caller ID was because of that pool-maintenance guy who'd started calling her a year-or-so back.

He should tell the police. It might get them off his back.

He pulled out the inspector's card from his wallet and dialled his direct line.

'Bandara.'

'Detective, it's Stan Andino here.'

'Mr Andino.' There was no hint of surprise in the man's voice, as if he'd been expecting Stan's call. Or perhaps nothing ever surprised the guy. He seemed to be one of those people who never got ruffled. The strong, silent type. 'How can I help?'

Another bloody student put their head around the door.

'Be with you in a minute,' Stan mouthed, waving Dimitri away.

'I was wondering if you'd be at the station around lunchtime. I'd like to show you something.'

'Sure. I'll let them know downstairs that I'm expecting you.'

The rest of the morning dragged, the blocks of clay taking shape at a glacial pace. Morag was the furthest along when the clock announced midday.

It annoyed Stan how gifted she was. And her phoney modesty. No doubt an attempt to stay on-side with her teacher, who couldn't but be shown up by her talent. Stan felt his use-by date keenly.

'Guys, I'm going to have to be strict about time today,' he said, handing the model her robe. 'I have an appointment.'

Dimitri pushed his chair back, clearly relieved to call it a day. His proportions were all out of whack.

Morag pouted. 'I'm really on a roll, Stan. How about I lock up after everyone's finished and drop the keys in at your place later?'

A murmur of consent rippled through the rest of the group.

Stan shook his head. The last thing he needed right now was a pert young woman popping round to his house.

'I tell you what, Zoe will be at the front desk until 12.30 pm. That gives you an extra half hour. You can leave the keys with her.'

He could sense his students' irritation, but he had more important things to worry about.

CHAPTER 39

STAN ANDINO

Stan sat in his car outside the police station for a full ten minutes. Finally, he got out. He was halfway across the car park when he stopped, like an insect trapped inside a glass paperweight.

He stared at the silver Audi parked two down from him. The number plate... It was Tibbie's car!

Stan floundered in disbelief and confusion, his legs suddenly limp like sapling branches.

Tibbie wasn't alive! He was losing it. Someone else must have driven the car there. Probably Austin.

He hoped it was. Maybe they'd bump into each other and somehow the current narrative would change. Austin would embrace him. Apologise. Say it had all been a big mistake. That the police had just confirmed Tibbie had tripped. Fallen. No-one else was implicated. Not even suicide.

A car tooted. Stan was still standing in the middle of the car park.

He gestured an apology and hurried towards the building.

The place made him nervous without adding Tibbie's car into the mix. But today he was initiating the visit. That had to be good, right? A bad guy would not place himself in the line of fire.

Then again, in movies the bad guy often hovered on the

periphery of the investigation, offering police unsolicited assistance. Bandara would have seen it all.

As the doors slid open, Stan nearly collided with a woman leaving.

'Janice!'

Tibbie's sister was on her phone, her expression open and unguarded. When she realised it was Stan, the shutters come clattering down.

She pushed past him.

'Jan, can we talk?'

'Hey, I'll call you back,' she said into her phone. Then to Stan. 'There's *nothing* to talk about. And do not presume you can call me Jan.'

He chased after her. 'Please, Janice. I know how it looks, but you must believe me—'

She swung round. 'Believe you? How many others did you take there? How many other floozies have you fucked above the ocean?'

'What do you mean? Where? I don't understand.'

They were standing in front of Tibbie's car. Janice fumbled with the key in the door.

'It has a remote,' Stan said, reaching for the keys.

She swung her arm away. 'Don't touch me!' Then she depressed the remote, successfully unlocking the doors.

'Please, Janice, can we talk like adults? Just for a minute?'

'I would have hoped you had more imagination than to take her to the same spot.'

'What are you saying?' Stan's voice cracked. 'I don't understand what you are talking about.'

'I told them.' She waved a hand towards the police station. 'That we used to meet there. Fuck there. Cause that's what it was, wasn't it? Just fucks.'

Stan closed his eyes. The fear that had gnawed away at him for thirteen years had just popped up like a Jack-in-the-box with a *Gotcha* grin. After Janice moved to Australia, it had been easier. Out of sight, out of mind. Stan had lulled himself

176

into believing his foolish indiscretion would be safe with the Tasman Sea between them. It wasn't, of course. Not when it involved someone like Janice. She was back and as unhinged as ever. A loose cannon. All he knew was that Carmen must never know. Never! It would kill her.

'Why tell the police about that?' Stan asked, holding the car door open. 'And now, of all times. It's not as though you were innocent. We were both consenting adults. Bloody foolish ones at that.'

'Fuck you, Stan Andino.'

He'd forgotten how fragile her self-esteem was. How easily she could feel slighted.

He clenched his jaw. He had to keep a lid on things. Maintain his composure. Janice had to be handled carefully. She was like a box of fireworks, always just one match away from an explosion.

'Jan, please. I absolutely do not want Carmen to find out. She's having such a rough time of things without this adding to her pain.'

'Well, you should have thought of that before putting your dick in places it didn't belong. And before you murdered my sister.'

'Jeez, Janice!'

'Do you mean to tell me it was just a coincidence that our little – what did you used to call it – *den of iniquity*, was where Tibbie spent her final minutes? Did you fuck her there, too, before pushing her over the edge? Easier, I guess, than having to pay back thirty grand!'

Stan's head was spinning, spots crowding his vision.

Janice yanked at the car door.

He held firm.

'Leave it! We're outside a police station, you stupid fool. Do you want to go down for assault as well as murder?'

He let go.

She pulled it shut and locked it.

Then she was reversing at high speed.

So, the police knew about him and Janice. And their secret meeting spot on the cliffs.

Far out! A moment of weakness with that witch (okay, a few moments of weakness) and his credibility, his marriage, his entire life was on the line.

He rubbed his forehead, trying to centre his thoughts.

As he stood there, he had the uncomfortable feeling someone was watching him.

He scanned the car park. Glanced over his shoulder. Looked up. Just in time to catch a glimpse of a dark figure stepping back from a window on the fifth floor.

CHAPTER 40

RAMESH BANDARA

Ramesh started each day with every intention of drinking the cups of tea that Dan, the division assistant, brought him. But something invariably got in the way, and by the time he clocked off there was usually a trail of half-drunk cups of cold tea in his wake. His busy schedule wasn't solely to blame. Tea was something Ramesh was particular about. A throwback from growing up in a Sri Lankan household. Properly brewed, leaf tea with powdered milk or a spoonful of condensed milk. Now that was something to get excited about.

He eyed the latest casualty. A disc of congealed milk was floating on top. Dan had threatened to stop including him in the tea run, so Ramesh closed his eyes, tipped his head back, and swallowed the dregs, slimy skin and all.

The meeting with Stan Andino had been interesting. Even more so, the one prior, with the deceased's sister, Janice Hyde. She was an odd one. Bolshy one minute, overly familiar the next. All the red flags were there. A woman he instinctively knew to keep at arm's length. *Allow yourself to be pulled into her orbit at your peril*, he thought.

Saying that, the information she'd shared was significant. And, added to the intel he'd received from ESR that morning, he might just have enough to lay a charge.

He mused at how often investigations uncovered

extramarital affairs, and how each discovery still surprised and left him feeling oddly disappointed and let down. As if he'd expected more of complete strangers. It was the fault of his parents. Vidu and Amilka had made matrimony look easy. Perhaps an arranged marriage was the answer after all, the choice of partner a collaboration of wisdom and culture, with religion affording the crucial ballasts.

Sometimes it felt like half of Auckland was having affairs. Perhaps there was more to why Emily had left him, after all.

He shoved the thought away before it imported a whole new angle to his grief.

Sex, never mind illicit sex, had been the last thing on his mind for some time now. The divorce, depression, and now the drugs to treat his depression, had killed off any stirrings down below. In fact, if he were honest with himself (which is what his therapist was trying to encourage) it went back much further than that.

It was said a woman made love with her mind, and a man with his body, but his mind had been getting in the way for a very long time. The thing was, sex and fun and food and laughter all seemed so superficial and selfish after losing a son. Just plain wrong.

Ramesh had two daughters, Talia and Nikita, whom he adored. But no child could ever be a replacement for another. It was not a case of either/or. There would always be a permanent place in his heart for Joshua Dinal Bandara. For his ten tiny fingers and ten tiny toes. Fingers that one night, without warning, turned cold.

He had been mulling over the information that Janice Hyde had just shared when Stan Andino arrived to show him 'a concerning text'.

'I mean, who would send something like this?'

Bandara had taken Andino's phone and scrolled down while the man looked on anxiously. No-one liked to relinquish their phone, even if they had nothing to hide. It was the closest one came to inviting a stranger into one's head. Into one's home.

'Who's your provider?' Ramesh asked, looking up. 'I'll get our telecommunications guys onto it. We should be able to track down the sender, unless it's come from a prepaid mobile that's already been destroyed.'

'I can't leave it with you,' Andino said, reaching for it like a child grabbing for a toy. 'It's got everything. My contacts, diary... everything I need to function.'

Ramesh handed it back. He wasn't too concerned. Anyway, soon the texts would be the least of the guy's worries.

'There are some sick pranksters out there. It's probably nothing more. Someone will be in touch. In the meantime, let us know if you receive any more.'

Andino hovered. 'I bumped into Tibbie Lamb's sister downstairs. I believe she came to see you?'

Bandara waggled his head, using the ambiguousness of the Sri Lankan mannerism to avoid answering the question.

Andino leant forward, his whole body urging Ramesh to reveal more.

'If you'll excuse me,' Ramesh said, moving towards the door. 'I'm expected upstairs. One of our receptionists is having a birthday shout.'

Ramesh brought his slice of banana cake back down to the office and ate it on his own. He'd never been very good at socialising with his colleagues. After all these years, there was still the fear of being put on the spot and having to share something about his personal life. Something that might mark him as different.

He could still remember his panic in Standard Three when it was his turn to share with the class what he'd done in the weekend. Other kids had gone to the beach, been to see a movie, played mini golf. How was he going to say that he'd gone with his parents to the Buddhist monastery for an alms-giving ceremony in memory of his grandfather?

His phone rang. It was Hilary Stark, of all people.

'How's life out in the community?' he asked, smudging lemon icing over the receiver.

'Too early to say.'

In-person conversations with Hilary had been challenging enough. Speaking with her over the phone, without any physical cues to soften the pauses, was even harder. He decided against mentioning her discourteous departure.

'I'm ringing about the case,' she said.

'The case?'

'The Lamb case.'

Ramesh felt a twist of anxiety.

'I've been thinking about it,' she said.

'Right.'

'Have there been any developments?'

'Last I heard, you were off the case,' he said, trying to get a sense of where the conversation was headed. 'In fact, off detective work altogether.'

There was a long pause.

'Things pretty quiet on the Family Harm front, then?' he asked, forcing a chuckle.

'No.'

'Well, good. I'm glad you're keeping busy.'

'So, have you made any headway?'

'Sure,' he said, trying to pinpoint exactly what he'd achieved since she deserted him. 'Though I'm missing having an astute partner to run things by.'

'I can come around if you need to talk anything through?'

He opened his hands in silent, confused exasperation.

'Really, I don't... Actually, that would be great. When are you free?'

'Tonight, after dinner if you like? Text me your address.'

'My home address?'

After Ramesh put down the phone, he navigated his way back through the bizarre conversation, searching for the real reason Hilary had called. Whatever her motivation, he was aware of feeling calmer. Just the prospect of running his thoughts by someone else. Someone who wouldn't judge him.

Since when had he ever needed someone to back him up before? Corroborate the calls he made? What's more, Hilary Stark was his junior. In experience and age. She was in her late twenties, early thirties at most. And she'd only been policing for a few years.

Come to think of it, he hadn't got around to asking what she'd done before joining the force.

CHAPTER 41

HILARY STARK

It was good to be out of CIB; there was less politics at Family Harm – fewer distractions and fewer toes to tread on. Hilary knew she had a lot to learn in terms of procedure in the new department, but she felt less out of her depth than she'd expected. Perhaps it was her own familiarity with the subject matter.

Strangely, though, it was not her new work that was preoccupying her when she headed home each night, but the Lamb case. It would not let go. That she'd been transferred in the middle of it hadn't helped; she was not someone to leave a job incomplete, be it a pile of laundry or a murder investigation. The abruptness of the transfer had felt like one final flip-off by CIB.

Her car's GPS was not much use when it came to finding Ramesh Bandara's house. He lived in a brand-new subdivision in Albany, not yet visible on her system. Fortunately, Google Maps helped out.

His place looked bleak in the white-bright light of a streetlamp; the patch of ground out front not even seeded with grass.

She rang the doorbell.

There was a loud crash from inside. Glass or crockery breaking. A few moments later Bandara appeared at the door.

'Hey! I wasn't expecting you quite so early. Come in. I was just finishing... finished my dinner.'

She looked at her watch. It was 7 pm. Dinner with her nan was always done and dusted by 6.30.

Bandara was dressed in jeans and a ribbed navy jumper. She had never seen him in proper civvies before. It felt weird, like spotting a teacher at the supermarket and realising for the first time that they led a life outside the classroom, too.

'Come in.'

Less than three strides from the front door and she found herself in a small galley kitchen. Fragments of china and what looked like cornflakes and milk were splattered across the black tile floor.

'Your dinner?'

'Afraid so,' he said with an embarrassed grin. He flicked on the kettle. 'Would you like a tea or coffee?'

'Have you got any green tea?'

He didn't, so she declined.

Stepping over the remnants of his meal, they moved into the living area – another compact space housing a television, a couch, and a dining-room table.

Despite the small size of the room, it still managed to look sparse and oddly disjointed. Around the table were four plastic chairs more suited to a hospital canteen. Up against one wall was an ornately upholstered wooden sofa, bookended by two inlaid side-tables. And in the corner was a giant white standard lamp that looked like it had been bought at a pop-art exhibition. It felt like a confusion of personalities. On the wall hung a large studio-style photograph of two honey-skinned little girls with huge brown eyes and wide Bandara smiles.

'Got to be honest,' Bandara said, sitting down at the table, 'I was a bit surprised to get your call.'

She shrugged. 'I don't like leaving a job half done.'

His face loosened into a smile.

'Shall we start with what we know,' she said, pulling up a chair and sitting down.

The table was covered in a PVC tablecloth with Christmas motifs over it. Christmas was five months ago.

'Straight to it, eh?' Bandara said, flicking back pages on a foolscap pad to get to the beginning of his notes.

'To summarise then: Carmen Andino is diagnosed with a brain tumour and undergoes a progressive personality change.'

Hilary took the baton. 'Unpredictable, all over the place, and, importantly, increasingly suspicious of her husband and her best friend, Tibbie Lamb.'

'Her fears are not entirely unfounded,' Ramesh Bandara said, stretching back in his chair. 'Stan Andino had strayed in the past.'

'Had he?'

Bandara nodded. 'Tibbie Lamb's sister told me she had an affair with Stan Andino some years back. And… wait for it,' he said, holding up a finger, 'their regular tryst spot was none other than the clearing off the cliff walkway, above where Tibbie Lamb's body was found.'

Hilary digested this new piece of information.

'What puzzles me,' Bandara went on, 'is the attraction of that place. I mean, it's pretty grotty as far as romantic spots go.'

'Maybe they wanted to rekindle their youth,' Hilary suggested. 'Feel like teenagers again. The risk. The thrill. Wild waves crashing below.' She was guessing. Her own teenage years had included nothing like that.

He laughed. 'Maybe I'm just getting old.'

'Do we know if Carmen Andino knew about the affair?'

Bandara confirmed she did. 'According to Janice, that is. After the affair ended, and we're talking fourteen years back, Janice wrote a kiss-and-tell letter to Carmen, spilling the beans on her hubby's infidelity. Interestingly, Carmen never confronted her husband about it, so to this day he doesn't know that she knows about it.'

'How can you be sure?'

'Janice Hyde rang me to tell me that she'd encountered Stan Andino in the station car park after she left my office.

I'd actually observed their interaction from my window,' he added. 'Anyway, she said Andino was terrified that she was going to reveal the truth to his unwell wife.'

'So, over a decade ago, Carmen Andino received a letter about her husband's wayward activity, in which, amongst other sordid details revealed, was the exact location of where he and his mistress used to meet up? Yet she never confronted her husband?'

Bandara shook his head. 'Though I think, based on the probability of human nature, we can assume she will, at some point, have checked out the place.'

'Pure supposition.'

'Human behaviour,' he said. 'I've seen a few spurned spouses in my time.'

Hilary shrugged.

'Fast-forward fourteen years,' he went on. 'We now have a woman with a brain tumour, who has become increasingly jealous and unpredictable, and suspects, rightly or wrongly, that her husband is having an affair with her best friend, Tibbie Lamb. I should add that, according to the good doctor, some tension around this predated Carmen Andino's tumour. She apparently not infrequently alluded, even if just in semi-jest, to her husband Stan having the hots for her best friend.'

'Yes, I see there's motive. But what else?'

'Carmen Andino has short, stubby fingers. The finger-shaped bruises found on Tibbie Lamb's upper arms were short and broad, an—'

'You cannot allow those bruises as evidence,' Hilary said. 'You yourself said they'd lost too much definition due to the delayed postmortem.'

Bandara put up his hand. 'I know, I know. But I'm looking at them more as corroborating evidence. For example, Eliot Bard's fingers are too long and skinny to have made those marks, even with spread accounted for.'

He stretched out his own hand. Ramesh Bandara had large, strong hands.

'Is Carmen Andino left-handed?'

He shook his head.

'So, you're prepared to use some of the features of the bruising to corroborate your theory, but not others. I thought you said that because the marks were more pronounced on the left, the person doing the gripping likely had a stronger left hand.'

'I know, I know. But variable hand strength is less convincing than finger shape.'

She rolled her eyes.

'Stick with me, Hil.' He cleared his throat, and felt a rush of heat to his face. 'Hilary.'

'You said before, Stan Andino had a financial motive,' she said, moving past Bandara's obvious embarrassment. 'We still don't know how much money Tibbie Lamb actually gave him over time. It might be more than just what the account reveals. Furthermore, it may have been intended to be a loan, not a gift as he is suggesting. We only have his word for it. Why is he no longer high up on your list?'

'Alibi,' Ramesh said, leaning heavily on the table. 'Tibbie Lamb's watch stopped at 9.46 am, which we can assume occurred on impact with the rocks. Other postmortem features corroborate this as the likely time of death.'

'Who is vouching for Stan Andino at this time?'

'He was taking a piece of pottery to a foundry in Avondale. I've just had this confirmed by Ross.'

'Randy Ross?'

He raised an eyebrow. 'Forget getting a separate Victim team, Scene Examination team, and Generally Enquiry team... Despite the headway we'd made before you left, I still only got a single assistant to replace you. Ross Dwight, who, as you well know, is as good as no assistant. Hope you're not feeling too bad about deserting me for greener pastures.'

Despite the headway we'd made. It felt good to be included in Bandara's 'we'. He was first man in CIB to ever share any credit with her.

'How did Dwight confirm Andino's alibi?'

'Staff at the foundry. Andino dropped in the pottery just before ten. It's on their CCTV footage. Andino could never have been in Browns Bay at 9.46 am, then made it across town in morning traffic.'

'Right, so, he's out of the picture,' she agreed.

Bandara went on to tell her about another development. A call from ESR confirming that the lipstick found at the suspected murder location, and which they'd assumed belonged to Tibbie Lamb, was in fact Carmen Andino's. 'Had her DNA all over it.'

'We're not beyond reasonable doubt,' Hilary said cautiously, 'but it's looking pretty damning.'

'No free passes from you, I see,' he said with a chuckle.

She smiled.

Bandara sat back. 'This is not the conclusion I want to reach. Carmen Andino is dying. She's got two young boys. She very likely did not fully understand what she was doin—'

'Detective Training 101,' Hilary interrupted. 'Don't let sentimentality get in the way. It messes with the facts. Leave it to the defence to challenge or prove insanity. That's not your job.'

Bandara jerked his head back, his eyebrows raised in surprise. Had she overstepped the mark again?

DC Stark seems oblivious to the chain of command within the department. Her manner is blunt and rude, especially when it comes to her seniors. DC Stark divorces herself from the camaraderie of her peers. She...

'Chain of Command. Pft' is what her nan had said to that progress report. 'Just a lot of epaulettes, male egos, and white noise. Don't let something like that distract you from your job, girl.'

Bandara nodded. 'You're absolutely correct.'

Hilary chewed her smile.

'So, we have a strong motive,' she said, emboldened. 'And DNA that puts Carmen Andino at the place in question.

She was also the last person to be seen with Tibbie Lamb. And her behaviour over the weeks prior was often irrational, aggressive and paranoid.'

'That's enough in my book to consider charging her.'

'It's not watertight; each of those factors could be plausibly explained away.'

'A punt I'm comfortable to take.'

Hilary shrugged. 'Fair enough.'

She pushed back her chair and stood up.

'You heading off already?'

'Unless there's anything else you need to cover?'

'No. No, nothing. Hey, thanks. It's been good to be able to run it by you.'

He walked her to the door.

'So, you do Christmas?' she asked.

'Christmas?'

'The tablecloth,' she said, tilting her head towards the other room.

'Oh. Right,' he said, his face relaxing. 'It's complicated.'

She waited.

'I was raised Buddhist. Or rather my parents were practising Buddhists. My mum still is. I'm not.'

'You chose Christianity?'

He shook his head. 'Not sure what I believe. But my wife, my ex-wife, she's Christian. So we sort of make it up as we go along. For the kids, you know.'

Hilary nodded.

'And you? Do you do Christmas?'

She shook her head. 'Not even in December.'

CHAPTER 42

STAN ANDINO

Stan found Carmen asleep on top of the bed cover, her head resting in a nest of pillows – no doubt something one of the boys, probably Reuben, had constructed. It was painful to think about what the kids were going through. Reuben, in particular. The lad was constantly trying to mediate, moderate, make better. As for Leon, Stan suspected his tough nonchalance was more a front behind which a frightened boy was hiding.

Carmen didn't look very comfortable, listing as she was to the left. If he didn't wake her, she'd wake up later with a wry neck.

He sat down heavily beside her.

She opened her eyes and gave him a skew smile.

He buried his head in her warm bosom, which smelt of neutral soap. More an absence, than anything. Of late, her signature smell had disappeared, as if her DNA had been diluted, or reconfigured by the drugs, the cancer.

'I love you, Carm.'

'Luuz ou, too, Shan.'

He pulled away, appraising her from a distance. Her face was lopsided; her mouth drooping to one side.

Twenty minutes later they were in an ambulance, tearing through the suburbs of Auckland, sirens keening.

The last time Carmen had been in the High Dependency Unit, it had been awful – the cold floor, hushed voices, the stainless-steel air. Yet this time Stan found some relief within its embrace, like a runaway finding refuge within a church. So long as he was in High Care with his wife, he didn't have to face what was going on outside.

'The scan confirms another bleed,' the specialist said, removing his John Lennon spectacles. 'Our focus now is to prevent it progressing.'

Reuben, his shoulders hiked anxiously around his ears, was stroking his mum's hair. Leon had gone home from school with a friend.

Carmen looked different. It wasn't just the disconcerting facial droop, but also her new weary detachment, as if she'd begun a gradual retreat.

Stan's phone vibrated in his pocket. Cell phones were supposed to be switched off. Something about interfering with the life-saving machines.

'Back in a minute,' he said, slipping outside.

He listened to his voicemail.

Mr Andino, Ramesh Bandara here. Can you please call me as soon as possible?

'Go away! Just go away!'

A cleaner wiping down the row of chairs in the corridor, looked up, disconcerted by Stan's outburst.

Stan dialled Bandara as he walked towards the window at the end of the corridor. The day had clouded over and a strong wind was tugging at the trees.

'Thanks for getting back to me. Are you and Mrs Andino at home right now?'

'No, we are not! Carmen has just been admitted to hospital with a brain bleed.'

There was a pause.

'I'm very sorry to hear that,' Bandara said, his manner suddenly less matter-of-fact. 'And I apologise for adding to your day like this, Mr Andino. But I need to inform you that a criminal case has been filed against your wife for the murder of Mrs Tibbie Lamb. She will be receiving a summons to appear in court.'

Stan slumped against the glass, his legs threatening to buckle.

'These are exceptional circumstances,' the detective continued. 'Nevertheless, a constable will need to come down to the hospital to deliver the summons. Is Mrs Andino *compos mentis*?'

'*Compos mentis?* What the hell? My wife has just had a bloody stroke and is fighting for her life.'

'You should know that we will not oppose an application for bail—'

Stan held the phone away from his face, looking at it as if it were an alien, then he hung up and slid down the cold hospital wall.

'You alright?' It was the cleaner.

Stan looked up, bewildered.

'You need help?'

He shook his head.

'Sick?'

'My wife… the police are charging her with murder.'

The man got on all fours, manoeuvred himself around, and sank down beside Stan, his short, pudgy legs and worn shoes right up close to Stan's. Together they sat in silence, staring into space.

Finally, after who knows how long, the man hauled himself up again, nodded gently, and shuffled down the corridor to resume his work.

Stan wasn't sure what was more terrifying. The fact that Carmen was going to be charged, or the relief he found in the detective's words, which meant that he wasn't going to be.

His phone beeped.

Another text.

About the money. I know you'll pay it back when you can. Tippy.

He dropped the phone as if it were a grenade, the screen cracking.

When was this nightmare going to stop? He felt like the unwitting target in some kid's computer game.

He put a hand over his mouth as if to deprive of oxygen the thought that was taking shape in his head.

He'd never before been able to comprehend those horrendous, once-a-decade news stories about an entire family being wiped out in a murder-suicide. Yet now it seemed the only way. The only way they could all stay together and be at peace. It was up to him. In his power to put an end to their suffering.

He'd do it while everyone slept. The boys wouldn't see it coming. There'd be no time to feel frightened. No time to register pain. Just *boom. Boom. Boom.* Then he'd turn the gun on himself.

Gun? What was he on about? He didn't even own a gun. Let alone know how to use one. Was he losing his mind?

Stan and Reuben sat in the car overlooking the lake. After the hospital visit, he'd driven down to the car park at the PumpHouse Theatre. A giant oak drowned the car in shade.

'Dad?'

Stan stared straight ahead.

'Dad?'

He turned to face his older son. Older by two minutes.

'I'm sorry, Reub.'

'For what? Mum's sickness is not your fault.'

'You don't deserve this. You and Leon don't deserve any of this.'

Reuben stiffened. A team of young rowers was hauling their boat out of the water.

Stan could feel his son's embarrassment at being seen in the car with his dad, who was crying.

'Reuben?' he said, enunciating his son's name carefully. 'The police think… they think your mum killed Tibbie. They are going to charge her with murder.'

Reuben turned to him, horror slowly spreading across his face. He fumbled with the door handle.

Stan grabbed his shirt.

'Let go of me!'

Stan held on with all his might as Reuben tried to wrestle free. 'Listen to me, we both know that if she did it, it was the tumour talking, not your mum. She is the kindest, most loving woman I know.'

Reuben's shirt tore as he broke free, then he was out of the car and running across the tarmac, past the little French café, through the grove of trees, and up the steep, grassy mound.

'Reuben!'

When Stan finally caught up with him, Reuben was sitting against a solitary tree in a sea of grass, the trunk blackened either by lightning or a fungus.

Stan's chest was heaving. He gulped for air. 'Oh Jeez!'

His son's cheeks were wet, but there was no sound to accompany his tears.

It would have been easier to deal with a tantrum. Reuben's defeated demeanour was more painful than any words.

Stan began to recite what he'd rehearsed in his head, the words spilling out of his mouth. He didn't know what else to do but walk his son into the eye of the approaching storm.

'I'm telling you all this because things are going to get harder before they get better. At school. With your friends. At home. I'm hoping we can keep Mum's name out of the newspapers. I'll have a word with Mr Morris. Give him the heads-up. Make your teachers aware of what's going on.'

Reuben sat there, as rigid as the trunk he was leaning against.

Stan continued. 'I'm not sure how Leon is going to react. I need you to be there for him. Especially at school.'

'So, the police don't think you did it anymore?'

Stan swung around. 'What? Reuben, I didn't kill Tibbie.' He grabbed his son's face in his hands. 'You hear me?'

Reuben jerked away.

'I would never lie to you. You must believe me!'

CHAPTER 43

ELIOT BARD

Eliot heard his name being called.

Dang it! He hadn't finished reading the comic.

He'd got to the surgery especially early, just so he could read at least one whole comic before his appointment. Austin had an entire shelf of them. And graphic novels.

The waiting room was packed, everyone there to see Dr Lamb. It was Austin's first week back at work after the horrible, horrible thing. The locum doctor who'd covered the practice while Austin was away – a grey woman with thin lips – had not been popular. Not with Eliot, anyway. She'd told him he had to work harder to get his blood sugar under control. Wanted him to come in for weekly reviews until his numbers improved.

It was spookily quiet for such a full waiting room. Laughing and talking did not feel right. Not after what had happened.

Eliot held onto his most serious frown.

'Hiya,' Austin said, patting him on the back. 'Come on through, mister.'

Even though Austin smiled, he looked different. Thinner. His face smaller.

Eliot hoped he wasn't angry with him for being the person to find his wife dead. He'd tried to do the right thing by giving back her hairclip.

'It's nice to see you,' Austin said, closing the door.

'These are from Mum,' he said, shoving a tin of his mum's homemade pistachio shortbread into his hands.

'She's a gem. Thank you.'

'They're my favourite.'

'I know they are.'

'Mum hardly ever makes them, because pistachios are really expensive. They are some of the most expensive nuts at the supermarket.'

'I'd offer you one,' Austin said, 'but I don't think you should be eating too many of these, do you?'

Eliot nodded, then shook his head.

'Maybe you can share them with Gwen?'

'Of course I will. Now, what are we doing for you today?'

Eliot looked down. 'The lady doctor who was here. Dr Robotham.' He felt his face go red. It was embarrassing saying her name out loud. Imagine having a name with bottom in it! At least it wasn't bum. Imagine Dr Robum.

'Yes,' Austin said, glancing at his computer.

Eliot pulled back his shoulders. 'She said my Hba1C wasn't very good.'

It wasn't that he was proud of the bad result, but he was pretty chuffed that he knew what Hba1C was. His mum was always going on about how important it was to be in charge of his own health, learn the right medical words, manage the diabetes himself… in case she wasn't around one day.

Eliot didn't like to think about that.

'Aha.'

'She said I had to get my glucose under control.' The phrase made Eliot think of a dog on a leash.

'Yes, I see that our old friend Hba1C has been creeping up again. Too much pistachio shortbread, eh?'

Eliot shook his head vehemently. 'I haven't had any. Only, like, just a funny-shaped piece on my way here. One of Mum's fails. That's all!'

'Let's see what your glucose is doing today,' Austin said

with a smile. He opened his drawer and rummaged around in it. 'Now where's my glucometer?' He sighed. 'This is what happens when you go away for a while. Everything gets moved around and muddled.'

'Austin, can I borrow you for a minute?' It was Gwen, his receptionist.

He pushed his chair back and left the room.

Eliot set off the silver balls on Austin's desk. *Click click click click.*

He pushed the tin of biscuits further away.

'I'll do a script for her as soon as I've finished with Eliot,' he overheard Austin say. 'By the way, have you seen my glucometer?'

Eliot lifted the net curtain and peered into the car park below.

Austin's shiny black Mercedes was parked in its usual spot. *Doctor's Parking.* Eliot loved fancy cars – Mercedes, BMWs, Audis, Jags, though he didn't like black cars. Black, poo-brown and turquoise were colours that made him anxious.

There were four other cars in the car park, including Gwen's battered green Mazda. And an old racing bike propped up against a pillar. The sort with downward-curved handlebars. Eliot used to have a bike just like it – a hand-me-down from his mum's old boss, Brian. He had so loved that bike. When he rode it, he felt like a pro – head down, bum in the air, feet spinning as he lapped the Olympic velodrome, the crowd roaring.

The last bit wasn't true; he'd never cycled around a velodrome. He didn't have the bike anymore either. The chain kept coming off and a man at the repair shop said it was time to put it out to pasture.

Mountain bikes were all the rage now, anyway. But they cost a lot of money. Eliot's mum said if he wanted one, he'd have to pay for it himself, which was not a happening thing. It would mean years of weeding Mr McDougal's garden.

Eliot's head started clicking. It was different from the

clicking silver balls. More like filing cabinets opening and closing.

'Here we go. Eliot?'

Eliot's brain pulled open another drawer.

Austin tapped him on the shoulder. 'Anybody home?' He was holding the evil finger-prick device.

Eliot pulled a face.

'Come on now, Eliot. You've done this a thousand times.'

'Whose bike is that?'

Austin followed Eliot's gaze out the window.

'Not sure. I think it might belong to Jeremy, Lila Nunn's caregiver. He's just dropped in to collect a script for her.'

Eliot, can you remember seeing or hearing anything unusual on your walk that day? Someone in a hurry perhaps?

'Now let's see what that glucose of yours is doing.'

'Someone might steal it if he leaves it there without a lock,' Eliot said.

Austin laughed. 'Not sure anyone would want to steal that. Looks pretty old, don't you think?' He reached for Eliot's forefinger.

Eliot hated that moment just before the puncture. The waiting for the spike to go in.

A bubble of blood swelled on the tip of his finger.

Austin swept the test strip across it, mopping up the red.

'I've seen that bike before,' Eliot said.

'Well, Jeremy does live in the neighbourhood.'

A number appeared in the small glucometer window. 'Hmm, Dr Robotham was right. You are running high. What dose of insulin have we got you on?'

'What?'

'Eliot, buddy, can you focus please? I've lost you to daydreams today.' Eliot pulled at his left ear.

'Have you brought in a record of your recent readings?'

'Forgot. Sorry. Don't tell Mum.'

'Look, mate,' Austin said, scrolling down the computer, 'I know it's hard to be disciplined about something you can't even see. I get it. Especially if you're feeling fine. But as I've told you before, glucose works silently, behind the scenes, doing its damage without you even knowing, till it's too late. You always need to be one step ahead of it. Like a super-smart detective. Okay?'

Eliot nodded. Squinted through the gauze curtains. Austin was not as much fun as he usually was.

'I'm going to increase your evening and your morning dose. We'll do it gradually. But I want you to record your readings twice a day until we've got it sorted. And no forgetting to bring in the chart next week. I'd like to see that the trend is headed in the right direction. Okay?'

Eliot sighed. Diabetes was such a pain.

Austin scribbled the new dose down on a piece of paper. Eliot folded it and slipped it into his jeans pocket.

'Make sure to tell your mum about the new treatment plan. And don't forget to thank her for the shortbread.'

He opened the door and tapped Eliot on the shoulder. 'Stay well, you.' Then he was calling in Jeremy, a super-skinny guy with dreadlocks pulled into a ponytail.

'Sorry to keep you waiting. Let's get you that script for Lila.'

The man smelt of cigarettes.

'I used to have a bike like yours,' Eliot said, as they passed each other. The guy turned. He had a long, thin chin like a cartoon character. 'Me?'

Eliot nodded. 'The racing bike outside. Is it yours?'

'That old donga,' the guy said, grinning. 'Afraid it is. Want to buy it?'

Everything about the man was thin. Even his teeth had spaces between them.

'Have you, like, ever cycled along the cliff path above Browns Bay?' Eliot blurted out.

'Maybe. Why?'

'I'm sorry to get in the way of a good conversation, Eliot,' Austin said, 'but I need to be getting on. Come on in, Jeremy. How's Lila doing?'

CHAPTER 44

CARMEN ANDINO

'Shan, can you shurn off jha eater?'

The small fan heater – an all-or-nothing device – had been a Boxing Day Sale special. When it was on, the room was hot and stuffy. As soon as you turned it off, however, the sphere of heat around it seeped quickly away, and the room chilled down.

Carmen lay propped against three pillows, trying to concentrate on what Warren Meiklejohn – the lawyer who'd been assigned to them by legal aid – was saying. He'd come to their home, because she was no longer up to going out. A fleshy fellow, with loose jowls and a comb-over, he gave the sense of having seen it all before.

'The police will definitely have more than just motive and anecdotally odd behaviour.'

'Like what?' Stan asked, his tone antagonistic.

He was not going to endear himself to the man, but Carmen didn't have the energy or capability to interrupt. Just the effort to make herself understood was exhausting. Things were too far along anyway; her head was a fairground of dizziness, nausea and meaningless words. She tried to pin down thoughts. Tried to grasp at the outline of herself. But there was so little of her left. Of Carmen the mother, the wife, the journo.

Meiklejohn shrugged. 'Perhaps they've identified Mrs Andino's DNA at the crime scene. Or have a witness. Who knows? Conviction does demand beyond reasonable doubt.'

'Back up a minute,' Stan interrupted. 'Surely the most important thing we need to focus on is not what proof they have, but Carmen's tumour. Her state of mind. Surely, she cannot be found guilty when her judgement, her personality, and her comprehension are all – were all – impaired.'

Carmen floated above the scene, watching the two men discuss her.

'I've spoken with your oncologist,' Meiklejohn said. 'She attests to the fact that the tumours resulted in significant cognitive impairment, which would have been compounded by the medication, particularly the highdose steroids. The radiation you received to your entire brain may have further exacerbated this. The term she used was…' He shuffled through papers. '…radiation encephalopathy.'

'May have? Of course, it did,' Stan said through gritted teeth. 'We have to go in with certainty. Conviction. Not some wishy-washy might or maybe or perhaps… Jeez!'

Carmen landed back in her body. She pounded her fist on the duvet. 'Fa God shake, Shan!'

Stan held up his hands in apology.

Meiklejohn waved his forgivingly. 'I say *may*, because typically, according to Dr Bell, radiation encephalopathy presents as more of a delayed side-effect. Sometimes a year or so out, if the patient survives that long.'

Stan's face collapsed like a punctured balloon. He was all over the place, like some preschool kid, his emotions on some out-of-control fairground ride.

'The thing is,' the lawyer went on, 'the extent of impairment is hard to measure. It's a subjective assessment. Dr Bell says that damage recorded on an MRI does not necessarily correlate with the degree of intellectual decline.'

'For fuck's sake, Warren! Just tell me what you can do for us.'

Carmen closed her eyes and tried to take herself back to the day everyone kept talking about. The day she and Tibbie took their last walk together. It was like beginning a 1000-piece jigsaw puzzle. Look for the straightsided pieces. Build the border. Then fill in the rest.

She could remember feeling annoyed with Tibbie. Really annoyed. Lots of little things about Tibbie had become irksome. But specifically on that day?

Strangely, every walk with Tibbie had merged into one and Carmen could not tease them apart. Tibbie wearing her cream hoodie and lime-green joggers. Tibbie wearing black leggings and a mauve merino. Tibbie spotting someone's pet parrot in a tree. Tibbie phoning to cancel on her. Tibbie taking Carmen for coffee and walnut cake in Browns Bay. Tibbie, unusually quiet and tearful. Tibbie talking about a phone call she'd had with her sister. Tibbie helping Carmen nick some fresh rosemary from a roadside hedge. Tibbie apologising because she had to leave Carmen halfway for some appointment. Tibbie looking healthy. Tibbie looking fit. Tibbie looking beautiful.

Beautiful Tibbie.

Beautiful Tippy.

Tippy! Tippy! Tippy!

'One step at a time,' Meiklejohn said to Stan. 'The police have made it clear they will not oppose bail, which suggests they are clearly cognisant of the difficult circumstances we find ourselves in.'

Carmen had spent two nights in the High Dependency Unit, before being moved to a private room. A constable had delivered the summons while she was still in hospital, but there were no handcuffs, no arrest, no policeman stationed outside her door. Just a piece of paper passed uncomfortably between hands.

'I suspect that even if we were to lose the case,' Meiklejohn continued, 'Mrs Andino would be looking at home detention.'

'Excellent!' Stan said, jumping up. 'No worries at all then. Never mind about her reputation. About—'

Meiklejohn stood up slowly, his very deliberate temperance a sign he was probably getting annoyed. 'Let's meet again on Thursday.'

'Shanks, Warren,' Carmen said.

She wished Stan would leave the room, too.

CHAPTER 45

ELIOT BARD

'Top of the morning, Master Eliot. Thought you might have decided to give today a miss.'

Eliot looked at his watch. 'I'm not late.'

'I know. I know. It's just feels like it because, well, I've been up since 4.30 am.'

'That's early.'

'Indeed, it is,' Mr McDougal said, beckoning Eliot to follow him.

Eliot dropped his backpack at the front door and followed the old man down the dingy corridor. 'If I can't sleep, Mum makes me a mug of warm milk.'

'I'm afraid warm milk would not have worked this morning,' he said stopping outside the laundry. 'Not with this little bugger making such a racket.'

He opened the door.

Eliot peered in. There, fenced off with washing baskets, was a small golden-haired puppy.

'Woah!'

'Eliot, meet Hazel.' Mr McDougal said, smiling so widely Eliot could see the top rim of his false teeth jiggling up and down.

'Is she yours? Is she?'

'No, she's Pauline's,' Mr McDougal said. 'I'm looking after her while Pauline is away for a few days.'

Eliot didn't get much gardening done, what with Hazel biting his heels and tugging at his trousers. All he wanted to do was keep cuddling her. She smelt of porridge and warm puppy.

'I wish Mum would let me have a dog,' he said, when they broke for morning tea.

'You don't need your own dog, now that we've got Hazel to look after. Bet your bottom dollar Hazel will be spending more time here than at Pauline's. I'm going to need lots of help. She's a feisty one. You can be Hazel's godfather.'

Eliot didn't like the word godfather. It sounded dark and mean.

Mr McDougal passed him a jam doughnut. 'I bought us a special treat.'

Eliot stared at the sugary ball with its bellybutton of raspberry jam.

He pouted. 'I'm not allowed.'

'Sure you are. Just this once. Everything in moderation.'

Eliot shook his head. 'My Hba1C is right off.'

'Your what?'

'It's this warning flag that tells the doctor how good my sugars have been over the past three months. Sort of like a school report card.'

'I see.'

'Anyway, mine isn't very flash, so Austin has increased my insulin. I promised him I'd record everything I ate.' He sighed. 'It's pretty shit.'

Mr McDougal looked taken aback. Eliot was also surprised by the way the swear word just made its way out of his mouth. But it was satisfying, too; he was nearly twenty-two years old.

He started to giggle as Hazel stuck her warm pink tongue in his ear; he was super ticklish.

Mr McDougal put the doughnut back in the box. 'I'm impressed by your willpower, boy. When we were in the army, we also had to be disciplined. It's a sign of strong character, that's what it is.'

Eliot sat up straighter.

'Austin says I've got to be like a detective. One step ahead of my sugars at all times.'

Suddenly he remembered. It was the detective bit that reminded him. 'Can I finish early today? I have to catch a bus to the police station.'

'To check your glucose?' the old man said with a wink.

'Don't be silly! I have to tell Detective Bandara something really important.'

Mr McDougal took a bite of doughnut, his eyes fixed on Eliot's.

'It's about the day I found Austin's wife. You see, I remembered that I saw a bike leaning against a fence on the cliff pathway. It was just like the one that belongs to this Jeremy guy, who looks after Lila Nunn.'

'You're not making much sense. Who is Lila Nunn?'

'A patient of Austin's. She's dementing.'

'And you think the bike might be related to Mrs Lamb's death?'

Mr McDougal's doubting expression took the wind out of Eliot's sails.

'I only remembered about it when I saw the bike outside Austin's surgery. It was this rusty silver racing bike and had red tape around the handlebars, which was starting to peel off. Detective Bandara told me to tell him if I remembered anything about that day. Anything at all.'

The yeasty smell of the doughnuts was getting to him. 'Maybe I could have just a half.'

Mr McDougal shook his head. 'Best not, eh? I've got a packet of roasted cashew nuts inside if you'd like.'

'No thanks.'

'Anyway, I think they've charged someone with Mrs Lamb's murder,' Mr McDougal said.

'Murder? For real?' All of a sudden, even thinking about the day he'd found the red-haired lady in the water was frightening.

'Some poor woman, who is apparently not very well in the head, did it.'

Eliot gaped.

'But best you don't tell other people. It's not common knowledge yet. I only know because Pauline's partner is a policewoman. And I'm telling you because it probably means the police have all the information they need.'

Eliot felt a gush of warmth spread down his front.

'No way!' he cried. 'Hazel's peed on me.'

Mr McDougal chuckled. 'Oh dear. She hasn't been toilet-trained yet. Never mind. Put her in the pen for a bit and come inside. We'll give your shirt a quick rinse.

By the time Eliot got home that afternoon he had so much to tell his mum about Hazel and his wet shirt and the tiny teeth marks on his legs and how much fun having a puppy was, that he forgot all about Austin's dead wife and the bike and the lady not right in the head who'd been charged with her murder.

CHAPTER 46

STAN ANDINO

Stan's bladder woke him. He stirred resentfully. It had been the deepest sleep he'd had in a long time. No dreams or restless legs, just pure blackout.

He stumbled to the toilet and relieved himself, then climbed back into bed. Checked the time on his phone. Another fifteen minutes before he had to get the boys up.

One new message.

A weight dropped to the pit of his stomach.

You and I both know Carmen would never have pushed me. We were best friends. The cancer didn't change that. Not guilty! Tippy.

The same sicko toying with him.

Stan read the text again. Then he pulled the duvet over his head and slid his feet towards Carmen's. They were freezing. He'd have to buy her bed socks; her circulation was terrible.

He pondered whether to show the police the text.

What was the point? They weren't on his side. Hadn't even followed up on his first complaint. So much for getting hold of his service provider.

He was tempted to play the texter at their own game, but Bandara had warned him not to. 'Such individuals are always after a reaction.'

Stan wondered if Janice was behind them. But when he thought about it, they were far too benignly worded for her.

The radio alarm burst into song. Stan swung a hand over to

kill it before it woke Carmen. He sat up, his heart pounding, his eyes trying to focus. A thin line of light had split the curtains in two. Another grey day.

'Pancakes!' Leon cried as he sloped into the kitchen, his white school shirt creased, his tie stained and off-centre.

'Thought you guys deserved a treat,' Stan said, wiping his hands on a dishtowel.

Reuben flopped down in his chair, dark rings under his eyes. 'I'm not hungry.'

'You sure? With sliced banana and maple syrup?'

He shook his head.

'I'll have his,' Leon said, ploughing into his serving.

'Can I make you some toast?'

'Nah.'

Stan scooped out the peppermint teabag steeping in a mug of boiling water. 'Leon, please take this to your mum. And remember, a gentle wakeup, not full-on for first thing in the morning.'

Leon took the mug from Stan and pantomime-tiptoed out of the room, tea sloshing onto the floor.

'Leon,' Stan growled.

Reuben rolled his eyes. 'Stupid asshole.'

Stan shrugged.

'It's like he doesn't even know there's anything different in our lives,' Reuben said. 'He's so selfish.'

Stan sat down beside his son. 'Listen, mate, we all have different ways of dealing with stress. Some people hide behind silliness, because they just can't cope with the truth. They still need lots of support and love; it can be pretty lonely running from the truth.'

Reuben looked up at his dad. For a moment Stan couldn't distinguish between his own pain and his son's; they'd always been so connected. He got how Reuben felt. Leon's casualness and apparent insensitivity were irritating. However, he had to keep reminding himself that deep down Leon was just a scared kid who'd hung on longer in Carmen's womb to delay facing the world. He was all loud, brash show, but ironically, the weaker twin.

A strange sound rose over the din of the old dishwasher on its rinse cycle. He and Reuben looked at each other.

It was a strangled sort of groan.

Then a crazed, anguished bellow came down the passage. 'Daaaaaaad!'

Stan froze, as if a power surge had tripped the switches and shrouded everything in darkness.

Leon's scream arrived in the room before he did, and it was an interminable few seconds before the boy caught up.

He burst into the kitchen.

'She's dead!'

'What?'

'Ma's dead!'

Then all three of them were charging down the passageway.

Carmen was lying on her side, a sagging undulation of body.

Her cheek had collapsed into a shallow pit and her teeth were protruding oddly, almost like a horse's.

Stan rested a hand on her forehead. Her skin was cold and waxy like linoleum.

He turned. Reuben and Leon were standing behind him breathing hard. In and out. In and out.

Their eyes clung to his, a silent morse code passing between them. Then all three slumped into the truth.

The journey that had started with a bottle of bleach and a black apron was over.

Stan put an arm out for each of his boys and pulled them in to him. The main mast of the Andino family had fallen. He was all that stood between them and a terrifying swell.

Leon held tightly onto Stan, his lanky body shaking, snot and tears sliding down his face, while Reuben climbed silently into the bed and snuggled up to his mother.

It was over.

Disbelief.

Grief.

Relief.

CHAPTER 47

STAN ANDINO

The funeral was a small affair. Just a handful of people. Friends had fallen like flies over the previous months, driven away by Carmen's craziness, the rumours, and finally the murder charge. The boys' social circle had shrunk, too.

Mr Morris, their school principal, was there, and three lads from the hockey team. Carmen's editor. A couple of Stan's pottery students, too. Also Dr Ngaire Bell; Carmen's brother, Richard; and Geoff and Pam, their elderly parents.

Stan sat in the front pew, a son on either side.

Carmen lay in a rented casket. He hadn't dared tell Richard. It was all Stan could afford.

'More eco-friendly', the funeral director had assured, trying to assuage Stan's guilt. Stan wondered who'd lain in it before Carmen. And who would occupy it after her.

He couldn't help reflecting on how different Tibbie's funeral had been. The extravagant floral arrangements. A church packed to capacity. Even Tibbie's dentist and hairdresser amongst the mourners. One of the checkout operators from the local supermarket, too. Tibbie had touched a lot of people. *A beautiful soul tragically taken too early* reiterated over and over.

Neither Reuben nor Leon was brave enough to speak, and

so it was left to Stan to try and bleach the stain that had spread over Carmen's entire life.

'She fought it as best she could… Wouldn't wish what she went through on my worst enemy… How she loved her boys.'

Richard read a poem. Then a pastor Stan had only met two days earlier was left to sum up Carmen in bland, generic terms.

As they made their way out of the church, Stan spotted Austin in the back pew. Warmth surged through him.

Austin stepped into the aisle and gave Stan a hug. 'Who would have thought we'd both be widowers before the year was out?'

Stan didn't want to let go. Austin felt so strong, so upright. He represented land Stan never thought he'd set foot on again. His friend, probably the only friend he had left, had come to bid Carmen farewell.

'Jeez!' Stan said, wiping his nose. 'I'm sorry. So sorry about all of this.'

Austin nodded. 'Life can be one cruel bastard.'

'Listen, about the money, I'm going to pay—'

'Let's not go there today, Stan. Right now, this is about you and the boys and their mum.'

'Thank you.'

Would he have been so forgiving of Austin?

As Austin moved away, Stan saw a familiar silhouette hovering in the doorway. It was Ramesh Bandara.

He clenched his jaw and ushered his sons outside.

'My sincere condolences to you and your boys,' the detective said.

Stan kept walking.

'Please know that in the light of developments, we've closed the case.'

Stan ruptured, like a high-pressure hose. 'Developments! My wife's death reduced to *developments*. Well, why don't you just fuck off? Do you think it makes any damned difference to us that the case has been closed? Do you? Carmen has been tried and found guilty by a kangaroo court through implication and rumour.'

Richard quickly shepherded Carmen's distressed parents to a nearby car.

'See the pitiful turnout here today?' Stan ranted, pushing himself right up into the detective's face. 'That will tell you how effectively you tainted my wife's reputation. She'll never be able to refute her epitaph. She… I mean, what do you think closing the case says? Eh? What do you think that says to every—'

Stan felt a hand on his shoulder. It was Austin.

'You're upsetting the boys, man. Hold it together. For them.'

Leon broke free and started sprinting across the lawn towards the main road.

'Leon!'

The kid kept running, dashing blindly across the intersection. A car hooted. Swerved.

Austin went after him.

Stan looked around for Reuben.

He spotted him leaning against the side of the church building, his shoulders curled in, his head hanging heavily.

'Just go,' Stan said, pushing past Bandara. 'You're not welcome here.'

The next fortnight passed in a blur. After Carmen's parents returned to Gore, Stan and the boys hunkered down. They all slept together in the lounge on mattresses pulled from their bedrooms. Woke late, ate takeaways, and played computer games. That's all Stan had energy for; his body and mind weighed down by an overwhelming lethargy and too many glasses of cheap red wine.

Austin had waved away talk of finances at the funeral. It was all the permission Stan needed to put the problem on the backburner.

They were living entirely on Tibbie's money. The amount

in the bank, not the cash he'd kept hidden in his underwear drawer. (No-one knew about that extra amount.)

The terrifying momentum of their life had stopped abruptly, like an out-of-control motorboat finally cutting out. And while it was a relief to find himself and the boys bobbing around in the ocean, Carmen's death – the reason the drama had resolved so cleanly – was not the outcome he'd have wanted. In another way, it was. He felt confused, conflicted, guilty, relieved, angry. So many emotions. So many unanswered questions. At the very least, Detective Bandara owed him some explanations.

What was the definitive proof they had of Carmen's involvement? How come Stan had been so suddenly excluded from the investigation, despite Janice's meddling? And who had sent the 'Tippy' texts?

There were days when Stan toyed with marching into the station and demanding answers, but he always chickened out. It was best to let sleeping dogs lie. Questions would only stir up murky sediment, and he risked bringing the whole goddamned drama back to life.

Two weeks after Carmen's funeral, Mr Morris rang to enquire after the twins. Stan knew it was time for them to return to school. As it was, theywere growing restless and bored. The comfort they'd derived from turning their backs on the world was losing its power. It was time for them to re-enter reality.

He had just dropped them off for their first day back, when his phone rang. Austin's number flashed up on his screen.

CHAPTER 48

AUSTIN LAMB

Stan's phone went to messages.

Austin hung up. He'd try again later.

He locked his car and climbed the back stairs to his surgery. Sylvia Stuart's Alfa Romeo was already cheekily parked in the disabled car park, twenty-five minutes early for the first appointment of the day.

Work was good the way it forced him to put one foot in front of the other. Like the silver balls on his desk, the perpetual motion left little room for reflection. It was definitely easier than the hours alone when his thoughts could expand, distend, rupture.

'Morning, Austin,' Gwen said, looking up from her desk and flashing a maternal smile. She'd been with him right from the beginning when he was just starting out as an eager young doctor. That she still wore the same mulberry-coloured lipstick was a reassuring constant. There was an order and tidiness in that. A safety.

Some of his patients had been with him for that length of time, too; those who were in their forties when he started out, now with narrowed arteries, stiff knees, and grand-children. No one said *My, you look far too young to be a doctor* any longer.

He sat down at his desk and flicked through the latest batch of blood results. He was not going to be hurried by Sylvia Stuart.

His phone rang. It was Stan returning his call.

'I was just checking in to see how you're all doing,' Austin said.

Stan hesitated. 'Okay, I guess.'

Austin pushed through the discomfort. 'I was at the boys' school last week giving a talk about immunisation. Had a chat with the principal, Morris. Great guy. He told me Reuben and Leon were still away.'

'They start back today,' Stan said, almost defensively. 'I've just dropped them off.'

'Oh, good. Good. It's a tricky thing, striking a balance between affording them the time to feel sad, and getting them back into normal life before they become stuck in the grief cycle.'

'Appreciate the concern.'

'Have you thought about getting some counselling for them, Stan? They've had a hell of a lot to process for thirteen-year-olds. I can recommend someone really good.'

'Yeah. Maybe.'

'Just something to consider.'

'Hmm.'

Stan's monosyllabic answers were disconcerting. Austin wondered whether it was low mood or even resentment talking; there was no straight road through grief.

He looked around. Gwen was in the doorway, waiting to speak with him.

'Five minutes,' he mouthed.

'Listen, Stan, why don't you and the boys come around for dinner Friday night? I'll get pizzas in. Reuben and Leon can watch a movie. It will be a chance for us to chat.'

'You sure?'

'I wouldn't have offered.'

'That would be nice. Really nice.'

After the call, Austin sank back in his chair and rubbed his eyes. Life! It could be so messy.

Gwen popped her head in again. 'Cath and I are joining forces to buy a Lotto ticket for the weekend. Want to come in with us? The jackpot is twenty million.'

Austin smiled. 'I thought you knew me better than that.'

'Twenty mill, Austin.'

'Ta, but I'll pass.'

Austin's childhood had been a never-ending game of Lotto. Was he going to cop a beating or would it be his lucky day? Spin the wheel. Was there going to be dinner on the table or would he have to hang around fast-food outlets, scrounging in the bin for people's leftovers? Spin the wheel. Was his mum coming home or would he be left to lie awake fending off the noises of the night? Spin the wheel. Was this going to be his forever school or would his mum and her new squeeze pack up sticks and move town again?

No, Austin did not want in on some Saturday-night lucky-dip. He would not be waiting for a sequence of random coloured balls to align; he'd worked too hard to eliminate chance from his life. Austin Lamb dealt in certainties.

CHAPTER 49

STAN ANDINO

Neither of the boys were keen on the idea of going to Austin's for dinner and they both sulked the whole way there. Stan was ambivalent, too. He'd messaged Austin earlier in the day on the pretext of telling him he would sort the dessert.

'I'll bring a tub of ice-cream and some strawberries. How many are you expecting?'

'Just the four of us.'

Thank God! Janice must have gone back to Australia.

Reuben was sitting in the front seat, balancing the punnet of strawberries on his knee. Stan could envision them tipping over any minute – the expensive, air-mile-eaters scattering in the footwell.

He didn't say anything. With teenagers you had to pick your battles.

That's what Carmen always said.

Leon sat hunched in the back seat with the ice-cream, sporting the black eye he'd earned the previous night at dinner.

It had begun with Reuben moaning through a mouthful of food. 'Why do we have to go tomorrow? It'll be so weird.'

'Yeah,' Leon chipped in. 'Like, I mean, Austin probably hates our guts cause of what Mum did.'

'She didn't do anything, stupid!' Reuben barked.

'Oh, so now you're the police expert.'

'Shut up, you loser!'

'You shut up.' Then in a low hiss: 'Son of a murderer.'

'If I am, so are you, you fuckwit,' Reuben had said, punching his brother in the face and knocking him off his chair.

'Stop right this minute!' roared Stan, his chest heaving. 'What would your mother think if she could see you both now?'

He helped Leon up off the floor. 'Just get out, Reuben. Go to your room. Go!'

'I'm not six years old!'

Rage flooded Stan's head. He lifted an open hand.

Stopped.

Scrunched his eyes shut. He'd never hit either of the boys. Not even once. Carmen had been the one to dish out the odd smack, but never him. What was he becoming?

'Reuben— please— just— do— as— I— say.'

Reuben must have detected the desperation in his dad's voice, because he'd shoved his chair back and stormed out of the room.

Austin opened the front door, dressed in navy loafers, jeans, and a crisp pink polo shirt, the Lacoste logo vouching for its provenance. Stan's T-shirt looked laundry-weary.

'Hey,' Austin said, pulling Reuben into a headlock. 'Good to see you.' He took in Leon's shiner. 'What happened to you, mister?'

Leon smirked and tossed his head towards his brother.

'Don't ask,' Stan said.

'Good brotherly love, eh?'

He shook Stan's hand, not in a formal way, but more an old matey gesture. 'Come on in.'

'I brought a bottle,' Stan said, shoving a supermarket merlot into Austin's hand.

Austin's exaggerated thank you was embarrassing. They both knew he preferred pinot noir, but Stan's budget couldn't cope with a good pinot.

'Hope you brought your togs, boys. The spa pool's just been valeted.'

They shook their heads in unison, giving their dad the evil eye.

'I'm sure I've got spares to fit you both,' Austin said quickly.

Ten minutes later the twins were soaking in the spa, while Austin and Stan sat out on the deck under the patio heater, drinking beer.

How surreal it was to be back in such a familiar setting. Familiar, yet strangely foreign; neither wife there to complete the picture. Two middle-aged, widowed men. Could the friendship truly recover or had the women been the glue before all the bad stuff started going down?

The Andino house spoke loudly of Carmen's absence. There were always dirty dishes in the sink, a mound of smelly washing in the laundry, pot plants turned wither brown.

Austin's house, on the other hand, looked as it always had. So much so that Stan wouldn't have been overly surprised if Tibbie had wandered in carrying a plate of hummus and home-made crackers. The curtains had been swept back in even, symmetrical swathes. Long-stemmed white roses filled a crystal vase…

Was it really so surprising? Austin was such a particular man. Not even the death of his wife was reason enough to let his standards slip. Saying that, credit was most likely due to the housekeeper Austin had no doubt kept on.

Stan felt exhausted thinking about all the effort required to maintain the status quo. Not that he was missing Carmen for the housework. It was more what the mess represented that bothered him. A physical manifestation of his family's breakdown.

Although for all the 'normality' of Austin's home, Tibbie's absence was palpable. The order felt brittle and the house hollow without her. Austin also seemed a little more ordinary.

Stan sighed, the beer starting to soften his discomfort. 'You're a big man, Austin.'

Austin dipped his eyebrows quizzically.

'I mean, I don't know if I could have been so forgiving.'

Austin shrugged. 'What Carmen did was not her. I know that. You know that. Yes, the consequences are bloody hard to accept. Pretty much impossible some days. I swing from acceptance to resentment in a moment. But Carmen's diagnosis was a death sentence for her and Tibbie. We all suffered because of the cancer. Not just Carmen. No-one could blame her for getting sick, so how can we blame her for the havoc cancer wrought on her brain and our lives?'

Stan had not been a prefect at school. He'd rationalised that such accolades were artificial and no real measure of a person or the success they might one day achieve. Yet now, as he listened to Austin's hugely empathetic response to an unimaginable tragedy, he realised that perhaps prefecture was a marker for what sort of human being you were and would become.

Austin had been a Deputy Head Boy at his school. As predictors went, the selection process had been spot-on.

Leon and Reuben finally emerged from the spa and stood dripping at the table while they scoffed an entire plate of sausage rolls.

'We better order these monsters some dinner,' Austin said, looking at his watch.

Stan was relieved; they usually ate much earlier at home.

Austin brought up the pizza menu on his phone and started reading out the options.

'We eat pretty much anything,' Stan interrupted. 'Only thing Leon doesn't like is blue cheese.'

But Austin persisted with the entire menu, and as Stan predicted, the extensive selection set off a fight between the boys.

'The seafood one. C'mon, Reuben.'

'Nah, I like—'

The doorbell rang, startling them all.

'Listen, you two, it's pretty rude to be fighting over what

pizza you want,' Stan said, after Austin had disappeared inside. 'Just make a bloody decision and get over yourselves.'

Stan heard a woman's laughter. Then Austin was back, Abby Manderson in tow.

'Never mind pizzas, guys. Look what this amazing woman has just delivered.'

The boys craned their necks to see what was in the large rectangular dish Abby Manderson was carrying.

'Chicken Marabella, no less,' Austin said with a smile. It was the first time Stan had seen Austin smile in a long time. It was good to see. 'You'll join us, Abby, I hope?'

The dish smelt amazing, but Stan felt a stab of irritation at the thought of now having to share Austin's company. Their honest, unedited chat had been just what he needed. The last thing he felt like was making small talk with Abby Manderson. Everything about the woman was loud. Her laughter, lipstick, her bust.

'Wouldn't dream of intruding. Anyway, I still have something in the oven I've got to get back to.'

She lifted a corner of the foil. 'Pop it in the oven for another fifteen minutes. And serve with baguette. I've got one in the car.'

Stan felt a wave of jealousy as Austin saw Abby out. The community had wrapped itself around their doctor. They'd see him right. Well-wishers had not dropped in with food at Stan's place for a very long time. After a delicious dinner, the inexpensive merlot surprisingly acceptable, too, Reuben and Leon settled into the media room to watch a movie, while Austin and Stan remained out on the deck.

The moonless night wrapped the men in a cocoon of darkness that was interrupted only by the orange glow of the patio heater. Austin had deliberately left the deck lights off so as not to attract insects, and the perfume from the garden seemed all the headier for the absence of light, as if the senses were usually in competition.

For the first time in what seemed like forever, Stan felt

hopeful. Maybe, just maybe, they could all get through this awful year and life would once again be good.

'Sometimes I feel so guilty about being here,' he said, turning to Austin. 'It should have been me. Carmen didn't deserve it.'

'Who deserves cancer?' Austin said, twisting a corkscrew into a second bottle of wine. A Central Otago pinot noir. Not even a screw-top. There was nothing under fifty dollars in Austin's cellar.

'The thing is, I wasn't always the best husband,' Stan said.

Austin refilled their glasses. 'We could always do better.'

Stan persisted. His secret had put a foot in the doorway, and now, after fourteen years, it wanted out.

'When Carmen was pregnant with the twins, I had an affair.'

The windchime jangled in the breeze. A morepork cried beyond the blackness of the garden. Blood pulsed in Stan's ears.

'Such a stupid, selfish thing to do. Poor insecure husband feeling neglected while his big-bellied, exhausted wife carried twins to term.'

Stan could feel Austin's judgement seeping into the silence that followed.

Austin cleared his throat. 'It's not uncommon,' he said evenly. 'Men straying while their wives grow babies. I didn't even have that excuse myself.'

Stan swung round. 'You?'

'Foolish men that we are.'

'Who? I mean, really? It's none of my business, but…'

Austin rubbed his nose, took a gulp of his wine. 'Same as you.'

Stan frowned, trying to find his way around Austin's words. 'What do you mean?'

'Janice, of course.'

Stan's head started spinning. He felt nauseous. Dizzy. Dry-mouthed.

'You and Janice? Tibbie's sister?'

Austin nodded. 'Yup. I shagged the sister-in-law.'

Shagged. Everything about Austin's confession. Even the language... None of it fitted with the image Stan held in his head of his perfect friend, perfect doctor, perfect pillar of the community.

'I share your regrets,' Austin said, his voice suddenly husky. 'Tibbie was everything I could ever have asked for in a partner. Everything.'

Stan was reeling; his world had just been tipped on its head. The certainty of day and night, summer and winter. Who his best friend was. The truth as he knew it.

'Were there others?'

Austin sniggered. 'I'm not that much of a degenerate.'

A noise behind them saw them both swing around. Reuben was standing by the open door.

'Hey!' Stan said, trying to sound chipper. 'Movie finished?'

His son's face was fixed like a waxwork. 'Nah. We having strawbs?'

'Course we are,' Austin said, jumping up. 'I'll just take the ice-cream out of the freezer to soften. We'll bring some through to you guys shortly.' Stan followed Austin to the kitchen.

Austin's skin looked yellowish in the harsh kitchen light and there was a large stain of Chicken Marabella down his pink shirt.

'Hope he didn't hear anything,' Stan whispered, tossing his head in the direction of the media room.

'Doubt it,' Austin said, pulling out the tub of vanilla bean from the freezer. 'We weren't exactly shouting.'

Stan took a knife from the magnetic strip above the stove. He knew it was hypocritical, yet he couldn't help thinking that Austin sleeping with his wife's sister was worse than his involvement with Janice. A bigger betrayal of trust. And betraying Tibbie, of all people!

He blinked, avoiding Austin's gaze under the bright kitchen lights. It had been easier to talk in the dark. He began hulling the strawberries.

'How did you know about Janice and me? I mean—'

'She told me. I came after you, as it were.'

Stan had always blamed himself. Believed he'd initiated the whole goddamned sleazy business.

Austin ran the dirty dishes under hot water, then packed the dishwasher – knives on the top shelf, forks facing down in the cutlery basket, big plates at the back, side plates to the front.

Stan's fingers were stained red from taking the heads off the strawberries.

How humiliating to realise that Austin had known about his affair with Janice for all these years. He wondered how many other people knew.

'Oh, that we could rewind the clock, eh?' Austin said, drying his hands with a sheet of paper towel. He scrunched it up and threw it in the bin. 'Tibs never found out, but I'll always feel bad about what I did.'

Austin's openness was disarming. For the first time ever, Stan felt on a par with the man. The scenario of artist/loser/loafer versus doctor/model citizen/sportsman felt outdated. Each was as flawed as the other.

And with that realisation came an even stronger bond. Their friendship for the first time in over twenty years felt real.

CHAPTER 50

ELIOT BARD

Eliot heard Austin Lamb's car pull into the driveway. His mum heard it, too, and made her way quickly down the corridor to the front door. It had been a scary start to the day.

Austin put his head around Eliot's door. His eyes were dark with worry. 'Are you okay?'

Eliot parked the barley sugar he was sucking in his cheek. 'S'pose so.' His mum told Austin how she'd come in to wake Eliot early, because she had an early start at work – 'meetings back-to-back' – and found him unresponsive. When she did manage to rouse him, his whole body was trembling and he was slurring his words.

'Yeah, like Mum said I was saying *thish ish nof whash*—'

That's when she'd given him an emergency glucagon injection to bring his blood sugar back up. It was super-painful.

When he was more awake, she'd made him eat a banana and two thick slices of peanut-butter toast.

'Well managed, Andrea,' Austin said, putting down his black bag and sitting on the edge of Eliot's bed.

His mum gave a nervous smile. 'I thought…' She became teary. 'I thought we were going to lose him, Austin.'

Austin reached for her hand.

Eliot found himself again thinking about what it would be like to have Austin as his dad, sitting there on his bed at the end of each day, and there every morning to wake him up.

He'd known Eliot since even before he was born. According to his mum, who liked to talk about Austin a lot, Austin used to put a horn-shaped stethoscope to her pregnant belly and listen in, just to be sure Eliot was doing okay inside of her.

It wouldn't be hard to make Austin his dad now that Austin didn't have a wife anymore.

'Perhaps we've increased your overnight insulin a bit too much,' Austin said, scratching his forehead. 'Either that or there's something else brewing that's playing havoc with your blood sugars. I wonder if we should admit you to hospital for a couple of days, just while we tinker with the doses?'

Tinker. Eliot liked that word. But no, he did not want to go to hospital.

He shook his head. 'I don't want to go to hospital.'

'You could have died, Elli.'

'Let's not build this into something it's not, Andrea,' Austin said, turning back to Eliot. 'But your mum is right. We need to be vigilant. I'd rather your sugars ran a bit high than too low.'

'High? But what about Hba1C and all that stuff?'

'I know, I know. It's the opposite to what I've been telling you.'

'And that locum lady.'

Austin chuckled and gave him a wink. 'Yes, and what Dr Robotham said.'

'I hate, hate, hate hospital.'

Austin patted Eliot's hand affectionately. 'I guess we could manage you from home. But I'd want you to ring into the practice with your sugars every morning and every evening for at least a week. Deal?'

Eliot nodded so hard his eyeballs jiggled around in his head.

His mum was not so happy. 'Today of all days I cannot miss work, which means Elli will be home alone all day.'

'Look, I think the disaster has been averted for today,' Austin reassured her. 'And Eliot knows what warning symptoms to look out for, don't you?'

'Yeah. Hunger, sweating, irritability, dizziness. Soon as I get any of those, I'll go eat a banana. Or two. Or three.'

'Perhaps you could ask your neighbour to pop in later to check on him?' Austin suggested. 'Give you peace of mind.'

His mum still looked unconvinced.

'You head on to work, Andrea. Really. I'll recheck Eliot's sugars before I go. Make sure he's one hundred percent. Otherwise, he can hang out at the surgery for the day. Read comics.'

His mum gave a long blink, her worry wrinkles smoothing. 'Alright.'

She kissed Eliot on the forehead.

As soon as she was out of his room, Eliot wiped it off. 'She's such a worrier,' he said, trying to wink.

'You're lucky to have a mum who loves you so much.'

He opened his black bag. 'Talking about comics, look what I found for you at the secondhand bookstore in Devonport.'

Eliot could not believe his eyes. A Tintin hardback: *Red Rackham's Treasure.*

'No way! For me?'

'Yup. Just for you. It's definitely a collectable.'

'You're the best, Austin. The best!'

Austin beamed as he passed Eliot the book.

'Ooh, that looks sore,' Eliot said, scrunching up his face.

Austin twisted his arm to get a better look at the blood-black scab on the side of his wrist. 'War wounds. I came off my mountain bike.'

Eliot sucked in an excited breath. 'What type?'

'Santa Cruz.'

'A Santa Cruz! Woah! They are, like, super-expensive.'

'It's not the cheapest bike on the planet.'

Bike… The silhouette of a thought appeared in Eliot's head. Suddenly its outline was marker-pen clear. 'I forgot!'

'What?'

'I forgot to tell the detective about that Jeremy guy's bike I saw at your practice.'

Austin face turned serious. 'Eliot, we now know how Tibbie, my wife, died. The police case is closed.'

'The thing is, I promised the detective that if I remembered anything about that day—'

Austin took Eliot's forefinger and pricked it. 'Here's hoping for a good reading.'

'A promise is a promise,' Eliot said, watching the blood bloom on his fingertip.

'What?' Austin said irritably.

Eliot carried promises around in a special bag in his head. His mum called it 'the bag of trust'. If you promised to do something, you had to do it. Like unpacking the dishwasher. It was a question of honour.

'I promised the detective.'

'Hmm, good. Your sugars have come right back up,' Austin said, running his hands through his hair. 'In fact,' he sighed, 'we've gone a bit too much the other way now.'

Blood sugars were such a drama. They were like the pirate ship at Rainbows End. Up, up, up, and then stomach-in-your-mouth back down.

Austin had his thinking face on, his lips curled in, his eyes moving from side to side like he was watching a game of tennis. 'You haven't yet taken your usual morning dose of insulin, have you?'

Eliot shook his head.

'Right, well I think you can give yourself a small dose now,' Austin said, straightening. 'Even out your sugars a tad. I'm also going to adjust your evening dose, to make sure you don't dip overnight again. Can you read that?'

Eliot squinted at Austin's scribble. 'Two out of ten for handwriting.'

'Maybe I should go back to school,' Austin said, with an odd voice.

Eliot laughed. 'Back to school! Back to school!'

But Austin didn't laugh. He didn't even smile.

He took out a blank sheet of paper and drew three columns. *Dose*, *time*, and *blood sugar.* 'I want you to give yourself half of your usual morning dose this morning.'

'Now?'

'Once you've washed your hands.'

Eliot jumped up. A person always had to wash their hands before injecting.

'Hang fire there, fellow. Start by making a note of the reduced dose here in the first column.'

Austin liked Eliot to keep his own records. 'Your body, your health, your life' is what he always said.

Eliot wrote down the dose in his neatest handwriting, then looked at his watch. 8.35 am.

'Perhaps write down nine 'o'clock,' Austin suggested. 'You've still got to wash your hands, and anyway nine will be easier to remember for tomorrow's dose.'

Eliot wrote 9.00 am in the second column.

On his return from the bathroom, Austin was on his phone. 'I'm not far off, Gwen. I can squeeze her in before my clinic begins.'

Eliot drew up the new, smaller dose of insulin and pulled up his pyjama top.

'Hang on,' Austin said, ending his call. 'I've another idea. I think I'd prefer you use a different-acting insulin this morning, just until you're out of the woods.' He pulled out a vial from his black bag, slipped on some gloves, unsheathed a fresh syringe, and drew up the new dose. 'Here, I can dispose of that for you,' he said squirting Eliot's syringe into a tissue and depositing the syringe into the sharps box by Eliot's bed.

He handed Eliot the new syringe.

Eliot was puzzled.

'I know it's confusing,' Austin said, not looking at Eliot. 'But it's just for today. To be honest, this is why I was keen for you to go into hospital.'

'Okay, okay,' Eliot said quickly, pinching up some of his

pale spongy belly before Austin could change his mind. Then he hesitated. 'It's not yet nine, though.'

'It'll be fine for today. Twenty minutes is neither here nor there.'

Eliot injected the insulin.

'Here, you can give that to me,' Austin said, capping the syringe and dropping it into his black bag.

'Naughty!' Eliot said, shaking his finger at Austin. 'Never put the cap back on a syringe. It should go straight into the sharps box! That's how we get needle-stick injuries. Remember?'

Austin stood up. He didn't look very happy at being ticked off. His eyes still wouldn't meet Eliot's. 'Text me your sugars in an hour, then again at four o'clock. Okay?'

Eliot nodded.

'Hey, Austin?'

Austin was already at the door. 'Yup,' he said, his back to Eliot.

'Will you please, please be my dad?'

Austin turned. His eyes looked too big for his face and his bottom lip was doing this strange twitching thing. Then he reached for the door handle.

Eliot was feeling a bit weird. 'Will you?'

CHAPTER 51

TERRANCE McDOUGAL

Terrance McDougal rang the doorbell.

'Come on, slowcoach,' he muttered, trying the front door.

He rang the bell again.

Eliot would no doubt have taken full advantage of the little medical episode that morning and be living up to his 'sick' status – lying in late, reading comics, or watching TV on his phone.

Terrance didn't blame the kid. Andrea was very strict and didn't cut him much slack. Eliot really needed a break from his mother's helicopter parenting, albeit well-intentioned.

Terrance made his way around the side of the house. He felt bad checking up on Eliot so soon. The thing was, he'd forgotten all about the RSA luncheon when Andrea called asking him to check on Eliot around midday. So, here he was doing his duty a few hours early.

He steadied himself on the low fence bordering the deck and swung one leg over, then the other, the minimal exertion robbing him of breath.

The sliding door was unlocked.

'Hello, hello!' he called, stepping inside. 'Just me.'

The house was still, except for the overly loud kitchen clock splitting the silence into seconds.

He cleared his throat. 'Eliot?'

Louder. 'Eliot?'

So, the kid had gone AWOL. Fair enough. He'd only be expecting McDougal to check up on him at midday. That gave him three-plus hours unmonitored. And fair enough! He was almost twenty-two, for goodness' sake. By the time Terrance had turned twenty-two he'd been making his own way in the world for several years and had seen more of life than what a North Shore suburb had to offer.

He felt for Andrea; it couldn't have been easy being a solo mum, especially with a lad like Eliot. But she was doing him no favours mollycoddling him. He was a bright fellow. Just needed to be given more independence. Needed to make a mistake or two. Learn the hard way.

Terrance looked around. The kitchen bench was covered in crumbs. A fly was exploring the inside of a banana peel. The lid had been left off a jar of peanut butter. Andrea was usually very particular about cleanliness. She must have had to leave in a hurry.

Her African violets lining the kitchen windowsill did not look in good shape; she was probably over-watering them. There was a power bill stuck to the fridge. Terrance couldn't help but glance at the invoiced amount. More than he paid for power. But there were two of them.

He peered up the corridor. Eliot's bedroom door was ajar.

Terrance shuffled towards it, curiosity more than anything driving him. It was a bit like walking past lit windows on an evening walk.

Eliot's room was warm and musty, and smelt like student digs.

The kid was lying at an angle across his bed, his mouth wide open.

Terrance reversed, feeling guilty for having intruded. How often did Eliot get to sleep in? At least he was home, and Terrance didn't have to report to Andrea that her son had gone walkabout.

He decided to make himself a cup of tea and wait for Eliot

to wake. Just so long as he could get away by elevenish, he'd get to the RSA on time, before all the good bits of the buffet had gone.

Terrance woke with a start. The phone was ringing.

He looked around disoriented, his mouth dry and furry.

A blue couch came into focus. A sliding door with a peeling flower motif. The old upright piano. Aah yes. The Bards' house. He must have dozed off after his cuppa.

He looked at his watch. He'd been asleep for almost an hour. If he wanted to get to the RSA, he was going to have to hightail it.

He hauled himself out of the armchair. Eliot would likely be up by now, but if not, he'd have to wake him.

'Eliot! It's me. Terrence McDougal,' he said knocking on the open bedroom door.

Eliot hadn't moved, his shape still a slant of torso and limbs, and his mouth still open catching flies.

Black spots started crowding Terrance's vision. He'd stood up too quickly. He steadied himself against the chest of drawers.

A small faux-silver sporting trophy teetered. Terrance fumbled, caught it, then went and dropped the blinking thing. It hit the ground with a crash, pieces flying across the room.

'Damnation!' he shouted, picking up the *Most Improved Player* plaque and severed silver torso.

'I'm so sorry. I'll get it repair—' Eliot had not stirred.

'Eliot?' McDougal said, shaking the boy's arm. It was cold.

McDougal lowered himself to the floor and put an ear to Eliot's mouth.

Instantly he was back on Fanshawe Street, kneeling beside a young woman who'd been knocked off her bicycle, her face colourless, her chest still.

All Terrance could hear was the sound of his own breathing. His own breathing. His own breathing.

CHAPTER 52

STAN ANDINO

Stan woke early. He hadn't closed the curtains properly the night before and Monday morning had rudely forced its way in.

He stared at the yellow-brown stain which had bloomed on the ceiling after the last heavy rain. He couldn't keep pretending it wasn't there. It was time to call a roofing contractor, or the damage would become a major.

Kaching! Yet another expense. One step forward, three back.

It had been a good weekend, though. Good, as in not goddamned awful. For so long, his days had been framed by awfulness, but this morning, save for the ceiling, he felt calm. Hopeful. Perhaps he'd finally reached the bottom and the only way was up.

He still felt a confusion of feelings towards Carmen. One side of the double bed was empty and cold. He was lonely. Achingly lonely. He'd lost his soulmate, lover, best friend. And yet, threading through this desolation was relief that most of the horribleness had died with her death.

Austin had reassured him that these conflicted feelings would change over time. That Stan and Carmen's many happy years together would ultimately win out over the horrendous past few months. And that hopefully the same would happen for the boys, too.

'If you took any family photos of Carmen when she

was sick, put them away,' Austin advised. 'Help Leon and Reuben establish memories of their mother you want them to hold onto. Only keep out photos of the good times. Talk about them. Embellish them with detail. It's amazing how susceptible to suggestion memory can be.'

He hoped Austin was right.

The dinner at Austin's had come as a real surprise. Not so much the sharing of food and wine like old times. Not even the honesty between them, which announced a new intimacy in their friendship. It was more the implicit forgiveness sewn into all these things. Austin's actions spoke of someone willing to look beyond the awfulness. Friendship didn't get truer than that.

As for the mysterious texts, they didn't bother Stan as much anymore. He'd largely managed to detach himself from the anxiety they sparked. Another one had come through just the night before, dinging as he was climbing into bed.

Sorry.

Tame. But puzzling.

The police hadn't pursued the texts further. Clearly, they were not a priority. Maybe, when Stan was feeling brave enough to face the detective again, he'd might remind him of his promise to track down the texter. He felt as if he was finally starting to move on, helped, as callous as it sounded, by the fact that Carmen had been cremated. He'd disregarded her wishes. Not that she'd ever formalised anything on paper. It had been just one discussion as newly-weds, about dying and wills and organ donation, the heavy topics broached with the academic ease of youth.

If she was to die first, she wanted to be buried in some beautiful place where he and any children they might have, could visit. She'd missed having that with her favourite grandmother; no physical place to go and pay homage.

The thing was, Stan couldn't bear the thought of the cancer growing like some organism underground. Irrational or not, he wanted it and the havoc it had wrought, burnt to a crisp. Gone.

He climbed out of bed and padded to the kitchen to make himself a coffee. It would be his first full day back at the Arts Centre. Nine until four. A regular working day. Back in the saddle again.

'I've got a chemistry assignment due the day we get back from holidays,' Reuben moaned as he climbed into the car after hockey practice. 'It's so unfair.'

Stan stopped at a red traffic light. Holidays already? Carmen had always been in charge of the school calendar.

The light turned green. 'Right, well, why not try and get the project done before the holidays then?'

'No-one says project anymore, Dad.'

'What?'

'I said, no one says project. It's an assignment.'

Stan turned right.

'Where we going?'

'I'm just swinging by the practice to drop off the togs Austin lent you guys on Friday night.'

'Do we have to? I've got so much homework!'

'I'll just be two tics.'

His plan was to return the togs and tell Austin about the direct debit he'd set up. Twenty dollars a week. All he could afford, but a measure of his commitment to repay Tibbie's money.

'Can't you do it another day?' Reuben grumbled.

But Stan wasn't listening. He was focused on the police vehicle reversing out of the medical practice car park.

The waiting room was empty, filled only with the chatter of radio talkback – just loud enough to ensure patient privacy, but not too loud to intrude.

Stan stopped. Swallowed. Started to retreat. Austin and his receptionist, Gwen, were behind the reception desk, locked in an embrace.

They both swung around.

Gwen tried to smile, then disappeared behind the file partition.

'Hi,' Stan muttered, feeling awkward, shocked, confused. 'I'm just dropping these off.' He lifted the bag containing the togs. 'Thanks again for Friday night.'

Austin stared at him.

'The togs you leant the boys.'

'Oh, right. Ta.'

'Sorry, I didn't mean to intrude,' Stan mumbled.

Austin shook his head. Put up a hand. 'We've just had some… uh…' His voice sounded strained. Choked. 'Bad news. About one of my most longstanding patients.'

Stan heard soft sobbing coming from behind the partition.

'Oh, jeez. I'm sorry.' He put the bag with the togs down on a chair. 'I'll leave you in peace—'

'No.' Austin's voice was like an anchor sinking into soft sand. 'Stay. Please.'

He sent Gwen on her way, reassuring her he'd do the computer backup, then pulled up a chair next to Stan in the waiting room.

He looked grey as he stared into the middle distance. 'Such a cool kid,' he said, shaking his head. 'Or I should say, young adult. He was always reminding his mum and me that he was twenty-one.'

'That's far too young to die. How did it happen?'

'He isn't dead.'

'No?' Stan was confused.

'He's in a coma,' Austin said, his voice husky.

Stan waited for more.

'I saw him just this morning. Right as rain. Well, he'd had a small scare, but he seemed to be good. Good. He was fine when I left him.'

It occurred to Stan how life and death were always in such close proximity. Two sides of the same coin. He couldn't begin to imagine the stress of Austin's job.

'I'm just angry with myself,' Austin said. 'I suggested we

admit him to hospital to get his sugars under control. I should have stuck to my guns. But he could be so damned stubborn.'

'You're a good doctor, Austin. One of the best. Sometimes things are beyond anyone's control.'

'Dad?'

They both swung round, any residual colour draining from Austin's face. He looked like he'd seen a ghost, but it was only Leon.

'What's taking you so long? Oh, hi Austin. Dad, I got a stack of homework to do.'

He'd clearly been sent as Reuben's emissary. Leon was never fussed about homework.

Stan got up. 'Austin, why don't you come back to our place for a bite? It will just be whatever – eggs on toast.'

Austin shook his head. 'Thanks, but I want to stop in at the hospital on my way home.'

CHAPTER 53

TERRANCE MCDOUGAL

Eliot's chest rose and fell as air was forced into his lungs and then noisily extracted. Terrance gripped Andrea Bard's hand tightly. His tremor was worse than usual, but it was hard to tell how much of the trembling belonged to him, and how much was Andrea's.

Terrance's thoughts were on a repeat circuit as he covered the same ground over and over. Thank goodness he'd gone around to check on Eliot earlier than asked. Had he done so at midday, Eliot might be dead. However, what if him finding Eliot early meant that the lad would live, but with brain damage? Terrance felt sick at the thought. If only he'd tried to wake the boy as soon as he arrived.

He was no stranger to death; his time in the Malayan jungle had seen to that. Yet somehow death during wartime was different. A recognised hazard. Losing a young life in the ordinariness of a regular day… that was something different altogether. He was still haunted by the death of the young woman knocked off her pushbike in front of him on Fanshawe Street, her lithe body animated by adrenalin one minute, the next limp and twisted on the tarmac.

He could not bear the thought that they might lose the boy. Eliot Bard was a stellar individual able to improve a person's day in an instant with his goofy enthusiasm and delightfully innocent quirks. He was no fool either. By gosh, he was no fool.

'Andrea?'

Austin Lamb put his head around the hospital curtain.

Terrance had met the doctor a handful of times over the years. He remembered him as being a suave, athletic fellow. Today, though, he looked grim, his eyes sunken into his head and his face pasty. The poor man had just lost his wife, yet his professional responsibility could not be easily paused because of personal tragedy.

Andrea did not look up.

'Doctor,' Terrance said, levering himself out of his chair.

Lamb put a hand on his shoulder. 'Don't get up. Please.'

'I should never have gone to work, Austin. Never!' Andrea blurted out, her gaze fixed on her son.

'I know how you must be feeling, Andrea,' the doctor said. 'But you can't blame yourself. We had no reason to suspect Elli would dip again so suddenly. After I got to work this morning, I even phoned a colleague at the hospital to tee up an appointment for him at the Diabetes Clinic, just to help fine-tune his regimen.'

He picked up the chart at the foot of the bed, as if desperate to have something to do with his hands.

'I should have been quicker off the mark,' Terrance said.

The doctor glanced up. 'So, you found him? What time was that?'

Terrance felt as if he was being asked to testify before a jury. He cleared his throat and grabbed his right hand with his left, to stop it shaking. 'Around eleven.'

'It's not your fault, Terrance,' Andrea said. 'It is definitely not your fault.'

But Terrance had been at the house for almost an hour before that. 'The thing is. You see. Well, I got there sometime before eleven. It was more like ten, actually.'

They both stared at him.

'Ten? I don't understand,' Andrea stuttered. 'I got a call from the paramedics just before twelve.'

Terrance's entire body was trembling now, as if the shakes

in his right arm had jumped the gate and were roaming free. 'I thought he was sleeping. Didn't want to disturb him.' His voice was rising. 'You said to check on him around lunchtime, but I had an RSA luncheon to attend, so I went over early. He was sleeping. Or so I thought. I stayed in the lounge and checked on him again about eleven. Eleven-ten. That's when…'

Andrea's face contorted with this new information, her expression navigating the territory of what ifs.

'Would that extra hour… could it… I mean… could it have made the difference?' Terrance asked.

Austin Lamb rolled his top lip under his bottom teeth. 'To be absolutely honest, yes.'

Terrance was reeling. His actions possibly having such terrible consequences.

'But why did his sugars dip so low in the first place?' Andrea asked. 'I mean, the paramedics couldn't even get a reading!'

The doctor coloured, as if he was now before the jury. 'Beats me. I suggested he take half his usual morning dose of insulin at nine, because his sugars had already started to rebound after the glucagon and big breakfast. I didn't want them to swing too high. I had to head off about 8.45 am to see another urgent patient at the practice.'

He walked round to Andrea. Rested a hand on her back. 'But I can assure you that such a small dose of his usual short-acting insulin would not have sent Eliot into a hypoglycaemic coma.'

She stood up, turned to Austin, and buried her head in his shirt. 'I just don't understand,' she said between sobs. 'It doesn't make sense.'

'It's possible our Eliot made a mistake with the dosing,' Dr Lamb said.

'But he's usually so goo—'

'Or there's something else going on in the background that is making his sugar control volatile. At the end of the day, Andrea, you must not blame yourself. The diabetes is responsible for this, not any one of us.'

CHAPTER 54

STAN ANDINO

'Apologies, in advance, Stan. But you know what they say, if you don't put your finger in it, you put your foot in it.'

Stan gave a half-hearted chuckle and tried not to squirm as he lay on the examination plinth.

He was not a willing patient. Needles and blood and all that stuff. Even the smell of antiseptic put the wind up him. Of course, he'd had to steel himself when Carmen got sick. He couldn't be feeling lightheaded at the first whiff of a hospital, when she was the one with cancer. Cancer. That word still sent a metallic fear through him.

The thing was, he'd noticed a change in his toilet habits for a few weeks now. He'd tried to ignore it, what with so much going down. He wasn't even sure until a week back if Austin would keep him and the boys on his books.

He'd mentioned it when they were at Austin's for dinner. Austin insisted Stan make an appointment. 'You're all Reuben and Leon have now,' he'd said. 'You've got to do the right thing by them.'

Austin removed his gloves now. 'Can't feel anything sinister. But it's probably prudent to get a colonoscopy. You haven't had one before, have you?'

A colonoscopy! Stan did not want one of those.

He got changed and sat down opposite Austin, who was

already typing up the referral. His friend looked haggard; the weeks of anguish were starting to take their toll.

'How are things at home this week?' Austin asked, almost robotically.

'Up and down. But you know…' Stan shrugged. It didn't feel right to be complaining, when Austin was clearly having a rough time of it, too. He wondered if the man had his own GP.

'How's your young patient? The one who was in a coma?'

Austin rubbed his palm across his mouth. 'Still hasn't woken up.'

'Jeez. I'm sorry.'

'Yeah. It's pretty fucked-up.'

Pretty fucked-up? Stan had never heard Austin speak in this way, nor look so defeated.

'I've taken up enough of your time,' Stan said, reaching for the referral.

Austin held onto it. 'Do you think you'll ever… I don't know… date again?' he asked.

'Woah! Left-field question, no segue required,' Stan said, with a grin.

If he were honest, the thought had crossed his mind, but at this stage it was confusingly tied up with finding a mother figure for Leon and Reuben.

He shook his head. 'You?'

'I never thought I would have been able to…'

Never thought. A silent 'but' hung in the air between them. Stan nodded. He understood. Same, same.

'I definitely wasn't looking for it,' Austin went on. 'You could have knocked me down with a feather.'

Stan felt as if his mind had momentarily wandered off and he'd been left behind somewhere in the conversation.

'You're kidding me?'

Austin was tracing imaginary circles on the desk with his forefinger. 'I know. So soon. It looks wrong.'

Austin had never cared what others thought, his

self-confidence verging on arrogance. And yet, here he was, tentative, embarrassed, almost asking for permission.

'Do I know her?'

'Don't judge me, Stan.'

'Me? Judge you! I'm in no position to do that. What's more, Tibbie would be happy to know you were doing okay.'

Austin ran his hands through his hair. 'You think so?'

'For sure! So, are you going to tell me who it is then?'

Austin scratched the back of his head and sucked his teeth loudly. 'The whole thing crept up on us unawares.'

Us.

'She would drop around to see how I was doing. Bring over a meal. That sort of thing. The friendship deepened. I—'

'Spit it out, goddamnit!'

'Abby. Abby Manderson.'

Stan swallowed. Nodded. Tried to smile.

'She's separated from her husband. You know that?'

Stan shrugged. Nodded again.

'The thing is, it's not like I could replace Tibs. Not ever! I mean, that would be impossible. But for the first time since this whole nightmare began, I feel almost happy. Am I a bad person for wanting to feel happy again?' Stan's head was spinning. Nothing made sense. Austin did not look particularly happy. Perhaps the ravages of the past months were only embedding themselves into his face now. It would take time for new love to plump out the hollows.

But Abby Manderson, of all people! The woman grated him. Her excessiveness, saccharine sweetness, her raucous, dominate-the-room laughter. Saying that, he was glad for his friend. Austin had had one hell of a time. He deserved some good in his life again. He did. Stan just hoped Manderson wouldn't wheedle her way permanently into his friend's life.

The man was in the throes of grief. Rebound relationships did not have the best success.

He stood up, slapped Austin on the shoulder. 'Good on you, mate.'

Then a thought struck him. He turned. 'Isn't Abby… isn't she one of your patients?'

Austin snorted. 'Used to be. Not anymore. Don't worry. It's all proper and above board.'

Stan forced a laugh. 'I'm pleased for you. I really am.'

CHAPTER 55

RAMESH BANDARA

Ramesh parked on the road. An ingrained habit when visiting private residences. If he had to make a quick getaway, it was no fun reversing up a driveway at high speed. It also allowed for the element of surprise. Furthermore, a police vehicle in a driveway was a sure way to get neighbours' tongues wagging, and he didn't want any sticky-beaks getting unnecessarily excited.

The visit was more to appease Terrance McDougal than anything else. The old guy, Eliot Bard's neighbour, must have been in his late eighties, early nineties. He'd caught two buses in to see Ramesh at the station and had been rather distressed. Apparently, Eliot was in a bad way in hospital. A complication of his diabetes. McDougal wanted to pass on some information on behalf of the kid, who was now in a coma. 'It's the least I can do for him, Detective.'

Ramesh had long ago learnt not to ignore unsolicited information and tip-offs; there was no room for complacency in his line of work. People's legitimate concerns always had to be addressed and checked out, even if only to be subsequently discarded. It was easy to get blinkered in the job, especially when on the home straight. And even more so after thinking you'd crossed the finish line.

He couldn't abide the idea of playing any part in a wrongful conviction, even unwittingly. It was a fear that had skulked in the wings throughout his career. He could remember his dad sharing something similar, about being terrified as a junior doctor of mistakenly certifying someone dead when they were in fact still alive. Each profession clearly had its bogeyman. Ramesh's fear of sending the wrong person down had grown huge and all-consuming during his depression. It had got to a point where he couldn't progress a single case without going back over and over it, in case he'd missed something. His need to reassure himself that he hadn't stuffed up became incapacitating. It's what eventually forced him into sick leave. He was much better now; the antidepressants had blunted these anxieties. But a grumbling background dread of stuffing up still threaded through his days.

Carmen Andino had not had to endure a trial, nor spend any time in jail. However, that she'd been implicated in a crime, extenuating circumstances or not, would without doubt leave a shadow over her sons' lives, influencing how they felt about themselves, the life-choices they made, their baseline level of happiness.

Ramesh didn't expect this investigative mission to yield much, but if nothing else, it would mean he would be able to sleep easier knowing that his original conclusion had been sound. There was also something about Hilary Stark's reserve when he told her he'd decided to lay charges against Carmen Andino that still troubled him. Something about how cautious and measured she was, her reticence almost challenging his conviction. She was good! Too bad she wasn't going to pursue her detective training.

The house was on a full section – an increasingly rare thing, with developers carving up any decent section into lots the size of postage stamps. Full sections were largely the prerogative of the wealthy now, or old people clutching onto the family home as extended family members and developers circled.

The bungalow had seen better days; the front door's sherbet-green paint was peeling, and the concrete steps were chipped. It would have been quite characterful in its day, with its bay windows and green joinery. Sadly, the decay paralleled the owner's health. According to Gwen, Lamb's receptionist, Lila Nunn suffered from severe dementia and required round-the-clock care.

Ramesh rang the doorbell and peered through the frosted-glass panel. A shadow approached.

He stepped back just as a young fellow, maybe in his late twenties, opened the door.

Ramesh held up the blue ID card hanging around his neck. The validation that only came with an official card. He wondered if it was the same for his fairer-skinned colleagues.

The man's face registered the same surprise everyone exhibited upon finding a police officer on their doorstep. But Ramesh was looking for more than mere generic surprise: That flicker of fear. The scramble to camouflage guilt. Even an overconfident charm.

'Hiya,' the guy said, fingering his tidy dreadlocks with long, bony fingers. Tidy dreadlocks, mused Ramesh – an oxymoron, if ever there was one. The man looked like an archetypal hippy, with twine bracelets on his wrists, metal earrings punched through his earlobes, and loose khaki clothing.

'Jeremy Booth?'

'Yup.'

'Detective Sergeant Bandara. Wonder if I might ask you a few questions.'

The man straightened. 'In relation to?'

'I'm tying up some loose ends on an investigation in the area.'

The guy shrugged. 'Sure. It's just—'

'Frederico!' A woman's deep voice boomed up the passage.

'Come in,' he said, ushering Ramesh inside. 'I can't leave my charge for long.'

Frederico? He thought the guy's name was Jeremy.

He followed him down the dingy corridor. A strong smell of urine and something vegetable-savoury hung in the air.

The corridor opened onto what would have once been the lounge, but in addition to a couch and television set, it housed a hospital bed, microwave, wheelchair, commode...

Locked behind a tray, in a sort of adult highchair, was a dishevelled old woman with leaky red eyes. In front of her was a plastic bowl of orange slop.

Note to self, Ramesh thought, *draft a living will*. He never wanted to be kept alive if he found himself in this wretched state.

'Navin!' the old woman cried, stretching out her hands and beckoning Ramesh over. 'Come, come.'

'She'll have mistaken you for some Indian friend or other,' the man said. 'It'll be less distressing for her if you just play along.'

'I'm not Indi—'Ramesh stopped himself. This was not the time to make such a point. He approached the old woman.

'Just in time,' she said, taking one of his hands in hers and massaging it. Her nails were embedded with grime. 'I thought you were going to miss dinner.'

'I wouldn't miss your dinner for the world,' Ramesh said, his father's words to his mother spilling out with the ease of memory.

Ramesh smiled to himself as he thought about his mother's crispy hoppers and delicious sour fish curry.

'Lila, would you like to watch *Sesame Street*?' the caregiver asked, wiping her mouth, and removing the plate of what looked like pumpkin porridge.

'Louder,' she cried.

He unmuted the TV.

Ramesh winced at the volume. 'Is there somewhere private we can chat?'

'I can't leave her unattended. But fire away. She's very deaf.'

Ramesh cleared his throat and glanced around the room. 'Do you own a racing bike?'

The man turned sharply. 'Yes… Why?'

'Do you have it here?'

'I keep it behind the shed,' the guy said, indicating vaguely outside.

'And how often *are* you here?'

'What did you say this was about?'

The old woman burst out laughing. Something on the screen.

Ramesh pulled back the net curtains and peered outside. 'As I said, just some loose ends to tie up in a homicide investigation. I'm following up on the sighting of a racing bike seen in the area.'

'A homicide!'

'Mind if I take a look at the bike?' he said, trying the French door.

'I don't have a key for that door. You'll have to go around the front.'

'Right you are. What did you say your hours are?'

'I didn't.'

'And they are?'

'Monday to Friday, seven till seven.'

'Long shifts! Ever get relief?'

The man's jaw softened. 'There's a night nurse, and then the agency covers weekends.'

'So, you can't get away during the day, not even for a half-hour break?'

Ramesh's empathetic tone was working. The man's guarded demeanour loosened.

'Lila's doctor prescribes sedatives, which I use sparingly. Typically, half a tablet after lunch will see her sleep for a couple of hours, freeing me up to do paperwork or anything else pressing.'

'Such as?'

Jeremy looked at his feet. 'I sometimes have to slip away to collect her meds from the pharmacy, if they can't deliver them, or, you know, pop down the road to buy milk.

Unofficially of course,' he added quickly. 'I'm never gone for much more than twenty minutes.'

Ramesh made his way outside via the front door. The back of the property was overgrown, the grass waist-high and the dark-green ivy rampant. He followed a thin track of flattened grass to the wooden shed on the back boundary. Around the side of it, out of sight from the road, was an old racing bike. Rusted metallic body. Red tape wound around the downcurved handlebars, the ends peeling off. It matched the bike Eliot had described to Mr McDougal.

On his way back to the house Ramesh spotted Jeremy Booth watching him through the net curtains.

'A bike very similar to yours was spotted near the scene of a homicide,' Ramesh explained, when they met again at the front door. 'A forensics team will be here shortly to examine it.' He smiled reassuringly. 'And likely exclude it from the investigation. Would you be willing to give us a sample of your DNA? It's nothing more than a mouth swab.'

'I guess. That's pretty full-on... Am I under suspicion for s—'

'Excellent. Thank you,' Ramesh said quickly, before doubt got the better of the man and made the whole process that much harder. 'One last question. Do you keep a record of when you give Mrs Nunn her "extra" medication? I'm interested specifically in Wednesday 29th May.'

The man hesitated. Looked down again at Ramesh's ID card.

'Wait here. I'll get Lila's notes.'

He returned a few minutes later with a lever-arch file.

Ramesh didn't like ring-binders when it came to evidence. A page could easily be removed or replaced.

Jeremy turned the pages. 'Here we are. The twenty-ninth.'

LN up through night with productive cough and fever 39.5°c. Increased resp rate. House-call am. Doxy BD for chest infection. 1st dose IV.

Ramesh was impressed with the hospital-like records kept for a dementing old woman living in her own home.

Lorazepam 2 pm.

He knew about Lorazepam. He and Emily had both been prescribed it after Joshua died.

'So you, what, went to the pharmacy to fill the script for the antibiotics?' Jeremy squinted at the page.

'Her first dose was given intravenously by the doctor. I guess I'll have gone to pick up her orals after lunch, once she'd had her sedative.'

'You guess?'

The man flushed. 'Lila's had three bouts of pneumonia in the past two months. It's hard to keep track. She has chronic airways disease.'

A grunting sound was coming from the lounge. 'Frederico, I need a poo!'

'Best I let you go,' said Bandara, waving the man away. 'Thanks for your assistance.'

Jeremy Booth hovered. 'Is that it?'

'I'll wait up on the road for forensics.'

CHAPTER 56

RAMESH BANDARA

Ramesh shut his office door and sank down in his chair. After the forensics had finished at Lila Nunn's, he'd dropped into the hospital to see how young Eliot Bard was doing.

Eliot looked less of a kid lying comatose in the hospital bed and more the unshaven, twenty-one-year-old man he was.

Ramesh didn't stay long. It was hard to see Eliot's mother leaning in so earnestly, as if willing her boy to get up and finish a race.

Ramesh was no doctor, but it had already been two days…

Loss of a young person was just wrong. A complete disruption of the natural order of life.

He and Emily had farewelled his three-week-old son in a very private service – parents, grandparents, priest, and of course Joshua in the tiniest of caskets. A bonsaied version of reality.

No one spoke about what their wee man had achieved. No friends squashed into uncomfortably upright pews. Just a blessing and the unconvincing promise of eternal life. And for the first time since Ramesh had flouted his parents' wish for him to marry a Sri Lankan woman and live a life aligned with their beliefs, he felt the loss of what he'd given up keenly. The embrace of a community. The scaffolding of a religion. Buddhism cultivated an acceptance of what could not be changed. A recognition of the importance of death in the cycle of life. Was a Christian farewell the right thing? Had he robbed Joshua of a safe rebirth?

He wondered now what demons Andrea Bard was battling as she held her son's hand.

The phone rang, interrupting his ponderings.

'Bandara speaking.'

'Ramesh, it's Nic from the lab. Can you talk?'

'About the cricket?' He knew Nic would be hurting after their dismal loss over the weekend.

'No! It's that racing bike.'

'What have you got for me?'

'Lots of the owner's fingerprints,' Nic said. 'As you'd expect.'

Ramesh nodded. 'Any others?'

'Nope.'

Ramesh lifted the lever under his chair. The chair dropped abruptly. He'd hoped for something else. Something definitive to hang his hat on.

'Did they match any of the prints lifted from the cigarette butts and other crap we found in the clearing on the cliff?'

'Afraid not.'

He could hear Nic chewing frenetically on the other end of the line. Clearly the guy was still battling with tobacco withdrawal.

'Thanks for letting me know. Appreciate it.'

'There is something else.'

Ramesh leant forward. Smoothed the crease between his eyebrows with his fingers.

'We found a trace of blood on one of the pedals.'

'On one of the pedals?' Ramesh repeated. 'Unusual place to find blood, unless the person was riding barefoot, or already had some on the sole of their shoe.'

He cast his mind back to Tibbie Lamb's postmortem findings. The pathologist had attributed all of her abrasions to the fall.

'Not that uncommon,' Nic said. 'I'm forever grazing my calf when I put my foot down to stop in traffic.'

'So, it's your blood then?' Ramesh said with a grin.

'Very funny.'

'First rule of cycling, Nic. Use your brakes, not your feet.'

Nic chuckled down the line. 'Thanks for the tip, Sarah Ulmer.'

'I suppose I'm going to have to wait a month of Sundays for the DNA. You know I'm already on borrowed time with the boss?'

'Leave it with me,' Nic said. 'I'll see what I can do. One condition.'

'Name it.'

'I don't want to hear about that bloody cricket score ever again!'

'Easy.'

And Nic was true to his word. He must have put in a rush request because Ramesh got an answer to the blood in record time. He owed him a beer.

CHAPTER 57

RAMESH BANDARA

As soon as Ramesh had put down the phone to Nic he rang Hilary. She didn't pick up, which wasn't surprising; she rarely looked at her phone during work hours. Saying that, she could safely be relied on to return his call at the end of her day. It had become a bit of an evening routine, the two of them talking through developments in the Lamb case which, like a lizard, kept regrowing its tail.

Hilary had been keen to accompany Ramesh back to Lila Nunn's house. In fact, she'd sounded almost enthusiastic, which was saying something for someone who rarely showed a skerrick of emotion. However, as Lila's caregiver only worked during the week, and Hilary was only free to pursue the Lamb case out of hours, Ramesh returned alone.

Dreadlocked Jeremy's defences were up, and he was a lot less forthcoming than on the first visit.

Ramesh mused how time could be a guilty man's friend, affording the opportunity for preparation to anticipated questions. But it could also be an innocent man's enemy, allowing fear and worry to nibble away at a person's calm and self-confidence. Which camp Jeremy Booth fell into was not yet clear.

The guy invited Ramesh into a sparsely furnished room off the main corridor. Melamine desk, chair, low-slung camping bed. On the desk was Lila's clinical file and a baby monitor.

The baby monitor caught Ramesh by surprise and took him straight back to the birth of Nikita, their second daughter. He'd thought the monitor would buy him and Emily some peace of mind after Joshua's death. But it only made things worse. They'd lie in bed listening to Nikita's every breath and grunt, the slightest hiss or crackle or absence of sound sending Emily dashing into the nursery. In the end, she chose to sleep beside the cot. And how could he blame her? He'd been naïve to think a piece of electronic equipment from Baby City could change the trajectory of their lives, their marriage. As the stats went, many marriages did not survive the loss of a child.

'Is this where you catch some shut-eye?' he asked, looking around the room.

'It's mainly for the night nurses,' Jeremy said tightly. 'I come here to do paperwork when Lila is sleeping during the day.'

Three-twenty pm. Lila was asleep now. Ramesh had timed his visit deliberately. An hour twenty after the old woman would have received her sedative.

With only the one chair in the room, both men stood as they went over the day in question again.

Jeremy had cycled to work from his house in Hillcrest, arriving for the shift change just before 7 am. Lila Nunn was not well; she'd been up all night coughing. Doctor Lamb was notified and a house visit scheduled for first thing that morning.

Jeremy paged through the clinical notes, then swung the file round to face Ramesh. 'The doctor came,' he said, 'changed Lila's antibiotics. Gave her the first dose IV.'

'And you went to fulfil the new script for the tablets that morning?'

'As I already told you the other day,' Jeremy said deliberately, the skin over his jaw rippling. 'I can't leave Lila alone when she's awake. I would have nipped out around this time to go to the pharmacy.'

'So, you never give her a sedative earlier? Say, in the morning, if the situation demands it?'

'Disrupting the routine of a dementia patient can have significant repercussions,' the caregiver said coldly. 'Routine offers security in a frighteningly discombobulated world. Anyway, as I said before, she'd had her first dose IV. There was no hurry. The next dose was only scheduled for the evening. It was a BD dosing.'

'BD?'

'Twice daily.'

Ramesh wondered whether the guy was trying to intimidate him with medical terms and words like discombobulated. Who used words like that?

'Right. So, you went out later that afternoon?'

'Lila's pharmacy is at Northcross. Ring them if you like.'

'Did anyone else use your bike that day?'

Jeremy swatted away air with the back of his hand. 'Like who? No-one knows where I leave it. You saw it yourself. It's well hidden from the road.'

'But it's possible?'

The guy gave a petulant sigh. 'Sure. Anything's possible. I wouldn't know, though, would I?' he said, gesticulating towards the windows.

The man had a point. The entire house was shrouded in thick net curtains, leaving Ramesh mildly claustrophobic. Unless a person was standing up close to them, the outside was a grey blur.

'What's your morning routine with Lila?'

'Breakfast. Shower. TV. Lunch. Sedative. Sleep—' The guy was definitely on his guard, his words spare, his tone clipped.

'The TV, is it always on?' Even with Lila asleep now, Bandara could hear the box blasting down the corridor.

'Yup, a reassuring constant. Though sometimes I mute it. The noise can do your head in.'

No kidding.

'And you shower Lila in the bathroom?'

The guy opened his hands. 'Where else?'

Ramesh ignored the sarcasm. That Jeremy was getting

worked up was not a bad thing. People made mistakes when they allowed their emotions to take over.

'Actually, mind if I use it. The bathroom, that is. Not the shower.'

'Across the way, first on your right.'

Ramesh closed the bathroom door and looked for a means to lock it. No bolt or key. In fact, the entire room appeared to have been modified with health and safety in mind – an extra wide doorway for wheelchair access, an open shower minus a lip, solid handrails next to the toilet and in the shower, lever faucets, and a sensor light, which came on as soon as anyone walked into the room. Just as well, too, because a tall metal cabinet had been pushed right up against the window, blocking out any natural light.

Ramesh mastered the cabinet's child-proof latch and peered inside.

The shelves were stacked with medical supplies. Bandages, incontinence pads, plasters, antiseptic solution, enemas, denture cleaner. Even a suture kit.

He leant into the shower and turned it on. An extractor fan automatically began sucking the air with a monotonous drone.

'Well, that's all for now,' Ramesh said, finally emerging. 'Appreciate your time.'

Jeremy eyed Bandara's water-splashed trousers. 'No problem.'

Wandering back up the driveway, Ramesh spotted a bonnet of mauve hair bobbing just above the creosoted fence line. He peered over, his gaze meeting that of tiny woman with coral-coloured lipstick and clip-on pearl earrings.

'Goodness me, you gave me a fright,' she said, dropping a few inches. She must have been standing on her tiptoes.

He chortled. 'And you me.'

'Is everything alright with Lila?'

'Yes. Yes. All good,' Ramesh said, with a doctor's certainty.

'I don't like to pry, but her family never visits. Never! I keep an eye on the poor dear. You're not family, are you?'

A classic sticky-beak. She'd no doubt seen the patrol car on the street.

'I guess you must get to see all the comings and goings.'

'I don't snoop, if that's what you are implying.'

'No. No.'

'I can't see over the fence. Not even from my porch. But you're lovely and tall.'

Ramesh was an exception to the rule. The average height for a male Sri Lankan was five foot six. His father always used to joke that the postman in Colombo had been very tall.

'I can recognise car engines, though,' Lila's neighbour said brightly. 'I'm pretty good at that. The night nurse has a VW beetle, and what a Teutonic racket that makes! Now the doctor's car, it's more of an expensive purr.'

'An expensive purr?' Ramesh said, trying to hold his grin. 'Mercedes is German-made, too, isn't it?'

She tilted her neck briskly. Clearly, she was not someone who took kindly to being challenged.

Not wishing to alienate her, he threw a wink her way. 'Chief Ops for the neighbourhood, I see.'

The woman gave a smoker's cackle, clearly delighted with the title.

'How about Ms Nunn's daytime carer? You hear him arrive and leave?'

'The one that looks like a Rastafarian. Hmm! My ears aren't that good, dear! He has a pushbike.'

'So, it's mainly her medical team that visit.'

'*Only* her medical team,' the woman said pointedly. 'It's a disgrace. And mark my words when poor Lila pops her clogs, all the family will come scurrying out of the woodwork.'

'I guess the doctor visits pretty regularly?'

The old woman sighed with melodramatic resignation. 'Goes through spells. Lately Lila's chest has been terribly bad. She has emphysema, you know.'

'Yes. A shame. Smoking's the culprit, they tell me.'

The woman pursed her lips. Ramesh had got a whiff of cigarette smoke from over the fence.

'Some weeks back the doctor was here more than he wasn't,' she went on. 'Such a dedicated physician, that man. And he's had tragedy to contend with in his own life, you know. It's always the good people. Not the degenerates or politicians.'

Ramesh raised his eyebrows quizzically. It was best not to interrupt a garrulous informant. She reminded him of his mum – an authority on everything.

'Lost his wife in May. Terrible business. She took her own life. Well, no one said as much, but you don't jump off a cliff unless, well, you know.'

'Hmm.'

'Poor man. And he's such a handsome fellow, too. You know, the day his wife died, he visited Lila.' She nodded emphatically. 'She was pretty crook. He spent ages with her. Even put up a drip. That's the sort of selfless person he is. Trying to keep Lila out of hospital at all costs. No matter that it meant more work for him.'

'He does sound very dedicated.'

'Not many like him these days. The old-school sort, despite his youth. He had to close his books at the practice a few years back, he's that popular.' She patted her hair. 'Little did he know that while he was being such a good Samaritan, his wife was likely in greater need of him.'

CHAPTER 58

RAMESH BANDARA

'I'm afraid he's double-booked all day, detective,' Gwen said briskly.

Ramesh knew he had his work cut out for him. Some medical receptionists required careful handling. There were those who took their role as gatekeeper of the fortress with unwavering dedication, sooner dying than burdening their boss with a pesky patient.

'Sorry to be a bother,' he said, sighing heavily. 'You might be able to assist me. Save me disturbing the good doctor.'

Gwen opened her eyes wider, not agreeing to anything until she'd heard the request.

'I'm just tying up a few loose ends.'

She beckoned him behind the counter, out of earshot of patients in the waiting room.

'Now this is what I call an organised practice,' he said, taking in the colour-coded files and immaculate tea-and-coffee nook.

Kill them with compliments. One of his boss's tips for extracting information from an unwilling participant. Which was ironic, considering his boss rarely complimented anyone.

'You must be very busy.'

Gwen raised an eyebrow.

She was one tough nut to crack.

'What time does the doctor start every day?'

'It varies.'

Ramesh mauled his thumb, trying to stifle his impatience.

The practice nurse walked in and switched on the kettle. 'Eight-thirty on Mondays, Tuesdays and Thursdays,' she volunteered. 'And ten on Wednesdays and Fridays.'

Gwen shot her a sharp glance.

'So, on Wednesdays and Fridays he begins his day after a round of golf?'

'Goodness no!' Gwen said, sniggering with disbelief. 'Those mornings are dedicated to rest-home visits and house-calls.'

'But if it's quiet in the community,' the nurse added, offering Ramesh a gingernut from the biscuit tin, 'he'll come in early to do paperwork. Other times it can be hectic out there and he runs late. Then we're playing catch-up all day.'

Ramesh couldn't resist; he loved gingernuts.

The surgery phone started to ring. 'Get that, won't you?' Gwen said to the nurse. It was clear who called the shots; *Practice Manager* was all but engraved on Gwen's forehead.

The women stood momentarily locked in each other's smiles.

'Lila Nunn is one of the doctor's patients,' Ramesh continued. 'Did he visit her on Wednesday, 29th May?'

'I'd have to check on the computer.'

She didn't move.

'I'd really appreciate that,' he said. 'And while you're at it, perhaps a list of other visits he did in the community that morning.'

Gwen sat down stiffly in front of the computer and began to scroll through the booking calendar as if she had all the time in the world.

Yes, she corroborated. Austin Lamb had indeed visited Lila Nunn that day before starting his clinic, in addition to seeing two patients at Rosalie House. No-one at St Mary's, though. 'It appears to have been quiet there that day.'

'So, three patients before ten? Is that the most he'd usually have?'

'It's highly variable,' volunteered the nurse again, now off the phone. 'In winter especially, he can have up to six or seven to see at each place.'

Austin Lamb's door opened and a yellow, leathery-looking man shuffled out.

'Cath, can you please—'

Ramesh caught the doctor's eye. Smiled. Gave a quick wave.

Lamb's face dropped.

It was a reaction Ramesh was not unused to from the spouses of victims. As the detective who'd led the investigation into the death of Dr Lamb's wife, he would forever be woven into the tragedy. Even though he'd worked alongside the doctor to help solve the mystery of his wife's death, Ramesh would have come to embody all the bad, sad memories. Most people just wanted to forget him, even if they were hugely grateful at the time. It was the epitome of a mixed emotion.

'Detective?'

'Morning, Doc. Don't worry, I'm not here for my haemorrhoids.'

No-one laughed.

'Your wonderful staff have been helping me dot a few i's and cross some final t's.'

Lamb looked bemused. 'I thought the investigation had wrapped up.' His brow smoothed. 'Anyway, glad they could help.'

The jaundiced-looking patient coughed. It was a wheezy, wet cough.

Lamb turned to his nurse. 'Cath, can you please do an ECG on Ron and send off a set of urgent cardiac markers.'

CHAPTER 59

HILARY STARK

Ramesh opened the door dressed in navy chinos and a white skivvy that outlined his strong torso. If this had been their first meeting, Hilary might well have taken him for a yuppie advertising exec, or an architect. Something trendy like that.

She passed him a large brown envelope.

'What's this?'

'Can I come in first?'

He stood aside.

She took stock of the lounge floor covered with index cards. 'You *have* been busy.'

'Talk about living the cliché, eh?' he said with a chuckle. 'Lone detective up all night, rearranging his thoughts on the lounge floor.'

She bent down to take a closer look.

'You got time for a cuppa?' he said. 'I popped out to get some croissants first thing. Used to be a bit of a Saturday-morning ritual with my girls…' He trailed off.

'Sure.'

'What'll it be? A cup of green tea and a croissant?'

'Do you have coffee?'

'Coffee?' he said, surprised.

Five minutes later, they were seated on Bandara's solitary couch, drinking coffee and eating French pastries.

'Croissants were the closest thing I could find here to the delicious buns of my childhood,' he said through a mouthful.

He shook his head, his eyes suddenly bright and alive. 'I can remember as a five-year-old the thrill of hearing strains of Beethoven wafting across the suburbs of Colombo, knowing the bread tuk-tuk was in the area.'

'Sounds a bit like Mr Whippy,' Hilary said.

Bandara wobbled his head. 'But it was not ice-cream on offer. The *choon paan* man sold breads and baked goods of every kind, including my all-time favourite, *Kimbula banis*. These amazing, buttery, crocodile-shaped buns covered in sugar crystals.'

She'd not seen him so animated before.

He sighed nostalgically. 'They were pretty darned delicious.'

She felt strangely awkward, as if she'd intruded on a private memory.

Ramesh wiped his hands on his trousers, picked up the brown envelope, and peered inside.

'I mistakenly took them with me when I got transferred,' she said. 'They've been in my car. Been meaning to return them. Don't tell the boss.'

He pulled out the five photographs. He'd seen them before, of course. Blown-up images of items found in the clearing the day Tibbie Lamb died. A crushed energy-drink can, a broken beer bottle, a strip of sateen ribbon, a tube of lipstick, and three cigarette butts.

'No-one's missed them.'

'I had another look at them the other day,' she said, taking them off him and spreading the photographs out on a spare corner of floor.

'Anything we didn't spot?'

'Most of the items appear to have been there for some time,' she said, spreading the photographs out on a spare corner of floor. 'Grubby, and the dust watermarked.'

'Except for the lipstick,' Bandara said, scrutinising one

photo, 'which we now know belonged to Carmen Andino, and so was probably dropped the same day the photos were taken.'

Hilary nodded. 'Anything else?'

He picked up a photograph of the ribbon – a short strip of coral sateen ribbon positioned alongside a ruler for scale. 'Looks pretty unspoiled, too.'

'Agreed. I'd say it hasn't seen rain or a single morning dew,' she said, unwittingly stepping on Bandara's arrangement of index cards.

'Please try not to stand on the deceased,' he said with a grin, straightening the card with Tibbie Lamb's name printed in bold black. 'But what would you use such a short piece of ribbon for?'

'You clearly haven't bought much jewellery, have you?'

He laughed. 'Have you been talking to my ex?'

'I checked out some local jewellery stores,' Hilary went on. 'And—'

'This coming from the woman who no longer wants to pursue her detective training!' he said, shaking his head.

Her research had revealed that Gordon's Jewellery chain used the exact same shade of sateen ribbon, which they ordered in pre-cut lengths for their variously sized gift boxes. The shortest length matched the strip in the photo exactly.

She'd visited one of the three Auckland branches during late-night shopping and checked through all the names associated with purchases over the previous six months. 'Customers are encouraged to sign up to a loyalty programme. They get an instant ten percent discount. Apparently almost everyone does.'

'And?'

'Nothing so far. I plan to head to their store out west later this morning. Want to come?'

'Sure,' he said, dusting off half a croissant's worth of crumbs.

The crumbs on the carpet left Hilary feeling uneasy. 'Are you inviting cockroaches to the afterparty?'

Bandara tilted his head and gave her an uncomprehending look.

'I can wait if you want to vacuum first,' she said.

Hilary had forgotten how much she hated crowded malls. And to add to the ordeal, the manager of the jewellery store was less than willing to assist. It was a Saturday morning. His busiest time. He had customers to serve.

They persisted; however, their search proved fruitless.

'Might be a dead end,' Bandara said, as she drove him home.

'There's still one more branch to check out in town. No point doing something in a piecemeal fashion. Either a theory is fully explored or not at all. I'll head over there one lunch-hour next week.'

He looked slightly offended.

She hadn't meant it as a criticism, so much as her just thinking out loud.

'We could go now, if you want?'

She shook her head. 'I promised my nan I'd take her to the Botanical Gardens in Hamilton for tea this afternoon.'

CHAPTER 60

STAN ANDINO

The kitchen stank of burnt garlic, so Stan opened the back door to let in some fresh air.

At every turn he missed Carmen. Entertaining without her felt like playing tennis with his feet. How had he taken her so for granted? He didn't want this life. Not the way it had turned out. He was the solo parent of two teenage boys, and a half-good, broke artist living on a loan from a dead woman, who his wife had been accused of murdering. It didn't get much worse than that.

'Won't be long now, guys,' he said, popping his head into the dining room.

'Sure you don't need any help, Stan?' Abby Manderson said, sliding her hand off Austin's lap.

It was odd seeing Austin with a woman other than Tibbie by his side. And yet, who was he to stand in judgement? People handled grief differently.

When he'd rung to invite Austin to dinner, he hadn't been prepared for his friend's response.

'Can we bring anything?'

We?

'No, no. I—'

'Hang on. Abby says she can do dessert or a salad.'

Abby Manderson. There, listening in on the call. So it was that serious.

'No really. Just yourselves. Come about seven.'

Stan was relieved when the boys were invited to a friend's overnight birthday gig. He wasn't sure how they'd react to Austin being with another woman. He could see it raising fresh fears for them, especially Reuben. Would his dad be looking to replace their mum?

Things were still fragile. Fragile enough that he'd even delayed talking to Reuben about the call he'd received from the detective.

He tipped the contents of the wok onto a platter. Strips of stir-fried carrot and bok choy fell to the floor.

'Shit!'

He stepped over the spill and carried the dish through to the dining room.

'Oh wow! Look at that. You're quite the chef, Stanley.'

Stanley? Everything about the woman grated.

'Better taste it first, before handing out compliments,' he cautioned, with forced light-heartedness.

Some days were easier than others. Days when he and the boys were moving forward, making up the rules as they went along. But there were others when everything felt hard, and the normal, casual life going on around them seemed disrespectful of their tragedy.

Austin refilled their glasses. He'd brought along two bottles – a Marlborough pinot gris and a stunning Central Otago pinot noir. Abby's glass was rimmed with red lipstick. She was a bright-red-lipstick sort of woman. Not Stan's type. But then, she didn't have to be.

Carmen had rarely worn lipstick. Never at home, and only occasionally when going out. She'd owned just one lipstick. A sort of nude taupe. How annoyed she'd been when she misplaced it, but she couldn't justify buying another. 'I'm losing my hair, for God's sake. What's the point of spending $65 on cosmetics? It's not like you can keep using it after I'm gone.'

Abby Manderson did most of the talking over dessert

– a thick, gluggy crème caramel Stan had bought at the supermarket. None of them could finish it.

'Stanley, hon, where's the powder room?' Abby asked, folding her serviette and pushing her chair back.

'Hope the boys have left it half-decent,' Stan said, indicating the first door on her right. 'I forgot to check.'

Austin helped clear the dishes.

'So, you guys are a proper couple?' Stan said, as he packed the dishwasher. 'It's great to see you happy again,' he added quickly, in case any hint of his ambivalence shone through.

'Look, I know it's weird,' Austin said, rearranging the fridge magnets. 'It feels a bit strange.' He shrugged. 'I hope Tibs is looking down with approval.'

'I got a call today from that detective,' Stan said, still staring into the dishwasher.

Austin dropped the Pooh Bear magnet. 'Hasn't that guy got anything else to do?'

As the magnet hit the floor, it split in two, Pooh's honey jar ricocheting across the room.

'Blast! I'm all thumbs today. Hope it wasn't precious.'

Stan waved it away with faux casualness. It was a magnet Carmen had bought the boys years ago. So yes, it was precious.

Austin threw the bits in the bin. 'The guy was ferreting around at the practice the other day, too. Talk about not knowing when to bow out and give us the space we need to get on with our lives.'

'Actually, he was following up on something for me. You know those crazy texts I keep getting?'

Austin looked blank.

'The weird ones supposedly from Tibbie? Well, he finally got around to tracking down who was behind them.'

'And it wasn't my reincarnated wife, after all?' Austin said, sarcastically.

Stan paused. Nothing about that comment felt right.

'It was Reuben.'

'Reuben?'

Apparently, it was ridiculously easy to do. Trace the number, that is. The detective had told Stan that his son had used his regular cell phone and simply blocked his caller ID. Nothing sophisticated. Not even a burner phone or changed-out SIMs, like in the movies. Just a kid bizarrely trying to make things right when everything was going wrong.

Stan couldn't be angry with the lad, even though the texts had added to the awfulness of the time. It was excruciating, the sadness of it.

'Poor kid,' Austin said. He patted Stan on the back. 'Your boys have been through a lot. But they'll come right; they're made of strong stuff.'

'You really think so?'

'I wouldn't say it if I didn't. You and Carmen have raised two fine young men. They'll be good.'

It was reassuring, the certainty in Austin's voice. 'Hey, how's the kid in the coma?'

Austin's face darkened. 'Not great. Apparently, he showed signs of waking up on Thursday. But they put him back into an induced coma because he's battling some hospital-acquired infection.'

Stan regretted bringing the subject up. Austin's benign demeanour had evaporated, and his face had again recaptured the angst of previous weeks.

Stan got to bed just before midnight. Cleaning up after dinner parties had been something he and Carmen had always done as a team – him on dishes, Carmen on surfaces and leftovers – a joint effort, followed by a whisky and reflections on the couch.

He lay in bed, lonely, his mind whirring. His phone vibrated on the bedside table.

'You're a good man, Stan. I know you'll give back the cash I gave you. Tippy.'

He scrunched his eyes shut.

Cash.

The other text had spoken about money, but this one expressly used the word 'cash'.

Reuben knew about the cash Tibbie had given him in the shopping bag. Knew that there would be no paper trail. Reuben had predicted what his father would do and was pre-emptively trying to set Stan straight. What an awful realisation… that a son could forecast the depths of his father's badness.

CHAPTER 61

AUSTIN LAMB

Austin drove down Constellation Drive at speed. It was after 7 pm and the traffic was light. He swung onto the highway and put his foot flat. Andrea Bard had left a message saying that the doctors had brought Eliot out of his induced coma. He was awake.

Austin had been double-booked all day and couldn't get away until now.

His phone rang, the dull drone reverberating through the car.

He glanced at the dashboard screen, before answering.

'Hiya,' he said. 'Did you get my message?'

'I did indeed, Doctor, and I'm not very happy about it. I've had chest pain all afternoon and have already removed my bra, ready for a full examination.'

He forced a chuckle. 'Sorry, hon.'

'Sorry! Is that all you've got to say for yourself?' Abby said indignantly. 'What, pray, is keeping the good doctor out so late?'

'You know the young boy who's been in a coma? He's awake.'

'Oh, that's excellent news, Austin.'

Austin changed lanes and took the Northcote offramp. 'Yes. It is.'

'You don't exactly sound overjoyed.'

'No, I am. I am. Just a bit distracted. That's all.'

'So, are you coming over?'

'I'm on my way to the hospital. To see him. He's not out of the woods yet.'

'Well, I'll keep my fingers and toes crossed – and all my other bits, too,' she said, with a booming laugh.

He smiled. 'Listen, after the hospital I think I'm going to head straight home and make it an early night. Just a bit weary. It's been a busy week. Sorry.'

She hesitated. 'Okey dokey. Well… good luck with your boy.'

Your boy. Your boy. Your boy.

Will you please, please be my dad?

The car behind hooted.

Austin lurched across the intersection and followed the road around and down towards the hospital car park. Ahead of him, set against the black of a moonless night, was North Shore Hospital – the iconic rectangular block with its horizontal white stripes and long lines of windows.

Eliot was alive behind one of those windows. Alive.

CHAPTER 62

ANDREA BARD

Eliot had fallen asleep again, and Andrea had to restrain herself from prodding him. According to the doctors, he'd turned the corner; his fever was down, his numbers were good, the brain scan encouraging. But she wasn't ready to trust other people, not even the doctors. Austin had told her Eliot would be fine the day she'd had to rush off to work.

Her son had skimmed too close to the edge, and every time he drifted off, she was gripped by panic, as if only she could anchor him to the shore. Let go and that would be it. She would not get him back a second time.

Almost losing Eliot had redacted everything else. For Andrea, the days when her son's life had hung in the balance *were* his life; the rest of his twenty-one years belonged to some other person.

The astute team of intensivists reassured her that Eliot was not going to slip back into a coma. Not under their watch. Of greater concern, they emphasised, was whether his brain had sustained any long-term damage. The likelihood of brain damage was apparently linked to the length of time his brain had been starved of fuel, which remained an unknown.

Eliot's CT scan had been 'unremarkable', and despite slow waves being recorded on the EEG, 'a measure of his brain's electrical activity', no discrete changes had been noted. These, the doctors said, were all good indicators.

They felt 'cautiously optimistic' about her son's prognosis and were keen to emphasise that improvements in his level of functioning could be expected for up to two years. However, Andrea could not focus on the future; she was still existing within the relief of her son being alive.

Eliot had no recollection of the days leading up to the all-sirens-blaring drive to North Shore Hospital, and he couldn't understand why he was there, despite her repeated explanations.

The doctors told her to be patient. Problems with memory were to be expected. Their hope was that any loss would be reversible with time.

Andrea sat sentry beside her son's bed, watching his chest rise and fall. He was breathing on his own, the relentless regularity of his breath a miracle, his body doing the same perfect work as a machine.

A hand on her shoulder startled her.

'Just me.'

She jumped up, wrapped her arms around Austin, and burst into tears.

He smelt good. Of citrus and sandalwood.

'Oh Austin. We've got him back. We've got him back.'

'Where am I?'

They both turned. Eliot was trying to sit up.

Andrea leant over him and caressed his forehead. 'Ssh. You're in hospital, love. Remember?'

'Hey, dude,' Austin said, putting up his hand to high-five Eliot the way he always did. 'You gave us quite a fright.'

Austin's hand hung there unacknowledged, his greeting like some arbitrary stop sign.

He lowered his arm.

'Why you here?' Eliot asked.

Austin's cheek twitched.

'I'm not sick, am I, Mum?'

'You have been,' Andrea said, pulling his top sheet straight. 'But you're getting better. How nice is it to have Austin visiting?'

'Do you come as friend or foe?'

'Only ever as a friend. You know that,' Austin said, punching Eliot playfully on the arm. 'Anyway, it's good to see you awake, man.'

'Good to see *you* awake,' Eliot said.

Andrea and Austin both laughed.

'It was touch and go for a while,' Austin said, scrutinising the window of the infusion pump. 'Your mum and I were so worried about you. Do you think maybe you mistakenly injected too much insulin?'

It was an odd thing for Austin to bring up, but Andrea suspected Austin was still feeling a bit awkward about how things had evolved the day Eliot slipped into the coma. About not insisting he go into hospital.

'We're not angry with you. But you're going to need to be especially careful in the future not to do something like th—'

'I don't think now is the time to be addressing this,' Andrea said firmly.

'Hey, Mum, look. There's a pipe coming out my penis,' Eliot said, pulling at the catheter.

'Eliot! Leave that alone. It's there to drain your wee.'

'Random! Have you got a pipe for your pee, Austin?'

'Ssh,' Andrea said, stroking Eliot's head.

'He seems to be doing okay,' Austin whispered into her ear.

She turned and with her back to the bed mouthed, 'He doesn't remember anything about that day. Nor the days leading up to it.'

'Nothing at all?'

Andrea shook her head, tears again filling her eyes.

Austin nodded. 'Some memory loss and confusion is to be expected, really. Eliot's brain has suffered a significant insult. I wouldn't be too alarmed if he comes out with some strange things.'

'Who is coming out?' Eliot asked.

'Nothing for you to worry about, Elli.'

Austin told her he would try and touch base with the neurology team involved in Eliot's care and get a clearer picture of his prognosis.

'Hey Austin, how come you're here? Friend or foe?'

Austin pulled a mock serious face. 'Just keeping an eye on you.'

'I'm just keeping an eye on *you*,' Eliot said.

Austin's phone started to vibrate in his pocket. He took a quick look at the screen, before switching it off.

'That detective,' he said, scratching his head irritably. 'Anyone would think he and I were a couple, the way he calls so often.'

'I'm going to be a detective, one day,' Eliot said, grinning widely.

CHAPTER 63

RAMESH BANDARA

It was 6.30 pm by the time Austin Lamb saw the last of his patients out the door. He'd told Ramesh that the best time to come was at the end of his consulting day. Ramesh had been waiting for over an hour.

Lamb looked weary. More tired than Ramesh felt. They both worked challenging jobs, though Ramesh imagined that the doctor's was more stressful.

The waiting room, emptied of people, felt strangely eerie, like a school building at night. Even the receptionist and nurse had knocked off.

'A cup of tea, Detective?' the doctor said. 'Afraid I've got nothing stronger.'

'Beggars can't be choosers,' Ramesh said, light-heartedly.

In fact, he didn't drink alcohol. Never had. But it took too much effort to explain. People seemed uncomfortable around a teetotaller. As if they were in some way being judged by the other's abstinence.

'I must say, I thought you were all done with us,' Lamb said, sucking his teeth. 'And yet you keep popping up.'

'I know, I know. I'm a bit obsessive that way. The thing is, working a case is a bit like moving house,' Ramesh said. 'The time-consuming part is finding a place for all the small things. It's not the big items – the bed, the couch, the cabinet.

It's where to put the brass ornament gifted by a distant aunt that gives one a headache.'

Ramesh had moved house fourteen months ago now. A relationship breakdown exacted more than just an emotional toll; divorce demanded the division of property. Even the ridiculously small stuff. He'd heard of one couple who'd had to get the court involved to help them divvy up their collection of garden gnomes.

'Doctor, you purchased an item of jewellery from Gordon's Jewellery in the city in January.'

Lamb was standing at the counter in the small kitchenette, waiting for the kettle to boil. He straightened. 'Excuse me?'

Ramesh repeated himself. Hilary had left a message on his phone that afternoon, saying she'd dropped into Gordon's city branch in her lunch hour, and bingo!

Lamb lifted his eyes to the ceiling as if trying to recall. 'Yes. That's correct. An eternity ring for my wife. A ruby eternity ring.' He rubbed his eyes with his fists. 'It feels like a lifetime ago.'

It was a lifetime ago. Tibbie Lamb's lifetime. However, Ramesh refrained from what would have been an inappropriate play on words.

'You're a finer man than I,' he said, pulling up a chair. 'Apparently, according to my ex, I could have done better on the romance side of things.' He rolled back and then forwards on the chair. 'Just as well my office chair isn't on castors.'

Lamb didn't react.

'Was it for a special occasion? The ring.'

'Uh... no, actually. Just a spontaneous gift. I'm a workaholic. Sometimes my lovely wife felt a little underappreciated.'

Ramesh nodded knowingly. 'So, it was a surprise then?'

'It was,' Lamb said, distractedly touching the kettle. He pulled his hand back in a hurry. 'Forgive my bluntness, Detective,' he said, rubbing his fingers, 'but what has any of this got to do with you?'

There was a long pause. Ramesh leant forward to show

Lamb a photograph on his phone. It was of the piece of coral ribbon stretched out against a ruler. Twenty-three centimetres long.

Lamb squinted at it.

'This was found at the clearing off the cliff walkway where we know your wife spent her final moments.'

Lamb put on his glasses.

'It's the exact colour and length Gordon's Jewellers use to secure their gift boxes.'

Lamb gave a cursory nod.

Ramesh did not hurry to fill the pause.

'And you are thinking, what, that it might be more than just chance?' Lamb asked, pouring hot water into two mugs, no teabag in sight.

'I'm not sure. But you have to admit, it is a bit of a coincidence, considering you bought your wife a gift from the very same jeweller.'

'No more, I guess, than finding a McDonald's or Burger King wrapper there. Tibbie occasionally ate takeaways, too.'

'When did you give her the ring? January?'

'No, no. Actually, only a few days before—' He stopped. Cleared his throat. Lifted his eyes. 'Before her death.'

'That's some months you waited. Were you having second thoughts?'

'I was keeping it for the right occasion,' the doctor said, looking around absentmindedly. 'We'd had a disagreement earlier in the week. About my long hours. I wanted to make up.'

He located the box of teabags and dropped one into each mug, then passed a mug to Ramesh.

The teabag was floating on top of the water, faint streams of colour leaching from it.

Lamb forced his teabag underwater with a spoon and held it submerged, the action strangely brutal.

'You know, Detective, I've been to hell and back this year,' he said, not taking his eyes off his mug. 'And I have really appreciated everything you've done to resolve how and why Tibbie died. But lately, your endless phone calls, your visits to the practice, your line of questioning... It's... well, it's off, for want of a better word. I almost get the feeling you think *I* might have done something wrong.' He looked up slowly. 'If this is indeed how you feel, I'd rather you came out with it and we addressed it head-on, rather than playing these silly and frankly upsetting games.'

Ramesh put up his hands in apology. 'I have been told I can be a bit like a dog with a bone. My apologies and thank you for indulging me.'

The doctor gave a concessionary nod.

'It's just that I'm terrible with surprises,' Ramesh continued. 'No good at keeping secrets, and certainly not for that length of time. I guess I would have given my wife the ring the day I bought it. But that's just me.'

The doctor looked at him impassively.

'Your wife was not wearing a ruby eternity ring when she was found,' Ramesh said, running through the postmortem findings in his mind. 'I believe she was only wearing a solitaire-diamond ring and a plain gold wedding band. Do you know if she had been wearing the new ring, or was she just keeping it for best?'

Lamb frowned, his eyes darting over this new information. 'I think so. I'm not a hundred percent sure. Are you suggesting someone might have stolen it before her body was discovered?'

'That, or it fell off in the fall. I've got a guy going over the site at low tide tomorrow with a metal detector, though I don't hold out much hope after this length of time.'

Ramesh smiled to himself as he visualised Ross Dwight cursing as the hems of his trousers got wet.

The doctor glanced at his watch.

'Of course, that doesn't explain the ribbon,' Ramesh said, taking a sip of the scalding tea. Some milk and sugar would have been good.

'I guess she might have taken the ring in its box to show off to Carmen. Those two shared everything, as close girlfriends tend to do.'

'A possibility,' Ramesh said, nodding slowly. 'Though, if it were me, I'd probably have worn it, rather than cart the box and ribbon around with me on a walk.'

Lamb tipped his tea into the sink.

'I'm grateful for your thoroughness, Detective. I really am. You found evidence of a gift that I can confirm I did give to my wife. It doesn't change anything. Tibbie is dead. And, personally, I do not need to know, or even want to know, the finer details of that awful day.'

Ramesh felt suitably chided. He could just imagine the furore if Lamb laid a complaint with his boss. As far as his boss was concerned, the case was closed.

'Furthermore,' the doctor said, fishing the hot teabag out of the sink and throwing it into the bin, 'I'd really prefer that you did not stir up the Andino family's pain again. If Carmen stole the ring, so be it. I'm not fussed. Her family's been through so much already.'

'Fair enough,' Ramesh said, impressed by the leaps the doctor was making to join distant dots. Also, his remarkable goodwill.

'Where do you ride?'

Lamb looked momentarily flummoxed.

Ramesh pointed to the photograph on the wall of Lamb on his mountain bike.

His face relaxed. 'Mostly Riverhead Forest.'

'Me too,' Ramesh said with a broad grin. 'Though it's been pretty muddy of late. I came off last week.' He lifted one trouser leg to show off a scab.

The doctor smiled thinly. 'War wounds. We all have them. But it's a lot of fun, or we wouldn't do it. Right?'

'Indeed.' Ramesh reached for the doorhandle. 'One final thing, doctor. Was it a good fit?'

'Excuse me?'

'The ring. A surprise ring must be quite a challenge. My

wife's engagement ring slipped right off her finger when I proposed.'

Lamb tapped the side of his nose, conspiratorially. 'There is an art to it,' he said, with a smile. 'Unbeknown to the wife, you take in one of her other rings for a size match.'

Ramesh shook his head in admiration. 'That's what you did? A master seductor, I can see. No wonder my wife left me.'

'Well, if that's all, Detective, I'll let you be on your way.'

At home, Ramesh warmed himself the last of his mother's goat curry in the microwave, then tipped it out of the Tupperware onto a slice of white bread. His mum was good the way she cared for him, dropping in meals once a week. He loved her food. Of course, he did. She was a wizard in the kitchen and the flavours swept him back to his childhood. He could still remember as a seven-year-old accompanying her around Auckland as she scoured the strange new shops for ingredients to rekindle her mother, her home, her beautiful Sri Lanka.

But the fact that, at the age of thirty-nine, the best meals Ramesh ate were still those his mother cooked for him was also a reminder of just how far he'd regressed. An independent, formerly married father of two slipping back into the habits of an overgrown bachelor.

Father of three.

He missed the girls hugely. But it made sense for Emily to be closer to her parents in Wellington, what with her going back to work fulltime. Of course, his own mother hadn't seen it that way. Even though she still got to see her granddaughters one weekend a month, when Emily brought them up to Auckland.

He sank down onto the couch, balanced the plate on his knees, and dialled Hilary. He wouldn't get a chance the next day what with it being the dreaded interdepartmental bonding day.

'I dropped in to see the doctor this evening,' he said, through a mouthful of curry sandwich.

'Are you sick?'

'No. Doctor Lamb.'

'Right.'

'He was happy to confirm that he bought his wife a ring from Gordon's, though seemed as puzzled as we are about how the ribbon got to the clearing. By his account, he gave his wife the ring a few days before her death. A kind of *sorry-I've-been-working-such-long-hours* sort of thing.' He paused. 'I suppose she could have taken the ring in its box to show Carmen Andino. Seems unlikely, but then again, what do I know? I'm just a man.'

'Unlikely,' she agreed. 'And I'm a woman.'

He smiled to himself.

'You eating?'

'Yes. Sorry.' He swallowed and pushed the bowl aside. 'I arrived home late and was starving.'

'It doesn't bother me. What's for dinner?'

'Goat curry.'

'Goat curry. That sounds adventurous,' she said. 'From your local Indian?'

He hesitated. 'Uh, the last of a batch I made on the weekend.'

How easily he'd lied! His days were spent in judgement of people who didn't tell the truth and here he was fibbing with ease, just because he didn't want Hilary to think less of him for relying on his mother for meals.

'Can you flick me the recipe?'

'I'm not sure it's worth the effort. It's pretty hard to get hold of good goat meat.'

He had no bloody idea where you bought goat, let alone how to cook it!

'Something I forgot to mention,' Hilary said, back on track. 'The jeweller said Austin Lamb took in one of his wife's other rings to ensure the correct sizing.'

'Apparently so,' Bandara said, pleased with himself for not having to rely entirely on Hilary for all the good intel. 'The good doctor's aptitude in matters of the heart left me feeling quite inadequate.'

'The thing is,' Hilary went on, 'the measurement the jeweller has for the ring is at least two sizes bigger than the circumference of Tibbie Lamb's right ring finger documented at post-mortem. And I don't think the body was in the water for long enough to account for the discrepancy. There were very few other signs of prolonged immersion.'

CHAPTER 64

RAMESH BANDARA

Ramesh had a restless night. Finally, in the early hours of the morning, he dragged himself out of bed and through to the kitchen to get himself some yoghurt. His indigestion was playing up, as was his old obsession. What had started as a seemingly irrelevant piece of information from Eliot Bard's elderly neighbour had grown into something bigger. And it was now casting a cloud of doubt over the conclusion he'd reached in the Lamb case. Had he got it wrong?

The thing was, the case was closed. New files had landed on his desk since. He needed to shift his focus.

A side of him wanted to leave things as they were. He was not immune to the satisfaction that came from a tidy desk, nor the need to reassure the public that the streets were safe. He well understood the departmental fatigue that set in when a case became protracted. But he also knew that if any one of these factors overly influenced his decision-making, the case and his ethics could be compromised.

Ignoring possibly random loose ends was an occupational hazard, especially among those who'd been in the job for a long time and had become work-weary and jaded. After years of living a life with the intensity turned up high, the job became just that, a job. A means to pay the mortgage, get a promotion, accrue leave. There was so much tragedy and deviance on offer every day, it was almost impossible not to become inured to it. To human crises. Both in the workplace and at home. In fact, some blunting of emotions was necessary to survive. But a blunted conscience? That was something different altogether. He had charged a dying woman with murder and sentenced her family to life. It was hard to move on from that.

Moonlight tampered with the darkness, silvering the faucet, the sink, the dishrack. He leant against the benchtop and ate spoonfuls of yoghurt straight from the tub.

If he had to keep working the case out of hours like some renegade TV detective, so be it. Starting the following day, which was scheduled to be an ITB day. Ramesh had never been a fan of the annual interdepartmental team-building thing, which he referred to as an MWT – a monumental waste of time.

Build a floatable raft with the materials provided and make it to the other side of the estuary, with some precocious young constable as team leader. Head out on a fishing charter for a few hours, despite weather that would make a duck seasick, then, while still feeling green around the gills, attend a cooking class to learn how to cook your embarrassingly scant catch.

Help teammates ferry boxes of alcohol across a deep gulley, then watch them drown in drink for the rest of the night around a campfire...

If he'd wanted to be a Boy Scout, he would have signed up as a kid. No. He'd call in sick and use the day to follow up on the new leads.

CHAPTER 65

RAMESH BANDARA

Stan Andino shut the studio door behind them and steered Ramesh outside. He'd sounded guarded on the phone. Hostile. All in all, it had been an odd conversation. Clearly everyone was getting sick of the detective.

'Did you talk to your son about sending those texts?'

'Not yet. Look, what do you want, Detective?'

'I wonder if I could swing by. Got a couple of questions that need clearing up.'

'Stop that!'

'Excuse me?'

'Sorry. I wasn't talking to you. Look, you've caught me at a bad time, Detective. I'm meant to be teaching a class in twenty minutes and I've still got to get the boys to school.'

'At the Arts Centre?'

'Yup. Leon, we're leaving in two minutes.'

'I'll drop in there. It shouldn't take long.'

And now here he was, Andino no more welcoming than he'd been on the phone.

'There's a nude modelling,' Andino said, explaining why he was leading Ramesh out into the car park to talk.

Bandara's interest was piqued. It had been a long time since he'd seen a woman naked. That was assuming the nude was a woman, of course.

Andino was looking podgier, his shirt creased, his posture defeated – a common reality for those caught up in the nightmare of a crime. After all the hype had died away and the sediment had settled, people were left to pick up the pieces of their lives. Personal grooming was often the first to suffer.

Andino made for the only tree in the car park that offered a meagre canopy of shelter. It was drizzling.

'I'm just trying to settle a few outstanding issues,' Ramesh began.

'So you said on the phone. Well, you can't take any more from Carmen. She's been well and truly deleted.'

Ramesh flinched. 'You had an affair with Tibbie Lamb's sister, Janice.'

Stan Andino looked around anxiously.

'What of it?' he said, trying to reassert his stolid stance. 'I'm not proud of it.'

'Your wife knew.'

Andino shook his head vehemently. 'No.'

'That wasn't a question. I'm telling you that she found out.'

The guy slumped back against the tree. 'What? How do you know?'

'She also knew where you and Janice Hyde used to rendezvous. Hyde wrote it all to her in a letter.'

'The bitch!'

Bandara waited a few moments to let the news sink in. 'It was always the same place, wasn't it?'

'You talk as if we did it a hundred times. Jeez! It was only… three, four times at most. Something I'll regret for the rest of my life.' He scooped his palm over his mouth. 'Carmen was carrying the twins. It was a difficult pregnancy. But I'm not trying to make excuses.' A strangled sob escaped.

'Did you always meet Janice in that same clearing just off the cliff walkway?'

Andino's eyes darted across this new information. 'So that's why Carmen went there with Tibbie?'

Bandara shrugged. 'Look, I can't say for cer—'

'Fuck Janice! The poisonous vixen. She has no scruples, that woman. I mean, what woman screws her brother-in-law?'

Ramesh frowned, trying to compute this new information.

'And there'll have been other suckers she led into her den. Her den of thrills,' he said, mimicking a woman's voice.

'Brother-in-law... You don't mean the doctor?'

Stan Andino cringed. 'I shouldn't have told you. Austin told me in confidence. But it gives you a measure of how low that woman was prepared to go.'

'He told you?'

Andino nodded. 'He's not proud of it either. He loved Tibbie to death. I mean, God, that's not the right word to use, but you get my drift. He adored her.' He gave another half-sob, half-groan. The guy seemed to be teetering on a breakdown.

'I'm glad for him that he's trying to move on. It isn't easy, I can tell you.' Andino wiped his nose on his sleeve and looked across the car park. 'Deserves it, poor bugger. He doesn't even have kids. Can't say I'm a fan of his new squeeze, though. But at least she's some company for him.'

'The doctor is seeing someone?'

Andino nodded as he blew his nose on his shirt.

Ramesh put a hand on Andino's shoulder. 'Hey, thanks for your help, Stan. I know it's been rough. Maybe you should consider taking a holiday with the boys? Get away for a while?'

Andino shrugged. 'If that's all, you'll need to excuse me. I've got work to do.'

Ramesh climbed back into his car. So, the good doctor was human after all. Oddly reassuring. It wasn't normal for a person to be flawless.

He picked up the list he'd drawn up the previous night. Next port of call – Rosalie House.

Ramesh started the car, then dialled Nic at Forensics.

'Hi, I'm away from my desk. Leave a message.'

Blast! Ramesh had just one free day to make some headway. It was only after he'd left a message and hung up that it dawned on him Nic would probably be at the interdepart-mental bonding day. If the guy checked his messages and blabbed about Ramesh doing work when he was meant to be puking into the toilet bowl at home, his boss would smell a rat.

He rubbed his forehead. Funnily enough, he *was* actually feeling a bit queasy.

He could hear his mother's voice. *That's what comes of fibbing, Ramesh. Bad karma.*

The traffic lights at the upcoming intersection were going to change and the Nissan in front of him was driving slower than his mother.

Ramesh turned on his siren, shocking the driver out of his coma.

The car pulled aside and Ramesh shot through. One of the perks of the job.

He was halfway across the intersection when a sharp, burning pain tore into his back. His mind scrambled around the agony, trying to make sense of what had just happened. Had he been shot?

He tried to pull over, but his hands, clammy and robbed of strength, slid uselessly over the steering wheel.

As the traffic light veered towards him, Ramesh closed his eyes. Then there was a *pop* and he fell forward into a ballooning cloud of white.

CHAPTER 66

HILARY STARK

'First bed on the left, beside the door.'

Hilary put her head around the drawn green curtain.

'Hey,' Bandara said croakily, his face breaking into a smile. 'Nice to see you.'

She wondered if hospital beds came in one size only; Bandara looked like an adult in a kid-size bed, his head and feet bookended by grey board.

As he tried to straighten himself, his smile turned to a grimace.

'Don't sit up on my account,' she said.

He pointed to the visitor chair. She sat down.

'So, you're in the dry docks for a while,' she said, putting the book she'd brought him on the side table.

'Not for long, if I've got anything to do with it.'

'A perforated duodenal ulcer is not to be scoffed at,' she said. 'According to Beth.'

'Beth?'

'My sister.'

'Well, if Beth says so.'

'She's a doctor. In Whangārei.'

Bandara raised an eyebrow. 'So, you've got a nan, and a sister who's a doctor in Whangārei. I'm looking forward to the next clue. Like what you did before you started policing.'

She looked up at the bag of blood suspended above his bed. It was nearly empty.

He followed her gaze. 'The second bag of life from a complete stranger,' he said. 'If I ever had doubts about donating blood…'

'What do you need me to do?'

He laughed. Then clutched his belly. 'Always to the point, Detective Stark.'

'Constable Stark,' she corrected.

'Ideally, I'd like my own pyjamas and toiletries,' he said. 'A bunch of ice-cold grapes would be good, too.'

She sighed. The last thing she had time to do was ferret around Bandara's place looking for his personal effects. She'd meant whether she could do anything in terms of the Lamb case.

'But I'll ask my mum to get them for me,' he said, quickly. 'She has the keys to my unit.'

'So, you have a mum and an ex-wife.'

'Touché.'

'What do you need me to do for the case?' she said.

He pointed to the drawer in his bedside table. 'Inside my wallet there's a list.' His eyes landed on the book she'd brought him. 'What's that? Homework?'

She picked up her very worn copy of *The Little Prince*. She'd had it for over twenty years. 'I want it back after.'

'Yes, ma'am!' he said saluting. 'Just as well you didn't bring grapes, too.'

'Have you read it?'

He scrutinised the title. 'Can't say that I have. Is it a kid's book?'

'Read it.'

She found his wallet and the crumpled piece of paper inside the sleeve.

Top of the list was 'Rosalie House – confirm Lamb visited 29th.'

'Your writing has deteriorated.'

'I blame the meds,' he said with a grin. 'They've got me on some pretty strong stuff.'

A familiar voice in the corridor caught them both by surprise.

'Well, well, well. Look who we have here,' the boss said, putting his ruddy face around the curtain. 'Two for the price of one. And both alive. Even better.'

The man smelt strongly of sweat and aftershave, neither winning the odour battle.

'Evening, sir.'

He was carrying a small arrangement of red and yellow carnations in a fluoro-pink cardboard vase. 'Not a great selection downstairs.'

Flowers from the boss? Bandara looked as gobsmacked as Hilary.

'I should go,' she said, standing up and slipping Bandara's list into her back-pocket.

'Not on account of me,' the boss bellowed. 'How's your new placement going? Not missing us, or rather Detective Bandara, too much?' he said with a wink.

Hilary felt herself colour. 'It's fine.' She turned to Ramesh. 'Look after my book.'

'Hey, thanks for visiting.'

'She's a strange one,' she overheard her former boss say as she made way out of the ward.

She slowed.

'Bet you're pleased to have Ross in her place. More fun to have around than that ice queen.'

She knew that's what they all thought of her, but it was still horrible to hear it out loud.

She hurried away before Bandara replied.

CHAPTER 67

RAMESH BANDARA

Ramesh was knackered by the time Hilary, his boss, and two other colleagues had come and gone.

'Had your share of visitors,' the guy in the next bed piped up when the nurse drew back the dividing curtain. 'And all in uniform. I'm guessing you're either a policeman or a really bad dude.'

Ramesh held his wound as he chuckled. 'Sometimes, I'm not so sure myself.'

'Nah, you're a clean skin. Don't look like you could be bad if you tried.'

Clean skin. A prison term for someone not yet tattooed. Bandara wondered about his roommate. The guy had the look of a heavy-metal musician who'd done some hard living.

'That stocky fella, he the big cheese?'

Ramesh nodded. He was tired. All conversationed out. But he didn't want to be rude. His neighbour hadn't had any visitors and he looked pretty crook.

'Yup, he's the boss.'

'You smoke?'

Ramesh shook his head.

'I'd fuckin' kill for a durrie right now.'

Ramesh was relieved there were no-smoking laws. He was

feeling seedy as it was, without having to contend with the smell of cigarette smoke.

'They think they can slow down my death. Get real! At least, if I could have a smoke, I'd go out happy.'

'Sorry to hear you're not well.'

'You think I'm in here on holiday, mate?' The guy started laughing – a deep throaty laugh which quickly turned into a gunge-trapping hack.

When he'd caught his breath, he pulled back his bedclothes to show off two bandaged stumps. 'My entrance ticket is diabetes. Yours?'

'A perforated ulcer.'

'A what?'

'Hole in my guts.'

'Sounds serious, man. Someone shoot you?'

'Stomach acid, apparently.'

'Far out! I'll stick with the diabetes.'

Ramesh didn't like having his predicament rammed home.

'Diabetes can be pretty bad, too,' he said. 'A young guy I know nearly lost his life after mistakenly injecting too much insulin. They're not sure yet if he's going to be left with brain damage.'

What was Ramesh trying to do? Make the poor guy feel worse.

'Yeah, can happen. Especially with the newbies before they learn the rules.'

'He wasn't a newbie,' said Ramesh. 'He's had the disease since he was a kid, or so I'm told.'

'Jeez, that's bad luck. Real bad luck.'

'Yes. Real bad luck.' Ramesh chewed his thumb nail, as he thought about young Eliot Bard. How diligent he was. A stickler for detail. Always eager to please and do the right thing.

'I say something wrong or what?' his neighbour said.

'Sorry. No. I'm just really whacked. If you'll excuse me, I'm going to try and catch some shut eye.'

'No worries. Hope you got earplugs. The fella across the way snores like a fuckin' steam engine.'

CHAPTER 68

RAMESH BANDARA

'Have you still got a sore tummy, Daddy?' Nikita asked, her little voice breathless on the other end of the line.

'It's getting better, missy. Much better.'

'So can we Facetime?'

'Maybe tomorrow. I'll make sure I'm looking sharp. How's school?'

'Gooood.'

'And Talia and Mum? Are they good, too?'

'Uh-huh.'

It had been a long, slow week. Recovering from surgery was no fun, especially when Ramesh started spiking fevers and had to be taken back to theatre to have a pocket of pus drained. The infection, second surgery, and sleep deprivation on a noisy ward had felled him. So, he was relieved when they finally moved him to his own private room. His relief was short-lived. Without the distraction of other patients, the days crept by at an even slower pace. He hung out for his daughters' calls from Wellington, but they only came in the late afternoons. And visitors tended to come in the evenings.

Since he was still nil-by-mouth, Ramesh didn't even have hospital meals to break the tedium. Instead, some thick creamy nutrition was pumped into his veins.

His mum was horrified that he wasn't allowed to eat any of the food she kept bringing in.

'Aiyo!' she'd exclaim every day. 'How can they expect you to get better without eating?'

However, she soon found other willing recipients. And it wasn't long before the nursing staff were swapping shifts to make sure these coincided with Mrs Bandara's visiting schedule.

As the days dragged by, all that was left for Ramesh to do was think and doze and think. He had never had so much head space before, and by the end of day eight he'd created an updated mind map of the Lamb case. If only he could act on it.

He felt as if it was he who had had both legs amputated. Hilary was his legs, but he hadn't heard from her since the first night. He was itching to call her, but knew she'd be getting on with the case when she could. She had her new position to focus on, and by all accounts Family Harm was no walk in the park.

Towards the end of the week, he discovered the book she'd left him in his bedside cabinet. It had been some time since he'd read a book, let alone one for kids. And he was quick to hide it away whenever anyone came into his room. But he persisted mainly so he could tell Hilary he'd read it. And perhaps in the hope of getting a glimpse inside her head; after all, she'd had the book for most of her life.

Finally, the following Saturday, just as he was taking his first mouthful of solid food – if puréed pear can be considered solid – she walked into his room in a lilac turtleneck sweater and jeans, her cheeks a little pink from having climbed the stairs. He had never been so pleased to see anyone.

'You're looking well,' he said. Her hair was down, making the angle of her fringe look less out of whack.

She pulled out his crumpled list. 'I've got news.'

'I'm feeling much better, thanks,' he said, with a grin.

'Austin Lamb was meant to visit Rosalie House on the 29th, the day his wife died, but rang mid-morning to say he was running late with his other house-calls and had to get back to his rooms. The charge nurse said he answered her patient queries over the phone and later sent through a couple of standing orders.'

'But Lamb's receptionist expressly said he visited two patients at Rosalie that day,' Ramesh said, jogging his memory.

'I double-checked with his office,' Hilary went on. 'The practice nurse confirmed from Austin Lamb's records that he saw two patients at Rosalie on the 29th and made a house-call to Mrs Lila Nunn.'

'Interesting. So, what he recorded differs from what actually went down? Either a deliberate lie to claim more for an in-person visit, or to afford himself an alibi for some unaccounted time.'

'Another possibility,' Hilary added, 'is that his nurse simply assumed he'd visited the patients in person, because of his cursory notes. I mean, if Lamb always saw patients at Rosalie on a Wednesday, and on the twenty-ninth he updated his notes digitally after discussing patients with the charge nurse, he might not have had any intention to deceive.'

The ever-measured Hilary Stark, reluctant to jump too hastily to any conclusion.

Ramesh passed wind. 'Jeez, excuse me!'

'Farting is a good sign.' Hilary said, her expression deadpan. 'Means your bowels are starting to work again.'

'Is that according to Beth in Whangārei?' he said, with a smile. 'Anyway, moving on, and I'm not talking about my bowels. Did you find out anything more about Abby Manderson?'

Hilary walked over to the windowsill and began deadheading an arrangement of flowers.

'She is not living at the doctor's house, but they are in a romantic relationship, judging by how they greet and say goodbye.'

Had Hilary been staking out Lamb's house? Ramesh pushed his puréed pears aside. The woman was a star. That she'd withdrawn from the detective training programme was nothing short of criminal. She was smart. Self-motivated. Uninterested in departmental politics. And dedicated to uncovering the truth.

'I've done a bit of digging,' she went on. 'Since Abby Manderson's divorce two years ago, she's worked in retail. Monday to Thursday at a high-end men's clothing store. You know, suits that cost over a thousand dollars. That sort of thing.'

Ramesh did not know. He'd only ever owned two suits in his life, and both were on special at Hallenstein's – shirt and tie thrown in, too.

A rattling sound from down the corridor announced the tea lady.

'Morning,' said the shiny-faced Kiki, who was wearing a bright turquoise and purple headscarf tied into a bow on the top of her head. 'And how are you today, Detective?'

'Ready to go home.'

He was desperate to get out of the place, but instead still had to rely on Hilary to drip-feed him information.

Kiki let out a boisterous laugh. 'I bet you are. But who will be there to make you the best cup of tea ever?'

Well, his mum would be, if she had anything to do with it. Though he was going to try and block all her attempts to come and stay. As much as he loved her, he knew it wouldn't take long for her to drive him crazy.

He turned to Hilary. 'Nothing has or will ever taste as good as that first cup of tea Kiki made me after a week of nil-by-mouth.'

'Nice pyjamas, Bandara,' Hilary said, with no hint of a smile.

Ramesh cringed. His mum had brought them in. *'I got them on special, Ramesh. Fifty percent off.'* That was no surprise; he couldn't imagine there was big demand for men's red koala-bear pyjamas.

'Tea for two?' Kiki asked.

Hilary nodded. 'Weak with soy.'

Ramesh was embarrassed by his colleague's bluntness. If people didn't know Hilary, her manner could come across as rude.

'No can do. Just milk from the cow,' Kiki said, with a generous smile.

'Black then.'

Someone needed to teach Hilary about pleases and thank-yous. Being shy or socially awkward, or whatever the reason, was no excuse.

'Fancy helping me abscond?' he said, after Kiki had left.

'No.'

'Only joking.'

They drank their tea in silence. Then Hilary got up, rinsed her cup under the tap, and made to leave. 'Anything else you want me to follow-up on?'

'Perhaps you could... actually, no. All good for now, thanks.'

And before he could ask when next he might see her, she was gone.

CHAPTER 69

RAMESH BANDARA

Ramesh edged across the seat and eased himself out of the taxi. 'Can you wait here, please. I shouldn't be long.'

'You must pay now. How do I know you won't run away?'

The driver's eyes widened as Ramesh flashed his police ID.

Ramesh shuffled into the shop.

A whisp of a man with a startled expression sashayed towards him, enveloping him in a cloud of aftershave. 'Afternoon, sir. How can I help?'

Ramesh glanced at his own refection sidelong in a mirror and tried to stand a little straighter. 'I'm looking for a suit to wear to my… my niece's wedding.'

The man's elevator eyes were scathing in their assessment of him, any retail charm rapidly evaporating.

It was time for Ramesh to share a partial truth or he was going to lose the guy. 'Excuse my dishevelled appearance; I've just been discharged from hospital.'

The man's expression swung from distaste straight to pity.

'With the wedding next weekend, I'm a bit short on time. I came straight from the hospital.'

'Take a seat, sir. I'll bring a selection over to you,' the assistant said, now in full mercy mode.

Ramesh must have looked worse than he thought.

He slumped down heavily into the chair. 'I'm fine. Really. Just had the stuffing knocked out of me.'

The fellow looked like he wanted to administer immunity juice and a cool flannel. 'Any specific cut or colour in mind?'

'Navy.'

Ramesh wanted to say navy and cheap; however, bringing up money in that sort of shop would lose him hard-earned credibility. What's more, he wasn't going to buy anything anyway, so what did it matter?

'You have a strong frame, sir. Nice wide shoulders. There are a couple of brands I have in mind. Their cut would be well suited to your... your excellent physique.'

'Actually,' Ramesh said, clutching his belly and giving a short, strangled cough, 'we shouldn't reinvent the wheel. A lovely lady helped me here a few weeks ago, just before things went pear-shaped. I think her name was Amy. No, Abby. Yes, Abby.

The assistant's face stiffened. 'That will be Abby Manderson. She only works weekdays.'

'Darn. We'd narrowed it down to three suits. I should come back on Monday. Hopefully she'll remember the ones I was considering.'

The occasional wincing worked a treat; he could see the young assistant was well and truly on his side.

'I am sure we can find something for you today, sir. Save you having to come back in the state you are in.'

Ramesh then let it slip that he'd been quite taken by this Abby Manderson and wondered whether she was already spoken for. He couldn't recall her wearing a ring.

The man pulled up another chair, his face suddenly animated. Ramesh had read him correctly; this was someone who enjoyed a good gossip.

Ninety minutes after he'd left in a taxi, Ramesh was back at the front of the hospital, feeling somewhat worse for wear. He staggered to the lift and made his way up to the ward. Had he been naïve to hope that his time AWOL would have gone unnoticed?

No sooner had he put a foot into the corridor, than he

was accosted by the charge nurse, who began reading him the riot act.

He pleaded guilty, but only to going outside for a cigarette. However, the rather fragile clemency she bestowed on him was instantly rescinded when she removed his wound dressing to discover that some of his stitches had ruptured and one corner of his wound was gaping.

'Really, Detective, I'd have expected more from you.'

As far as Ramesh was concerned, bursting open his abdominal wound might just have been worth it.

Abby Manderson had by all accounts been very distracted since the start of the year. 'Head in the clouds,' said the young sales assistant. And dropping heavy hints that she might not be working at the store for much longer. 'We all assumed she was seeing someone,' he said, glancing in the mirror and smoothing his hair. 'You just know, don't you?'

Then, more recently, he told Ramesh, she started sporting a ruby eternity ring. However, she'd been most coy about its provenance.

'Say no more! If you get my drift.'

Yes, Ramesh got his drift.

'Funny thing, though,' he said, holding up a finger. 'She's been slightly subdued of late, despite the bling on her finger. She's usually got a lot of energy. A lot.' He took a considered breath. 'Who knows, sir, timing-wise, you might just be in with a shot.'

Ramesh thanked him. Asked him to put the suit on hold. Said he'd left his wallet behind in the rush but would ring in with his credit card details later to arrange for it to be delivered.

He felt a dart of regret that he wouldn't be buying the suit. The young man knew his stuff; the suit looked darned good on Ramesh, even if he said so himself.

The assistant helped him out to the waiting taxi.

'Forgive me for being forward, sir,' he said, just before closing the door, 'but in my opinion, you could do better than Ms Manderson. Just saying.'

CHAPTER 70

HILARY STARK

She arrived early. The zoo car park had been her idea. She'd suggested to Bandara they meet there after her half-day of training in Point Chevalier.

It was a long time since she'd been to the zoo, the place her nan used to bring her and Beth every weekend in the months after their dad killed their mum. Hilary was eight at the time and stopped talking. For a year, maybe more, she lived inside the safety and silence of her head, only speaking to the animals.

Bandara pulled up alongside her and wound down his window. He looked peaky, more angular, his honey-brown face paler. 'Glad to be back in the saddle?'

'Am I ever? Taking it easy is overrated.'

She didn't for a moment believe he had been taking it easy; his ten days convalescing at home would have been a free pass to continue investigating the Lamb case.

'So, where to from here?' he asked, getting out of the car, his movements guarded.

She gestured to the zoo's entrance.

'Inside? Guess the zoo's as good a place as any,' he said.

A wheezy woman with a triple chin let them in for free. 'Police and firefighters, no charge. You guys are our heroes.'

As the turnstile clunked forward, Hilary felt that same

sense of relief she'd felt as a child, the city and all its malice peeling away.

'Let's start with the meerkats,' she said, hurrying ahead.

'This from the woman who usually gets straight down to business!' Bandara called after her, already out of puff.

They bought lemonade ice-blocks at the cafeteria, then found a bench near the meerkat enclosure.

'They can eat scorpions, you know,' she said, taking a teeth-tingling bite of her ice-block.

'Scorpions? Impressive.'

'They tear the tail off,' she said, mimicking the brutal gesture. 'Scour the body with sand to rid it of residual venom. Then, dinnertime!'

'You're a fund of useless information, Detective Stark.'

'Constab—' She turned. Someone was calling her name.

It was one of the zoo veterinarians.

'Long time no see, Hilary Stark. How's the force treating you?'

She shrugged.

He put out a hand to Bandara. 'Hiya. I'm Roger.'

Bandara introduced himself, and before Hilary could think how to steer the conversation away from the inevitable, Ramesh had asked the question.

'So how do you guys know each other?'

She started kicking at the dirt, the dust dulling her polished boots.

'Hilary was one of our best carnivore keepers,' Roger said. 'We were gutted to lose her. But she was destined for greater things.'

'I know that feeling,' Ramesh said.

As they walked back towards the exit, Bandara turned to her. 'Best carnivore keeper, hey?'

Hilary tried not to smile.

'You'll let me know on Monday what time, once you've got the go-ahead from the big guy?' she said, as they stood in the car park, the real world coming back in focus.

'Yup. I can't see how he'll have an issue with you being there. Anyway, he's eating humble pie, right now, after I brought him up to speed.'

'Hard to believe.'

Ramesh turned to her. 'Thanks for everything, Hil.'

She felt herself colour as she pulled her door shut.

'Be in touch Monday,' Bandara mouthed, fumbling with his door handle.

CHAPTER 71

RAMESH BANDARA

They were in a side-street, parked out of view. Hilary was late. She was never late. And Ross was rabbiting on about some hot new recruit.

'Mate, can you cool it? I'm trying to get my thoughts in order.'

Ross put up his hands in mock defence. 'Whew, bit tetchy today, are we?'

Ramesh didn't need the young upstart to remind him. He couldn't mess this up. This was his chance to make good. Though he knew there were some things he would never be able to alter.

'Why do we need that stuck-up bitch here anyway? She's not even on the team.'

'Because she's done a hell of a lot more legwork on this case than you. And if I hear you refer to a female colleague in that way again, it'll be a disciplinary referral.'

'Woah. Take it easy. Must be your time of the month, sweetheart.'

Ramesh clenched his fists. Then he caught a glimpse of her in his rear-view mirror, striding up the road towards them.

He turned to Ross. 'You stay here.'

'Ah c'mon. Where's the fun in sitting in the car?'

Ramesh ignored him and got out.

Hilary gave a quick nod. 'Ready?'

'Let's do it.'

She led the way.

'Detective,' Gwen said, through a mouthful of sandwich. 'Hope you're not here to see the doctor. He's running very behind.'

'We'll wait.'

Gwen eyed Hilary out of the corner of her eye.

Somewhere a baby was crying.

Lamb's door opened.

'Cath, can you give me a hand, please?'

The nurse put her head around the back partition. 'One minute.'

A shadow swept over the doctor's face when he spotted Bandara.

Thirty minutes later a young mum holding her baby in a capsule emerged, followed by Lamb.

'Thank you so much, Austin.'

'Let me know how grumble-guts gets on,' he said, tickling the infant's toes.

Ramesh mused how much easier it was to do his job when people looked like criminals. Austin Lamb did not look like a murderer.

Gwen turned her back and whispered something to Lamb.

'I'm afraid I'm not going to be able to see you today, Detective,' Lamb said, walking over to where Ramesh and Hilary were seated. 'In future you will need to make and pay for an appointment. Otherwise, those who really need my services miss out.'

'I have made an appointment,' Hilary said, standing up.

Gwen shook her head.

'Hilary Stark. First appointment after lunch.'

'Oh, right!' Gwen said, flushing. 'My apologies.'

Lamb looked thrown and quickly disappeared into his consulting room.

Twenty minutes later he emerged, making a show of dusting down his shirt of crumbs.

'Come on through, Ms Stark,' he said, pointedly excluding Ramesh. As soon as the consulting door closed, Ramesh leant over the reception desk.

'Just to give you the heads-up,' he said, 'you might want to cancel the doctor's afternoon clinic.'

Gwen jerked back her head. 'I can't do that,' she said in a low voice. 'You cannot just come in here, erect some red cones, and announce that the road is closed. This is a medical practice.'

She picked up the phone.

'That won't be necessary,' Ramesh said, then knocked on the doctor's door and let himself in.

'May I join you?'

Lamb peered over his glasses. 'You've lost weight, Detective.'

'Perforated duodenal ulcer,' Ramesh said, patting his stomach a little too vigorously. It was still surprisingly tender. 'But I'm on the mend.'

Lamb's face registered the gravity of the diagnosis.

'I'm assuming this is not a medical consultation,' he said tersely.

'We're here about your wife's murder.'

Lamb gave a laboured sigh, rearranging his pen at right angles to his notepad. 'This is getting out of hand, Detective. If you keep showing up here, I am going to have to lodge a complaint with your superiors. It's not acceptable anymore. This is my place of work. I'm beginning to feel like the adversary in all of this, which of course is crazy! I think, somewhere in your zeal for your job, you've lost your way. Now—'

'Doctor, we have some further questions for you about the day your wife died. It might be easier if you accompanied us down to the station.'

'Now? Are you out of your mind? I've got a job to do. Patients to see. Any further communication will have to be through my—'

'We can come back with a warrant, if you'd prefer. But

that's just prolonging things. And it could get a bit messy if you've got a waiting room full of patients.' Ramesh smiled. 'Hopefully we can resolve the outstanding issues today and finally close the door on this investigation.'

Lamb hesitated.

'Would you like a few minutes to make the necessary arrangements with your staff?'

In his experience it was best at such times not to present too many options, but to act as though there was only one way to resolve things.

As they drove to the station, Austin Lamb seated in the back beside Ross – a punishment in itself – Ramesh spied the tiniest crack in the doctor's demeanour. He'd seen it before. There was something about a ride in a police car.

CHAPTER 72

RAMESH BANDARA

Hilary and Ramesh sat on one side of the table, Lamb and his lawyer on the other. It was late. They'd been delayed waiting for Lamb's lawyer to arrive.

Ramesh could already see that the interrogation was going to have to spill into the next day. And as they weren't charging Austin Lamb with anything yet, extra time would only be to the man's advantage.

'We found a trace of your blood on the pedal of Jeremy Booth's bike,' he said, opening with an irrefutable fact. No preamble or gradual escalation of questions. 'Do you know how it might have got there?'

Lamb's demeanour switched instantly from aloof and dismissive to cautiously engaged. Maximising the element of surprise and speaking the same language as a man of science seemed to have worked.

The lawyer whispered something in his client's ear.

Lamb shook his head, indicating he was not overly concerned. Then he rested his elbows on the table and steepled his hands in front of his mouth. 'Indeed I do, Detective.'

Ramesh knew the doctor would be no foolish blabber. He didn't have the chaotic, unhinged aura of someone about to capitulate. Aside from his brief outburst at the medical practice, he'd been calm and contained. Any information he volunteered would be to one end only – damage control and self-preservation. Ramesh knew he had to remain vigilant and play the good doctor at his own game.

It was a tricky path for them both to tread. Without any absolute, definitive proof, it was going to be a game that could easily be lost with one careless comment. Ramesh had to keep his cards close to his chest, as did Lamb. If Ramesh offered up too much too soon, Lamb would have time to recreate the truth to fit the evidence provided. Similarly, if Lamb offered up information that proved contradictory to what Ramesh already knew, he would be digging his own grave. It was a careful dance, neither in a hurry to lead.

'Before we get to the blood on the bike,' Lamb said slowly, 'perhaps I should fill in a few other gaps.' He smiled thinly.

Ramesh dipped his head in acquiescence.

'One morning,' Lamb began, as if beginning a fairy tale, 'and I'm talking about some time before Tibbie's passing…'

Passing. An unemotive word, cleverly chosen.

'I left my phone at home. Gwen got hold of Tibbie and asked her to drop it in at the rooms. These days, whatever one's line of work, being without one's phone is like being without a limb, don't you think?'

This was not an anxious, 'I'm innocent' account of events, but one pitched more in the style of a dinner party story embellished for maximum satisfaction and enjoyment.

'Tibbie was en route to my rooms with said phone when a text came through for me. Unfortunately, she breached my privacy and read it.'

Breached my privacy! This guy was something else.

The room was quiet except for the ticking of Hilary's large analogue wristwatch.

'It was – how shall I put it – a rather personal text.'

'Personal?' Ramesh prodded.

'Yes. From a former patient. Abby Manderson.' He turned to include everyone in his gaze. 'Female patients can sometimes be hard to ward off.'

Ramesh glanced over at Hilary, whose eyebrow was raised in a peak of disbelief.

'I'm not trying to make excuses,' Lamb said quickly, reading the room. '*Mea culpa.*' He rocked back in his chair. 'I'm a fallible, hot-blooded bloke. Guilty as charged.'

The man was brazenly toying with them by using words such as *guilty*. He was clearly enjoying his own performance.

'Guilty of having an affair.'

Nothing quite like a limited admission of guilt to restore a man's credibility.

Lamb was convincing, it had to be said. The way he'd framed his story in honesty left him looking good.

'The blood on the bike?' Hilary said, reining him in.

Ramesh clenched his jaw to stop himself smiling; Stark wasn't having a bar of the doctor's dramatics.

'If you'll indulge me a little longer, Constable,' Lamb said with a smile. Constable. He'd taken note of Hilary's rank and was using it as a put-down under the pretext of being polite.

'It was tense for some weeks,' Lamb went on. 'Tibbie kept threatening to leave. It could have gone either way, to be honest. I'd been a fool. I loved my wife and couldn't bear the thought of losing her.'

Couldn't bear the thought of losing her. Losing her. Losing her.

Bandara was suddenly back inside the day Emily left him for good.

After all the toing and froing, the last link had been so brittle, nail clippers could have broken it. With just a few things left to collect from the house, the necessary papers signed, and all arrangements for their girls worked out and diarised, it had been a hug and a bumbled goodbye. Then Emily had walked away down the garden path, the girls' pink plastic dolls house in one hand, a pot plant in the other.

There were things he'd wanted to say, but for so long the right words had been unable to come out, and with such a backlog, articulating them at such a late stage would not have made any sense.

'On the morning of the 29th I was in a rush,' Lamb went on. 'I had an urgent house-call on top of my usual rest-home visits.' He laid both his hands flat on the table in front of him. Surprisingly squat hands for an otherwise angular, athletic-looking fellow.

'As I was heading out, I suggested to Tibbie we meet at nine-thirty in the small window of time I had between house-calls and the start of my clinic.'

'The time she usually walked with Carmen Andino?'

'Hmm,' Lamb said, pressing his lips together, as if contemplating his wife's daily charitable chore. 'I suggested she cut their walk short just this once.'

'So, you visited Lila Nunn, then took her caregiver's bike?'

Lamb nodded sheepishly.

'Answer the question aloud, please,' Hilary said.

'Yes! Yes, I did,' Lamb said, exaggerating each word. 'It was a bit cheeky, me borrowing Jeremy's bike, I know. But it saved me having to negotiate the morning traffic. Not infrequently I leave my car parked at Lila's house and walk down to Rosalie House, which is just a couple of blocks away. Sometimes, if I've been in a rush,' he said, assuming a slightly mortified expression, 'I've been known to borrow the lad's wheels. This'll teach me for not coming clean with him.'

'And your blood on the pedal?' Hilary said, her monotone voice persistent.

'I believe my foot slipped off the pedal. The sharp corner scraped my calf, nicking my skin and my rather good pair of Rodd & Gunn trousers. I've yet to get them repaired.' Then, as if filling in for the less cycle-savvy in the room, 'It can happen more easily when you're not wearing cleats.' Ramesh felt a moment of panic. There was no doubt as to who was steering the interview. It wasn't Hilary. And it most certainly wasn't him.

'Where did you agree to meet?'

'I suggested the clifftop walkway as I figured it would be convenient for both of us,' he told them, 'as well as a suitably picturesque spot for the surprise I had in store for her.' An apology and a gift – the eternity ring purchased some months earlier, which was symbolic of his enduring love for her.

'So, you chose the very same place where you and her sister, Janice, would meet in secret – what was it? – thirteen years ago now?'

The doctor's cheeks coloured, his eyes running ahead.

'I… that's…' He laughed, clearly uncomfortable.

'A word with my client, please?'

But they could not afford pauses. The doctor was too quick a thinker. Any respite would simply afford him the opportunity to slither out of their grasp, and right in front of the boss, who was looking on from another room by video-link.

'We can keep going,' Lamb said, reading Ramesh's unarticulated objection. He clearly wanted to appear amenable and keen to placate.

'A grotty clearing on an overcast day,' Hilary said, her timing impeccable. She had a knack of cutting Austin Lamb down to size every time he thought he was ahead. 'Wouldn't a restaurant or café have been more appropriate?'

'On the contrary,' the doctor replied coldly. 'Tibs loved surprises. We used to pick out secret rendezvous for each other's birthdays and anniversaries. A silly little tradition,' he said, with chuckle.

Tibs.

Ramesh and Hilary had spoken with a number of Austin Lamb's former schoolfriends and medical-school colleagues. By their account, Lamb was renowned for his performing and public-speaking skills, landing the principal part in many a school production and medical-school review.

'He could bluff his way out a detention, that guy,' said one friend. 'Not that he ever found himself in one. Prefect material from early on.'

'Austin was the first of us to start dissecting the cadaver,' volunteered a medical school mate. 'Nothing phased him. The guy was focused and single-minded when faced with any difficult task. He didn't let emotions get in the way.'

'An absolute charmer' was a former physics teacher's assessment. 'High IQ and EQ, which can be a rare thing in super-bright kids. He could read a room. Personally, I think he should have made Head Boy.'

A charmer. Could read a room. Single-minded. Unemotional. Focused. Persuasive.

'I'm confused as to why there were none of your fingerprints on the racing bike,' Ramesh said. 'Admittedly, it was examined some weeks after you say you used it, but I would have expected a few at least. Did you wipe it?'

The doctor smiled broadly, like a quiz contestant confident his answer would win him the big prize.

'Gloves.' He paused. 'May mornings are chilly.'

'It's not like we live in the Northern Hemisphere,' Hilary interjected.

'I always wear woolly gloves when I'm out and about early in the day,' Lamb continued. 'Have you ever had a doctor examine you with cold hands, Constable Stark? Not a way to endear yourself to a patient, I can tell you.'

'So, you get to the cliff walkway,' she said, pushing through his verbal padding.

'Yes. I left the bike against a bench and waited for my wife.'

'In the open or hidden in the clearing?'

A flash of unease flickered across Lamb's face.

'On the path, I think. Tibbie arrived almost concurrently. Is that relevant?'

'You can't rem—'

'I apologised to Tibbie again,' Lamb said, speaking over her.

For the first time, Ramesh got a sense of how the doctor might react to being challenged outside of an interrogation room. There was cold aggression in the way he wrestled for control of the conversation.

'But surely—'

'I told her how much I loved her. That I wanted to make a new start. Gave her the ring I'd bought.'

'Yes, the eternity ring,' Hilary said, with emphasis on the word *eternity*. 'All wrapped up.'

Ramesh sat back, allowing the Hilary–Lamb dynamic to play out. Lamb would not be used to a woman who was not in awe of him. Who did not respond to his charms.

'Yes, all wrapped up,' Lamb said flicking something off his nostril.

Hilary folded her arms. 'Just to clarify, did you not say to Detective Sergeant Bandara you'd given the ring to your wife a few days before she died?'

Ramesh cleared his throat to mask a chuckle. Hilary was mocking Lamb's sarcastic attention to rank.

'I think I've made it pretty clear that my story differs from what I first told you,' he said impatiently, looking only at Ramesh. 'I knew how it would make me look, admitting I'd been to the place where my wife…' With an almost goofy expression, he shook his head. 'How many times have I watched some detective series on television and bemoaned that a suspect did not tell the truth about a minor misdemeanour, thereby implicating themselves in something bigger?'

'Was she pleased with the ring?' Hilary asked.

Lamb shook his head. 'She was still angry. Hurt.'

Hilary lifted her shoulders and hands as if that was a no-brainer.

'She threw the box on the ground. And… and…' Lamb faltered. Closed his eyes. 'She ran to the edge.'

Everyone in the room's breathing seemed to synchronise. One breath in. One breath out. In and out, as if the interview room was doing the breathing.

'Then she jumped. No warning. Nothing. She just jumped.' His voice was flat. Defeated.

Ramesh was reeling, as if he'd just witnessed Tibbie Lamb end her own life.

It was not the horror of the act that got to him, but the fact that the doctor's account of events was plausible. Entirely plausible.

Lamb closed his eyes. Sunk his head into his hands. Released a stuttered sob.

'I think my client has probably had enough for one day,' Lamb's lawyer said, his pragmatic words a rude intrusion. 'As Dr Lamb has not been formally charged with anything, can I suggest we resume in the morning?'

Ramesh hesitated. Wondered about his boss watching in the next room. Was he even still there, or had he given up on Bandara?

He couldn't object. Lamb was no flight risk. Yes, guilty of perverting the course of justice, but possibly nothing more.

'Tomorrow at nine then.'

'One last question,' Hilary said, overstepping her rank.

Ramesh did not want to make a scene; however, Lamb's lawyer was less amenable.

'I'm afraid this is not—'

'Why didn't you call 111?'

Austin Lamb rubbed his hands down his trousers. His eyes were dark and earnest.

'I'm not proud of my actions,' he said slowly. 'I was in shock. She was dead. I felt responsible. Confused.' There were tears in his eyes.

'How could you be sure she was dead?'

'She was splayed out on the rocks below, in a pool of blood. You don't survive a fall like that. I've seen enough dead bodies to know.'

CHAPTER 73

ANDREA BARD

Andrea had bargained with God to let Eliot live. That was all she'd asked for. She could cope with anything else life threw at her.

When he'd woken after three days in ICU, she'd been ecstatic – his eyelids lifting like theatre curtains on bemused green eyes. But then the doctors put him into an induced coma because of a severe infection his body was battling. And his life remained in the balance.

She stayed vigil by his bedside, only going home when forced to, and then just for a few hours of broken sleep.

On Eliot's fifth day in hospital, Andrea was discussing his progress with a specialist when two of her colleagues from work arrived to visit, flowers and cards in hand. Not permitted into ICU, they were shown to an area to wait for Andrea. When she went out to find them, she overheard them talking.

'I hate to say it,' one said in a hushed voice, 'but it might be for the best if he, you know, were to pass away quietly. He's a strange kid. Has had his fair share of issues even before this happened.'

'At least Andrea could get on with her life,' the other concurred. 'I mean who wants that sort of responsibility hanging around your neck? An overgrown kid who will never, let's be honest, never leave home.'

Andrea had wanted to burst into the room raging. Did they think that her life was less than theirs because she'd given birth to a child with challenges? That her love for her son was somehow diluted because of his difficulties? His death easier to accept?

Instead, she forced herself to be civil, and only after they'd left did she lock herself in a toilet cubicle and crumple to the floor sobbing.

Two days later, with Eliot's infection finally under control, the doctors woke him up.

Once the initial euphoria settled, Andrea's prayers changed.

Please heal his brain, God. I can deal with anything else. But please don't let the damage be permanent.

One minute Eliot was calm and attentive, the next, overwrought about some minor change in routine. 'I hate that stupid stuff. It tastes like the toilet cleaner. No! I won't. You know I only like mint-flavoured toothpaste!'

His short-term memory had been drastically affected. He could remember nothing about the weeks leading up to the hypoglycaemic event, nor, it seemed, was he easily able to retain new information.

Various specialists cycled through the ward. A neurologist recommended that, when Eliot was discharged, Andrea erect whiteboards around the house to serve as reminders for Eliot. Ticking off activities with a red marker pen (make bed, wash hands, lock front door) would help reinforce habits, while they waited for time to hopefully reverse some of the damage. 'It could take anything up to two years to regain his premorbid level of functioning. That is, if it's going to happen at all.'

An occupational therapist recommended an identity bracelet engraved with Eliot's essential contact information. And an endocrinologist arranged for a special glucose monitor, which could be attached to the skin and afford minute-to-minute glucose readings.

'Not that way, Mum. Dr Hay's office is left.'

Eliot had a follow-up appointment with the diabetologist, and they were negotiating the maze of corridors at the medical specialists' centre.

'I don't think s—' Andrea stopped. Turned to look at Eliot, her mouth agape. 'You... you remembered the new doctor's name!' And that his office was off to the left.

The doctor was pleased with Eliot's progress, too.

'All looking good,' he said, making notes. 'Now I'd like to try and shift you from the short-acting insulin to a new, slightly longer-acting one. Means you won't have to inject quite as often.'

Eliot shook his head. 'No! I don't want to.'

'I thought you'd prefer fewer jabs.'

'I don't want to change! I don't want to change!' Eliot said, flicking his forehead with his fingers.

Andrea put a hand on his arm. 'Hasn't Dr Hay managed to get your sugars to the best they've been in ages?'

Eliot nodded.

'Well then. I think he knows best.'

'But it's bad. It made me sick.' Eliot looked around in panic. 'Austin tried the same thing and I nearly died.'

'What's bad?'

'The new stuff! Like, I went all wobbly and sweaty and funny in the head. If Austin hadn't been there, no one would have found me, and I would have died. I would have, Mum.'

'You're getting confused. This is a new kind of insulin.'

'I'm not getting confused!'

Dr Hay scrolled through Eliot's file and brought up his hospital discharge summary.

'There's no mention here that Dr Lamb changed your insulin, Eliot. Just that he recommended you have half your usual morning dose—'

'I know! He prescribed half the usual dose and told me to fill it in for nine o'clock on the chart.'

Dr Hay nodded as he looked at the scan of the handwritten chart the paramedics had found at Eliot's bedside. 'Correct.'

He swung the computer monitor towards Eliot. 'But the insulin was the same type you'd been injecting all along.'

'You're not listening!'

'It's okay, Elli,' his mum said, trying to appease him. 'It can be confusing.'

'I filled it in there,' Eliot said, pointing to the first column, 'even though it was before nine o'clock, but Austin said nine was an easy time to remember for future doses. Then he changed his mind, like you want to do now. And he gave me a new insulin. He said it would work better just for that day. He even squirted out the stuff I'd drawn up. That's when I went off and Austin went all blurry.' He sucked in a big breath. 'If he hadn't got me to hospital, I would be dead, dead, dead!'

'Austin didn't take you to hospital, my boy. It was Terrance McDougal who found you unconscious.'

CHAPTER 74

AUSTIN LAMB

Austin did not sleep well. He'd put off Abby coming around. Told her he was coming down with something and didn't want to pass it on to her. The truth was, he didn't want to have to bring up the fact that he'd been interviewed at the station. An interview that was to be resumed the following day.

It had been a stressful enough time for the two of them, Abby struggling with guilt at being 'the other woman' now that Tibbie was dead. Talk about her moral compass kicking in well after the fact.

'Society has no sympathy for a mistress, Austin. Not even if she's filling a gap in a marriage that has irretrievably broken down. But add to that the wife committing suicide, I'd be crucified if our affair came out now!'

So, the less Abby knew of any police involvement the better.

The police knew he'd been dishonest about the day Tibbie died. First saying he'd given her the ring a few days before, then admitting giving it to her on that fateful day. And being with her when she jumped, no less. Perverting the course of justice would have its penalty; however, Austin had enlisted one of the best defence lawyers in town. If anyone could get him off, Mark would.

Austin was up early, dressed and waiting for Mark to pick him up for round two at the station, when he received a text informing him that the interview had been delayed until the afternoon. Apparently, DS Bandara had been called away on other business.

Austin found the delay reassuring; clearly, he was no longer a priority.

Fortunately, he'd managed to get a locum in for the rest of the week, so he didn't have to get Gwen to shuffle patient appointments again. It did annoy him, though, how the detective could be so blasé about disrupting other people's lives, with such little regard for the consequences.

He mooched around the house for a bit, before deciding to hop in the spa pool; he had tights knots in his neck.

At 2 pm the four of them were again seated at the table in the small, windowless interview room at the police station.

Austin felt calmer and more relaxed than he had the day before. The detective appeared friendlier and less stressed, too. The only one who remained as intense as ever was Bandara's sidekick. Austin was familiar with her type. Blunt. Aggressive. Without an ounce of femininity.

And as if to prove a point, she was the one to begin.

'So, you did not call 111 after your wife jumped. Instead, you chose to leave the scene.'

Chose to. She was underlining his free will.

He met her gaze straight on. 'I never imagined I would react the way I did. I was in shock. Knew Tibbie was dead. I was afraid how it would look. You can understand that, surely? A sort of unwitting hit and run,' he said, looking over to Bandara. 'Except that, I wasn't culpable of anything more than trying to make up with my wife after having an affair.'

He ran his thumbnail along a crack in the table. 'Once I'd left the scene, it was even harder. How would I explain it? And then, well, the longer… the more time distanced me from what had happened, the more mired in the situation I became.'

'This is where it gets interesting,' Hilary said, after a long pause.

Detective Bandara had taken a backseat and seemed to be following lazily for the ride. Was he simply indulging his junior? Giving her some practice in a case he knew was going nowhere?

'You make the decision to let an innocent person take the fall. Carmen Andino. One of your patients and closest friends.'

'Before we move onto that,' Ramesh Bandara interrupted.

Austin felt a dart of satisfaction at the detective pulling rank. It was time to put the precocious constable in her place. 'You didn't mention having any physical contact with your wife in the minutes before she jumped. She caught you unawares.'

'Is that a question?'

'Well, did you have any physical contact?'

'Yes,' Austin said, knowing instinctively it was the right answer. Clearly they had something to suggest contact had taken place. 'As in a kiss when she arrived, if that's what you are asking.'

'No. I'm more concerned about the bruising noted on your wife's arms in the configuration of handprints. Stocky handprints.' Bandara looked pointedly at Austin's hands. 'It seems she was gripped with some force.' Austin was still thinking how to best answer Stark's question about Carmen, when this one hit. He breathed in slowly and smiled, while trying to centre his thoughts.

'Which question would you like me to answer first?'

The detective put up his hand like an eager kid and reciprocated Austin's smile. For a brief moment Austin wondered whether this sequence of questioning had been rehearsed, like some sort of charade. But he quickly dispensed with the idea; it gave the detective too much credit.

He frowned. Told them that the only thing he could think of was that on the morning of Tibbie's death, or perhaps it was even the day before, she'd been walking backwards in their dressing room, 'which is raised a few steps higher than our bedroom level'. She hadn't realised she was about to step back over the stairs, so he'd lunged forwards to grab her. 'How awful to think I might have left bruises.'

Bandara jotted something down, then looked up. 'Just to clarify, you grabbed her like this, front-on.'

'Correct.'

He sucked his teeth loudly. 'I'm confused. You see, the way the finger and thumbprints encircled Mrs Lamb's arms would suggest she was gripped from behind.'

It was hot and stuffy in the little room, which smelt strongly of pine and minerals. Austin had smelt the cheap cologne on the detective before. Clearly the man didn't earn enough to be able afford a more refined fragrance.

Austin cast his mind back to what Tibbie had been wearing that day. Her tight-fitting, long-sleeved mauve merino and leggings. It was unlikely that her corpse had been undressed before being taken to the mortuary.

'Tricky thing, drawing conclusions from bruises only noted at post-mortem,' Austin said. 'There's always cutaneous spread to account for.'

He saw the constable shoot Bandara a glance.

Austin relaxed back in his chair.

But Stark was clearly determined not to let him enjoy the moment, and she was back at him with the Carmen question. How could he have thrown his close friend and patient under the bus?

'That is not the person I am,' Austin said, taking his glasses case out of his pocket and removing the soft cloth inside. 'I never once implicated Carmen. You may remember I was supportive of the initial hypothesis that my wife might have taken her own life. Which I can now confirm, she did. *You* are the ones who raised suspicions about Carmen Andino. You are the ones who got it wrong.'

'And *you* remained silent.'

He took off his glasses and cleaned each lens in turn. What his 'silence' would mean for him was unclear. But Mark would no doubt work his magic.

'What happened next? After your wife jumped?' the female asked.

'I cycled back to Lila Nunn's. Got my car and went to work.' His voice trailed off. He shook his head. Closed his eyes. 'If I could have that time over.'

'You returned to your car which you'd hidden where?'

The relentless motion of Stark's questions was deliberately dismissive of any emotion he expressed. And her choice of words, such as *hidden* instead of *parked*, were clearly designed to needle him. Well, he wouldn't give her the satisfaction of rising to the bait.

He told her that he'd parked behind the garage in Lila Nunn's driveway, where he not infrequently left the car when he had additional calls to go on to at Rosalie House.

'The driveway winds naturally around to the back of the building,' he went on. 'An odd configuration, as if the builder got it wrong and built the garage back to front.'

Ramesh Bandara suddenly came to life. 'One thing perplexing me, Doctor,' he said, 'is how Jeremy did not hear you leave after you returned his bike.'

'He'd have been showering Lila,' Austin said, without a second thought. 'That's her morning routine. Shower from nine-thirty to ten-thirty. Which is why I always visit Lila first on my rounds, otherwise I'd be left waiting till she'd finished showering.'

Bandara seemed well satisfied with Austin's response, as if he'd been hoping for the answer Austin gave.

'Yes, it would be hard to hear a car leaving from the bathroom on the far side of the house,' the detective said. 'What with the shower and extractor fan going.'

Austin felt a prickle of unease. Was Bandara implying Austin had thought through the scenario in advance of the day?

'Water, Doctor?' the detective asked, spacing out the four glasses stacked beside the jug.

Water? Why offer water when the interrogation was surely drawing to a close? There wasn't much more ground to cover. Was there?

CHAPTER 75

RAMESH BANDARA

Beyond reasonable doubt. That's what the boss wanted. What any murder charge required to stick. Yet all the evidence Ramesh and Hilary had presented so far had been explained away by Austin Lamb credibly. Each time the man had managed to wriggle free.

They should have called his bluff about the bruising. Implied it had been noted and photographed at the scene. Instead, Lamb had made an 'educated' guess that no-one would have looked under Tibbie's long sleeves until she'd been undressed at the mortuary. He'd assumed poor police procedure. And of course, he also knew about cutaneous spread after death. He was, after all, a doctor.

Without an eyewitness to the crime, Ramesh knew that nothing short of a confession would change the narrative. And that was seeming less and less likely.

'If we could return to the ring for a moment. The somewhat ill-fated gift for your wife.'

The doctor sighed, as if humouring a less intelligent being.

'Last we spoke I was very impressed by the lengths you'd gone to, to keep the ring a surprise, while still ensuring it was a perfect fit.' He turned to Hilary. 'Doctor Lamb secretly took one of his wife's other rings to the jeweller for sizing.'

Hilary feigned being impressed, but she was no actress.

'What I don't understand,' Ramesh said, 'is why the ring turned out to be two sizes too big for your wife's ring finger.'

Lamb narrowed his gaze. He put a forefinger to his lips.

'Sadly, Tibbie never got to try on the ring,' he said after a long pause. 'If any crime was committed, it might be that the jeweller made an error with his sizing gauge.'

His calm confidence spoke of a man who knew the police did not have anything concrete on him. He was enjoying playing them like a fiddle.

'I'm not a pathologist, Detective,' he said, before anyone could fire another question at him. 'But I hope you have more to go on than my wife's finger width determined at postmortem. I'm not sure how accurate a corpse's finger width would be after suffering blunt trauma on rocks and then being submerged in salt water for a time.'

The doctor might have been a smart man, but did he not appreciate how inappropriate the word corpse sounded under the circumstances? It was as if he'd momentarily forgotten which hat he was wearing. Doctor or grieving husband?

'Nor have you bothered to find out which finger the eternity ring was intended for,' Lamb continued. 'Perhaps you measured my wife's other rings,' he said, as if working through the scenario himself. 'But it seems you simply assumed it would be for her right ring finger, and not, for example, her left middle finger.'

Ramesh could not refute any of what Lamb was saying, even though he knew from the conversation he'd had with the assistant at the suit shop, that Abby Manderson had been seen wearing a ruby eternity ring and so had likely always been the intended recipient of the gift.

However, even this did not implicate Lamb in his wife's murder; it simply corroborated the fact that the man had been having an affair. What Bandara couldn't understand, though, was why Lamb even bothered to give the ring to his wife, when he'd always intended it for his lover?

'It fitted Abby Manderson perfectly,' Hilary said, not giving the doctor the luxury of resting even momentarily on his laurels.

'You've got to be joking!' Lamb said, his voice rising for the first time. 'This is nonsense. Absolute nonsense!' He swung around to his lawyer, his eyes flaming, like a cornered bull. 'My relationship with Abby Manderson is off-limits. Off-limits! It has absolutely nothing to do with any of this.'

Hilary made fleeting eye contact with Ramesh. *Strike one.* Lamb had just lost his equilibrium.

Ramesh looked down at his lap. Sighed. Then slowly he lifted his head, letting his gaze soften and the edges of his vision blur. It was time for Austin Lamb to feel that it was just the two of them in the room. Lamb needed to forget about the relentless, brilliant Hilary Stark. The conversation had to feel intimate. Safe. Man-to-man.

'The hardest thing must have been deciding to kill the boy.'

Lamb stared at him, his suave handsomeness dissolving like a sandcastle on the incoming tide.

'What!'

'I think you know, Austin,' he said, using Lamb's first name for the first time.

Lamb's eyes darted around the room.

'I'm not sure if I mentioned that Eliot has regained his memory of the events leading up to his coma?'

Lamb blinked. His cheek twitched.

'You gave him a different type of insulin on the morning in question, didn't you?'

'Different type!' Lamb sniggered. 'A different *dose*! A *smaller* dose, in view of the kid's recent hypoglycaemic event. I think you'll find that to be sound medical practice!'

'I was of the understanding that—'

'Apologies for interrupting, Detective, but you are a layman. You have no understanding of the finer nuances of medicine. You can't be expected to. But that you have the audacity – no, the negligence – to base a case of... to imply attempted murder, no less, based on your... your limited understanding. I'm appalled. Rest assured, I will be taking this further!'

Ramesh was close. It was time to summon his own acting skills. After all, he had played Tony in *Westside Story* in Form One.

'As I was saying,' Ramesh said, his voice level, kind, empathetic, 'Eliot drew up the smaller dose on your initial recommendation. However, you subsequently got him to discard this, and you drew up insulin from your own medical supply, with a new syringe. Insulin that was different both in its duration of action and dose.' He cleared his throat. 'Once Eliot had injected it, you capped the empty syringe, put it in your black bag, not in Eliot's sharps box, to dispose of the evidence. And you left.'

The doctor pressed his left hand firmly onto the desk, as if trying to counter its trembling.

'So, now you are relying on some handicapped kid's memory, after he's been in a coma for a week, Detective?' he said, shaking his head. 'You can surely do better than that.'

'You loved him, didn't you?'

The doctor's mouth opened.

'Pftt!' he said, in an attempt at derision.

The room was quiet except for the sound of Austin Lamb panting, and Hilary's loud wristwatch ticking.

'You loved him like a son,' Ramesh said quietly.

Like a son.

Austin's face collapsed, the guy ropes severed.

Ramesh had him. The right word at the right time had found the pocket of guilt that weakened an otherwise meticulous, cold-blooded man.

The doctor closed his eyes. Dropped his head. Forced rigid fingers through his hair.

Finally, Austin Lamb looked up, his face drawn and grey.

'I never imagined… it was just… he was going to ruin it. Ruin everything. Don't you see?'

He melted into his seat.

Was that relief Ramesh spied in the doctor's eyes? Playing at the truth was an exhausting business. Like trying to keep a boat afloat in a storm. Capsizing was in many ways easier.

CHAPTER 76

AUSTIN LAMB

Tibbie was perfect. Everyone said so. Intelligent, caring, interested, interesting. And a stunner to boot, which, as much as Austin hated to admit it, was one of her most essential qualities; she was seen to be a catch before people even got to know her. Her looks endorsed him, like a prefect badge on a blazer.

When they started dating at school, Austin felt as if he'd won the big prize at a tombola. A Willy-Wonka moment, which hinted at the possibility of realising far-fetched dreams. Maybe, just maybe, he could escape his past and curate a respectable life. Securing Tibbie was like Day One of The Creation. She was the core of his new life. A perfect snowball set rolling. Next, Austin made Deputy Head Boy (tick), and then gained entrance into medical school (tick), each step up the ladder taking him further from the bog of his childhood bubbling below.

Ironically, though, the very qualities that made Tibbie a catch also threatened their early relationship. The attention she attracted was sometimes hard to brook, and, not infrequently, Austin felt as if he was on her arm, not she on his. A Princess-Diana-Prince-Charles sort of scenario. No secret who the crowd adored.

With time this changed. Austin qualified and quickly

gained a following of adoring patients. His standing in the community grew. Dr Lamb the all-rounder – caring doctor, sportsman, philanthropist, antique clock restorer. The power balance equalised. In fact, it might even have started to shift in his favour.

What took some years for Austin to realise was that Tibbie had come into the marriage with her own baggage. She, too, had been trying to escape her childhood. One in which she'd enjoyed abundant privilege, but very little love. Desperate for affection and approval, she was wired to please. And once Austin realised this, it became easy to manoeuvre her in whichever way he chose. Not that it was necessarily calculated or even conscious.

He only hit her once. They were in Fiji, on holiday with the Andinos. She'd been flirting with Stan by the pool. Said it meant nothing. 'Just a bit of foolishness after one too many cocktails.' However, he'd seen the hungry, flattered look in Stan's eyes. The loser!

The slap left no obvious mark, but still, he decided it best for Tibbie to remain in their hotel room for twenty-four hours until she was ready to come out smiling.

There was only one real stumbling block in their marriage. Children. Tibbie did not want a family.

Austin never got to the bottom of it. His wife seemed to adore other people's children, and they in turn adored her. Perhaps she did not feel confident to change the template on which she'd been raised. Maybe she thought Austin's affection for her would be diluted if children came along. Possibly, she worried that pregnancy would take its toll on her female form. Whatever the reason, on this point she was unmovable.

The standard line they offered to those who nosily enquired was that they couldn't get their heads around bringing children into an already overpopulated and hostile world. But behind closed doors, it was a different story. The I-want-children/I-don't debate was protracted and played like background music on repeat.

Over time, they settled into the confirmed status quo; however, it was always the first topic to flare whenever they argued, which admittedly was not often. They were largely good together and, as many people put it, 'a power couple'. Austin bided his time, feeling certain Tibbie would eventually capitulate.

He did not foresee the disruption that Janice would have on their lives when she came to stay for a couple of months to get over yet another disastrous relationship. Foxy, flawed, volatile Janice offered herself to Austin on a plate, and he simply could not resist. Perhaps deep down, he wanted to hurt Tibbie the way she'd hurt him for so long. Anyway, he did what most men would do if there was zero chance of their spouse finding out. (Well, Janice wasn't exactly going to tell her sister she'd been sleeping with her husband. There was safety in the proximity of family fucks, after all.)

The secret trysts imported an unexpected excitement and novelty into Austin's very responsible and respectable life. The coarseness of it, the risk, the mind-blowing sex.

Then Janice returned to Australia and life went back to before.

Well, not entirely; she had stirred something in Austin. In fact, she'd flipped the coin for him, turning Tibbie's perfections from virtues into vices. Janice's thick thighs, lipsticked innuendos, and meaty mauve nipples captured Austin's curiosity. And Janice pushed back. Tibbie never did (except in regard to having a family). A dissatisfaction had crept under Austin's skin and would hang around for the years to follow.

Then one day, out of the blue, after yet another argument about starting a family and Tibbie's inevitably declining fertility, she finally gave in and agreed to come off the pill. Austin could not believe his ears. His relief was immeasurable, as was the love he again felt for his wife. At last, he could see the remaining pieces of his perfectly designed puzzle slotting into place. Austin – the doctor, loving husband, and family man.

Tibbie did not conceive immediately, and Austin rationalised that it was her body readjusting after such a prolonged period of contraception. He hoped they hadn't left it too late; however, the last thing he wanted to do was add further stress to an already fraught topic.

He felt quietly confident that the odds were still in their favour. The biggest challenge had been aligning their intentions. Now, it was just a matter of time. That's what he was always telling his patients who were trying to get pregnant. 'Get on with living your life. It will happen, and often when you least expect it.'

Months and then years passed, but Austin didn't dare broach IVF. Finally he realised children were not to be, and he quietly bound and boxed his disappointment, packing away his hope with clinical resignation.

When Tibbie's mother died, the two sisters inherited equally. Janice, however, who was still single, between jobs, and in debt, believed she was entitled to more than a half of the estate. As far as she was concerned, Tibbie had no need for the money, married as she was to a wealthy doctor. Things came to a head in a bitter, long-distance phone call, during which Janice outed Austin's infidelity with her years before.

Tibbie was devastated. Devastated. The revelation ripping the scab off her childhood fear of abandonment and rejection.

Austin managed to placate her, if only just.

Things were more complicated, though, than first met the eye. By the time Tibbie learnt the truth about Austin and her sister (some eleven years after the fact), Austin was bedding someone else. Abby Manderson. He knew his protestation about the Janice affair – 'just once in a moment of weakness' – would not wash if Tibbie ever found out that he was in fact embroiled in a second affair. Even Tibbie had her limits. Though to be fair, Austin had kept a clean slate for the twelve years between Janice and Abby. Regardless, he knew that if Tibbie were to find out about Abby, his marriage would be over.

It was a tense truce, and life had to be negotiated a lot more carefully.

Austin had always thought he was the one doing wrong, until Carmen made *that* comment about Tibbie having a coil!

Tibbie, of course, denied it. Put it down to Carmen's tumour-riddled brain. But Austin knew. Knew his wife too well. Her expression. The way she'd blushed. And it didn't take much ferreting on his part to confirm the truth: a simple call to Tibbie's doctor to moan about some new bureaucratic requirement for GP practices. Then, as a casual aside, 'a quick query from Tibbie' about when her IUD was due for replacement.

The answer flicked a switch in Austin's head and there was no going back. Here he had thought they'd been trying unsuccessfully to have children, when all the time his wife had been having the last laugh. The last laugh. The last laugh.

Divorce was not an option. Not for Austin anyway. He would not risk losing his standing in the community, something he'd worked so hard to achieve. As for splitting their assets…

So, he was forced to carry on as if he knew nothing of her lie. But all the while his resentment festered.

At least the discovery of Tibbie's deception relieved him of any guilt he harboured about his affair with Abby Manderson.

The pretence continued for both of them, until Austin slipped up and left his phone at home one morning.

When Tibbie read the sexting between Abby and Austin, she was furious. Told him she was leaving. Started to make concrete plans.

Austin was clear in his head about one thing: she was not going to be the one to do the leaving. He would be the one to determine how things went down. In fact, he'd already been scheming how to get rid of Tibbie, after learning about her gross betrayal of his trust.

It hadn't taken long for him to realise that Carmen's brain tumour was in fact a gift horse he could not look in the mouth. Carmen was going to die anyway. If he planned things correctly, Carmen would take the blame for murder. And while he felt bad about framing his most longstanding friend, he knew the law would be more forgiving of a woman with cancer, than a bitter, philandering husband.

How wonderfully Carmen played ball – aggression, violent outbursts, paranoia, memory loss, as if on cue. In the end, the poor woman had zero credibility and all the motive in the world. She even dropped her lipstick in his consulting rooms during a seizure. He could not have asked for more.

CHAPTER 77

AUSTIN LAMB

Hearing the undergrowth rustle, Tibbie turned. She was waiting in the clearing, her back to him.

Austin sat down on the smooth curve of boulder in the middle of the clearing and patted it, beckoning her to join him.

It had been drizzling and the shorter strands of her hair had frizzed, so that a fine auburn halo framed her face.

She looked at him. He could see the hurt crouching behind her almost smile. But Tibbie was like a puppy, easily mollified by any show of affection. He pulled out the small giftbox wrapped in green and tied with a coral satin ribbon. Apologised again for his lapse. Promised that his affair with Abby was over. That he'd do anything, absolutely anything in his power to make it up to her.

She stared at the gift in her lap, her eyes filling with tears as she hesitantly untied the ribbon.

There wasn't much time, but this could not be rushed.

Austin kept one ear to the path, listening for walkers. The drizzle had been an unexpected bonus, though he couldn't get cocky; there would still be the die-hards out with their dogs despite the weather.

Tibbie gasped as she opened the box. The ring looked stunning, nestled there in a bed of puckered white satin. An eternity ring to reaffirm his undying love for her.

With his encouragement she tried it on. It was too big. Of course, it was.

He told her he would take it back and get it resized.

As she handed him back the box, the ribbon fell to the ground. A gust of wind grabbed it and carried it towards the ledge. She jumped up to retrieve it. Tibbie, ever the collector of mementoes. Champagne corks, birthday cards, little pieces of fake holly…

Austin shadowed her.

The ribbon landed less than a metre from the cliff edge.

'Careful,' he said coming up behind her and grabbing hold of her upper arms. He didn't have much of a head for heights, but this was no time for weakness.

He tightened his grip.

'You're hurting me, Austin,' she said trying to unpeel his fingers. 'I'm fine.'

Then he was manoeuvring her closer to the ledge.

'Austin! What are you—' she said, pushing back against him, her voice twisting through annoyance, confusion, then panic.

He held firm, his thick fingers pressing into her soft flesh.

Then he shoved.

Tibbie stumbled. Caught herself. Arced backwards.

He stepped in, side-on, and with his shoulder gave her another nudge.

Tibbie's cry was like a bungy-jumper's – short-lived and quickly lost to the wind. The sort of cry a stranger might hear, but instantly doubt themselves, because the sound had already been stolen by the breeze.

Austin grabbed onto a crooked pōhutakawa branch and peered down into the water below, catching a glimpse of Tibbie's body sprawled on the rocks before a wave swept over her.

It had been unexpectedly easy. No contingency plan needed. He'd rehearsed the scenario so many times in his head, anticipating every possible speedbump that, in the end, it was something of an anticlimax. Almost akin to handing in a thesis – all the hard work done, the final presentation a mere formality.

What Austin had not been prepared for was the emotional chaos of the ensuing weeks – the onslaught of attention from patients, extended family, and the police. Nor had he fully appreciated quite how the Andinos would react. It was everybody else's emotions that started to take their toll on him, and for a while he felt as if he might lose his footing.

Of course, Abby was there through it all. Though her guilt at being 'the other woman' in such morbid circumstances proved an annoying distraction. She, of course, had no idea that he'd been involved in Tibbie's demise. A secret was only as good as those entrusted with it.

Initially she was reluctant to continue where they'd left off, which beggared belief. What had happened to all the dreams they'd had for a future together? Had he just knocked off his wife for naught? He persuaded Abby that he needed her more than ever, and that Tibbie would have wanted him to be happy, her suicide, simply a measure of her instability.

He gave Abby the eternity ring as planned, though changed the scenario of its delivery to avoid suspicion on her part. Instead of her finding a naughty surprise hiding in his underpants, he gave her the ring over a quiet dinner, tearfully affirming his love for her and his commitment to their future.

The sex was not quite as good in the weeks that followed. Abby kept getting visions of Tibbie watching them do it, which was a bit of a lustkiller. As for Austin, the excitement that had come with the illicitness of before was slightly muted. He was hopeful things would ramp up again with time.

For all the human distractions and intrusions, Austin felt a quiet pride in his achievement. A reminder that if he set his mind to something, be that burying his past, gaining entrance to medical school, or committing the perfect murder, he could succeed. It was a heady feeling, being savvier and more powerful than most. Being… invincible.

Eliot's involvement was an unexpected setback.

CHAPTER 78

RAMESH BANDARA

'I would have done anything for him,' Lamb said quietly, all the hubris gone. They were into their second hour of interrogation, and everyone in the room was exhausted. Ramesh had not been party to a confession like it before. A complete outpouring, as if a dam wall had burst.

In Ramesh's experience, eliciting a confession was often about establishing a rapport with the accused. And he'd been impressed by how Hilary had known the exact moment to step back. She had clearly appreciated that her absence of rapport with the doctor meant he would do anything to defy her, and she did not want this to sabotage the final stage of the interrogation. However, Ramesh knew that for the someone like the doctor, a man who'd spent his entire life shaping the truth, he'd need more than just rapport. He would need to find Austin Lamb's Achilles' heel.

'Why did he have to go and spot the bloody bike?' Lamb said. 'He's just so damned observant, that kid.'

Ramesh nodded. Eliot most certainly was.

'I thought that if I didn't pay his questions much attention, he'd forget about it. I should have known; Eliot never forgets anything.'

'You've been in his life since the beginning, haven't you?' Ramesh said.

Lamb nodded.

'I was newly qualified when Andrea Bard joined my practice.' He tossed his head back and sniggered. 'Barely out of med-school nappies. She'd just moved into the area and was nearly at term. I looked after her in the final weeks of her pregnancy. My first pregnant patient. A solo mum at that. I was excited. Idealistic. Felt that I could make a difference. Help give her kid a good start. Break a cycle I understood too well.'

He shook his head as if watching the event that would change his life unfold on screen.

'Her waters broke in the early hours. I thought, with her being a first-timer, it was likely to be a protracted affair, so I reassured her and told her that I'd swing by first thing in the morning and give her a lift to hospital.'

His voice had turned husky. Ramesh poured a glass of water and pushed it towards him. Lamb ignored it.

'I went back to sleep. Forty minutes later she called again. She was wanting to push. By the time I got there, she was on the bathroom floor, baby's head crowning.' He sucked in a stuttering breath. 'The cord was wrapped twice around Eliot's neck. I panicked. Felt my inexperience keenly.'

Ramesh could relate. He'd been out of his depth on more than one occasion in his early years as a detective. Being a newly qualified professional was a terrifying thing when it came to dealing with human lives. The weight of expectation. The responsibility. A layman didn't differentiate between a doctor or a detective with one year's experience or ten.

'It was not a straightforward delivery. I've often wondered whether, had I done things differently, Eliot might not have had all... had all the issues he's had.'

So Eliot Bard had come to represent a failure in Austin Lamb's life. The man who'd spent a lifetime striving for perfection – perfect life, perfect wife – blamed himself for the bungled, imperfect delivery.

'I've had a lot to do with Eliot over the years,' he said,

his demeanour somehow almost lighter for the burden he'd just shared. 'He's had various physical and mental challenges. Thankfully they've not been as severe as they could have been.

'Andrea and I greeted each milestone with relief and excitement.' His face broke into a smile. 'And all the time our young Eliot wielded his magic – the quirky, open, funny, honest, intelligent and authentic kid that he is.'

If that wasn't an admission of love, Ramesh did not know what was.

Lamb was already in too deep, he told them, when he realised Eliot could scuttle everything. Not only would Lamb go down for murder, but Eliot would witness his hero, his honorary dad, his 'bestest' friend, fall from grace. Neither was conscionable.

'I didn't know what to do.' He made an odd sound, a half-sob, half-belch. 'There was no solution. No way out!'

His eyes looked dead as if he'd just seen himself in the mirror and perceived the monster he'd become. He'd attempted to murder Eliot, the kid he and Tibbie had never had. The kid he desperately loved. The kid he'd been determined to afford a better childhood than his own.

'But the thing about impulsive plans,' Lamb said, tapping his forefinger on the table as if giving some sort of professional assessment, 'is that they are less likely to be watertight.' He looked up at Ramesh. 'Eliot didn't die.'

Ramesh nodded. This was a moment to pause over. The moment that would send Dr Austin Lamb down.

'I bet you thought you'd lucked out when he woke from his coma, without any memory of the events?' Hilary said, breaking the spell.

CHAPTER 79

RAMESH BANDARA

Stan Andino sat on the brown corduroy couch flanked by his sons. The room smelt of new carpet. It was a pleasant beige, with a generous pile.

The boys had changed since Ramesh first met them. Like choir boys losing their pure voices, they'd shed their innocence for gawky limbs, pimply faces and whiskered chins. There was a flatness to their affect, which was particularly marked in one lad, his eyes holding onto a cold cynicism.

Andino looked like an overgrown kid himself. Three kids on the couch.

He didn't offer Ramesh a drink. Ramesh would have declined anyway.

'Thanks for agreeing to meet with me. I know you all lead busy lives.'

It was one of those inane things you say, like a comment about the weather. A meaningless opener to temper hostilities and awkwardness. Something Hilary could be better versed at.

She'd accompanied him for support, but he'd asked her to remain outside in the car. This was something he had to do alone.

Not wanting the small, lopsided family to have one more moment of unnecessary anxiety, Ramesh got straight to the point.

'I'm here to apologise,' he said, shoving his hands under his thighs. 'We... I... made a mistake.'

The three looked at him with weary distrust.

'We now know with absolute certainty that Carmen, your wife and mother, did not murder Tibbie Lamb. I am extremely sorry for any pain I have caused in the process of reaching this conclusion.'

The heat pump was on high, and hot air billowed the rust-orange curtains.

'More information has come to light, and we now have in custody the person we believe to be guilty of Tibbie Lamb's murder.'

Stan Andino started to cry. A silent, wet shuddering.

The boy on his left rubbed his back. 'It's okay, Dad. It's okay. I knew she didn't do it.'

'How did it go?' Hilary asked, as Ramesh climbed into the passenger seat.

'Let's get out of here.'

She drove them down to the Milford marina and pulled into a park opposite the mirror-still water.

Ramesh wound down his window, inviting the rhymical clang of masts and buoys into the car. The sun was warm on his arm.

'Not sure I'm up to this job anymore,' he said, trying to get comfortable in Hilary's very cramped little car.

'Of course you are.'

He shook his head. 'Doctors have a saying. *Primum non nocere*. First do no harm. I reckon we should abide by that, too.'

'Don't go getting overly sentimental on me,' Hilary said. 'You can't make an omelette without breaking eggs.'

Ramesh chuckled. That was Hilary Stark for you.

'We caught the bad guy,' she said.

Yes, they'd caught the bad guy.

She reminded him of a child, the way she lived in the present, said what she saw, called a spade a spade.

He admired, too, the way she kept moving forward. The only direction that would lead somewhere. There was a lot to be said for that. And the way she never gave up on a question until she'd got an answer.

He turned to face her. 'Two things.'

'Yup?'

'*The Little Prince.* It's an awesome book.'

'It's good, right?' she said, a wide smile disrupting her serious expression.

She looked lovely when she smiled.

'You remind me of him,' Ramesh said.

'Who?'

'The Little Prince. Your wisdom, wilfulness. Your honesty.' He wanted to say her childlike naïvety and kindness, too. 'And your bloody refusal to give up on a question.'

She blushed.

'What's the other thing?'

'What do you mean?' he said.

'You said you had two things to tell me.'

'Oh.' He pulled his shoulders back. Slapped the dashboard with an open palm. 'Hilary Stark, you cannot give up on becoming a detective. You're too damned good.'

She turned away. Reached for the key in the ignition.

'Want me to drop you home?' she asked.

He shook his head. The boss had given him the afternoon off.

'I need to pick up a rather flash suit I ordered. But after that, how would you fancy spending the afternoon at the zoo?'

ACKNOWLEDGEMENTS

Dr Anthony Falkov for talking me through the various treatment options for a patient with brain tumours. Dr Tim Koelmeyer for sharing his forensic pathology expertise. Dr David Galler, for generously answering my questions about ICU scenarios. Amali Fonseka for her wonderful insights into Sri Lankan culture. Dr Barbara K. Lipska and Elaine McArdle for their book, *The Neuroscientist Who Lost Her Mind: A Memoir of Madness and Recovery,* which affords a unique look into the psychological and physical journey of someone battling brain tumours. Nadine Rubin Nathan for representing my writing with such passion. Louise Russell and all the team at Bateman for their backing and great expertise in bringing another of my books into the world. Keely O'Shannessy for designing, as always, such an awesome cover. And my dearest family, who are there for me in so many ways, whenever I venture out of my writing room.